FIENDS IN HIGH PLACES

THE HIPPOSYNC ARCHIVES
BOOK 1

DC FARMER

WYRMWOOD
BOOKS

COPYRIGHT

First published 2014 as The 400Lb Gorilla by Wyrmwood Books 2014

Second edition published by Spencer Hill Press 2016

This edition published by Wyrmwood books 2024

A CIP catalogue record for this book is available from the British Library

eBook ISBN - 978-1-915185-26-6
Print ISBN -978-1-915185-27-3

Published by Wyrmwood Books.
An imprint of Wyrmwood Media.

EXCLUSIVE OFFER

WOULD YOU LIKE A FREE NOVELLA?

Please look out for the link near the end of the book for your chance to sign up to the no-spam-guaranteed Readers' Club and receive a FREE DC Farmer novella as well as news of upcoming releases. HERE ARE THE BOOKS!

FIENDS IN HIGH PLACES
THE GHOUL ON THE HILL
BLAME IT ON THE BOGEY (MAN)
CAN'T BUY ME BLOOD
COMING SOON
TROLL LOTTA LOVE
SOMEWHERE OGRE THE RAINBOW

PROLOGUE

MOST SENSIBLE PEOPLE, those blessed with a modicum of self-preservation, would avoid crossing a poorly lit park at night or in the dark, predawn hours. Places where there were lots of bushes, trees, benches, where other…people might secrete themselves for a variety of nefarious or unsavoury reasons.

Especially when the weather was foul. Especially when the lighting of such areas left a lot to be desired in the form of no less than two broken street lamps. Oxford city council would, no doubt, get that sorted out quickly. But this cold early morning, the repairs were yet to be requisitioned. All the more surprising, therefore, to see an elderly, solitary gent sauntering through the gates along the dimly lit paths at a time in the morning when most people were still abed.

One might excuse this eccentric gentleman for not noticing the presence of several small, hooded figures stirring in the shadows as soon as he entered. Figures who were slowly, stealthily, moving to form an encircling mob that travelled unseen with the man towards the middle of the park.

Small people in hoods, for anyone with a television or who ever read the news, usually meant raucous behaviour at best, thuggery and violence at worst. Who would not have been sickened by the spate of brazen shoplifting sweeping the country. An activity that the more libertarian commentators and media liked to blame on inflation, poverty, and the shops themselves as having such alluring content. But which most people recognised as being nothing more than opportunistic greed. And yet, the portly man did not seem to notice the gaggle of hooded figures until one of them moved to stand in front of him to physically block his path.

'Oh, excuse me,' said Eric Porter. For anyone who knew the man, this obliviousness to his surroundings came as no surprise. He was a man whose waking hours were spent contemplating things that the rest of us did not. And he did all this so that we, the remainder of the population did not have to. The point was that he was not very good at mundane things like remembering to put the correct shoes on the right and left foot, remembering to comb his hair, where he left an umbrella and all the other things that less-eccentric people were troubled by.

However, on glancing around, he finally realised that he had wandered into a situation that he might be better off avoiding. On confronting the lead hooded figure, after his apology, Mr Porter turned around to retrace his steps only to find the way blocked with more hooded figures.

'Ah,' he said. 'Oh dear. What is my niece going to say to all this.'

It was at this point that his attackers moved in.

CHAPTER ONE

CLOSED HEAD TRAUMA is about as much fun as nude paintballing. There is nothing remotely enjoyable about your brain being bounced around inside your skull like a ping-pong ball in a goldfish bowl. And since normal grey matter has the consistency of a chilled egg pudding, the outcome is seldom positive. Damage can range from a very nasty headache to a borg-like half-life, totally dependent on technology to feed and breathe. With luck, it's possible to recover with nothing more than a touch of memory loss, which may not always be such a bad thing. After all, sometimes it's a blessing not to remember every detail of the day your life gets thrown into a blender.

Matt Danmor was a blender survivor.

To top it all off, they'd diagnosed some retrograde amnesia. And since the details of what happened after the car left the road were pretty sketchy, they'd slapped on the label of post-traumatic memory loss for no extra charge.

In truth, it was all a bit of a blur. Matt's recovery was slow and inconsistent. Even months afterwards, as his bruised mind repaired itself so that the picture became less like a half-finished jigsaw puzzle and more like a stuttering magic lantern show, certain stark recollections would return with a vengeance to wake him sweating, pulse pounding in the dark watches of the night. Sensations like the juddering thump of the car turning over twice, or the sharp metallic odour of petrol soaking slowly into his trousers, or the sickly rose bouquet of the air freshener leaching all over his upside-down forehead, or the pitiful relief he'd felt when the fireman wielding the Jaws of Life finally cut through the screeching metal to grab Matt before he passed out.

He'd regained consciousness at the hospital. There, the thing that stood out like a Klingon in a bikini, the one abiding memory he had of those first couple of hours as they tried to work out which parts of him weren't broken, was his MRI scan.

He'd mumbled half-conscious responses to their questions about him having any metal in his body, 'Are you absolutely certain, Mathew?' as they whipped off his watch, festival wristbands and his Celtic cross pendant. Then they'd slid him into the machine's cylinder and started the buzzing, metronomic scan. Matt had been woozy and sick, though mercifully free of pain, thanks to whatever it was they'd shot into him. Confused, he'd started to believe that they were burying him alive to the sound of Burke and Hare playing the bongos on his sarcophagus but had clung on to reason just long enough not to make an arse of himself by screaming to be let out.

Yet it wasn't the scan itself that was the issue; after all, who in their right minds would object to having the protons of their body's water molecules tweaked into different eigenstates so long as it revealed all the broken bits? No, it was what happened immediately afterwards that had threatened his sanity.

When it was over, the mechanised table slowly eased him out, and someone took his hand and asked him if he was okay. He'd mumbled a grateful, 'Yes.' and looked up into a pair of kind green female eyes in a quite attractive, dusky-grey face. Quite apart from her unusual complexion, there were two things about this woman that stood out. The first was that she wore the strangest-looking diaphanous green robes, which flowed about her like mist. The second was that her feet went clip-clop on the hospital tiles when she walked.

Matt had squinted down and been reassured by what he saw in a half-conscious, altered-state kind of way. After all, if he had a pair of woolly legs and hooves for feet, he'd be doing the two-empty-coconut-shell-tango when he moved, too. It was only later that he would put his decision not to scream down to the confusion brought on by his parlous, opiate-dulled, post-traumatic state.

'Just rest,' said the woman in a soft Scottish accent. He struggled for a woozy label. Was she a radiographer? A goat-nurse?

But he'd taken her advice and shut his eyes, deciding that the presence of a genetic hybrid in the X-ray suite of a busy NHS hospital was not something he need concern himself with at that moment. He simply stored it away as something he would think about later, when he didn't have to worry about whether he was going to live or die. He must have drifted off because when he next opened his eyes, he was in a hospital bed with his leg in traction, his right arm in a sling, and his watch and necklace back on—the wristbands, he later learned, were considered too much of an infection risk and incinerated.

Of course, when the hours and days and weeks of later arrived, so that Matt did think about his clip-clopping Florence Nightingale, he decided to keep his own counsel. He filed the goat lady away in the mental drawer labelled Side Effects: ignore. After all, opiates were a wonderful thing when you were all banged up, but they did have a bit of a reputation for inducing the odd hallucination. Besides, Matt had other sea creatures to barbecue—like learning to walk again and wipe his arse with his left hand (not necessarily at the same time).

Memory of the goat lady didn't fade, exactly, but the inclination to tell anyone about it did because Matt had absolutely no desire to see some smart Alec trying to keep a straight face while saying, 'You're kidding.' or 'Must have been your nanny.'

It was there in the quiet moments, though, always ready to come to the surface, challenging Matt to find an answer to it all. Not that there were any answers to find. Not then.

———

MATT'S BONES HEALED QUICKLY, but his brain took a bit longer to function normally again. His experience in the MRI remained in the mental drawer where he'd left it. Putting things into drawers, however, only means that when you do rediscover them, they're usually covered in fluff and stuck to a blob of Blu Tack.

One winter's morning in a city famed for its university and the fifth-highest rate of bicycle theft in the country, something happened which caused Matt's mental drawer to spring open and reveal a *very* large, *very* fluffy, *very* sticky blob. Not to mention a huge and wallowing iceberg of weirdness.

And, like the shortsighted lookout on the *Titanic* of destiny waving blithely at the ever-nearing iceberg of fate, by the time Matt noticed it happening it was far too late to do anything about it.

CHAPTER TWO

ALL IN ALL, it was an okay shift, as A&E night shifts went. The usual gaggle of fate's victims walked, hobbled, or were wheeled bleeding and in pain through the doors of Accident and Emergency. There were the inevitable clutch of drunks, a couple of sprained ankles, a four-year-old with a split pea up his nose, and three myocardial infarcts. Not forgetting the evening's main entertainment, in the form of a corpulent gentleman of indeterminable age who'd had an altercation with a cucumber. Accidents happen, of course. Sheer bad luck, he tried to explain, that his epileptic partner was holding the cucumber at the very moment that the video they'd been watching had, literally, gone on the blink.

Unfortunately, said partner had not turned away in time. The result of the subsequent stroboscopically induced convulsion was a flesh mock-up of a Soyuz spacecraft violently docking with the International Space Station, as the charge nurse so very nicely put it to the naïve med student who had picked up the case. No one asked why the man was dressed in a baby-doll nighty and a thong. After all, if someone walked in wearing scuba-diving gear and holding a spear gun, with an arm missing and a shark's tooth hanging from the stump, the scenario wouldn't need much explanation. The same principle applied with the man in the nightie. Not funny for the watery-eyed patient, yet gut-achingly hysterical for the staff. There followed a fun half-hour of swapped war stories about pan handles, light bulbs, and even a dentist's drill, all infamous for having found their way into an orifice designed more for things leaving than entering. All about as PC as male-only clubs, of course. But then, a sense of gallows humour was compulsory for a job in A&E if you wanted to survive. The giggles only ended—and even then, after a fresh wave of guffaws—when the radiographer who had taken the X-rays muttered that she preferred her cucumber in Pimm's with ice.

Preferably, though, not that particular cucumber.

Matt had joined in with the laughter, but it was he who took a cup of tea to the cucumber man, knowing that when you were bedridden and in pain, whatever the cause, a kind word or deed went a long way. He had first-hand experience of that, even if his Florence Nightingale had walked with a pronounced *clip-clop*. The charge nurse saw him approaching the curtained cubicle and grinned.

'You've got a good heart, Matt,' he said. 'When you've done that, check the saline cupboard, would you? The OD in four will need an IV in a moment, and you-know-who's already on the warpath.'

As always, aspirin overdoses meant urgency. The longer salicylates sat in the stomach, the greater the damage. The one good thing from the patient in four's point of view was that she'd used half a bottle of Absolut vodka to wash them down, after a plateful of chow mein. Consequently, she'd thrown up most of the tablets in a sticky mess, which steamed pungently in a cardboard kidney dish at the foot of her bed. Still, she needed observing while they waited for blood gases and salicylate levels, as well as some Fair-Isle-jumper-wearing type from Psych with the time to listen to the catalogue of woes responsible for such a cry for help. Right now, though, she needed a drip, and some bright spark had filled the saline cupboard with bags that were past their use-by date. Which meant Matt, as the duty porter, had to fetch some more.

Now, everyone knows that eight hours into a nine-and-a-half-hour night shift, something happens to your brain. The tiredness gland begins secreting the neurochemical equivalent of cotton wool, turning the world into a slow-motion video punctuated by jaw-popping yawns. It's at about that time that concentration begins to fizzle out and die.

Two seconds either way and it wouldn't have made any difference; Matt would have seen it, or missed it, or done the paso doble around it. But as luck would have it—and bad luck had been having it an awful lot with Matt Danmor recently—just as he returned from stores with two arms full of saline bags, a nurse pushing a trolley bearing a minor ops tray stepped right into his path.

Instruments flew up in the air and skittered over the floor with clattering finality, bloody swabs fluttered to the corners like fatally injured doves, and Matt and the nurse let fly ear-burning curses.

Matt squeezed his eyes shut, groaned inwardly, and waited for it. He knew what was coming, and *you-know-who* didn't disappoint. A head popped out from behind the curtain of cubicle four, where the aspirin overdose still retched.

'Oh, for God's sake, don't tell me. Danmor strikes again. Can't you do anything right, you klutz?'

If he were asked, which he never would be, for the moment that the night really went pear-shaped, that would have been it. The moment when Matt experienced the full-on accusatory disdain of Giles Roberro—sorry, *Doctor* Giles Roberro, as he constantly reminded anyone who forgot to add that little ego-massaging prefix. He glared at the mess on the floor and then again at Matt, anger sparking in heavy-lidded eyes that didn't suffer fools at all, let alone gladly. He treated anyone non-medical, which meant the vast majority of people he came across, with vitriolic contempt of the 'what had once passed through a dog and is now underneath one's shoe' variety. Worse, for some reason Roberro had singled out Matt as someone deserving of his special attention. And for 'special' read unpleasant in the extreme.

'How am I supposed to work like this?' Roberro demanded before adding with exaggerated slowness, as if Matt were a three-year-old on a naughty stool. 'We. Need. A. Bag. Of. Saline.'

Face burning, Matt retrieved a bag from the survivors he'd stacked on the desk. Roberro snatched it from him, irked by not being able to find further fault. Even so, it was asking the impossible for him not to throw in a few patronising comments.

'Find this one all on your own, did you?' he said with a sneer. 'Manage to walk all the way from here to the stores without a GPS, did we? My, your mummy will be proud. Oh, and we need some really important shredding of documents done, and some even more important coffees made. So chop-chop, Mathew. If you're good, I'll let you play with sphygmo cuffs again later, eh? See if you can cut off the blood supply to your head by wrapping it around your neck.' The last word emerged through snarling teeth. He sent Matt a maniacal grin and promptly disappeared back behind the curtain where he muttered, loud enough for everyone to hear, 'Is it a policy in this hospital to deliberately employ moronic wannabe porters, or have we just been singled out for special treatment?'

Sweat prickled Matt's neck. The fleshy part of his thumb stung from where the nail of his forefinger had dug into it. His eyes flicked down to an ophthalmoscope on a side table. For one teeny-tiny second, he toyed with the idea of seeing if its handle might work as a worthy cucumber substitute for good old Dr Roberro, but he dug the nail in a millimetre more and the moment passed. It generally did. Rita, the staff nurse responsible for wheeling out the minor ops trolley, five feet one and sixteen stone under a cherubic smile, made eyes to the ceiling and mouthed, 'Arsehole.' as she tilted her head towards cubicle four.

Roberro's ego was a huge and loose-bowelled elephant in the room, one that left crap in big piles all over the place. Working with him was like trying to test hobnail boots on a floor made of eggshells. Whatever you did, the end result was invariably an unsatisfactory fiasco. Doctors were busy people and they dealt with stress in different ways. Some ranted and raved, some went inside themselves to a place where everything was wound so tight you could use it in the timpani section of the Royal Philharmonic. Roberro just became a total git who expected everyone to forgive him for it because he played the difficult-job card so expertly.

Arsehole.

It wasn't even as if Roberro was a good doctor. He was just a loud doctor. The last time Matt looked in a textbook, he'd found nothing in there that could be cured by shouting. Even as he found gloves for the clean-up, Matt's face burned once again with sullen anger. Roberro had come up with the double whammy there. Moron was bad enough, but the real twist of a barbed dagger in the gut came with that one word, 'wannabe.'

CHAPTER THREE

MATT's blue porter's shirt was soaked from the saline episode, and under it the leather thong of his pendant felt soggy too. He went to his locker, took off the necklace and stuffed it into his backpack, changed his shirt and went back to work.

He managed to avoid Roberro for the rest of the shift, but at seven-fifteen, on his way to clock off, the morning took a final nose-dive. He was busy packing away his sandwich box when he sensed a presence in the doorway of the porter's lodge (a cupboard) that he took his breaks in. He looked up and flinched as an involuntary, but thankfully incoherent, yelp leapt from his throat on seeing what stood there.

Linda Marsh was Oxford General Hospital's Hotel-Services Manager. A person blessed with features modified by the performance-enhancing drugs that had also given her a statuesque body, in a discus-thrower sort of way. A champion body builder in her spare time, she was not someone you wanted to be hugged by.

Or at least Matt didn't. Not that he was in any danger of that happening. Underneath Linda Marsh's hard exterior beat a heart of granite wrapped up in a personality that would have been at home inside Stalin. Ex-Navy, she had the vocabulary and tone of a nicotine-addicted, gravel-gargling

Tourette's victim. In his pigeon-holing imagination, Matt had renamed her head cheerleader for the Uruk-hai.

Noting Matt's reaction to her unannounced presence—a reaction she was perhaps not unfamiliar with, Ms Marsh's beetle brows furrowed into a scale model of the Mariana Trench. 'What the shee-ite is your problem?'

Matt tried a laddish laugh. It got mangled on the way out into a hysterical giggle. 'I thought you were someone else,' he stammered, airbrushing out the mental image of a mountain troll that popped up in his head.

'What the bollocks happened with the saline and that trolley, Danmor?' she growled, hands on hips in the lodge doorway. Matt hadn't known people could growl until he met Linda Marsh, who did it in a harsh, north-east accent to boot. 'Infection control have been on at me already. That trolley had been used on a junkie with a head laceration. Could have been any soddin' thing on those swabs you managed to plaster all over the floor. Looked like the soddin' Somme in there.'

'One of the nurses pushed the trolley out just as I walked in,' Matt explained, knowing it sounded pathetic. 'Just a bit of bad luck, I suppose.'

'Bad luck? Bad soddin' *luck*? What is it with you?' she snapped. 'If this was a ship, you'd have been overboard weeks ago.'

'Overboard?' Matt groped for understanding.

'Yeah. Like the shite Jonah that you are.'

Matt opened his mouth to speak, but nothing emerged.

'You *do* know who Jonah was?'

'Yes, I—'

'He was an unlucky twat, too. Got his leg bitten off by a whale. Served him bloody right for huntin' the bastards, if you ask me.'

Matt considered explaining the difference between Jonah and Captain Ahab for all of two-hundredths of a second, then flushed that thought down the mental pan, together with the image of Herman Melville rotating in his grave and tearing at his hair in mental agony. It needed two extra pulls on the chain to get rid of that one.

'Look, Danmor.' Marsh's voice dropped lower than an adder's abdomen.

Here it comes. Must be all of five days since I last heard this.

'I don't need to tell you how much of a gamble it was taking you on.'

'I'm really very—'

'Someone with your background isn't exactly top of the soddin' A-list, you know?'

Cow.

'Yes, I—'

'Like I said.' Marsh pulled her shoulders back. 'I've stuck my soddin' neck out big time. I don't usually go anywhere near anyone with a history of…like yours.'

'I know. And I'm more than grateful, honestly. But it was just an accident.'

Marsh's mouth dropped open and she cut him off in mid-explanation. 'Jesus H. Christ. *Accident*? Like the brake just happening to slip on the wheelchair with that cataract patient on the back stairs was a shitty accident. Lucky, she lost just the one eye, if you ask me. And what about *accidentally* settin' Mr Sanji's hair on fire in ortho theatre? Oh, and let's not forget postin' twenty soddin' stool samples through the General Office letterbox. That *accident* took the soddin' biscuit.'

'First-day jitters?'

Marsh fixed him with a pair of feral eyes. 'Tell me you're not a card-carrying lunatic, Danmor.'

That was a toughie. Final answer? Matt wasn't entirely sure. There were moments when he looked around and couldn't quite remember where he was or why he was there. Absences was the official term given to those terrifying lapses, and considering what he had been through they were perfectly understandable. Yet the aching feeling of displace-ment that lingered when they'd passed didn't seem to be less-ening—a vague, tantalising, edge-of-consciousness awareness that there was something Matt should know which might explain all of this. But he had enough sense to realise that admitting to any weaknesses at all was a sure-fire way to lose this job.

'No, I'm not. I'll get better, honestly. I'm sorry for all the hassle.'

'There's still three months of probation to go in this job. You remember that the next time you decide to throw a minor ops tray all over the floor, right?' Marsh glared at him like a python eyeing a cornered coypu.

Matt swallowed. 'Be off my trolley if I didn't,' he said, because he felt he had to say something. As rapier wit went, it was about as effective as a paper stab-vest, but then he knew it would be. Jokes and Ms Marsh were not comfortable bedfellows. It was as if humour had woken up one morning, taken a look at the head on the pillow next to it, sworn blind never to drink five alcopops in an hour ever again, and fled the chamber white-haired and screaming.

'I mean, I'll try. Really, I will,' Matt said. Then added, 'There is one thing I wanted to ask you, though.'

Marsh fixed him with another stare, and Matt could have sworn his feet were turning a little granite-like.

'It's just that…well, Dr Roberro seems to have taken a bit of a dislike to me.'

'How?'

'Calls me a cloth-eared, hopeless, total waste of space who should have been aborted to spare the world the risk of contaminating the gene pool, that sort of thing.'

Linda Marsh grunted. 'Bit of light-hearted banter never hurt anyone.'

'Threatening to brand me with the resuscitation paddle because I hadn't stirred his coffee is not what I call banter,' Matt said.

Marsh shook her head. 'You need to stand up for your soddin' self, Danmor. It's the only way to get any respect in this world.'

'Oh, so if I stood up to you and told you where to go, you'd respect me?'

'No, I'd kick you in the balls and fire your arse for insubordination.'

'But—'

'Survival skills, Danmor. That's what you need to develop. When I was on night manoeuvres, I made sure I knew my enemy. Once, I captured a whole platoon without firing a shot.'

Probably turned to stone on catching sight of your face.

'I've never had a day's trouble with Roberro.' Marsh smiled, pulling her shoulders back. Matt imagined the walls of Isengard starting to shake and shiver.

'That's hardly surprising,' he blurted.

'What's that supposed to soddin' mean?'

'It means that you're more used to handling people like him,' he explained, backpedalling so fast he almost tripped over himself. 'What with your military background, and all.'

Linda Marsh was looking at him as if he'd just stepped off the nine-thirty-five express from Jupiter. If fire had started coming out of her nostrils, Matt would not have been at all surprised.

'Now listen here, Danmor. Roberro is a doctor. Remember that. He is a highly qualified, dedicated member of staff and we are here to support him in his role as a direct patient carer. He is also a total prat and a waste of bloody space and the chairman of the Trust's nephew. That puts him at the top of the soddin' food chain in the law of the jungle. Got that?'

'So, he won't be shocked to wake up one day with a poison dart in his neck,' muttered Matt with an attempt at a smile. It bounced off Linda Marsh's anti-humour force field like a tennis ball. She shook her head and turned to leave but hesitated in the corridor, turning back to pin Matt with a full-on glare. When she spoke, it was more an order than a question.

'Almost forgot. Jim's asked for next Saturday night off. You can cover him, can't you?'

Matt's gut fell into his socks. He knew he'd been caught off guard. 'Ummm,' he mumbled.

'Thought so. That's settled, then.' She turned away and hurried off, leaving Matt with an impotent frown.

Great, he thought and tugged hard at the straps on his rucksack. *Bloody great.* Yet another all-nighter, and on a week-end, too. He should have said no, but with that thought came the dread realisation that he had no reason to refuse. Matt's current social life was like the Sahara—desolate and unpopulated. He threw the rucksack over his shoulder and headed for the exit, wanting very much to be out of the place. He grabbed his cycle from the rack and headed off into the still, dark morning.

The hospital was pretty quiet at half past seven, it still being too early for most of the day staff to have arrived, and traffic was light. As he pedalled past the entrance to A&E, Matt saw Roberro flirting with one of the med students, a buxom girl with dark circles under her eyes from nights spent shadowing her mentor. Matt caught Roberro giving her a lizard smile, his hand straying to the head of his bloody stethoscope, his finger rolling along the chrome chill ring that held the diaphragm in place. As a sensuous hint, it was about as subtle as a Christina Aguilera video. Christ, was that bloody thing grafted to Roberro's neck? Why did he have to brandish it like a shaman with his totem? Okay, maybe a stethoscope was a bit more useful than a skull on a stick, and comparing Roberro with a witch doctor might be a bit harsh. Then again…

Fleetingly, just before he flew past and out of sight of the A&E, Matt saw the med student's eyes stray to Roberro's suggestive finger and nod. Just brilliant. He wanted to turn around, ride into the reception and scream at her: *It isn't worth it. Letting him paw you won't make you a better doctor.*

But by the time he'd stopped the bike, they'd disappeared into the labyrinth of the hospital.

CHAPTER FOUR

MATT PUMPED his legs and sped out of the hospital grounds to
flee the pall of depression descending over him. The chill,
dank January morning didn't help, with thick, low clouds
delaying the onset of dawn. Nor did the thought of returning
to the crappy two-room flat off the Iffley Road he rented with
its promise of early morning TV, and the latest world-shat-
tering events surrounding celebrity tiddlywinks with the stars,
or whatever other such mendacious bollocks passed as news
these days.

Matt's heart descended to a point somewhere around his
knees. The truth was that the TV was his only companion in
an otherwise empty flat. He suddenly couldn't face it. Not yet
anyway. The events of the last hour and a half at the hospital
needed to work themselves out in his head before he went to
bed. At least on the bike there was traffic and wind, and the
psychologist had said that when he felt like this it was best to
go for a walk or do something physical, rather than just dwell.

It had been the psychologist's bright idea to go back to
work. Immerse himself in daily life. Do something that
involved meeting lots of people. Not that Matt considered a
portering job a long-term option. As careers went, it held
about as much appeal as being an alligator orthodontist, but it
was hospital-based and a valid first step back on the "road to

recovery." Matt cringed at the phrase. Yet he'd taken the advice and applied for the portering job in a city where he knew no one.

Oxford had seemed as good a choice as any, in that he'd always loved the spires and the pinnacles. On school trips he'd been seduced by the hidden-away quadrangles and passage-ways that led to the secret chapels, halls and alleys. Away from the high street, with its nod to retail modernism, lurked an older world of cloisters and passages that might lead almost anywhere. Indeed, there were quiet corners of this city that had remained unchanged for five hundred years.

It was to those that places Matt was drawn time and again, to feel the stone of the old city wall under his hand or feast his eyes on neo-gothic finials from a long-gone age. He felt at home there, walled in by the ever-changing Cotswold limestone that lined the narrow, winding streets, finding comfort in his solitude, like an animal in some ancient stone burrow.

He exhaled with gusto and let the cold January air sting his face with a wake-up slap. Out on the road, it was a little easier to take the mental step back needed to look at why he was so pissed off with Linda Marsh and Giles Roberro. It wasn't difficult. He was there in Oxford because he had wanted a fresh start, a chance to recover from the derailment his life had suffered. Too old to have contemporaries at university there, and with no relatives in the area, the chance of bumping into anyone who might do a double take and say, 'Matt! Long time no see. I heard you'd been in a nasty acci-dent…' were slim. Or so he hoped.

So, when Roberro called him a 'moronic wannabe.' the derailment had done a quick and unwelcome house call in his head, tweaking at his paranoia. The obvious thing to do would be to leave. Marsh was a bigoted arse and the Gener-al's HR department was so unprofessional that it had let the details of his past history leak out to an idiot like Roberro.

Yet something kept him turning up for his shifts. A vague awareness that working was, indeed, aiding his 'road to recovery.' even. But was it worth all this grief so that, when he went back to the slot they were keeping open for him at the med school in Bristol, Matt could look them in the eye and tell them he'd done something vaguely paramedical while he recovered? Or was it pure stubborn defiance that dragged him out of bed every morning and kicked him through the General's doors for yet another dose of Marsh and Roberro, like a stick of seaside rock with 'mule' printed right through it?

He took a left on Observatory Road, the doubt an insomniac serpent, writhing and coiling. Was he reading too much into this? Had Roberro simply assumed that *all* twenty-seven-year-old porters hankered after a white coat and a stethoscope, aiming 'wannabe' his way on general principles? Or did he know that Matt had been a second-year med student on the Graduate Entry Course at Bristol until a year ago?

That would be a difficult one to sort out. Asking the git outright was out of the question. If Roberro didn't know and then found out, things would be three times worse. As for Marsh, she *had* taken a gamble with him, so Matt could almost forgive her the self-interest. After all, employing someone who'd been in hospital for six months after a messy RTA was a gamble. Especially since two of those months had been spent as a voluntary patient in a psychiatric unit. Okay, her way with words left a lot to be desired, 'Are you a card-carrying lunatic?' was about as subtle as Dick Van Dyke's Cockney accent. But it got the message across all right.

Matt pulled up at the junction of Observatory Road and Walton Street to turn left. There were blue flashing lights and a queue of traffic ahead. Looked like an accident. Matt grimaced at the irony but pressed on. He managed to weave his way forward between the static cars until he could take a right on Jericho Street, just as an ambulance with all the trimmings appeared on the scene.

Definitely an accident.

Matt's pulse did a quick fandango, and his mind slid unbidden down the potholed lane of empathetic memory like an Olympic luge with a faulty brake. What if the driver came to and found that his girlfriend was not in the car with him? What if she wasn't there because the paramedics had taken her first? What if her mashed-up limbs were more mashed up than his? What if her injuries were so bad that…

Matt shook his head to clear it. No point in revisiting this. No point at all. Better to seek out a distraction and turn away from this whole line of thinking. He'd moved on, hadn't he?

Yeah, right.

Traffic thinned the nearer he got to Jericho itself. So why he didn't carry straight on instead of turning left, Matt had no idea. Turn he did, though, forcing his mind to anticipate the bacon bap at the mobile café near the station. He'd stuff it in the rucksack and head on up the canal towpath for a couple of miles, just to clear his head. Maybe head towards Duke's Cut and then back to Wolvercote. After the rain they'd had, the weir at the Carp Inn would be in full flow this morning. He liked the weir. Liked its raw power. He often found himself standing near it, watching the water swirl and froth, wondering what it would feel like to be in that water with all that tumbling, sucking, boiling force about him.

A sudden rush of despond washed over him like a slew of filthy water. Who was he kidding? He knew what the weir was all about and it had nothing to do with admiring the power of nature. It was about making it easier on everyone he left behind if it looked like an accident. His three brothers and a sister (averagely close—Christmas, Easter and christenings de rigueur) would be upset of course, but would accept the accident scenario with just one or two transient and quickly dismissed doubts. At least tumbling into the weir was plausible as an accident, unlike an aspirin overdose, or the slow death of paracetamol, or a smashed skull at the bottom of the suspension bridge at Clifton…

Matt pedalled a bit faster. It had been a bad morning, but he still had things under control. Even so, he'd go to the weir just to reassure himself that it was there should he need it.

Hart Road was empty of traffic. He slowed down as he

approached the junction with Great Clarendon Street and happened to glance to his left as he pulled up to a stop. He was parallel to St Barnabas' School. Right at the south-eastern corner was a kids' playground with a log cabin, swings, and a roundabout. What it was that made him look across he'd never know. At this time in the morning, with the grey dawn yet to pour colour into the day, it should have been empty. But look across he did. What he saw made him slam on the brakes and skid to a full stop.

Matt's breath stuttered in his throat. He blinked and rubbed his eyes. Surely not. But yes, there was no denying it.

Someone was strapped to the roundabout, arms and legs splayed open like a double wishbone.

CHAPTER FIVE

It was a children's play area, so it was slightly less incongruous to see a handful of kids in there too. Why they were standing around chanting was anyone's guess. It added a very odd vibe to the scene. And the cherry on the weirdsville cake was the kid on top of the roundabout straddling the splayed victim, brandishing what looked like a small scimitar in both hands.

Matt would have been the first to admit that Oxford was an interesting city, full of very bright people who knew as much about the real world as a life dedicated to theoretical quantum physics or medieval Ottoman architecture of the Balkans might allow. Which was to say, not much. He saw them in the street every day, dressed in clothes chosen from a charity shop by a visually challenged chimpanzee. Perfectly polite, but as eccentric as a box of croakers.

He had not yet, however, seen anyone sacrificed. Let alone sacrificed by a group of children.

The thought struck him that this might be a school play being performed in atmospheric outdoor conditions by some idiotically enthusiastic school drama group. But, he couldn't for the life of him see any teachers or camcorder-wielding parents. No, it was just a bloke splayed on the roundabout and the chanting children and that wicked-looking knife…

His pulse accelerated to a thrum.

At that point, he did what any youngish bloke who had no experience of kids other than a couple of nephews and a niece under ten would do. He looked up and down the street to see if anyone else might take the responsibility and groaned at seeing not a soul. Cursing, he pushed his bike up onto the pavement and shouted a half-hearted, 'Oi, do your parents know you're out here?'

Linda Marsh would have laughed herself apoplectic. Even Matt, on hearing himself actually say it, realised instantly that, as an authoritative reprimand, it carried about as much weight as a rice-paper hammer. No parent in their right mind would have got up that morning and shooed little Shane or Olivia off with, 'Now, don't forget your pencil case and oh, have a good sacrificial ceremony in the park on your way to school, won't you, darling.'

Matt's shout, though, did get a reaction. They didn't flinch, but neither did they jeer or tell him to bugger off. With an eerie synchronicity, the children all turned towards him and hissed like cornered cats. At least, hiss was what his brain came up with, even if as adjectives went it was a tad under-stated. Because with the hiss came a sudden gust of wind that blew Matt onto his backside with an ungraceful and painful thud.

There was something else on that wind, too—a very unpleasant sweet and sickly smell, redolent of something furry that had given up the ghost and was now providing a generous banquet for a whole generation of maggots. But that registered for the briefest of moments in Matt's head. Like most rational human beings, when confronted with inexplicable slips or clumsiness, Matt blamed either bad luck or the weather. And because he was fed up with blaming everything on the former, he opted for an overenthusiastic south-westerly as the cause of his ungainly sit-down. *What were the chances of a gust of wind picking up just at that minute and blowing us over, eh?* chortled that bit of his mind that held the anchor chain of his sanity firmly in its grasp and was reluctant to let go. The sheer ignominy of falling down made his face burn with embarrassment; he'd been humiliated twice already that morning by experts, and he was buggered if he was going to let it happen again. Especially not by a bunch of kids.

Mouth clamped shut, Matt got up. He could see that the entrance to the park was twenty yards away on Great Clarendon Street.

'Right,' he said, brushing himself off, his face set as he strode along the railings with new purpose, noting how the children all followed him with their eyes as he marched. 'I'm coming in. Whatever evil little game this is, I'm not playing. And you'd better all be gone by the time I'm in there, or so help me…'

He turned into the park. None of the children had moved. This close, Matt could hear that the hiss they'd all produced earlier on continued as a low, sibilant, droning note. None of them seemed the slightest bit bothered.

Matt hesitated. A swell of doubt and disquiet sloshed over him as he tried, desperately, to formulate a plan of action. He couldn't quite make out how old any of them were because of their hoods. Indeed, in the grey light they all looked very similar, except for the one with the knife, who hissed the loudest and who had the meanest look in his eye, with a monobrow to boot.

'Right,' Matt said again. 'I've warned you.' He reached for his mobile and brandished it. 'I have police and social services' number here. You leave me no choice.'

That part wasn't even a bluff. He'd lost count of the times that someone had asked him for the number in the hospital, so he'd stuck it in his contacts. It didn't matter that there would be no one there at this time. It didn't look like this crowd of kids had any idea what time it was, anyway. He pressed the dial button and a jolt of something—static, he supposed—shot up his finger. Matt dropped the phone.

More shitty luck? A power surge on the network just at the wrong bloody moment?

'Shit,' Matt said, shaking his hand.

A malevolent grin had spread over the lips of all the children at the same time.

Now he was really miffed. 'Okay, you've had your chance.'

The kid with the knife raised his chin and hissed a little louder. The circle of kids below shifted to form a line facing Matt. As one, they pulled down their hoodies a little further.

'Oh yeah?' Matt said in a voice full of don't-even-think-about-it. He looked around for a weapon and found a two-foot length of branch. He realised with a sudden flash of clarity that turning to run was probably the best option, but there was still that bloke on the roundabout, and Matt would put money on him and the stick being the victim's only hope.

'I'm warning you,' Matt said. 'I've never hit a kid, but I'm willing to make an exception if you lot start anything.'

The kid with the knife lifted his chin once more—this time to scream. At least, that was the word that best fitted the cacophonous noise that emerged. Several things happened at once. The line of kids began to run forward just as a flock of crows, startled by the scream, took off from a tree at the edge of the park. Matt raised the stick in both hands and tried not to think of the headlines:

Hospital porter gets six years for assaulting children.

Or worse:

Card-carrying lunatic jailed for child assault.

'Oh shit,' he said, as out of the corner of his eye he saw the kid with the knife raise it up once again to finish off what he had started before Matt butted in.

'Shit, shit, SHIT!' Matt said again, as the noise of the crows above demanded his attention. They weren't just cawing now; they were cawing for England. Cawing and wheeling together around a tight knot in the air, just above where the kid with the knife was staring and screaming out that unearthly ululation. Wheeling and…well, doing what birds generally did from a great height.

The knife wielder stopped screaming and started spluttering. The line of Stepford kids came to a halt as well. Their leader was in trouble, because the sloppy bowel contents of thirty well-fed and feisty Oxford crows was finding its target. Matt could hear the wet slaps as the stray bombs from the crow squadron hit the roundabout.

Nasty.

He didn't think it for long, though, because the knife-wielding leader was in dire straits. He clawed at his eyes, choking and spitting. He stumbled off the roundabout, the knife clattering from his hand. The other kids seemed momentarily paralysed, and Matt saw his opportunity. He stepped forward with the stick in his outstretched hands and thwacked the half-blind leader gently on the backside.

'Go on, bugger off back to wherever the hell it is you came from.' It was nothing more than a tap, yet the effect was electrifying. The bird crap victim went rigid and then began to shake and quiver like a twanged ruler jammed into a desk. The movement became more and more violent, accompanied by another half-hearted hiss, this one cut short by a nause-ating gurgle. It was perhaps the most distressing thing Matt had seen or heard in many weeks, if you discounted the bloke last Tuesday in A&E who'd tried to circumcise himself with an electric kitchen knife.

The other kids reacted as one. They picked up the convulsing leader and ran with him towards the bushes, ignoring Matt completely. He, meanwhile, could only gape open-mouthed at what was happening.

Afterwards, Matt liked to think that they disappeared into the small copse of trees along a path to their gang HQ. But, what he really saw was a sort of gap open up in the air, into which the kids all ran. He wasn't paying that much attention though, because his eyes were riveted on the quivering bird-crap-coated kid, who appeared to be splitting in half as they carried him. A grey-white appendage poked through the material of the kid's sweatshirt and tried to unfurl itself. There was a snapping noise, more whiffs of *eau d'abattoir* and then... nothing.

The kids had disappeared. The silence that fell got top

marks for eerie, punctuated by a distant echo of the cawing birds. A car sped past on Great Clarendon Street. From behind him, Matt heard a voice from the roundabout.

'Excuse me? Do you think you could untie me? I am so very grateful for your help, and I realise that this is most inconvenient, but you see, lying here is doing nothing for my lumbago.'

CHAPTER SIX

MATT TURNED to peer at the face straining up over a broad chest. Not a young face, jowly and clean shaven, but one that looked irrepressibly cheerful, under the circumstances. The weird first impression that registered was of a deconstructed panda—above the face was a full head of snow-white hair, but the eyebrows beneath were bushy and black.

'Hello?' said the man again when Matt failed to respond. His eyes swivelled warily back to the spot where the kids had all disappeared.

'DO YOU HAVE A HEARING IMPAIRMENT?' the man asked.

'Sorry,' Matt replied, finally hurrying over. 'Sorry. Just hang on while I untie these…' He grunted in concentration.

The knots securing the man's wrists and ankles to the handles on the roundabout were tied with what appeared to be rough rope. But when Matt tried undoing them, he was disconcerted to find that the rope had an oddly hairy feel. Also, the more he tugged at the knots, the tighter they became.

'You will need a blade.' The man winced as the rope contracted around his wrists.

'Blade, right.' Matt began tapping his pockets and looking

back towards his bike, wondering if he had a penknife in the little tool kit under the seat.

'I think you'll find that the one they dropped will be sharp enough,' the man said, just managing not to make it sound too patronising.

Matt's eyes strayed to the scimitar thing lying on the ground. The blade was pewter-grey, the handle leather-bound and worn. It looked like one of those toy plastic ones that came with a shield and a Roman helmet and cost 99p back when Woolworths had been a magic emporium full of cheap treats.

Yet it didn't feel much like plastic when Matt picked it up. In fact, the handle was strangely warm to the touch, and the thing sang with a metallic *zing* when he hefted it. The curved blade was a bit awkward to use, but incredibly sharp. In fact, he didn't even have to do any sawing. The fibres of the rope melted away at the knife's touch. Within seconds, Matt had freed the man's hands; he sat up with a groan and began massaging his wrists as Matt went to work on his ankles. Two more swipes of the blade and the rope fell away, the fibres writhing on the ground as if they'd been burned. The man swung his legs over and stood, swaying. Matt took a step back to survey the children's would-be victim. Without warning, the man let out a hiss of air, swooned, and sat back down heavily. Matt reached forward only to be waved away.

'No, it's nothing. Pins and needles in my foot, which will pass, I'm sure.' The man smiled and held out a hand. 'Porter's the name.'

'Mathew Danmor. People call me Matt.' Matt shook the hand. It was smooth and dry.

Porter tried his feet again and didn't wince this time. Like Matt, he wasn't tall; unlike Matt, he had a full figure. He was clean shaven and wore a three-piece suit of sage green over a white shirt and a red-and-black striped tie. There were highly polished brown brogues on his feet and, from the way he held his back straight when he stood, Matt would have put money on there being a bit of military in his background.

'It goes without saying that I am delighted to meet you, Matt Danmor,' Mr Porter said.

'Are you okay?' Matt asked. 'I mean, they didn't…'

'No, they did not. I am perfectly fine, thanks to you.' Porter smiled and glanced at a splash of crow guano glistening on the elbow of his suit. He brushed it away, and Matt frowned. Despite the fact that the roundabout resembled something that thirty crows had used repeatedly for target practise, Mr Porter had managed to emerge almost unscathed.

'Should I call an ambulance?' Matt asked.

The morning light was brightening by the second. Matt found his phone near where he'd dropped it. It was cool to the touch and lit up when he pressed the power button.

'Ambulance? Oh, I don't think that will be necessary.' Mr Porter beamed.

There was something about that smile. Matt found himself reminded of moving to a house in Bristol with his family when he was six and being made to fetch a ball that his brother had just kicked into next door's garden. The ball had taken a deflection off Matt's shoulder and so, despite his protestations, retrieval responsibility was his. There had, up to that point, been no introductions. In the time it had taken to walk through the garden, out on to the street and up to next door's front door, Matt's brother had graphically described the neighbours as potential cannibals, vampires, zombies, or a combination of all three, the whole fabricated gory lot embellished with blood-curdling descriptions of the acts they had perpetrated, and *would* perpetrate, on Matt.

Quaking with fear, Matt had rung the doorbell. The door creaked open to reveal a septuagenarian man with twinkling eyes who'd listened to Matt stammering his request without protest. The man fetched the ball, while his silver-haired wife rustled up two chocolate biscuits and a glass of lemon squash, much to Matt's delighted relief and his brother's chagrin. The neighbour, whose name was Wil, exuded warmth and good humour and became Matt's friend from that day on. But it was Wil's eyes Matt always remembered. Full of kindness, oozing wisdom and a glint that—even at an early age—taught Matt that his brother's taunts and petty niggles were just meaningless drops in the cosmic ocean. Matt caught a glimpse of that exact same wise and sanguine look in Porter's eyes as he smiled. He didn't seem to be that bothered about what had been about to happen to him. Which, of course, made him either a saint or a complete grade-A head case.

'What about the police?' Matt said. 'I know they're pretty hot on knife crime.'

'Yes,' Mr Porter said dubiously. 'Still, no harm actually done…'

'No harm?' Matt protested. 'They were about to make you into a kebab.' He held the knife up. 'I mean, just look at this thing.'

Mr Porter fussed with the top button of his shirt. 'The thing is, I do try to avoid the authorities here in Oxford if I possibly can.'

It was such a bizarre and incongruous thing to say that, for a long ten seconds, Matt didn't speak. Finally, he managed, 'Are you on the run or something?'

'Only from Mrs Porter. Her punishment for the wrong proportion of Tanqueray to Schweppes is severe in the extreme.'

Matt didn't laugh. 'Those kids weren't just calling you names. They were—'

'I know.' Mr Porter held up his hands. 'And, strictly speaking, we should absolutely contact the police. But one also has to consider how they might react to such a story.'

'What do you mean?'

'Where are my attackers?'

'On the street somewhere.'

Mr Porter nodded but his lips had gone very thin. 'Much as it irks me to say this, imagine yourself a police officer called to the park by an elderly gentleman and a young man. There are ropes on the ground. They'll find a knife on you. Tainted as they are by the worst aspects of society and its vices, they will, undoubtedly, look for…other explanations.'

Matt stared at Mr Porter in horror. 'You mean—'

'A tiff between two admittedly unlikely lovers after a little jogging, exactly.'

'Jogging? You mean dogging.'

'Do I? Yes, of course I do. Regardless, one partner takes umbrage and calls the police with a ridiculous story just to cause embarrassment to the other.'

'But—'

'Matt, please don't think that I am implying anything, but if you have had dealings with the police at any stage in your young life, you must know that they are programmed for cynicism.'

Matt had, indeed, had dealings with the police in A&E on a regular basis, so he knew that Mr Porter was right. They wouldn't see the young Samaritan having rescued the respectable man from The Hannibal Lecter Under Twelve Admiration Society. They would see an old queen and a rent boy.

'And obviously, there's the knife,' Mr Porter added. 'It would take some explaining.'

Matt stared at the blade and immediately hid it behind his back while glancing out to the street to see who was watching.

'But those kids…' Matt began, unsure of how to finish it.

'Indeed, those…kids.' Mr Porter nodded and sent another sympathetic smile Matt's way. 'My office is just a few streets away. I don't know about you, but I'm starving. Have you had any breakfast yet?'

On cue, Matt's stomach did an impression of a mountain lion warning off a rival.

'Excellent,' Mr Porter said and started walking towards the park entrance. 'We're down near the canal. First left off Albert Street.'

Matt stared after him, confusion simmering in his brain. What the hell was going on? After all that, was he meant to simply follow this bloke? Half of him wanted to walk away, but the other half was too intrigued and bewildered by what he'd just witnessed for that. Besides, he really was quite hungry.

Matt picked his bike up from where he'd left it on the pavement, and they walked down Clarendon Street, Mr Porter striding along at a fair pace with Matt pushing his bike alongside, silence hanging between them.

'I think it has stopped raining,' said Mr Porter eventually. 'I wouldn't be at all surprised if the sun made an appearance later this morning. I think we've had enough precipitation for a good while, don't y—'

Matt stopped walking. 'Look, Mr Porter, I'm genuinely delighted that you're unharmed, but I think I'm going to explode unless I get some answers here. Why were those children trying to stick a scimitar in your chest?'

'Children, yes,' Mr Porter said but with an odd, faraway expression. 'How many did you actually see, Matt?'

'Eight. Seven on the ground and Charlie Manson organising the spit roast above you on the roundabout.'

'Shall we cross here?' Mr Porter suggested, guiding Matt across the road.

Exasperated, Matt followed.

'Children,' Mr Porter mused as they walked. 'In a play area. Clever, that.'

'What?' Matt said.

Mr Porter didn't slow down or stop. He strode along like a major on the way to inspect the troops. But he cleared his throat as if he'd come to some sort of conclusion.

'Matt, you look like a nice, normal sort of chap.'

Yeah, thought Matt, casting his mind back to his usual cursory glance in the bathroom mirror that morning. He had looked normal. At least, the mirror hadn't cracked or anything. But then, a crate full of black mambas looked just like any normal old crate until you opened the lid and inspected the contents.

'What's that supposed to mean, exactly?' Matt asked.

'It means that sometimes you just have to accept what you find as…what you find.'

'Not following,' Matt said.

'Well, clearly, I was the victim of a magging.'

'A magging?' Matt said. 'I think you mean mugging.'

'Exactly. They wanted thingummy…um, you know…'

'Money?' Matt suggested.

'Yes, money. They wanted money.'

'Muggers usually threaten, take the money and run. They don't stand around howling at the sky and hissing at each other.'

'Perhaps they were hissing to express their disapproval at your intervention.' Mr Porter was almost running now. Matt got the distinct impression that he was fishing in uncharted waters with an illegal pole.

'Well, they weren't rehearsing a scene from *Jack and the Beanstalk*, I know that,' Matt argued. 'To me, they looked like a bunch of very small but determined psychopaths.'

Mr Porter took a sharp left and, panting, drew up outside a heavy wooden door in a red brick wall. It was an oversized garage of the lockup-under-the-arches-at-Waterloo Station School of Architecture. It had a curved, sludgy brown roof and a sign above the door that read *HIPPOSYNC ENTER-PRISES*. Still wheezing slightly, Mr Porter opened the door and stepped inside.

'You can leave your bicycle here; it will be quite safe.'

CHAPTER SEVEN

INSIDE, a coir mat with *Welcome* written on it was the first thing Matt saw. A long corridor ran the length of the building, with four sets of doors on either side, plus one at the end facing the entrance. There were no windows, just three fluorescent strips, which illuminated the corridor with a garish light. One of the bulbs flickered constantly. The walls were a drab green, and the doors looked old and heavy and gleamed with shiny brown paint. On the wall near to the welcome mat was a cartoon sign hanging at a jaunty angle from a blue drawing pin:

You don't have to be mad to work here, but it helps.

MATT HAD SEEN the same sign a dozen times in as many cramped and joyless offices. Someone's idea of a good laugh, no doubt, but one that, in Matt's experience, evoked nothing but groans of contempt for its banal clichéd message. At Hipposync, someone had seen fit to cross out, '…but it helps.' and amend it with, '…but we are equal opportunity employers.'

Under the poster and underlined in red was:

Avoid accidents in the workplace. Protection must be worn at all times. Lost talismans must be reported to Mrs Hoblip immediately.

'I SEE someone has a sense of humour,' Matt said.

Mr Porter peered at the note and nodded. 'Unfortunately, it is not Mrs Hoblip. She had hers surgically removed at eighteen months of age. Bit of a fad in those days amongst her…' Mr Porter stopped mid-sentence and cleared his throat again. 'But overall, we run a pretty tight ship.'

'You're not related to someone called Linda Marsh, by any chance?' murmured Matt, but Mr Porter didn't answer. He was already striding up the corridor.

'I'm right at the end,' he said over his shoulder. Matt followed, reading the signs above the doors: *Citizenship*, *Asylum*, and *KOL*.

'What's KOL?' Matt asked.

'Knowledge of Life. Your lot have become very strict on settlement applications.'

'You're something to do with immigration, then?' Matt asked, as light began to dawn in his head.

'Something, yes.' Mr Porter nodded with a funny little smile. They passed another door, this one with *DC Farmer, Scribe Services* stuck on it in embossed blue Dymo tape.

'Writes stuff down. In 450 languages. At the same time,' said Mr Porter.

Matt toyed with asking, but by then they'd arrived at a door that had *PORTER* written above it in big gold lettering.

'Here we are,' said Mr Porter jovially as he opened the door and stepped inside. 'The one place where I can feel absolutely safe.'

Matt had time to appreciate that the office was much

bigger than he'd expected it to be before his legs went from beneath him. A second later, he was face down on the carpet, more shocked than hurt. In fact, the landing had been surprisingly soft, while the sudden, overriding sensation he had was not of agony but of fresh pine. It was everywhere. Not the overpowering, eye-watering disinfectant reek that was used with such little success to try and mask the ammonia stench of urine in men's toilets. No, this was zesty and fresh. The smell, combined with the prickling in his cheeks, led to him realising that the carpet was full of real pine needles. Feeling like an idiot for tripping, Matt tried to lever himself up. But something was sticking into the small of his back, stopping him from moving, and he realised with dumb amazement that he hadn't fallen: he'd been thrown.

From behind him, he heard Mr Porter speak. 'Kylah, please. There is absolutely no need for this.'

'Look at the alarm. It's gone haywire. I'm telling you, he's packing iron.' Girl's voice. Youngish. No nonsense.

'Even so, give him the benefit of a little doubt. This is not the way to treat guests.'

The pressure on his spine eased and he swivelled his head around to see Mr Porter looking highly embarrassed but extending a hand to help him up. Matt brushed pine needles from his jeans and brow, looking around properly for the first time. The room was cluttered. Well…half of it was. Big windows looked out across an open stretch of yard towards the canal and the towpath on the other bank, and it was this view that cut the room in two.

On one side of the windows, the room was a junk shop box room where dressers, wardrobes, hatstands, and stacked chairs lined the wall. The other half looked more like an office—all clean lines, light wood, filing cabinets and a pine desk. Very business like. Much like the girl who stood in front of the desk, glaring at Matt with almost unbridled hostility.

'Matt Danmor, this is my niece, Kylah.' Porter made the introductions.

Matt wanted to say hello, but it seemed someone had

squirted superglue onto the roof of his mouth. Instead, he contented himself with an imbecilic nod while he studied the girl and tried to work out something drop-dead witty to say.

She was no more than five foot two, dark-haired and olive-skinned. She wore a tight black cardigan over a white blouse and black trousers, in a non-provocative way that still somehow did enough to show that she had all the right bits in all the right places. Miss Hipposync Enterprises 2024 of that there was no doubt. And, like all those girls on calendars or in films or magazines that he looked at and harmlessly fantasised over, completely out of Matt's league. On one level, knowing that helped. But it still took another ten seconds until, finally, his brain decided to lend a hand and put him out of his misery by ungluing his tongue, though it still felt like it had at least one granny knot in it.

'Was it something I said?' he mumbled. If he'd hoped for a chortle or even a twitch at the corner of her mouth to acknowledge his stunning repartee, he was disappointed.

'Where's the iron?' she demanded.

'Iron? Like, in getting the creases out of clothes? Not my strong point actually…'

'I mean the ferric stuff,' snapped Kylah. 'Rusts in the rain. Made from ore by smelting.' She made the process sound like something heinous.

Could be a wind-up, thought Matt. But the look on Kylah's face was straight from the Mel Gibson-as-Wallace, leading-the-Scots-into-battle school of aggression. He made himself think harder.

'My dad gave me a small tyre iron I carry on my keyring,' he said. 'It's in my bag.' He started undoing the buckles of his rucksack.

'Stay right where you are,' Kylah ordered, and Matt noticed that she held something in her hand. It was long and had a bulbous, egg-shaped end, which glowed a yellow-green colour as Matt watched. 'Put the bag against the wall and stand away from it. Now.'

Matt did as he was told, realising that this day probably

couldn't get much weirder if a headless horseman burst in and asked for directions to the Bodleian. Kylah moved toward the rucksack, and the glowing thing in her hand glowed ever brighter. A second thought struck Matt. Weird as the day was turning out to be, it was well worth it to be able to watch Kylah moving with cat-like grace across the floor.

She chose that moment to look up at him with suspicion written all over her face, and Matt prayed he wasn't dribbling. Apparently satisfied that he was not going to rush back and undo the buckles, she hurried to another room (which, from the noise of taps running, Matt assumed was a bathroom), from which she emerged with a wet towel. Gingerly, she threw the towel over the rucksack so as to completely cover it. Matt noted that the glowing egg thing glowed a little less as she did it.

'Kylah is also head of security here at Hipposync,' Mr Porter said with an apologetic air while making his hands into claw shapes and baring his teeth. Matt couldn't help noticing that he did this with one eye on Kylah to ensure that she didn't see. She shot him a suspicious glance, but Mr Porter knitted his fingers together and his expression melted back into serene amusement. 'Right, I promised you a breakfast. Full English suit you?'

'Uh, yes. Think I could manage that,' Matt said.

Mr Porter got to his feet. 'Okey-dokey,' he said with alacrity and moved with surprising speed towards the door. 'I'll just go and sort that out with the canteen while you explain to Kylah all about this morning's little…situation.' With that, he was out of the door and whistling down the corridor.

'Uncle Ernest?' Kylah yelled after him.

'Canteen?' said Matt.

The whistling receded, leaving Kylah to mutter under her breath before she turned towards Matt.

'What situation?' she asked through clenched teeth.

Matt couldn't help but notice that her eyes, though currently full of unmitigated frustration, were large and expressive and of an extraordinary bright blue, flecked with little motes of yellow gold.

'Has anyone ever told you that you have the most amazing eyes?'

All the saliva turned to sand in Matt's mouth. What the hell was he thinking of? Christ, that sounded like number four in the world's top twenty crap chat-up lines. He'd never said anything like that to anyone in his life. He felt himself turn crimson from the knees up.

'That's not very polite,' Kylah said.

Matt hesitated. He had expected derision or even a 'puh-lease' br sh off. He had not expected a sour accusation of bad manners.

'I mean it,' he stammered. 'They're amazing.'

'Amazing is one way of describing them, I suppose. The kids at school preferred 'goggle-eyes' or 'straighty.' My parents were going to get them squinted, but the apothecary said I'd grow into it.' She shook her head. 'You good-looking ones are all the same. You think you're better than the rest of us just because of some lucky genes. Please keep your sarcastic comments to yourself, and let's get back to the situation, shall we?'

Matt frowned, tried to smile and found the smile freezing on his lips. It was a piss-take, obviously. Some sort of deconstructed feminist irony number she was doing on him. It had to be, because the alternative was that she was suggesting that she was somehow not a traffic-stopping stunner, while he was not bad-looking. Laughable, but then why was there no sly stuff-that-in-your-pipe-and-smoke-it smile on her lips? All that Matt saw was the slightly disgruntled look of someone feeling a little fed up with her lot, not liking having it shoved back in her face. Still, whatever was happening, it definitely wasn't going the way he'd meant it to.

'Look, I didn't mean to—'

Kylah held up her hand to stop him in mid-apology. 'What situation?' she asked again, very slowly.

'Mind if I sit down?' Matt asked feebly. The tilting world was making him a little lightheaded.

Kylah gestured towards a chair.

'Right. Situation. Right,' he babbled. 'Difficult to know where to begin. Maybe it started with the exploding saline bags…or with seeing Roberro trying to seduce another med student…or maybe it was the accident on Walton Street. Or, maybe it really only started with the kid howling on the roundabout as he held this over your uncle's chest.' Matt reached for the six-inch long blade he'd stuffed in his belt. 'Could have done me a real injury throwing me down like that with this thing where it was. Doesn't bear thinking about.' He put the curved blade on the table in front of him, and saw Kylah shoot up out of her chair like she'd been electrocuted. The glowing egg-wand thing was now a pulsating orange like a miniature sun.

Someone knocked on the door. Kylah looked from the weapon to Matt and then back to the weapon again. All Matt could do was shrug. She backed away and, still looking at the scimitar, opened the door to her uncle. Mr Porter struggled in under the weight of a huge tray laden with plates and silver platters. The smell of cooked bacon was almost palpable.

'Here we are,' said Mr Porter. 'A Mrs Hoblip special.' He put the tray on a sturdy-looking oak desk and dabbed at his face with a handkerchief, smiling. 'I see that you two are getting on well. Excellent.'

'Mr Danmor—'

'Matt.' Matt earned a frosty glare for his trouble.

'Matt,' Kylah said, 'was about to tell me about this morning's situation. We've got to this part.' She pointed at the blade.

'Ah,' Mr Porter said, the smile fading from his face quicker than Matt could have said, 'psychopath on a roundabout.'

'I don't need to tell you that this is a machara,' added Kylah, glaring at her uncle.

'Not a scimitar, then?' asked Matt.

'No,' explained Kylah. 'Scimitars are longer. Swords rather than daggers. This evil little weapon is the favourite of the Ghoulshee.'

'Blimey,' Matt said blankly. 'I thought they made handbags.'

'Ghoulshee, not Gucci,' Kylah snapped. 'The machara is a lethal weapon.'

'Hmm, machara, yes,' Mr Porter mused. 'I feared it might be. So, fried or scrambled eggs, Matt?'

Matt turned his gaze to Mr Porter, who was smiling pleasantly again.

'Um…scrambled, I think.'

'I'm going to scream very loudly in a moment,' Kylah said, with quiet menace.

'Now, Kylah,' Mr Porter said in what Matt assumed must be his firm voice. It sounded about as firm as soggy cardboard to Matt, but then he had a feeling that Mr Porter didn't do ranting and raving. Somehow, he didn't need to. 'Matt has done me a very big service this morning and I have promised him breakfast in return. So, let's all eat and Matt can tell you the story as we avail ourselves of Mrs Hoblip's skill with a frying pan. Oh, and there's coffee and toast for you, my dear, as I'm sure you haven't eaten yet,' Mr Porter added.

Kylah let out a nasal sigh and shook her head. But she took the proffered cup.

CHAPTER EIGHT

THE FOOD WAS DELICIOUS. Matt wasn't quite sure why, but it was, without doubt, one of the best breakfasts he'd ever tasted. Was it the ambience in the room, redolent as it was of old wood, leather and fresh pine? Or was it that Kylah was sitting not ten feet away, munching toast and sipping coffee? While Matt concentrated hard on not dripping too much bacon fat on his T-shirt, she somehow managed to make munching toast look incredibly elegant.

'Situation, remember? I'm still waiting for an explanation,' she said after several moments of silent, or as in Mr Porter's case, not so silent, chewing.

'Right,' Matt said and put down the sausage he'd just pierced with his fork. He started with the saline incident, giving Kylah a blow-by-blow account of his day right up to the point at which he'd seen that grisly, grey appendage trying to poke its way out of the dagger-wielding kid's sweatshirt. By the time he'd finished, her mouth had set into a line of grim irritation, which she vented on her still merrily chomping uncle.

'How many times have I asked you not to walk through that park when it's not yet light, Uncle Ernest?'

'Too many times for me to remember, Kylah. However, it

was *almost* light and I must have the exercise, as you well know.'

'Buy a rowing machine.'

Matt decided this needed clarification. 'Excuse me, but I get the impression that this attack was not exactly unexpected?'

Kylah and Mr Porter exchanged glances. Mr Porter answered, 'Not entirely, no.'

Kylah stared at the…*wand*. The egg was glowing faintly. 'Are you sure you don't have any more iron on you?'

'It's possible he has traces in his teeth or nails in his boots. It's of no consequence,' Mr Porter said with a dismissive wave.

'Could someone please explain to me what the hell is going on?' Matt didn't mean it to sound so plaintive, but it did, even to his ears.

'Kylah?' prompted Mr Porter.

She looked at her uncle, aghast. 'He doesn't have any clearance.'

'For what?' Matt asked.

'For this.' Kylah waved her arms to take in the room. 'You shouldn't even be here.'

'Why? What exactly do you do here?'

Mr Porter chuckled. 'We publish esoteric texts here at Hipposync. Things no one else will touch.'

Kylah shook her head. 'At least that's what it says we do at Companies House. But what we really do is highly confidential. You'd have to sign an official document…'

'I don't have any problem with that,' Matt said, aware that there was a lot more going on here than was visible on the surface.

Kylah took a good twenty seconds to think before she spoke again. 'Okay. I'll tell you what it is we do here, if you allow us to use some equipment to extract the information about the attack from your memory.'

'Extract?'

'Yes. It allows us to copy what you saw, so that we can analyse it.'

'Like some sort of memory video?'

'Yes. Something like that.'

Matt shook his head in wonderment. 'Technology these days, eh?'

'So, you'll agree to that and swear to it?'

'Like I said, no problem. Now, what's so hush-hush about this place?'

Matt peered at Mr Porter and saw that, though a smile still played on his lips, it had become a sad, wintry shadow of itself.

'What are you?' Matt pressed. 'MI5? Special Ops? What?'

'None of the above.' Kylah sighed as she said it. 'My uncle, Mr Porter...he's...this is really quite difficult.'

'Nonsense,' Mr Porter chided her. 'Matt, what is it you do again?'

'Ah, that's where it's sort of ironic. I'm a porter, too. At the hospital. For the time being, anyway.'

'And do you know where the name Porter comes from?' Mr Porter beamed.

Matt nodded. 'Got an A in French GCSE and did a degree in English before I decided on medicine. So, *portier*, from the French. Doorkeeper.'

'Very good, Matt.' He nodded and sent his niece a smile of approval.

Kylah took a breath and decided to get it over with. 'Hipposync Enterprises.' she said, 'is a front for the Department of Fimmigration.'

The elongated silence that followed was punctuated only by the moist chewing noises of Mr Porter enjoying his breakfast.

'You did say Fimmigration?' Matt asked.

'Yes,' said Mr Porter. 'As in Fae immigration.'

'As in Fae for faeries?'

'You're really quite etymologically sharp, Matt. Did you know that?' Mr Porter was beaming now.

'Okay,' Matt said and laughed. He didn't like the hollow sound it made. 'This is a wind-up, right?'

'You wanted to know, and we're telling you.' Kylah was all business. She reached into a drawer and pulled out a green stone attached to a leather strap. 'We monitor movements between here and there. The term Fae tends to cause the same sort of reaction as you just exhibited. But the people on your side couldn't come up with anything better. Hipposync, for want of a better word, is an embassy. Strictly speaking, you're sitting in a chair in another dimension at this very moment.'

'Another dimension?'

Kylah shrugged. 'It's the easiest way to explain it. I could have gone for Avalon or Otherworld, Tír na nÓg, or Mag Mell. I mean, they all boil down to the same thing. We watch who comes in and out and keep an eye on who's here already. I have to admit, it's mainly one-way traffic. There are very few of your lot going through, due to the fact that you can't normally see us and therefore don't really know of our existence. So, by and large, it's our lot who want to come this way.'

'Our lot? You mean…'

'*Homo elementus* comes the closest, if you like Latin.'

Matt didn't. Nor did he like having the Mickey taken out of him. And this was all wearing very thin.

———

HE ALLOWED HIMSELF A WRY SMILE. This was all complete bollocks, but the breakfast was top notch, and Kylah was pretty good at keeping up the charade, as well as being very pleasant on the eye. He didn't see any harm in playing along for a while.

'So, what about what happened this morning?' he asked. 'What was all that about?'

'Ghoulshee separatists. They're fundamentalist Fae. They feel repressed and are fighting for their rights,' Kylah said with a look on her face that suggested that the toast she'd munched was, in fact, dried guano.

'Which are?' Matt finally bit into the very juicy sausage.

'The usual stuff that always arises when you're motivated by emotional resentment of rival communities,' Kylah said. 'They want parity for their language, freedom to practice their religions, and an end to political suppression.'

'Sounds reasonable.'

'Put like that it does, doesn't it? However, these are Ghoulshee we're talking about here. An end to political repression means they're looking for the release of some political prisoners.'

'So?'

Mr Porter looked up from eating a slice of marmalade-laden toast. 'Most of them are in jail here, convicted serial killers. Apart from the one or two who are successfully running local councils.'

'Parity for their language sounds okay too, doesn't it?' Kylah added. 'Except that they have this way of screaming that leads to certain death. And as for religious practices, what they want is the freedom to come here at least four times a year to harvest victims for the torturous and cannibalistic rituals that pass for their worship.'

The sausage in Matt's mouth did not have quite the flavour he thought it had all of a sudden. He pushed his plate away, rinsed his mouth out with some tea, and took a deep breath. This had gone far enough. A laugh was a laugh, but this was bordering on deranged. He'd make his excuses, thank them for their hospitality, and mosey on up to the weir for a reassuring look at his exit strategy.

'Right,' he said to an expectant Mr Porter and his attractive niece. 'Thanks for the breakfast—'

'But you're thinking that we're making this up as we go along,' Kylah offered, 'and oh, is that the time? You really must get going. Am I right?'

'In a nutshell,' Matt said, blinking several times.

'I don't particularly care if you believe me or not, but the fact is you witnessed a Ghoulshee incursion this morning, and an attempt on the Doorkeeper's life. Even you should see how getting rid of one of the five would be a huge political blow.'

'Five,' said Matt, who now had one eye on the door. He made to get up but couldn't. His backside seemed welded to the leather.

Mr Porter took over from his niece, attacking a mushroom with vigour and seeming not to notice Matt's writhing struggles. 'Five of us. We're sort of a family firm, but by this time none of us can remember when we divvied things up, or how. We keep in touch, though, solstices and equinoxes mainly. Although there are cards at Christmas, too.'

'Right,' Matt said, using both arms now to try to lever himself to his feet. Still nothing.

'I know that this is difficult material,' Mr Porter added. 'It must seem like we're both escapees from the local solarium.'

'He means sanatorium,' Kylah said, in an aside that hadn't seen rain for a thousand years. 'And there's no point trying to get up until we've used the pentrievant. You agreed to that, and it's a binding metaphysical contract.'

Matt sighed. 'Is this some sort of cult? Only I've donated to "help the terminally deranged" already.'

CHAPTER NINE

'Lunacy,' Mr Porter said, smiling as widely as ever. 'That's a fairly standard human reaction when faced with incomprehensible supernatural explanations. All I can say to you is that you should try to remember the "children" we saw this morning and rationalise them, if you can. I mean, did they look in any way human to you?'

This was off-the-wall stuff. But the answer to Mr Porter's question was very definitely no. They had not looked human. But neither did a lot of kids between the ages of ten and seventeen these days.

'Exactly,' Kylah said, noting the absence of any denial from Matt. 'The really interesting thing about all of this is why you saw them in the first place. The Ghoulshee should be invisible to the human eye. That's the real conundrum here.'

'*I'm* the conundrum?' Matt said, eyebrows up. 'Look, tell me where the hidden camera is so we can get this over with. Truth is, I've been at work all night and the charade is beginning to wear a bit thin.'

Mr Porter shook his head. 'No hidden cameras, Matt. This is the truth.'

'You *did* ask,' Kylah said. 'There are thousands of us over here. Mostly well-behaved, because we all know that if we transgress, back we go.'

'Okay, okay,' Matt said, feeling himself slide into a mildly angry humouring-the-weird-people mode. 'Let's assume that I believe you for one minute. Why? Why would your lot want to come over here? I mean, I presume you can do stuff, right? Give people tails and horns? Magic carpets? Water into wine? I mean, I'd have thought that the world was your oyster.'

Mr Porter sighed. 'You'd think so, wouldn't you? But you see, Matt, the problem with a society based on supernatural powers is that it isn't aspirational. Some of our people are very good at teleportation; others can heal cuts with a poultice and some runes; one or two can eat a whole child in one sitting.'

'Dreables.' said Kylah with a little shudder.

'But the point is,' continued Mr Porter, 'it's innate. There's nothing you can do about it. You get what you get when you're born. Yes, there are courses on skill development, but basically, it's pot luck. That tends to breed resentment. Whereas your lot,' Mr Porter gave Matt an indulgent smile, 'you're all born the same, with certain notable exceptions like Einstein or Pelé or Eddie the Eagle. That means you're all aspirational. Anyone can be anything. Our lot find that very attractive. Look at the mobile phone. We don't have anything like that. Yes, we have some people who can communicate by thought projection across continents, but day to day, we rely on carrier pigeon or men on donkeys. Here, any idiot can use a mobile phone.'

'Plus, here is where the gold is,' Kylah added.

'Gold?' Matt asked, trying to keep up.

'Why do you keep turning my statements into questions? It's very irritating.'

'Kylah,' Mr Porter warned.

Kylah glanced at her uncle and then turned back to Matt with a smile that might as well have had plastic stamped on its underside. 'Gold is highly prized, not only for its rarity but because it is supernaturally inert. In other words, despite what the alchemists all claim, they can't make it from anything.'

This is bollocks, Matt thought. *Bollocks with a capital B in heavy type and underlined.* Still, he couldn't help but respond to their nonsense with a little bit of argument. 'What do all your people do here? Read palms? Gaze into crystal balls?'

'That's a little bit patronising, Matt,' said Mr Porter as he sipped his second cup of tea.

Matt shook his head and shrugged. 'Humour me.'

It was Kylah who answered. 'We're into everything. Finance, politics…'

'Very big in alternative medicine,' Mr Porter added. 'Take homeopathy. One of my nephews started the whole thing in the seventeenth century. The King's Head in Canterbury, I believe it was. He bet his friend that he could turn five shillings' worth of ague cure into £10,000 by diluting it to buggery and getting the punters to buy it. Of course, he cured the first five by giving them the proper strength, but after that you were lucky to get one molecule in three million of the stuff. Bright spark was my Sam. Huge profit margin, too. Set the trend, of course. Now they're all trying to outdo one another with ever more bizarre scams. Trouble is that your lot will pay for anything. I mean, we don't mind as long as it doesn't do any harm, and if there's one thing the punters like, it's a good listener. In effect, it's merely sympathetic magic. I expect they're still doing reiki, are they?'

'My sister's into it.' Matt nodded, feeling sweat break out on his forehead as he tried to make his legs respond to the order to get up.

'That was Sam's brother Tobin's idea. That's sibling rivalry for you.' Mr Porter gave an indulgent chuckle. 'Do anything to cop a feel, would Tobin. Gallstones of a bear, crystal healing.' He shook his head. 'You couldn't make it up, could you?'

Matt smiled and looked around for the exit sign.

'It's still very tribal, though,' Kylah said. 'For example, there are lots of soothsayers in finance. Unfortunately, someone sent them rams' entrails instead of goats' in 2008. But as you know, what goes up must come down.'

'Are you saying that the global financial meltdown was all down to a sheep's intestine?' Matt asked, trying not to let his jaw drop open more than it already had.

Kylah shrugged. Mr Porter had moved to look out of the window, whistling softly.

'But hang on a minute,' Matt said, giving up his struggle for a moment to pursue a strand of their twisted logic. 'Rewind. Your nephew, Sam? You said he had a *real* cure for the ague, whatever that was.'

'Probably malarial fever,' Mr Porter said. 'Used to have mosquitoes here, you know. Endemic in the Fenlands.'

'Well, anyway, my point is that if there was a cure, why not use it instead of trying to trick people?' It wasn't brilliant as rational arguments went, but it was the best he could come up with at that moment.

Mr Porter shifted his ample bottom in the seat, but Kylah nodded and lifted one eyebrow. 'That's the one thing about our lot that you need to understand. Caprice is what we're all about. Trickery is a way of life. You lot have altruism; our lot have mischief and fraud. It's what makes most of our people tick.'

'Nice,' Matt said. 'So, the bloke I work next to on the day shift might be a bloody warlock intent on swapping people's X-ray results.'

Kylah shook her head in a derisive fashion. Her eyelashes really were long. 'That's just silly.'

'Oh, sorry.'

'Warlocks are strictly military. You're far more likely to come across one of the undead working in the mortuary, and the worst they get up to is swapping the labels on corpses' toes. It's a bit of a giggle, that's all. Very sociable lot, the undead.'

'This Ghoulshee lot don't sound very sociable,' Matt muttered. He wanted to add the words, 'even if they exist.' but held them in check.

Mr Porter nodded. 'They do not believe in a symbiotic

existence. In fact, they have openly expressed their political will to create a Ghoulshean state across both dimensions.'

'That would mean cancelling Christmas, would it?'

Kylah shrugged again. 'Christmas, Easter…night and day.'

'Bit of luck for you that I turned up when I did this morning, then,' Matt said, plastering on a grin. 'But now, if you don't mind, I'd like to leave. So why don't you get on with your thought…thingy?'

It should have read *Bedlam* above the entrance and not *Hipposync*, but they were good. Matt had to give it to them. March hares though they may have been, they had all the answers. L. Ron Hubbard would have been very jealous. But enough was enough. He'd play along, let them do their new-age thought retrieval crap and get out of there quicker than you could say sleight of hand.

'Okay.' Kylah picked up the green stone on the strap. 'This is completely painless, I guarantee. And yes, at least five CCTV cameras will have seen you walk in here with my uncle, so we're not going to do anything nasty to you, okay?'

Relief rippled through him on hearing that she'd read his anxiety and was on his wavelength. 'So, this will let you see what I saw this morning?'

'Exactly. I'll be able to run IDs on the perpetrators and get them back to our people on the other side.' Kylah stood and walked towards him. Was that a softening of her expression?

'What's it like on your side, then?' he asked, deciding to indulge her as she moved behind him to strap on the pentrievant.

'Good fun in daylight. Night times are spent indoors behind a garlic wreath with a hemlock bat. We have our issues, just like you do.'

Matt noticed that Kylah's nails were painted a royal blue. Her fingers were cool on his forehead as she adjusted the stone.

'I owe you one for saving my uncle's life,' she whispered close to his ear.

Her breath was warm. It made his throat tight. 'It was nothing,' he croaked.

And, in truth, it *had* been almost nothing. Apart from shouting a bit and tapping a brat on the arse with a stick, he'd done very little. But another part of him, the part that had noticed the yellow flecks in her eyes, knew that there were very few occasions in life when one of the truly unattainable ones was this close. And even fewer occasions when he'd done something even quasi-heroic. So even if she was as flaky as a piece of salted cod, it was a now or never moment.

'I uh…don't suppose you fancy a drink sometime, do you?'

'Hmmm,' she said. Amazing, how one syllable had such a capability for stopping you in your mental tracks and turning your vague hopes into something that smelled like what was left at the bottom of a milk carton after ten days on the windowsill in July.

Realisation sat up and waved at Matt. There was bound to be a boyfriend with designer stubble, a perma-tan and a bank account the size of Luxembourg. Maybe even a castle in Transylvania.

Kylah's eyes had become even bigger ovals of confusion. 'I don't think—' she began.

'Sorry,' Matt said, in that way he had of apologising for assuming he'd committed the despicable crime of social ineptitude. 'Stupid of me.'

She kept looking at him as if he was a puppy behind bars in a dog compound. A strange, niggling disquiet began scratching at the inside of his skull.

'You're a nice guy, Matt Danmor. But Fae and humans are not a good mix, and I haven't had any reason to question that maxim so far.' Her eyes searched his and they seemed full of genuine regret. 'I'm sorry.'

The scratchy niggle grew into a jolt of panic as Kylah's

finger reached out to touch the green stone to the centre of his forehead. Was this a huge opportunity he was about to wave goodbye to?

'Hang on a minute,' Matt said and put his hand on her wrist just as the pentrievant touched. 'Wait—'

CHAPTER TEN

IT WASN'T EVEN RAINING; that was the most puzzling thing. Why else would he be here holding his bike like a TWOT in a trance under the dripping branches of a sycamore on the canal towpath, if not to hide from the rain? It was as if he'd just come round after a bloody fit or something. But if it had been a fit, he'd be on his back frothing at the mouth, or at the very least twitching like a pithed frog, wouldn't he? Matt glanced at his watch. Almost nine-thirty. Bloody hell. Two and something hours since he'd had that riveting conversation with the Uruk-hai cheerleader back at the General.

Matt groaned. *Oh Christ, please don't let this be some crappy escalatory consequence of the accident.* All he needed now were random cognitive blackouts on top of feeling like crap almost every day and being as clumsy as a ballerina in clown shoes. *Am I really going to have to tell that bloody psychologist that I'm having memory lapses?*

He r. oved out from under the sycamore, considering that option for all of two seconds before chucking it down the pan. No way was he going to give the psychologist the pleasure of that oh-so-irritating, I told you so, smile. He'd rather eat his own head. But where the hell had all that time gone?

In his past, his student past, whole chunks of time could slide by when Matt had been under pressure for a test or revising something he enjoyed. But at least when it was done, he'd had the benefit of knowing the names of all the nerves in the upper arm or the gist of the coma-inducing Krebs cycle. Even then, though, there'd never been anything like this big, gaping hole where his recollection should have been.

He looked at his watch again. Yep, now it was eight-thirty on the dot. Matt forced himself to think. He'd cycled away down Observatory Road; he remembered that bit. And then there'd been the accident on Walton Street. Yes, and then…it was no good. He knew that the plan had been to grab a bacon bap and head up to the weir, but now a headache was pounding away behind his left eye. What he craved were two paracetamol and a bed. He did not feel the slightest bit hungry; in fact, he thought he could taste the last remnants of some very nice sausages on his palate. He hadn't been to the bacon butty van already, had he?

Matt sighed, wheeled his bike around and mounted. On his left he could see the tower of the church in Jericho and the fronts of the few low buildings on St Barnabus Street jutting out onto the wharf. He glanced at them as he passed but gave them no more than a fleeting millisecond's thought. Why should he? He'd never been inside any of them. Didn't know what they housed. Didn't care.

On the bike, Matt kept his head down and bypassed the usual morning traffic by negotiating the smaller streets and alleyways. It took him twenty minutes of hard pedalling before he approached the right turn off Iffley Road into Fairfield Street. His flat there consisted of two rooms on the ground floor of an end-of-terrace house. The street itself was narrow with cars always parked along it, making it a complete nightmare between seven-thirty and ten every morning.

As with most of Oxford's rented accommodation, the flat had been remodelled to suit the high turnover in this archetypal student town. In other words, it was cramped, badly designed, and about as welcoming as a Guantanamo toilet. A bolted-on lean-to at the rear housed a lecturer in ancient history. Upstairs was a bachelor bursar to one of the colleges. Lots of young men visited the bursar, ostensibly to discuss their student loans, but Matt suspected there were all sorts of withdrawals and deposits going on up there that had nothing to do with finance.

Matt opened the front door and kicked away the morning's post before stooping to pick it up. Most of it was for people who hadn't lived at the property for years. Of today's mail, only two items were addressed to him. One was an electricity bill, the other an invitation to a timeshare junket where he was guaranteed to win a microwave! Yeah, in exchange for signing up for one week in an apartment in the Costa del Ripoff in February, which was a snip at £5,000 a year. Wow, sometimes it was difficult to believe how lucky a bloke could be. Matt crumpled the letter in his fist and threw it into an overflowing black refuse sack in the hallway, strategically stationed there for such eventualities.

He stuck his key in the door off the entrance hall that led into his flat and leaned his weight on it. As usual, it stuck on the warped laminate flooring two feet into its travel. The stuffy smell of years of occupation hit him, together with the stifling heat of the storage heaters, which were always on, no matter what Matt tried to do to shut them off. He dumped his rucksack and shut the door. He needed a cup of tea and something for his headache.

CHAPTER ELEVEN

THE FLAT WAS TINY. It was six paces from the bay window looking out on Fairfield Street to his kitchenette. The sink, a cooker, about a yard of work surface, and a fridge were inelegantly shoehorned into an alcove. Behind that, the bedroom itself was furnished with a gigantic king-size bed that could accommodate a small horse (and, judging by the way it sagged alarmingly in the middle, probably had) and allowed room for the most minuscule of bedside tables. Most of Matt's worldly possessions were on that table. A French window, specially designed to allow in draughts no matter which direction the wind was blowing, led out onto a gravel patio big enough to hold Matt's bike, so long as he kept the front wheel at right angles to the frame. The bathroom opened off the bedroom and down some steps and contained a pale pink suite the colour of an anaemic grapefruit. The showerhead dripped constantly, and the only window in the room that might have allowed any sort of ventilation had been painted shut at about the time of Noah.

Advertised as an ideal flat for a couple, it would have been if that couple were either conjoined twins or under three feet tall. If you were in any way normal, in that you might require some me-time away from your partner for anything longer than twenty seconds, the place would have driven you bananas within a week. But as a bolthole to doss and exist as a single man about Oxford, it was fine. Fairfield Street was, Matt kept telling himself, a temporary solution to a temporary situation. The thought of it being anything else appalled him. Yet he knew that, for some, renting a place like this as a couple was often a first step in their quest to aspire to something better.

He'd rather eat crow shit.

An alarm sounded in his head. The words crow shit bounced off the inside of his skull like a pinball, setting off lights and bells. Not his usual choice of comparative reference at all. So where exactly in his mental lexicon that little scatological descriptive gem had been dragged out of, he had no idea. Matt poured water from the kettle, squeezed the steeping teabag with a spoon, added some sugar and milk, and sat on the sofa.

Memory lapses. Unusual phraseology. What next? Matt reached across and flicked on his iPod, which was charging on a speaker system dock. He pressed shuffle and waited. The song that came on put a tin hat on it. The Automatic's metaphoric tilt at the demon of drink and drugs, *Monster*.

Unbelievable. Not his choice. Someone else's. The very someone he was trying his level best to forget.

Silvy.

What the hell would she have made of 71 Fairfield Road? The answer was that Matt was clueless. In the few weeks that their relationship had lasted, there hadn't been time to catalogue an extensive list of her likes and dislikes. They'd spent too much time making love, eating, making love, drinking, and having your actual amazingly wild fling (making love). But she had kept humming, 'What's that coming over the hill,' by said Automatic after she'd heard it once on the radio in his car. She'd kept on singing it, so he'd downloaded it for her.

Silvy.

The girl he'd fallen head over heels for. The girl he'd been driving home with and who hadn't been in the passenger seat of the overturned car he'd woken up in after the accident. The girl no one could trace to any ambulance or hospital, and whom the calm psychiatrist suggested had been a figment of Matt's imagination, even calling it, 'delusional depression.'

Matt remembered the enthusiasm glinting in the chap's eyes as he said that. An enthusiasm that belied the even expression he'd maintained. He'd been pleased with his diagnosis, Matt could tell. Unusual in someone quite so young, he'd explained, but not unheard of. Probably respond to a dibenzothiazepine, he'd added. And so, Matt was prescribed a drug with the crass and cringe-inducing name of Deluquel. Amazing to think that a drug company, which had spent millions steering the thing through the murky layers of government red tape it needed to navigate to get onto the chemist's shelf, could not have come up with a better name than bloody Deluquel.

Matt hated the things. They made him drowsy, made his mouth dry, gave him constipation and blocked his nose. Worse, they made him exist in a cloudy, buzzy world where nothing mattered quite as much as it should. But he could have put up with all of that as long as they helped him forget about Silvy.

The problem was, they didn't. He could not forget Silvy. She was as real to him as the steaming cup of Typhoo in his hands.

Up until Silvy, there had, of course, been a few others— few being the appropriate adjective. Some he had really liked, but they never seemed to like him with the same passion. Others were more relationships of circumstance—aimless dalliances that waxed and waned like pieces of driftwood on a spring tide. Matt hadn't slept with all of them—scratch that, he hadn't slept with nearly enough of them. Even when he had, the Richter-scale tremors he'd been led to believe might happen never did. Perhaps, he rationalised, it was because he was such a late developer in the romantic sense.

Up until he was almost seventeen, he'd paid scant attention to girls, even while his schoolmates spent every waking moment playing CLF. *Cherchez La Femme* would have sounded way uncool, even amongst the bright top set who were his contemporaries, whereas the acronym was obscure enough to make it sound acceptably like a rap band to the uninitiated. In fact, Matt found the whole flirting thing a bit like a meta-physical forum on ethics in journalism: a complete bloody mystery. Often, he chided himself for not having paid enough attention to at least recognise romance when it sat up and tried to love-bite him on the leg. That was, he suspected, the main reason why he was so crap at it. Perhaps it was lack of confidence based on the way he had looked—still looked— average, at least to his own eyes. His face, Matt supposed, wasn't bad. Some of his ephemeral girlfriends had even called him cute. And he was working on trying to get rid of that expression he sometimes caught himself wearing, the one that showed how crushed and disappointed he was these days at what the world was dishing up.

Silvy blew all that angst and self-doubt out of the water with one devastating smile. She'd been physical, always touching and wanting to be touched. She was taller than him by an inch, and even taller when she wore the kind of heels she liked. Part of the appeal, Matt knew, was the way she'd done all the running. She'd insisted on long walks on the beaches, and even longer weekends staying in doing nothing except eating pizza and ice cream in bed. Well, almost nothing.

Silvy had urges, and she responded to them like any animal would. At least, any animal that didn't give a tinker's cuss about anyone watching. At the end of the long walks, Silvy would invariably find a dune to lie down on. In bed, Silvy would find something interesting to do with the ice cream (and, on one very memorable occasion, an olive). It was exciting, liberating, and so the psychiatrist had said, a total bloody fantasy.

Matt sipped his tea. Its hot sweetness massaged his tongue. He knew he should go to bed. He knew he should take his Deluquel and try to sleep, in the hope that when he woke up things would be better. He knew that running this video over in his head was a total waste of time, and that the patronising psychologist who was dishing out the therapy had shown him ways of pressing the stop button before it got into full swing. But remembering Silvy and the few things they'd (apparently not) done in those few weeks together didn't seem like so much mental agony to Matt.

That, he surmised, was the nub of the problem. He reached into his rucksack and took out the necklace she'd given him on their second date. It was still damp from the exploding bag of saline. Attached to it was a pendant. Matt still wasn't sure how best to describe it, except that it was a looped cross inside a circle, and it was white gold and had hung around his neck on the leather thong from the day she'd given it to him. It looked Celtic, or so he'd supposed. But when he'd asked Silvy, she'd shrugged and said, 'It's pretty. Wear it for me.'

It was quirky and ornate, just like Silvy. When he'd shown it to the psychiatrist as proof of Silvy's existence, the bloke had simply stared at it impassively. Matt even toyed with the idea of trying to find out where she'd bought it, to see if the shopkeeper might remember her, but there were no markings at all that might help in that search. He could have bought it himself anywhere. At least, that's what the look on the psychiatrist's face had implied.

Matt could understand that look. After all, what the psychiatrist saw was this bloke who'd survived an awful crash, obsessed with a long-legged blonde with a supposed libido the size of Mount Etna, waving a pagan symbol on the end of a bit of leather as the only evidence of her existence. What was worse was that Matt could not furnish any photos. Silvy hadn't liked having her photo taken. She'd told him that some Native Americans believed photographs stole their souls. He'd waited for her to laugh. She hadn't, although he'd felt one building up inside him. But he'd swallowed it down and nodded instead.

There was something about that Teutonic accent of hers

that lent gravity to everything she said. Made it all sound so plausible. And besides, anyone who looked like Silvy, and did the things that Silvy did, was allowed to have the odd foible, as far as Matt was concerned. Christ, she could have more foibles than a fencer's kit bag, so long as she kept taking him for those long walks on the beach. True, they hadn't mixed with any of his or her friends. She'd never mentioned any of her own and he hadn't minded. They'd been too caught up in each other, Matt argued when the psychologist had inquired. But the answer he gave had not satisfied the shrink. He'd put a different spin on the whole thing, implying that it was also not beyond possibility that the bit of Matt's head that controlled sexual fantasy had been jolted into overdrive as part of his post-traumatic stress.

Matt squeezed his eyes shut. They had all the bloody answers. Trouble was, they were all the wrong ones. He let his fingers roll over the pendant, slipped it back over his head and went to the bathroom. There was ancient lino on the floor that looked like an off cut from a Jackson Pollock exhibition (had he done anything with lino?). It didn't do to stare at it for long because the shapes and stains began to writhe with a life of their own if you did. Matt blew out air and reached for the knob on the bathroom cabinet door. Inside was a haphazard collection containing an arrangement of razor-blade cartridges, shampoo, toothpaste, an unopened box of non-steroidal anti-inflammatories (for when his legs hurt too much after the bike), and a bottle of Deluquel. He took the bottle out and looked at the label, his mouth a thin line.

'Sod it,' Matt said to the bloke who looked back at him in the mirror.

Matt eased a couple of tablets out. For some reason, his headache was abating, but it wouldn't do any harm to help it along. He took the tablets back to the tea that he'd placed on the floor in front of the sofa and gulped them down. Outside, a drizzle greyed out the day.

He switched off *Monster* and found some Kings of Convenience instead. The melodious strings of *Toxic Girl* bathed his ears. It was the soundtrack to his life.

'Sod it, sod it, sod it,' he said and threw off his clothes, searching for some not-too-sweaty shorts in the laundry basket. He put on his running shoes before he had a chance to change his mind. Three miles along the river would give him the best chance of sleeping. Besides, endorphins were much better for you than bloody Deluquel. Everyone knew that.

Even a mature second-year med student who'd survived a car crash on an empty road in good weather involving no other vehicle, and whose lovely blonde passenger had disappeared from the face of the earth.

CHAPTER TWELVE

THE AFTERNOON SHIFT after a night on was, in many ways, a lot worse than the night shift itself. Matt had managed, at most, four hours of sleep, so he was tired even before he started. Added to that was the fact that afternoons meant you turned up for work at the point when everyone else had their eyes firmly fixed on five o'clock and out the door. Still, working three to ten wasn't too bad, he supposed. Especially since Roberro was on nights all this week, which meant that the git wouldn't be making an appearance until seven.

As soon as Matt arrived, he was sent up to geriatrics to take a patient to the mortuary. It wasn't the first time, so he'd mastered the dead-body nerves a while ago. But it did mean that he was hooking up with Flynn, a twenty-year veteran of the portering service, who was gold-star material when it came to skiving. It always took two to transfer a corpse, and if Flynn was involved, you could bet that it would be a fairly cushy number. Flynn had the florid look of a ten pints of Guinness a night man, and drifted through his shifts with a minimum of effort. He was always up for mortuary duty because it was a great way to kill at least half an hour doing nothing but wheeling a trolley of inanimate flesh along miles of flat passageways.

After fifteen minutes of negotiating corridors full of visitors and staff, most of whom bowed their heads respectfully on seeing them, they reached the service lift, which would take them down to the underground maze of tunnels that led to the mortuary. Matt stood at the rear of the 'corpse cart' an adapted trolley with sides and a lid, while Flynn wheezed at the front.

'Ever thought about working in the mortuary, Mike?' Getting Matt's name wrong was another of Flynn's endearing little qualities.

'Not really.'

As usual, Flynn didn't wait for Matt's answer. Listening wasn't one of Flynn's strong points, either, along with hygiene, a basic understanding of the English language, tolerance, or a sense of humour. Not forgetting compassion.

'Bloody cushy number, if you ask me. Stiffs come in, you tag 'em, then hand them over to the coffin jockeys. Don't even have to listen to them whingeing on about their bloody cancer and stuff. Only thing puts me off is the unhealthy atmosphere, you know, down in the basement, like. Dark all the time. Never see daylight. Can't be good for you.' Flynn proceeded to hawk up a cigarette-fuelled chunk of decayed lung lining and expectorate it neatly onto the floor in the corner of the lift. They completed their descent with a lurch, and the lift doors opened. Moments later, they were pushing the trolley along a corridor lit by flickering fluorescent lights, between lines of hissing pipes. Flynn had given up all pretence of pulling the trolley; even the trailing hand he'd pretended to steer with was quickly abandoned, leaving Matt to do the lot. Apart from the hiss of the pipework, the bowels of the hospital were eerily quiet.

'Too spooky for me,' Matt said and decided to throw in, 'and with limited prospects. Bit of a dead-end job, don't you think?' The pun flew straight over Flynn's head like a squadron of Canada geese heading south.

'Ah, but that's where you're wrong, Mike,' Flynn said, as Matt had known he would. Flynn was one of those people who would argue over anything. Even, more often than not, when you'd agreed with a point he was making. It tended to make conversation with Flynn highly exasperating. 'Could be a real money spinner, but Alf and Dwayne—well, you know Alf and Dwayne. I mean they're good blokes, don't get me wrong. But they're too precious about it all. Don't know if being precious about corpses is quite right, know what I mean? People can get funny ideas. You know…haemophilia and that.'

Matt knew he meant necrophilia, but pedantry had no place in conversations with Flynn, either. Life was way too short.

'Almost went into business once, did me and the boys down here,' Flynn continued. 'I had this idea, see. Touched by an Angel, I was going to call it. Brilliant, it was. Get Dwayne and Alf to make the stiff look nice with a bit of makeup and that, and then take a picture of it and paste it into a Bible scene. You know, like *The Last Supper*, or *Joseph's Dream*? Something tasteful for relatives to remember them by. And if they didn't like the Bible—say they were Muslims or Buddhists—we could've done something with pyramids and a camel. Maybe even some pandas. For a fee, of course.'

'They weren't interested, I take it?' Matt said, shaking his head in disbelief.

'Nah. Lacking in enter-prune-arial spirit, that's their problem. Said the hospital governors wouldn't approve. I ask you.'

Imagining propositioning grieving relatives with a cheesy portfolio of biblical scenes sporting a variety of Aunt Madges and Ednas as Mary Magdalene filled Matt with a shiver-inducing disquiet. Screaming silently at the bullshit Flynn came out with was the only thing that helped.

'You've met Alf and Dwayne, though, eh, Mike?'

'Yeah, couple of times.'

'You know the drill, then. Go with the flow. They're harmless enough. Go back a long way, do me and Alf and Dwayne.'

Flynn pushed through the mortuary's wooden swing doors with their scarred metal facings and let them clatter back against the trolley with no attempt at helping Matt through. The mortuary reception was a table in front of a squat line of filing cabinets. Everything was spic and span; all paperwork was filed away in labelled box-files, while an ancient PC played a tranquil fish tank screensaver. Another set of doors led to the mortuary proper. Flynn pushed those doors open, calling ahead as he did so.

'Aye, aye. Shop?'

The mortuary's main room had low ceilings and was well lit. At the centre stood a large stainless-steel table with drains and hoses. Through another door were the fridges. Chairman of the Board's *Give Me Just a Little More Time* boomed out from a Bluetooth speaker system on the post-mortem table. Flynn did a little shimmy as he walked through the door, completely at odds with the rhythm of the song, and said, 'I love the Four Tops.'

The smile that crept over Matt's face at hearing the music died into another silent scream.

Two men looked up as they entered the room. One was a giant of a man. At six-four, twenty-one stone, sporting a full beard and dark-rimmed eyes in a podgy face, Alf didn't ever say much. In fact, Matt hadn't heard him say anything, ever. However, the other attendant more than made up for his partner's reticence.

'Well, well, if it isn't WMD Flynn. What poor mug have you brought with you?'

'It's Mike,' said Flynn. 'You met Mike?'

'Mike?' said Dwayne looking past Flynn towards Matt with a puzzled frown. 'Flynn, his name's Matt. As in Mathew.' Dwayne shook his head in despair at Matt.

'Whatever,' Flynn said. The chances of Flynn ever admitting a mistake were as remote as the average hill town in Nepal. 'Got a customer for you. Eighty-eight-year-old, heart attack. Found him DIB.'

'Her name is Mrs Settle, and she's eighty-seven,' Matt said, sending Flynn a questioning frown but getting a blank look for his efforts. 'Cause of death was pneumonia. But the "found dead in bed." bit is right.'

'Exactly,' Flynn said with stunning disregard. He proceeded to unwrap a chocolate bar and eat it while peering under the shrouds covering a couple of corpses.

'We got the word from Ward Nine,' Dwayne said, shaking his head. Matt was struck by the sympathy in his voice. 'Been expecting Mrs Settle. Alf, why don't you and Flynn sort the paperwork? Matt can help me move Mrs S.' It was couched politely, but there was no doubt that it was an order rather than a request, delivered with Dwayne's customary cheerfulness.

Alf nodded and began to walk towards Flynn, who looked for a moment like he might object, having visibly flinched at the suggestion of doing something that involved the word, work. But then he did the maths and realised that paperwork, although distasteful, did not involve anything physical. Besides, Alf was already moving towards him. So, like Napoleon faced with the advancing Russians, retreat was the only option. Dwayne watched them leave the room.

'Lazy sod,' Dwayne said as the doors to reception swung shut behind them. Up close, Matt saw that Dwayne's complexion, like Alf's, was parchment-white, with dark circles around his eyes accentuated by a liberal application of mascara and lots of jewellery. A cursory count gave up a figure of nineteen piercings in all, eyebrows, cheek, tongue, lips all glinting in the harsh light. Dwayne fetched a long, solid plastic board, which he began to slide under Mrs Settle as Matt tilted her. In seconds, the board sat half on the corpse cart and half on the mortuary cot.

'On three,' Dwayne said, and he pulled while Matt pushed. The Patslide was a very simple piece of kit that relied on the very low friction between cotton sheets and its smooth plastic coating, which meant that patients of any weight could be slid across from one bed to another easily. All it required was that the puller and the pusher brace themselves to overcome the initial inertia of the body. Once the mass started moving, it did so effortlessly.

So why, this time, Matt's back foot began to slide the moment he applied pressure to the inanimate Mrs Settle, he had no idea. But slide it did, losing purchase and causing him to lunge forward. Instead of using enough force to push her three feet, Matt's turbo thrust was enough to put her into the next county. The result was that Mrs Settle shot across towards the surprised Dwayne, who ended up frantically juggling the stiff corpse that now jutted out, rigid as an ironing board, its top half hovering precariously over the edge of the mortuary cot.

'Shit, shit, shit. Sorry,' Matt said, yanking on the sheets to bring Mrs Settle back from the brink. To his credit, Dwayne said nothing, the strain on his face preventing speech for a couple of very long seconds, until Mrs Settle had…settled.

'That was close,' he said. 'Not easy explaining how a corpse breaks its neck after death.'

'I slipped,' Matt said, mentally cursing his rubbish luck once again.

Dwayne came around to Matt's side of the cot, knelt down, and picked up a plastic chocolate wrapper, which had provided the banana-skin effect between Matt's foot and the polished mortuary floor.

'You into Lion Bars, Mathew?'

Matt shook his head.

'What odds would you give me for this being WMD Flynn's break time confectionary of choice? The bloke is a bloody disaster. If he was a horse, he'd be forty thousand tubes of UHU by now.' Dwayne pulled the sheet back from Mrs Settle's face to reveal the grin of her rigour-stiffened features. 'Poor thing. I mean, look at her hair for crying out loud. Those bastards on Ward Nine haven't washed it for days. She'll have to have the works.' He strode, using quite short steps and bent elbows, to a whiteboard and wrote up *SETTLE-WCB.*

'WCB?' asked Matt.

'Wash, conditioning, and blow-dry. To be honest, I could do without it this afternoon. There's a couple coming in from a fire and they'll stink the place out. All that fat running everywhere—'

'But Mrs Settle,' Matt said, dragging the conversation back to the point at which his mind had hit a speed bump. 'I mean, who is going to mind if she doesn't have her hair washed?'

'Mind? Her, of course. If she could speak it'd be the first thing she'd say. Just because she's dead doesn't mean she doesn't want to look her best,' Dwayne sounded piqued.

'Fair enough,' Matt said.

'I'm surprised at you, Matt. You're spending too much time with the likes of Flynn. Even if there's little dignity in the way they die, down here they can have dignity by the sackful.' He tweaked at a nose ring, his expression softening. 'We all have a calling in life, Matt. Yours, I would say, is not tied up with transferring corpses onto slabs in mortuaries. But while you're doing it, you might as well do the best you can, eh?'

Matt frowned, more in surprise than disdain at what he was hearing. *Wisdom in the Mortuary* would be a great name for a book. That, or *Dwayne the Philosopher Mortician*.

'Do you believe in bad luck, Dwayne?' Matt asked, sensing that Dwayne was someone who might not scoff as he began stripping the sheets from Mrs Settle, ready for the laundry.

'Of course, I believe in bad luck. I've got more four-leaf clovers stuck in my bobble hat than you've had hot dinners.'

Matt was quiet for a few seconds, and then asked, 'So, do you think that someone could be doomed to be permanently unlucky?'

'Doomed. That's an odd thing to say, Mathew. I'm not so sure about doomed, but it's possible to have more than your fair share, I suppose.' Dwayne put out a hand and his fingers touched Matt's arm. They were icy cold on his skin. 'Luck's a funny thing, though. All depends on how you look at it. Take poor old Watkins over there.' Dwayne nodded towards a human shape under a white sheet on the other side of the room. 'Retired for one year, and then drops dead from a massive heart attack as he is about to putt for the best round of his life on the eighteenth hole.'

'That's unlucky,' Matt conceded.

'You might think so. But when we opened him up, we found an aneurysm the size of a plum in his head. That bursting would have won him a "cabbage-stuck-in-a-bed" first prize. His heart would not have had to do anything much and he might have survived for a few more years yet, dribbling and having someone change his nappy twice a day—if he was lucky.' Dwayne grinned. 'And once that was explained to him, he was a much happier bunny,' he added under his breath.

Matt looked up. 'What did you just say?'

Dwayne looked up, his face all mock innocence. 'Who, me?'

The moment was lost as a shout emerged from the vicinity of reception.

'Mike.' Flynn appeared in the door. 'Ready?'

'Two seconds,' Matt said and began bundling the sheets into the corpse wagon.

'Yes, hurry up, Matt,' Dwayne said, making eyes to the ceiling. 'You don't want to keep a busy man like Flynn waiting.'

Matt grinned and watched as Dwayne went to the iPod and changed tracks. D:Ream's *Things Can Only Get Better* started up as Dwayne began removing shampoo and conditioner from a cupboard.

'One question,' Matt said as he began to trundle the corpse cart out. 'Why Horizon Flynn?'

Dwayne picked at a small scab on the mast of the sinking ship tattooed on his arm and grinned. 'We gave him that name when the coalition were in power. Horizon as per the Post Office? You know, flashy but—'

'—completely bloody useless,' Matt said, finishing off Dwayne's sentence for him with a grin and a nod.

'You're a smart bloke, Matt. Things'll work out. You'll see.'

CHAPTER THIRTEEN

In the lift, Matt considered telling Flynn what he thought he'd heard Dwayne say about Mr Watkins, but just as he got round to mentioning it, the radio on Flynn's belt crackled into life and the switchboard asked him to go the car park to help transfer a pregnant woman to the delivery suite.

'Top car park,' Flynn explained to Matt with a grin. 'Long way. If I go via the main entrance, I'll have time for a fag before I get there.'

'But that way's twice as long,' Matt pointed out.

'They don't specify a route, do they?' Flynn tapped his nose. 'You've got a lot to learn, Mike.'

Not from you, though, said a wary voice in Matt's head. 'Personally, I'm always ready to learn, although I do not always like being taught.'

Flynn looked at Matt with suspicion. 'Someone say that did they?'

'Churchill,' Matt said.

'That bloke from stores?'

'No, Churchill. World War II Prime Minister?'

'Nah, doesn't ring any bells. Sure you got that name right, Mike?'

Matt didn't bother to say goodbye as the lift stopped and Flynn walked off with no offer to help return the trolley.

Flynn was the ghost of Matt's future. An ignorant, bigoted, lazy sod of a ghost who represented the very worst aspects of what lack of ambition and total absence of any aspiration could lead to. Matt had no doubt that Flynn knew how many paid sick days he could have every year, took them all, and did so with a guiltless conscience and an immense pride in his achievement. He'd steal ten minutes at the beginning and end of the day, never volunteer to do anything he wasn't asked to, and considered it all his right as a working man to do so. And if Matt wasn't careful, unless he got his act together, he might be Flynn in twenty years' time.

Shuddering at the thought, Matt got out and began trundling the corpse cart back to its station on the fourth floor. He thought about Dwayne, and about what he'd said, and knew that Horizon Flynn was pretty much as wrong about everything and everyone as it was possible to be. How did people get like that? Was it simply pig ignorance? Or did they have to work at it? For Flynn to badmouth Alf and Dwayne was more than a tad hypocritical. As far as Matt could see, the mortuary was the most efficient and positive place he'd come across in the hospital, which was as madly arse-backwards as things could possibly be.

Matt frowned again at the memory of what he'd heard Dwayne say about Mr Watkins, but then shook his head. Of course, Dwayne hadn't said that Mr Watkins had been reassured by being told he'd had a narrow vegetative-state escape. The bloke was already bloody dead. If Dwayne hadn't said it, Matt had either heard it wrong, or made it up. And as far as Matt knew, his hearing was fine. Great. So now he could add inventing weird imaginings to his long list of mental glitches. The psychologist was going to have a field day at their next meeting.

A&E stayed quiet until around eight, when the punters decided that tea was over and with nothing special on the box, now might be a good time to get all those niggly little ailments sorted out. He caught a glimpse of the Uruk-hai cheerleader as she was leaving the building and got a thousand-yard stare for his trouble. But Linda Marsh was clearly not in the mood to stop for a chat.

As regards Matt's luck, things weren't too bad, if you discounted Mrs Settle and the Lion Bar wrapper and an episode in the men's toilets when the cistern overflowed after Matt had flushed it. It had taken a wedged kidney dish on top of the ballcock to sort that one out but sort it out he had. Roberro didn't even dip onto his radar until later. He'd seen the sphincter strutting about, whispering sweet nothings into the med student's ear at every opportunity. Though, judging by the smirk on his face, they were likely to be as sweet as lime vinegar.

By nine-thirty, things had quieted down again. The punters who chose to be ill at eight had decided that enough was enough and, faced with a further two hours' wait, had buggered off home to self-medicate with paracetamol and wine. Meanwhile, the poor sods that would be there at two a.m., having fallen over and cut their heads open with a full cargo of lager or cheeky Vimtos on board, were only just setting out from home for a night on the town.

Word had gone out on the floor that there was to be a crash drill sometime that evening, but it had yet to happen. With a bit of luck, it would be after ten when Matt was on his way home to bed. The only slight, niggling concern he had, as nine-thirty came and went, was that Roberro had been designated the trigger, and Roberro was enough of a prat to pick the worst possible moment for Matt.

At nine-forty, as Matt returned from wheeling a patient with a twisted knee from X-ray, the med student put her hand on his arm. This close, Matt saw that she wore a lot of foundation, through which small excrescences had begun to poke. But her eyes were big, her lipstick was freshly applied, and she flushed a pleasing pink when he looked up at her.

'Matt, sorry, but the woman in Cubicle Three has just left and there's a bit of a mess.' She made a face.

Matt shrugged as he parked the twisted knee. 'I'll sort it.'

He couldn't remember the woman in Cubicle Three, but

unless her visit had involved some significant fetching or carrying or wheeling or pushing on his part, there would have been zero contact. The curtains were still drawn, the bed unmade, scattered tissues on the floor. No bodily fluids—that was one good thing. But there was something on the floor between the wall and the locker adjacent to the bed.

Matt had seen lots of things on the floors of these cubicles, ranging from used needles courtesy of junkies who thought they might as well shoot up while they waited for someone to set their broken arms, to a lump of human waste moulded into a perfect tennis ball courtesy of a schizophrenic (he'd been nicknamed Novak by the staff).

But there were also less esoteric items that found their way to the least accessible corners. Things that were forever falling out of handbags and hurriedly grabbed coats when people got the all-clear to leave. Perhaps it was his past experience of lost phones and keys, or that he was still distracted by Dwayne and Horizon Flynn. Whatever it was, he didn't bother with the plastic gloves that hung in boxes on the wall. After all, it was obvious that these items had slipped out of a pocket or a bag and rolled under the locker.

Squatting to reach them, he felt for, and picked up, the Chapstick and comb first, then reached blindly for the long pink thing with the fingers of his left hand.

It felt smooth, if a little tacky to the touch, and he had to feel for it to get a hold. It was only when it was out from under the locker that he realised that it had an unscrew able bottom and a battery compartment. Then, after he'd had it in his palm for at least twenty seconds, the acrid smell caught in his throat and made his eyes water.

His shoulders slumped, and he went slack as the sick realisation of what this was sank in.

He groaned and managed to utter, 'You cow.' Though, the med student was nowhere near enough to hear him— before th crash alarm sounded.

At that point, it all became perfectly clear. The dildo was about the thickness of a very large banana, and Matt's hand was very well wrapped around it. That meant lots of contact area. And the person who had smeared the bloody thing with superglue knew that, too.

Outside the cubicle, people were running around, rushing to the crash drill, which his pager was telling him was in the minor ops room. It was a timed exercise, and they were expecting him there. The stopwatch was pressed when the last member of the team arrived, and he was as much part of that team as the anaesthetist or the nurses. Matt hesitated in the cubicle, running mental fingers over the very pointy tips of the dilemma he hovered above. He could slope off, wrap a blanket around his arm, and pretend that he'd never heard the alarm. That route led straight to serious disciplinary action. Might as well hand in his notice here and now.

Or he could tough it out, penis in hand.

There was only one thing he could do.

They were all in place as he walked through the door to the minor ops room: anaesthetists, medics, nurses, med students, and, of course, Roberro.

'You're late,' Roberro said.

Matt nodded. 'Had a spot of bother with some super-glue.' There was no point trying to hide it, so he waved his trophy for all to see. 'Seems like the lady in Cubicle Three is missing a friend.'

The laughter went on for several minutes. One of the nurses asked if she could touch it. Someone else suggested that the woman in Cubicle Three might have been a Hobbit, as Matt had clearly found 'Dildo Baggins.' which segued with a guffaw into, 'What am I going to do without my precious?' The med student wouldn't look Matt in the eye.

Roberro was in his element, however, calling Matt a moron for falling for that old trick, waiting for the other stuff to die down before spitting out, 'Still, that proves it. We always suspected you were a bit of a prick, Matt.' It got a laugh, but one tinged with a couple of derisory jeers for its banality. 'Bet you've never held anything that big before, eh?' Roberro added. The laughter dwindled to one or two giggles.

'Still, we all know what to call you now, eh, Matt?' Roberro leaned in, his malicious eyes gleaming with triumph as he bellowed out the word as if he were on the terraces at Chelsea, or wherever the hell it was he came from. 'Wan-ker. Wan-ker. Wan-ker.'

No one laughed at all that time. As Matt glanced around, he could see that they were all uncomfortable with this little tableau, suspecting for themselves what Matt already knew to be the truth: that the whole thing had been set up just for this moment. So that Giles Roberro could stand there and call Matt a spiteful name. All the doctors had been to med school and qualified in puerile humour. But mostly people matured out of it, at least until reunion nights. So, to see it so blatantly trotted out again like some old and sick pantomime horse was uncomfortable. Particularly in what was meant to be a professional environment and close proximity to the general public. But Roberro couldn't see it. He dished out the lumps because he was in a position to do so. And he did it behind a skin so thick it would require an armour-piercing shell to get through to him.

Well then, thought Matt. *Lock and load.*

'Funny you should mention names,' said Matt. 'Because this thing has one already.' He held up the marital aid. Now that he'd stopped waving it about, it was clear that a piece of flesh-coloured dressing tape had been applied. Matt ripped it off with a flourish. Written along its length, like *United States* on an Atlas rocket, was the word *GILES*.

This time, the laughter was genuine. Everyone howled. Everyone, that was, except Giles Roberro. He turned purple, became progressively flustered, and tried unsuccessfully to dismiss the drill. But no one wanted to leave in a hurry, not when they really were enjoying the joke. In the end, it was Roberro who left first, muttering to no one in particular, 'Some of us have actual work to do, you know.'

Several of the female nurses volunteered to get Matt's hand free.

'No,' said the charge nurse. 'I can see the video on

YouTube now, and the comments that'll follow. Come on, Matt, in here, out of the way.'

It took five minutes of superglue remover and gentle prising to get Matt's hand free. There was no pain; they'd had lots of practice with sixth-form toilet seats and tender bums over the years. 'Quick thinking, putting Giles's name on it like that,' the charge nurse said.

'He's a git,' Matt answered. 'Okay, a laugh's a laugh. But with him…' He shook his head. 'And what is it with him and women? He never seems to have any difficulty. Is it charm?'

'Charm? Yes, if charm was spelt P, E, R, V, E, R, and T. Most of them give in after a while to shut him up and stop him bothering them. You need to watch your back, though, young Mathew. He's got it in for you.'

'But what the hell have *I* done?' Matt asked in a plaintive soprano voice.

'You're male, young, the girls think you're cute, and the other staff all like you. You're stealing the golden boy's light. What more reason do you want?'

'Oh, for crying out loud, that's pathetic.'

With one final bit of kneading, the dildo came free and the charge nurse held it up. 'Hit the nail on the head there, Mathew. That's Giles Roberro for you. Pathetic.'

CHAPTER FOURTEEN

IT WAS FOOD FOR THOUGHT, and Matt chewed it cud-like for the remaining twenty minutes of his shift. It was as he was leaving, threading his way along the corridor towards the main reception area, that Roberro pigeonholed him. There was no one within five yards as he moved in close, wearing a grin bright enough to burn a hole in the ozone layer. To the casual observer it would have looked like a couple of mates bidding each other good night. But Matt could see the real fury under the fixed smile and feel it in the powerful squeeze of Roberro's fingers on his arm.

'You ever do anything like that to me again, and I'll break your arm,' Roberro promised.

'Don't tell me—De Niro in *The Godfather: Part II*?'

Roberro squeezed Matt's arm a little harder. 'I mean it, fuckwit.'

Matt returned the squeeze on Roberro's biceps. 'Know what they say? If you can't stand the heat, don't throw stones.'

Roberro looked momentarily confused, but then shook his head. Both men released their grips as a nurse passed by. Roberro waited until she'd turned the corner before continuing. 'You think you're the Alsatian's testicles, don't you? Always the unfunny answer. I've got some advice for you,

Wannadoc. You'll never make it. Too clumsy. They're not going to let you near patients, you klutz. So go and teach English to the refugees, there's a good moron.'

Blood was pumping through Matt's head. He wasn't sure whether he should laugh out loud or thump Roberro in the face. The guy was a joke. A childish, bigoted prat. And there was no doubt now that the git had somehow accessed his file. But Matt sensed, too, that violence was what Roberro wanted. Grounds for dismissal. Exactly what Matt didn't need on his CV. How on earth they had managed to let this idiot get through med school was beyond him. Okay, the days of putting medics on pedestals were long gone. They'd been political scapegoats and the subject of spin for far too long. Overbearing and superior had replaced knowledgeable and humane a long, long time ago in the British way of thinking about the medical profession (which put Matt at the top of the throwback league when it came to motivation). But he also knew that some still clung to the idea of an oath, which had been put forward twenty-four centuries before. Doctors were in privileged positions and, as such, should show a degree of probity, set a good example, demonstrate a degree of moral fibre. The downside was that when doctors fell from grace, they often did so spectacularly. Okay, Roberro was no Crippen or Shipman, but Hippocrates would have had him shot on sight. And it was that which irked Matt the most.

'Tell me, Giles, have you been an arsehole all your life, or have you matured into it?' As a scathing riposte it lacked almost everything, but as a from-the-gut insult, it did the trick.

'Keep going, fuckwit. We'll see what you can come up with as a joke when you're shovelling crap from the blocked toilets next week.'

'The toilets aren't blocked,' Matt said.

'They will be on your shift.'

The fingernail in the palm trick wasn't doing it for Matt. He could hear the enamel of his back teeth squelching and grinding together. 'Give me one, just *one* reason why you're being such a total shit, other than the fact that you're a complete twat. I'd really like to know what I've done to get under your skin.'

Roberro snorted. 'It's a jungle out there, turd-face. People need to know their place in the food chain. My job is to educate you and help you understand that whatever you do, you're going to fail.' He formed his fingers into a gun barrel and used his thumb to mimic the hammer coming down. 'Ergo, *scaevitus*. That's Latin for total loser.'

'Sounds like Latin for total crap from here,' Matt said.

'You pathetic little oik,' Giles sneered. 'Piss off back to whatever little provincial backwater pond you crawled out of with the rest of the algae.'

Matt's fists were balled tight. He was close, so very close, to smacking Roberro one right in the mouth and screw the consequences. But something stopped him. His ears felt odd, as if they were going to pop, and there was a distinct tingling in his scalp. It was difficult to put his finger on it, but he got the weirdest impression that something had changed.

They both saw her in their peripheral vision at the same moment, swivelling their eyes like target rangefinders to stare. She stood looking in from the reception area, her smile confident and happy, cheeks tinged red from the cold. She walked straight through the security doors and no one tried to stop her as she strode across the floor. Matt saw that Roberro seemed to have lost control of the muscles in his lower jaw before he realised that his own mouth was gaping open, too. She moved straight towards them, her eyes dancing with amusement. It was Roberro who took the chance. Never one to miss an opportunity of playing the macho medic card, he looped his stethoscope around his neck and moved forward to meet the girl before Matt had a chance to move.

'I'm sorry, this is a restricted area,' Roberro said, but with enough saccharin to sweeten a bag of lemons. 'Have you booked in? Here, let me help you.'

He took her arm and tried to steer her back towards reception, still wearing his best winning grin. The girl didn't budge. She looked at his hand on her arm, then at him and spoke, very calmly. 'I don't remember giving you permission to touch me.'

Roberro pulled his hand back as if it had been scalded, his smile curdling into crushed consternation. The girl gave him a glance that you could have shaved with an ice pick before turning to Matt and breaking out a hundred-watt grin.

'Hello, Mathew,' she said and walked towards him, not stopping until she had both hands on his cheeks and was kissing him full on the mouth.

Matt was paralysed. Totally dumbstruck. For two seconds, he couldn't even respond to the kiss. But being male and heterosexual, things soon started stirring, and he returned it with interest. She was the whole package—the look of her, the feel, the smell. Especially the smell. It was one of the things he'd missed the most. He never had found out what perfume it was she wore. She'd been vague about it when he'd asked, but it was a heady mix of wonderful aromas—bergamot, vanilla, amber and chocolate, and something else from his past that seemed able to reach in and press lots of his buttons without asking. The kiss wasn't bad, either. It was a warm, hungry, wild kiss full of promise and desire.

But then, that was her all over. That was Silvy.

CHAPTER FIFTEEN

MATT PULLED BACK to look at her and then pulled her to him in another crushing hug. She writhed under his fingers.

'I cannot breathe, Mathew,' she squealed, pushing his hands away and laughing.

'But how…when…*where* have you been?'

Silvy put her fingers on his lips. 'Not here,' she said. Same accent. Same Marianne Faithfull like, deeper-than-you'd-expect voice. 'Come on. Let's get out of here.'

She pulled Matt after her and he drank her in as he followed, inhaling her delicious bouquet. Despite it being January, her legs were bare under her coat, and the backs of her knees looked soft and tanned, drawing stares like a kebab-shop rotisserie drew bluebottles. Matt's head spun with questions, but it was such a sublime moment he didn't care.

Silvy was here. Silvy. Real and warm and actual.

'Wait,' he said as they walked through the exit doors. 'I forgot something.'

Matt turned and hurried back to the reception desk. It was manned this evening, behind a screen of protective glass, by Isla, a hardboiled no-nonsense Scot who, having grown up in Glasgow, took no crap whatsoever from the drunks and the manipulative junkies trying to bag another hit. Which was just as well, as it was they who made up the majority of A&E's dysfunctional population at this hour. But Matt must have had a wild look in his eye, because even Isla took a step back as he approached.

'Matt, what's wrong?'

Resisting the urge to howl like a wolf, he asked, in between his gasps for breath, 'Can you see that girl out there?'

'You mean the one that was trying to eat your face in the clinical area five minutes ago?' Isla said.

'Yes, her.'

'Of course I can see her.'

'Yesss,' Matt said, making a fist of triumph.

'Are you feeling all right?'

'Better than I've felt for a long time. Isla, listen to me. I want you to take my mobile phone and take a photograph of us. She hates having her photo taken, so you need to be a bit sneaky.'

'Okay, but—'

'I know. I will explain it to you one day, I promise. Would you, please?' Matt handed over his mobile. 'Battery's almost flat, but there's enough juice for a snap and I've put it in camera mode already. Just point and press this button here. I'll be outside with her.'

Isla hesitated. 'But it's your phone. Won't you want it back?'

'Nah, I'll pick it up tomorrow. Thanks, Isla.'

The idea of a photograph had come to Matt out of fear and paranoia. If he had a photograph, he could at least stuff it under the nose of that sniffy psychologist, even though he knew she'd have something dubious to say about it. And yes, of course it was possible to stage a brief encounter moment with any old slapper willing to pose for a snap. But he would know. Every time he looked at it, he would know that she was real.

Matt turned and hurried back to Silvy. They stood under the brightly lit awning of the main A&E entrance, and once more he held her away, staring, grinning like an idiot as he turned and twirled her. Then he kissed her again and, making sure she had her back to Isla in the reception area, saw the flash go off before he closed his eyes to enjoy the kiss once more.

'You have nice lips, Mathew,' Silvy said when they broke off. It made Matt smile. She was always saying stuff like that. Little compliments that sounded off-kilter, as if she were surprised. As if it was all new to her.

'Okay,' Matt said. 'Now what? I've got a million questions. We need to go somewhere where I can talk my bloody head off.'

'Where is your car?' Silvy asked.

'Totalled in the crash. Never got around to getting another one.'

'Totalled, yes. I am sorry.'

An awkward silence opened up between them, and it was Silvy who broke it. 'So, we will get a taxi. I would like a steak. I hear the Carp does an excellent rib-eye.'

'Getting a bit late,' Matt said, glancing at his watch and then frowned. 'How do you know the Carp?'

Silvy shrugged. 'It is not my first time in this city.' Then she grinned, and Matt found himself grinning, too. It was more than infectious; it was contagious. Fifteen minutes later, Matt stood at the bar of the Carp Inn, smiling with gratitude at the barmaid as she took his order for food. The kitchen had stopped taking orders ten minutes before, but she'd bought his story, which was that his girlfriend had flown in from abroad this evening and her plane had been late arriving and they were starving. Because it was a half-truth, Matt found he was able to sell it pretty well. At the bar, he kept looking around to make sure Silvy was still there.

She was, looking amazing in a short jean skirt, Ugg boots, and a low-cut T-shirt under a tight cardigan.

He leaned against the bar to quell his trembling, picked up the two pints of cider he'd ordered, and went back to her, sensing a big, stupid grin on his face, where there should have been hate and suspicion and ire. Those were the emotions he'd dreamed about hurling at her (along with several knives and an anvil) should they ever meet again. Of course, having been told by the psychologist that Silvy wasn't real, the chances of that ever happening had been remote. Even so, it had given Matt huge vituperative pleasure to imagine it. Now that she was sitting here, however, all that bile had boiled away like so much steam. In fact, it was all he could do to stop himself from climbing up on the table and dancing a jig.

Through the window over Silvy's shoulder, the world outside was going downhill. The wind had picked up, and people huddled against the plummeting temperature as they hurried to and from cars in the car park. Matt Danmor couldn't have cared less. Inside, it was warm, and his world, so banal and ugly not an hour before, was suddenly the best place in the universe to be. Silvy was sitting opposite him. Blonde, beautiful, smelling fantastic, *and real*. Matt's brain gave another whoop. He wanted to shout it out. Scream the word at the top of his lungs.

Those lips, that hair, those legs, all *real*.

Four little letters that meant he wasn't a lunatic. He took a healthy swallow of his drink and smacked his lips. Sod the Deluquel; he'd moved on to a real mood lifter—a pint of Old Rosie's cider.

'So,' Matt said, holding up his glass. 'Here's to you, Silvy. Back from the dead.'

A warm smile played over her lips. 'You are so funny, Mathew.' She held her glass up and they clinked before she brought it up to her mouth and downed half the pint in three swallows.

'I can't tell you how mind-blowingly amazing it is to see you again, but I have to ask—'

'Where have I been?' She finished his sentence, looking at him over the rim of the pint glass.

Matt smiled, despite himself.

Was this Silvy being frank, or—and this new thought

floated out from behind a rock like a vicious moray eel—conniving and treacherous?

'Mathew,' Silvy said, her gaze steady, 'I know that I have a lot of explaining to do. After the accident…well, I had to go away. When I came back, I started looking for you right away. You must believe that. But I couldn't find you anywhere.'

'When you say you had to go away, where to? Did you run because you didn't want anyone to find you? I mean, how did you get out of the car?'

He'd wondered about that, of course, like he'd wondered about every single second of his time with her. The 'hiding from the authorities' theory had presented itself as a viable scenario, along with 'alien abduction' and 'figment of his imagination.' All equally valid as insane theories went.

Silvy shrugged. 'I was thrown clear. Luck, I suppose.'

Luck? Screamed a voice in Matt's head. *Did luck stop you coming to the hospital and finding me afterwards? Was it luck that made you completely untraceable on any bloody database in the country?* The voice wanted him to be incandescently angry, but he couldn't. Breathing in Silvy was like being dragged along to a Barry Manilow concert—despite a cast-iron determination to despise the whole thing, halfway through you found yourself singing along to *Copacabana* and then before you could say, 'Oh Mandy.' it was too late and you were cheering like a good'un.

'So,' he asked, composing his thoughts, 'was it something to do with not wanting to be found? I mean, are you here illegally?'

'Something like that,' Silvy said and swallowed some more cider before shifting over and snuggling up close. He caught another waft of that evocative perfume and drank it in while she spoke. 'There is so much to talk about, I know. But all I have been thinking about is how it was before. Those few weeks we had together, I was so happy. Now that I have found you again, I want so much for us to be like we were before. For a short while. There will be time for explanations, I promise.'

'So, you want me to pretend like nothing happened and pick up where we left off, is that right?' Matt asked, pulling back, unable to hide his incredulity.

'It is all I have been thinking about. I know what you must be feeling, but can we? For maybe half an hour, while we eat and drink. You and me. Please?'

She had a pleading look in her eyes. He'd seen that look before when he'd needed to get up for a lecture and she hadn't wanted him to.

'Maybe I *am* insane,' Matt muttered.

Silvy smiled. 'You haven't changed.'

'Oh, yes, I have. In all sorts of ways.'

'Please, Mathew. Later, I will tell you everything you want to know, I promise.'

Matt frowned. How bloody crazy was this, all of a sudden? He had every right to demand a blow-by-blow account of what happened that night, but on the other hand there was something weirdly appealing in remaining ignorant for a smidgen longer. He'd been in limbo for so many months; another half an hour would make bugger-all difference. Drinking Silvy in was like rediscovering a favourite wine after years of bad harvest. She was very pretty. And her perfume was bewitching.

'Okay,' he said. 'Let's eat, drink, and be merry for half an hour. I reckon I deserve that, too.'

She smiled and put her hand on his thigh under the table. 'I have missed you so much.'

She obviously hadn't changed. And if Matt needed further evidence, the way she laid into her steak five minutes later was proof positive. They laughed and joked and touched and drank, oblivious to all those around them while the pub gradually emptied. By eleven-thirty, they were full of food and more than a little drunk.

'Shall I ask them to ring for a taxi?' Matt asked.

'Yes, why not?' Silvy said.

'To where?' It was a question so loaded that it almost exploded in Matt's brain.

'Yours?'

'Fine,' Matt said, trying to swallow and hoping he'd at least put his running gear in the laundry basket.

Silvy looped an arm in his. 'Come on. Let's go outside until the taxi comes. I think it has started snowing.'

CHAPTER SIXTEEN

THERE WASN'T MUCH, a fine dusting, but it seemed to please Silvy. It had turned very cold, and their breaths plumed like thick smoke as they clung to each other for warmth. The Carp had a terrace much frequented by students in the summer months, but this time of year the umbrellas were all furled and tied with rope, chairs upended on their tables. To Matt and Silvy's right was the stone bridge carrying the road over the weir; to their left, a footbridge led to a river island housing a weather station.

'Let's go onto the footbridge,' Silvy said. 'I love looking at the white water coming over the weir.'

'They've probably locked the gate,' Matt called after her as she hurried down to where the footbridge began.

'Open,' she sang back, and he watched as she walked out over the water. Matt went after her but hesitated before taking that first step onto the bridge. Was it only this morning that he'd had an absence attack that had left him confused and depressed? This morning after work that he'd toyed with the idea of cycling up here to feed his despondency? He shook his head in disbelief. Here he was, at that very spot, walking onto it in a moment of fun and contentment, as far removed from the dark dejection of a dozen or so hours ago as it was possible to be.

Yet an echo of that feeling brushed over him, as unpleasant as a hanging cobweb kissing his cheek. He'd walked alone onto this bridge many times. Walked and stood, watching the weir, imagining himself in the water, feeling its surge, his body twisting and rolling, his mouth spluttering, instantly disoriented as the power of it churned about him. So many times he'd imagined that last second of giving up the fight and inhaling and choking. He looked up. A half-moon emerged from behind the scudding clouds and lit up the edge of the cloudbank like a silver ribbon. And there on the bridge stood Silvy, smiling at him.

'Come on, Mathew. Don't be such a baby.'

He placed one foot on the footbridge. Something wet caressed his cheek. He looked up and was greeted by fresh snow coming down with a vengeance. With it came a strange and deathly hush. Even the noise of the late leavers from the pub diminished to a distant jangle of dampened laughter and jeers. Silvy stood watching him, patient and unflustered by the snow. Still, the half-moon beamed its cold light onto her hair. It was breath taking and magical as she held out her hand to him. He stepped forward and her long, cool fingers intertwined with his. She slid her free hand beneath his coat and felt through his T-shirt for the pendant.

'You still wear it,' she whispered.

'Always,' he replied.

'Promise me you will,' she said and kissed him again. But this one was oddly chaste, starkly different from the passion-filled hunger of before. He leaned forward to respond with a little more interest, but she turned away to look at the river and the water boiling through the weir gates.

'I know this place quite well,' Matt said, following her gaze. 'I come up here, sometimes. Since the accident, that is. I love it when it's like this after the rain. In full flood.'

The snow fell thick and fast now, blurring the pub lights and turning people into fuzzy shapes.

'I used to wonder what it would be like in the water. Helpless, giving up to the force of it.' Matt glanced at her, but she kept her eyes on the weir. 'You probably think I'm a coward. It's a coward's way out, isn't it?'

'Is it?' she asked, the words soft, her eyes flint.

It was a stepping-off-the-escalator-with-your-eyes-shut moment for Matt. His brain was flying along in half-pissed contentment, but Silvy's words required more than a bit of clear thinking if they were to make any sense.

'What do you mean?' he asked. The wind had picked up, swirling the snow about them. Matt pulled his coat tighter.

'After the accident, remember I told you I went some-where?' Silvy said.

'Yeah.'

The wind was now howling.

'I died, Matt. After I pulled the wheel and we hit that tree, I died. But you survived. That wasn't what was meant to happen.'

The steak and cider churned in Matt's stomach with a sickly swoop. 'What do you mean?'

'My injuries were horrific. A broken neck; ruptured internal organs. But, for me.' she smiled a smile of terrible calmness, 'dying isn't that bad.'

'Dying isn't that bad? Who are you? Miss Blonde Zombie 2024?' Yeah, that was it. Try turning it into a laugh. That usually worked. But no one was laughing here. Not this time. He had to shout now to be heard above the squall. 'Come on, hitting your thumb with a bloody hammer isn't that bad. But dying is…well, it's *dying*. What could be worse than that?'

She turned her eyes towards him. They were silver. Odd that, because there wasn't any moonlight anymore. 'Believe me, there are many things worse than dying, Mathew.'

He was going to ask, 'Like what?' but something caught his attention on the island side of the footbridge. It wasn't easy to see through the snow but, yes, there were people there. Small people dressed in robes. They looked a lot like a chil-dren's choir. And then he realised that he couldn't hear any sounds from the Carp anymore because of the strange roaring noise coming from behind the stone bridge on the far side of the weir.

A bucket full of ice spilled into his gut and he shivered violently. 'Right, this is getting *way* too weird. What's going on, Silvy?'

'When I died, someone fixed it for me to come back.'

'Big bloke with a scythe and a white horse?'

Silvy didn't so much as smile. 'When you come back, you will be so much stronger. Like me. We can be together for always, Mathew. All you have to do is jump.'

Matt looked behind him. There were now more 'children' on his end of the footbridge as well. He peered at them through the whirling, driving flakes. They looked at him with unblinking eyes. All with identical, fresh-faced stares like a bunch of disturbing Russian dolls. That was worrying. Beneath him, something was happening to the river. The water level appeared to be falling. That was even more worrying. Then, something Silvy had said earlier suddenly rang a very large alarm bell inside his head, too.

'Hang on, did you say, "after *I* pulled the wheel and we hit the tree," before?'

'Yes.'

A simple word, 'yes.' Simple, but loaded with oh, so much terrifying meaning. And as Matt stared at her in disbelief, he saw something move behind her eyes. Something restless and unsavoury which turned the ice in his gut into a glacier. Matt took a step back, but his brain was having a bit of trouble assimilating the whole package. An involuntary laugh escaped from where it cowered deep in his throat. It was meant as a 'Good one, Silvy. Now let's go home to bed'-type laugh. Instead, it rushed out as a shrill warble of fear.

'It is time, Mathew,' Silvy said and stepped back. At least that was what Matt's brain wanted to believe, because admitting to what actually happened was grounds for sectioning. Silvy began drifting back, at a rate of knots, about a foot off the ground, still with that sad little wistful smile on her lips. One second, she was next to him. The next, she was standing amongst the choirboys of St. Clone's on the far side of the footbridge. At the same time, the roar from the other side of the weir doubled in volume. Beneath him, the river had dwindled to a trickle. Where the hell was all that water?

The answer came in the form of a frothing white wall of river twenty-five yards away accelerating towards him. He looked at Silvy and saw her smile tilt upwards to the sky as she and the choir opened their mouths and screamed (or was it wailed?) like banshees. Lots of things were happening in Matt's brain at once. Panic and terror, but most of all anger.

Silvy.

Too good to be true, bloody Silvy.

He should have known. Should have realised that someone like her was never going to bother with him unless there was a very good—or very bad—reason. Too good to be true; too beautiful to be real. And here he was on a footbridge in the snow with a Thames tsunami heading his way. By any stretch of the imagination, that added up to deep doo-doo. But Silvy? Not an English language student at all, then. That meant one very important thing as far as Matt was concerned.

Every single crap incident in the last year was her fault.

He wanted to hurl abuse at her. Wished he had those knives and the anvil. But all he could think of was her pendant. He reached for it, bundled it in his hand and drew back to throw it as the water struck. He thought he heard the tone of the godawful noise they were making on the bank change. He didn't speak whatever language it was, but if he were a betting man, he would have put money on the fact that it changed with that one note from triumph to despair.

Then, the cold fury of the wave broke over him and the handrail in front of him snapped off with a crack. It buried itself in his midriff. His feet left the footbridge, lifted bodily by the power of tons of water as it drove onwards. There was a bend in the river ten yards behind. The bank, he remembered, was dotted with huge sycamores. He expected to tumble down the far side of the wave at any moment, headfirst into a churning brown mass, and be dragged under to join the grasping roots and bits of old bike that conspired to tear his flesh and trap his limbs. But the handrail kept pushing him back, keeping him high on the crest. He went ten, twenty, thirty yards backwards and the wave kept growing. He could look down, see the river and the bank, even the Carp with its lights still burning as the water swept by.

Maybe he should have screamed, but there was too much frothy water spraying into his face as the wave finally peaked. He hovered thirty feet above the river proper now, and he could feel the power beginning to diminish. Any second, the thing was going to curl over, come crashing down and bring him with it. He closed his eyes and flailed his legs. He began to feel the weight transfer, the momentum changing from a force pushing back to a tilting fall as gravity kicked in. He reached the apex, his back arching, ready to plummet. Matt had air enough in his lungs for one last yell.

'Silvy, you—'

Thump!

His back crunched against something solid. And then the water wasn't lifting him or pushing him or sucking him down anymore. In fact, there wasn't any water at all. The pressure on Matt's back eased and he fell forward onto the fifteen-foot length of handrail still wedged under his armpits, but even more wedged now in something solid, high above the riverbed. Below him, the water roared past like a charging beast. And then, there was only river. A thick, oily, silent slick in full flood. Like it had been five minutes before. Matt swayed—or rather, the handrail swayed—while his legs swung in the air like a clown on a trapeze.

He risked a look behind and felt for whatever it was he'd thumped into. The snow stopped falling to allow the moon to slide out and shed its light on the mayhem. He was up a tree. Specifically, one of the huge sycamores overhanging the river, with the handrail wedged firmly in its branches. Matt pushed himself back on trembling arms to collapse in the elbow of one of the tree boles. He lay there panting, his limbs shaking from a shuddering mix of cold and adrenaline.

Not dead, he thought.

Not bloody dead. And from somewhere inside his head, a little voice said, *Now, what are the chances of that?*

Matt laughed out loud.

He was wet and he was cold, but most of all: he was NOT dead.

CHAPTER SEVENTEEN

BELOW, on the remains of the footbridge, he thought he could see something in the vague shape of Silvy disappearing into a shimmering bit of air. Odd, but bearing in mind what had gone before, not unexpected. From the direction of the Carp, came screams and shouts as people emerged to look at what was left of the weir and the footbridge, and realise that the pub had miraculously avoided a very wet end. Matt considered yelling for help, but then thought about trying to explain why he had decided to do an impression of a colobus monkey on this of all nights and thought better of it.

Instead, still shivering badly, he scrambled down the tree in the semi-darkness. The first twenty feet or so were easy, but then the trunk thickened, so that near the bottom he was forced to hang from a low branch and dangle. Matt fell, bent his knees and rolled. He sat up, checked himself for sprains or breaks, found none, and began walking. He stayed in the shadows and passed two fire engines, an ambulance, three police cars, and the beginning of a milling crowd set on enjoying a bit of a disaster. He could have rung for a taxi, but he was still sopping wet, so he jogged to keep warm. It freed his mind to think about what had just happened, and boy, was that an uncomfortable process.

Silvy was real, because other people had seen her. Of that

there was no doubt. Roberro, the prat, had even touched her. So, tick the 'real' box in red ink. But a real *what*? That was the six-million-euro question. Matt headed back towards town, thinking of what had happened on the bridge. Thinking of Silvy the meat-loving sex goddess transforming into an evil Snow White twin, complete with an entourage of at least seven vertically challenged…things. And 'things' was exactly the correct improper noun because, when they'd howled at the sky, they had neither sounded like, nor looked like, any human he'd ever seen.

Matt got to the top of Woodstock Road and, despite bouts of severe shivering, kept going. The weather had driven everyone indoors. He was miles from his flat, but it didn't matter. His brain, Deluquel-free at last and sober from the river dousing, was trying to get a handle on things now that it had some new data.

Ok, so Silvy was real-*ish*. But hadn't she said she'd come back from the dead? Matt listened to the arguments raging inside his skull and heard his head throw them all out as insane. But there was no denying the evidence of his own eyes and ears, not to mention the evidence of his sopping-wet clothes. During his cosy little evening out with back-from-the-dead Silvy, he'd strayed off the path of the here and now into a there and then, which was not the world as he knew it. She'd admitted to causing the crash, for crying out loud. Not only that, but she'd also tried to kill him all over again, hadn't she?

The MO of this most recent murder attempt was the most difficult thing to take on board. A knife to the heart, okay. A brick to the back of the head, possibly. But a thirty-foot freshwater tsunami was unconventional, to say the least. So unconventional that, whenever Matt's brain got to that bit, it stalled and sent him off in search of something he could cope with. But no matter how hard he tried, there was nowhere else to go, and he found himself trotting through the white, silent streets a bit quicker, with regular over-the-shoulder glances to see if any very small people wearing calf-length hoodies were following him.

By the time he reached the General, the snow had come back with a vengeance, lying an inch thick on the ground. Matt retrieved his bike and stuck his head down against the wind. He made it back to the flat through a deserted Oxford in twenty minutes but was seriously cold when he got there. He got in, drew the blinds, stripped off and promised never to slag off the storage heaters ever again as he hunched intimately up against one in an extremely ungainly pose. When the circulation had returned to his hands and feet, he put on some old joggers and made a mug of tea, drank it scalding hot, made another one, and waited while his limbs slowed from a shake to a quiver as he sat on the sofa, analysing how lucky he had been.

Lucky.

Not a word Matt had associated with himself for quite some time now. That was the biggest problem of all, as far as believability went. For the last fourteen months, Matt had been a klutz—Captain Ahab's Jonah, to quote Linda Marsh. Tonight, though, Matt had won the lottery-rollover-mega-bingo top prize and cheated death. That did not compute.

Matt was still pondering that incongruity when he finally stopped shivering, yawned, and then yawned again. Exhaustion and its sneaky little friend shock were knocking at his mental door. Bed beckoned. Matt took the hint. He upended his cup in the sink and, as he did so, his eyes fell on a thin worm of brown leather attached to an encircled golden cross, sitting next to the drainer.

Silvy's pendant.

Somehow, it had still been wrapped around his forearm and wrist as he'd reached to fill the kettle. He'd used trembling, numb fingers to disentangle it and had forgotten all about it until now. He picked it up and studied it. The clasp on the necklace had broken, and the link holding the pendant to the leather gaped. Unbelievable to think that the thing hadn't been lost altogether in the water, let alone remained wrapped around his arm.

The one thing Silvy had ever given him—not counting her body and two attempts on his life. The bin, overflowing as usual, beckoned at his feet. He dangled the pendant over it. There was a space between the new tea bags and the congealed remains of a plate of macaroni cheese, but he hesitated. The pendant had become as much a part of him as the small mole on his left buttock and his bigger left ear. There was a jeweller in the shopping centre in Headington. He could get it fixed there. He might never wear it again, but at least it would be in one piece. And it had a lot more significance now that Silvy had solidified into a lot more than a lump of undigested, gristle-induced imagination.

Matt yawned so wide he almost dislocated his jaw. He stumbled into bed. It felt warm and welcoming and he fell asleep immediately. Within an hour, and for the first time in many months, he was dreaming Deluquel-free dreams. After months of sanitised, tranquillised sleep, they came thick and fast, and began with the main feature.

Silvy.

A collage of Silvy laughing, munching on raw steak, naked in his bed. It was pleasant, non-threatening, until the scene in the car happened along. It was blue, a humble little Fiat Bravo called Spike, with two occupants: Matt and Silvy. *Monster* boomed out of the speakers, Silvy singing along to it, happy, legs crossed in the passenger seat next to Matt. It was night; the towel they'd used to lie down on in the dunes was still covered with sand on the back seat. There was no traffic.

'Thanks for a lovely day, Mathew,' Silvy said and kissed his cheek.

'It was a pleasure,' he said. 'Really was.'

'I wish it could go on forever.' She stretched back, and her breasts pushed forward against her T-shirt in a way that made it a very big struggle for Matt to keep his eyes on the road.

'Nothing lasts forever,' Matt said. He could feel the sloppy grin on his face.

'No. And I am sorry.'

'What for? That things don't last forever?'

'No,' Silvy said. 'For this.'

It was a classic schlock-horror moment. Hysterical, if it hadn't been so horrific. Two people in a car on a quiet country road. One turns away, and on turning back has a face like something from a crack-fuelled nightmare. Except Silvy didn't do the melodrama. She didn't turn away. She sat there while Matt checked his mirrors, before turning to her for an explanation.

'Sorry for wha…AAARGHJESUS.'

It was a meeting Linda Marsh for the first time on acid, moment. Silvy wasn't Silvy anymore. Her blonde hair had disappeared, and in its place was a moving, weaving cornrow of red snakes. Hungry, ice-blue eyes with vertical black slits for pupils. Her skin was alabaster and almost transparent, her mouth lined with needle teeth.

Matt's scalp contracted in terror. His body, meanwhile, didn't simply flinch. It tried to jump backward out of the car, and would have succeeded, but for the seat belt and the door. Matt let go of the wheel, every sinew in his body desperate for escape. He watched the thing put out a claw—there were just the two fingers—and grab the wheel in a convulsive jerk as it turned its grinning face to the sky and howled.

Matt woke with a sweaty start, panting, feeling like he was in a very bad B movie. He got up and drank some water from the sink in the bathroom. The clock read 3:33. He could feel his heart racing as his mind did its usual bout of rationalisations. Was this a nightmare or a delayed recollection of actual events? Matt closed his eyes and shook his head slowly. He really did not want to know the answer to that one.

Which only left the problem of getting back to sleep. He'd read somewhere that you needed dreams to prepare you for the trials and tribulations of everyday life. You were unlikely to face the monsters of your imagination in actuality, but in case you did, your subconscious had already done an am-dram production of it so that there was a subliminal script filed away ready for immediate access in your amygdala. Some people said you could control your dreams, train yourself to become lucid while you drifted through REM sleep— or the more vivid non-REM variety. That was all well and good, but the thought of being lucid with Silvy doing her gorgon act didn't fill him with enthusiasm.

Matt thought of drifting on a boat on a nice blue sea, sun above, coral shallows below, bobbing along with a warm breeze in his hair. Pretty soon, he'd gone off again. But there were more dreams waiting to ambush him. No more of Silvy; she'd gone back into her box for the night.

No, these were just weird.

It was morning and he was on another footbridge. Not the one at the Carp, but he knew it well enough. This one crossed the canal in Jericho within sight of St. Barnabus. He wasn't alone. There were two people next to him. His legs didn't seem to have any bones, and his eyes wouldn't open. He could hear and smell, though. His two companions struggled to support his jelly form. One smelled of pine needles, along with something more exotic. The other smelled of fried bacon and wheezed quite a lot.

'We need to get him to the other side,' said Pine Needles.

'Do we really?' puffed Bacon. 'Can't we leave him here? I mean, he can see his velocycle.'

'It's called a bicycle, and no, we can't. It's only a few more yards. And we need to hurry up. I think he's already beginning to come round.'

'Oh, all right. All I can say is that this is doing my lumbago no good at all. I shall have to have some of those marvellous little buttons…what are they called, again?'

'Aspirin. They're called aspirin. And I don't like you using so much of their stuff, you know that. Why don't you ask Mrs Hoblip to cook up a toad-bile poultice?'

'Ah yes, Mrs Hoblip's lumbago poultice. That panacea for so many ills, and the cause of a great many more, unfortunately. You seem to have conveniently forgotten the last time. The look on that plastic surgeon's face is one that is burned onto my retinas. And skin grafts are no fun either, I can tell you. Really, Kylah, I'm surprised at you.'

'All right, all right, I'll get you some aspirin. Now, let's do this, please? Ready?'

Matt felt his feet dragging on the wooden walkway. Felt himself leaning against the bike. And then woke up in his own bed wondering who the hell Kylah was, and why that name, Mrs Hoblip, rang so many bells.

CHAPTER EIGHTEEN

MATT STAGGERED out of bed the next morning, showered and dressed, got on his bike and headed off towards Headington shopping centre. The jeweller was a small, rotund man with one tuft of hair on the top of his head. He wore a moth-eaten brown, green, and yellow sweater that looked as if it had been worn every day for most of the last century. Matt retrieved the pendant from his pocket and showed it to the guy as he explained what needed doing.

The jeweller looked at it, nodded, and said, 'Two hours.'

Matt headed into town. Out on the bike, he began to feel better as he got to the end of Cowley Road and hit the city proper. He cycled up to the General, found Isla, and retrieved his phone; the battery was, as usual, pancake flat. Time he sorted the damned thing out once and for all. He rode back into town, parked and locked the bike before joining the Oxford throng on foot. It was at that point he realised that what he'd seen that morning was not confined to Independent Television, but also seemed to be out in what passed for the real world.

Something big in fancy dress was going on. Matt saw a couple of witches with green faces and warts the size of ten-pence pieces cackling outside Agent Provocateur. Another one stood in front of him in the queue in Boots the Chemist. He was on the point of asking her what it was all about when he glanced down and saw that she had ten tubes of haemorrhoid ointment in her basket. That put an end to any thoughts he had of engaging her in conversation; he had a gut feeling that someone who needed that amount of anal pain relief might not have the sunniest of dispositions.

There was an eight-foot-tall hairy outside Starbucks. The yeti suit was well insulated, since he/she was the only customer daring to brave the elements at a pavement table, reading *The Guardian* and laughing like a drain. But it was when he entered the phone shop that weird became full-on bizarre. The thing that served him had gone to a lot of effort, and must have been in makeup for two hours, at least. They had blue skin and dead white eyes, with corneas that looked like they'd been in a microwave on high for far too long. Their coat—which was seaweed, studded with barnacles and covered in slime—dripped water everywhere, leaving small puddles wherever he stood.

'That's fantastic,' Matt said.

'What's that, mate?' asked the thing.

Matt read the badge pinned above the remains of a festering crab on its chest. It said, *DEAN.*

'Your costume, Dean. Bloody brilliant.'

'Look, mate, we're really busy, so…'

'So, what exactly is this? Are you being sponsored? Something worthy, is it?'

Dean peered at him, doubt causing the clammy-looking skin on his forehead to wrinkle and his tone to become tetchy and tinged with suspicion.

'Was it a phone you wanted?'

'Okay,' Matt said, with a grin. 'If that's the way you want to play it, that's fine by me. What's available on upgrade for someone on an Ocelot 25 contract?'

Dean launched into a well-practised spiel about Nokias and iPhones vs Samsungs, but Matt couldn't keep his eyes off the invertebrate life forms on Dean's coat. When one of the whelks on his elbow sent out a proboscis and latched on to a cockleshell next to it, Matt let out a yelp of astonishment. 'That's amazing.'

'Something funny, mate?'

'Okay, I realise that you're at work and stuff but...oh come on, one of your whelks just—'

The look on Dean's waterlogged face could have stopped Big Ben.

'Fine,' Matt said with a shrug, 'I'll go for the simplest of the lot. Give me something basic.'

'No problem,' Dean said. 'Want me to transfer your contacts?'

'Please,' Matt said and handed over his old mobile. Dean pressed some buttons, tutted and then rummaged in a drawer until he found a charger and plugged it in. After fifteen long seconds, the device chimed into life.

'Can you actually see through those lenses?' Matt asked.

'Lenses?' Dean muttered.

'Yeah, those contact lenses. I'm amazed you can keep them in.'

'I don't wear contact lenses,' Dean said.

Matt grinned and winked but stopped short of a nudge.

'So, I'll put your phone contacts onto the SIM card and then copy that onto the new phone, but all your photos will go, okay?'

'Ah,' Matt said. Of course, there was one photo that he might want to look at, but what was the point? Silvy was old hat. Whatever they'd had together had been washed away on a thirty-foot wave. But curiosity got the better of him. 'Hang on, before you get rid of them, there's just one snap I want to check out. Is that okay?'

'Be my guest.' Dean handed the phone back to Matt, who scrolled to his media file. 'Yeah, here it is,' he said and called up a thumbnail of him and Silvy in the entrance of A&E the night before. Had it really been less than twenty-four hours? He waited while the photo loaded. Yup, there he was with his arms around...what? Not Silvy. The image was blurred and looked more like a wheeling sandstorm than anything else. In the middle of the blur stood a shape, all angles and…were those folded wings protruding from her back?

'See, I knew the thing was on the blink. I mean, look at that?' He held up the phone so Dean could see.

Dean stared and very, very slowly, turned his blind white gaze on Matt. 'Is this a wind-up?' he whispered.

'A wind-up? I wish it was. I would have been better off with a wind-up. The battery on this is crap. I mean this phone is only ten months old—'

'Look, pal,' Dean said. 'I don't know what this is all about, but you're making me feel really uncomfortable here.'

'Sorry,' Matt said, miffed. 'But it's a bit rich telling me that you're uncomfortable when it's me that's standing here being served by the creature from the blue lagoon. I'm trying to show you how useless this two and a half mega-pixel camera is. That's supposed to be me and my girlfriend—'

It was then that Matt glanced up and caught his reflection in a mirrored wall behind the phone display.

Something cold shuddered down the backs of his legs, made his toes tingle.

In the mirror, he saw himself holding his rubbish phone next to the fantastical Dean. Except that Dean's reflection wasn't there. In his place stood a tallish, sallow, bespectacled youth, with carefully styled hedge-backwards hair and a bad case of acne.

'Shit,' Matt said.

'Here, use these,' Dean said out of the side of his mouth. He held up a pair of dark-rimmed glasses.

'What are they?' Matt said.

'Granite resin rims. Didn't they tell you about that? You know, looking through a hole in a stone and stuff?'

Matt, whose brain now raced along at two hundred miles an hour and was fast approaching a bend, considered the advice with his usual scepticism and wanted to hurl a 'What do you take me for?' sneer at Dean. Then, he thought of the witch with the pile cream in Boots, and Hillman the imp on

Dawnbreak, and realised that he was in no position to be throwing that sort of sneer around.

Dean's suggestion, laughable though it was, merited at least one go. After all, only Dean was going to laugh like a hyena if he tried on the glasses and looked a pillock. He took them, saw they were lensless and put them on. The photo of Silvy changed from a blurred grey shape into…blonde, luscious Silvy. He looked across at Dean and saw, not something with an address care of Davy Jones's locker, but an anxiously frowning youth. It was only after two minutes of this that he realised his mouth was wide open.

'So,' Dean said, eventually. 'You won't want the photograph, then?'

'Yes,' Matt said in a castrati wheeze. He cleared his throat and repeated, in a lower tone, 'Yes, I want it, thank you. I'll buy a memory card for the new phone, so if you could transfer it over, I'd be very grateful.' Matt waited while Dean did what he needed to behind the till. He had a thousand questions, but this was neither the time nor the place. Besides, Dean didn't strike him as the forthcoming type. Matt waited while Dean put the new phone in its box in a carrier bag, handing it over with a smile. As Dean the youth, it was quite a nice smile. Matt whipped off the glasses to see that, as Dean the creature, the smile was a glimpse into a fishy maw that Matt didn't need.

'And it's Black Lagoon, by the way. Not blue.' Dean waved away Matt's offer to return the glasses. 'Keep them, I think your need is greater than mine.'

Matt gave him a wintry smile and left. He walked along the street, contemplating this new twist. If he had this right, the things—and there was no other word for them—he kept seeing in the street were not people in fancy dress.

Not only that, but from the way they drew no responses or stares, everyone else was seeing them as normal-looking people, just as he was through the stone-rimmed glasses. But why was he seeing them for what they really were, and what the hell *were* they? He turned a corner into Brasenose Lane and stopped. The two witches window-shopping at Agent Provocateur earlier were coming towards him. He slipped on the glasses. The witches became two very ordinary and attractive women in their early twenties, who looked like any of the scores of similarly attired women rushing to or from lectures, or shopping, or chatting, all around him. All it needed now was for a soundtrack of *The Twilight Zone* to kick in, and his day would be complete.

What do you mean, day? How about week? Or month? Try a year?

Matt heard the voice. It belonged to the whining little Pixie Of Negativity that lived inside his head, which always laughed like an orang-utan whenever Matt gave in to the megrims and headed up to the weir. Today though, the PON sounded as if it was trying a little too hard with the put-downs and the jibes. Okay, what was happening was off the scale weird, and he understood it about as much as the mathematics of fractal crystallography, but there was no denying this concrete *something*, where for months there had been nada, limbo, an almost comatose bewilderment. Wasn't that better?

Well, no.

Matt crossed the road and wandered into Whitewells bookshop. Cramped and claustrophobic, it nevertheless had lots of nooks and crannies where a quarter of a century could pass without anyone disturbing you. That was about as long as he might need to get to grips with being in this current episode of *Weird Tales*. Matt grabbed a paperback from the three-for-two table and found a quiet seat in which to sit down and 'read' while he tried to gather his thoughts. That was easier said than done, because they were scattered all over the ten-acre field of his mind and weren't responding to the well-trained collies of reason and logic he'd sent out to shepherd them in.

After perusing the shelves for five minutes, his pulse began to slow, but he did a quick stone-rimmed-glasses check of his fellow browsers, just to be safe. He came up with nothing but a normal-looking bloke with a knitted scarf and glasses hovering around the Sci-Fi section, and a gaggle of pale coping women dressed in painted work boots and flowing coats looking up sociology texts.

Okay, Matt. So, you can see things. Ergo, you're gifted.

No, that was just twaddle. Nine-year-olds who could play all of Rachmaninoff's piano concertos without sheet music were gifted. What Matt was experiencing wasn't a gift. It was a curse. An important one, too. *How* important he had no idea, but something scratching away behind his eyes told him that it was. Yet it hadn't fazed Dean in the slightest.

Thinking of Dean sent him off on another tangent. What on earth was he doing working in a mobile phone shop, anyway? In Matt's experience, phone shop employees consisted of people between jobs of the waiting-for-something-better-to-come-along variety, or derailed bankers, or maybe the odd student. In Dean's case, a *very* odd student. At that point, someone opened the fridge door in Matt's head and the light came on. Is that what he was seeing? Students? The PON felt obliged to contribute.

In Oxford? Bah humbug. Surely not, sir. Preposterous idea.

Matt told it to shut up and wondered if there might be an actual college—a St Elsewhere's offering human studies to aliens. If there were one, the open day must have been mind-bending. That thought was weird enough to allow Matt to drag the scattered ewes of his thoughts back to his own predicament. Gifted or cursed, that was the question. There were no answers in the paperback, which was just another serial killer shocker, this one about a murderer who chose his victims by what yoghurt flavour they bought at the supermarket, and, after ten minutes of more wool-gathering, Matt left it on the seat and walked back out into the daylight.

CHAPTER NINETEEN

HE CYCLED BACK to his flat and was almost there when he remembered the pendant. Instead of turning left down Fairfield Street, he went straight on to Headington. The jeweller was hunched over a desk with a loupe stuck over one eye. He looked up, climbing off his stool as Matt entered the shop.

'There's good news and bad news,' he said.

Matt shrugged. He was, by now, ready for anything.

'Firstly, I have fixed it. Simple job, really. Replaced the clasp and soldered the linking ring. No, it's the pendant itself I wanted to talk to you about. You did say it was gold, didn't you?'

'Isn't it?'

'Buy it abroad, did you?' The jeweller's smile was a tad patronising.

'It was a present.'

The jeweller sucked in air through his teeth. In that lugubrious hiss was years of having to disappoint gullible punters like Matt with news that their foreign-bought sterling silver crucifixes were, in fact, nothing but bits of old sardine tin. He fetched a large, illuminated magnifier and placed the pendant on the counter in front of Matt, tilting the magnifier towards him so that he could see.

'The workmanship is very basic, but it's interesting, to say the least. If it isn't a reproduction, then it could be very old, indeed.'

'Right,' Matt said.

The jeweller pointed to a bit of lumpiness on the surface, working at it with tweezers. Something flaked off.

'Gold leaf,' he said. 'It's all over the surface, but if you look at the rims of the circle…' The jeweller pointed with his tweezers. Matt could see that the rims looked darker than the rest of it.

'What does that mean?'

'I might have said that the metal is showing through where it's worn on the rims. But having looked at it carefully, it looks to me as if the gold leaf has been laid on so that the rims are deliberately exposed.'

'Exposing what?'

'Looks like gold, feels as heavy as gold, but it isn't. It's iron.'

'Iron?'

'Yes. And that would support it being genuinely old, since it isn't the kind of technique modern knockoffs use. I mean, *really* old. Like museum old. I'd look after it, if I were you. Who knows, it might be worth something even though it isn't gold. That'll be £10, please.'

Matt paid and watched the jeweller wrap the pendant in some tissue paper, before taking it back and stuffing into his pocket. On his way home, he topped up on the basics at a supermarket where there were as many security guards as checkouts. He took a hand basket and filled it with eggs, milk, cereal, bread, cheese, and a couple of pizzas. He saw one goth couple who might have fit the bill *à la* Dean, but when Matt put on his stone-rimmed glasses, they stayed the same. It was the way they chose to look. Chalk that one up to a misguided taste in music and a hopelessly optimistic view of what those facial tattoos were going to look like in thirty years' time.

MATT HEADED BACK to the flat, put on some Foo Fighters, and tried to get his head around exactly what the hell was happening. After an hour, he had more questions than answers on the pad he'd decided to use as a jotted *aide-memoir*.

Who, or what, was Silvy?

Why did she want him dead?

Why had she lied about the pendant being gold, and why had she insisted he wear it?

Why had he started seeing things everywhere, and why did no one else seem to mind?

Matt made a cup of instant coffee and, as he stirred in the milk, realised that he sort of knew the answer to that last question, having seen Dean's reflection in the mirror. But it was an answer he had shied away from because it meant…it meant that when everyone else looked at Dean, they saw the geeky phone salesman. It was only he, mental Matt, who saw the thing from the deep.

And of course, there was what Dean had said.

'Didn't they explain that to you?'

They? Who the hell were they?

Matt went round in mental circles for another hour before summoning up enough effort to stick the pizza in the oven. He played some Royksopp while he waited and then sat on the sofa to eat.

He had the psychologist's number. The offer of support was there at any time during office hours. What he was supposed to do when the PON struck at two a.m., he wasn't sure. Howl at the moon? He chewed on his pizza and thought about it hard. The woman would listen, as she was trained to do, and then…and then what?

Things you're unlikely to hear a psychologist congenitally devoid of a sense of humour saying:

Delighted to hear that Silvy is not a figment of your imagination. Sheer bad luck that she's an entity capable of conjuring up walls of water. Still, these things happen. And as for seeing things differently, don't worry about that. It is, of course, possible that you're the one that sees things the right way. It's more than likely the case that the rest of the world are labouring under the misapprehension that the earth is populated by people just like them, when, in fact, it's full of otherworld freaks. How wrong they are, eh, Matt? Ha ha. Thank God you stopped the Deluquel when you did. They could have been preventing you from seeing things as they truly were. Narrow escape, there.

The pizza crust turned to cardboard in Matt's mouth. There was only one real conclusion to draw from all of this, no matter how you picked at the detail. He didn't need a prat of a psychologist to tell him what it was.

He'd lost it, big time.

Okay, there were some small-print issues that were doing his head in, such as Dean implying, because Matt could see him, that he was one of them. Terrific. Was he going to wake up one morning with his skin sloughed off to find that he was a green-lipped mussel? It didn't bear thinking about.

He sat up, mulled it over, drank too much wine on his own, and went to bed. His dreams were full of witches with green faces and creatures from the deep, but at least his conversations with them were intelligent and non-threatening. He even got some share tips from Hillman the imp. The most vivid dream was a replay of him on the canal bridge hearing and smelling (but not seeing) Mr Bacon and Miss Pine Needles.

Matt awoke at first light, depressed but determined, more convinced than ever of what he'd concluded the night before —that he'd gone completely mad. He ate raisin wheats (two bowls full) and kept the TV off. By seven-fifteen, he'd unlocked his bike and was heading into town, certain there was only one place he could go to put an end to all of this.

The snow had all but gone, but a sharp frost had painted the pavement white, and the other brave souls who had ventured out that Saturday morning were swaddled against the elements. Matt chose a route through the centre of town, navigating the High Street to Brasenose and the Bodleian, took Park Road to cut through the Banbury and Woodstock Roads to Little Clarendon Street and Jericho. His curiosity had been piqued by the dream featuring Miss Pine Needles and Mr Bacon. He was convinced that the Mount Place footbridge had been in it, so why not take a look at it in daylight? After all, it led to the towpath and his final destination.

He was heading north when he first saw the other cyclist coming towards him, slowing and pulling towards the centre with an arm out to indicate a right turn. He didn't give her a second thought as he motored through the crossroads of Albert Street and Cardigan. The last thing Matt expected was to hear a muffled yell, before finding himself thrown over the handlebars as the other bike broadsided him. He was aware of a couple of oaths escaping his lips, before hearing the crack as his helmet met with the road. He rolled, saw a galaxy of stars, and ended up on his arse facing back the way he'd come, stunned but intact. The other cyclist was hurrying towards him.

'I am *so* sorry,' she said, kneeling. 'Are you okay? I have no idea how that happened. I lost my balance. It was like something hit me from the side.'

Matt got gingerly to his feet and shook out his limbs, arched his back, and shook his head. Nothing broken. 'I'm fine.'

The woman stared at him with what were, even to Matt in his slightly woozy state, quite amazing eyes. He gave her his best brave smile.

'Honestly,' he said and took off his helmet.

'Oh,' the other cyclist said, with what could only be described as a moment of horrified recognition. The only thing missing as confirmation was an added, *'it's you.'*

'Do we know each other?' Matt asked, with a brow like a field on a ploughing day.

'Uh, no.' She said it quickly. 'Don't think so.'

Matt shrugged and reached for his bike. It had been in worse spills down mountain paths. As he righted it, he saw something on the ground the size of a Frisbee, with sharp, spiky protrusions. He bent to peer at it.

'Is this yours?' he asked.

The woman looked down and screamed, 'DON'T TOUCH THAT!'

Matt recoiled at her sheer intensity, standing back as she went to her cycle and fished out a battered old piece of Hessian sack, which she threw over the Frisbee. Gingerly, the woman used her boot and the tips of her fingers to get the thing wrapped up before carefully dropping it in a pannier.

'What is that thing?' Matt asked.

'This? It's a…piece of art. That's what it is.' This was accompanied by another too-bright smile. 'From my collection. Must have fallen out of the pannier when we collided.' A car pulled up and flashed its lights at them. 'We'd better get out of the road.' The girl pushed her bike towards the pavement. Matt followed on shaky legs.

'I'm really, really sorry,' the girl said again as they mounted the pavement.

'It's okay,' Matt replied. 'These things happen.'

'Not to me.' She sounded like she meant it.

Matt held out his hand. 'Matt. Matt Danmor.'

'I'm Kyeee…aren.'

'Kyearen? Are you Australian?'

The girl giggled. 'No. And it's just Karen. I get a little stammery under stress. So, Matt, were you off to work?'

'No. Morning off. I was about to go up the towpath to the Carp.'

'The Carp?' Her smile became a frozen grimace. 'Bit early, isn't it? And on a day like today, too.'

Matt frowned. 'What's wrong with today? It's dry and bright. Ideal day for a bike ride.'

Karen looked bemused, but then recovered. 'Yes, well, you could look at it that way. But there'll be lots of walkers on the towpath. Bit of a nuisance on the bike.'

'Not at seven-thirty in the morning, they're not.'

'No.' She glanced down, and then up again. 'Shame you've got a flat tyre then, isn't it?'

Matt looked down at his bike and groaned at the deflated state of his rear tyre, which, he could have sworn, had looked fine a minute before.

'Listen, there's a café in the boatyard. Let me buy you a cup of tea. I'm beginning to get cold out here.'

CHAPTER TWENTY

MATT SHRUGGED and followed Karen for fifty yards to The Breakfast Barge, a low brick building with wooden picnic tables outside and Formica-topped tables inside. The day's specials had been written up on a blackboard in yellow chalk. Most of them featured eggs, chips, beans, and Spam in a variety of combinations.

'You grab a table,' Karen said. 'I won't be a minute.'

Matt went inside and found a table by the window. He took off his jacket and helmet before glancing outside, where Karen was trying surreptitiously to push the Hessian-encased piece of 'art' into the canal with the toe of her boot. It plopped in with a hiss of steam. She stayed to make sure it sank before looking up and down the canal to see if anyone was watching. Satisfied, she sauntered back towards the café. It left Matt forlornly wondering if he'd been born with a weirdness magnet implanted in his brain. Even the people who smashed into him by accident were bloody odd.

But he forgot all about that when she came in and took off her helmet. When you're male and twenty-seven, you tended to forgive girls who are five-two, dark-haired, olive-skinned, and dazzling without their cycle helmets.

'Tea or coffee?' she asked.

Matt mumbled something that sounded like 'tea' and

watched her move towards the counter. He willed himself to keep his eyes on the back of her shiny black hair, but he gave up after she'd taken two steps, and let his gaze fall to her very nice compact bottom.

Stop it, said the PON. *The woman almost killed you five minutes ago.*

When Karen came back three minutes later with two steaming mugs, he'd chided himself into trying not to think about her in any way other than a mutual victim of circumstance.

'So,' she said, blowing over her tea with both hands cupped around the mug in a way that made Matt forget how to swallow. 'You were telling me about the Carp.'

Matt sipped at his tea and decided that waiting two minutes for it to cool might be the best way to avoid first-degree burns to his lips and palate. 'It's not the pub,' he explained. 'It's the weir that's the attraction. I like looking at it. I like the sense of power it has.'

'Well, you'd have a job this morning, because they've cordoned the whole thing off. Some sort of freak surge the other night. Caused a bit of damage, I understand.' She said it all so casually, as if that sort of thing happened every day.

'More than a bit of damage,' Matt muttered.

'Oh, so you've heard about it, too?'

There was a moment when Matt considered not speaking. A moment of vague doubt about the wisdom of saying anything. But in the end, there wasn't any choice. Karen was lending him her ear, and it was all Matt needed. He opened his mouth and out the words tumbled.

'Not just heard about it. I was there when it happened.' It was a simple enough statement. Not one you'd expect to result in someone dropping a very hot cup of tea, and then jumping up and back to prevent the stuff from scalding her.

'Blast,' Karen said and fetched a cloth from the girl behind the counter to wipe it up. Matt found himself smiling despite the near miss. He didn't know many people whose response to an exploding mug of tea was, 'Blast.'

'Sorry,' she said, sitting again when it was all cleared up. There was still half a mug of tea left, and she clutched it to her again with both hands. 'I thought I heard you say that you were actually there for a once-in-ten-thousand-years natural phenomenon that no one can explain, and for which there are no eyewitnesses. Silly me.'

'You did hear me say it. That's because I was there. But you don't want to hear me twittering on about the weir…'

'Yes, I do,' Karen said quickly, before adding, 'I mean, there are so many rumours and stories. I'd like to know the truth. You know what they say, there's no smoke without—'

'A pyromaniac. Look, if I tell you, you'll think I'm stark raving mad.'

Karen focused those big eyes on him. 'Try me.'

So, he told her. And in the telling, it all came out. About Silvy and the Carp and the tsunami. And about the vertically challenged clone choir, and him being deposited up the tree. About him now seeing people that looked like they'd lived underwater most of their lives serving customers mobile phones. It was easy. Much easier than telling it to the psychologist, because Karen listened with a resigned kind of sadness. As if it wasn't bizarre. As if it were a story she'd heard before and was all the more tragic for having heard it again.

'See, told you I was mental,' Matt said when he'd finished.

Karen, however, didn't push her chair away and make excuses to leave. By rights, she should have been smiling and backing away, nodding slowly and saying, 'Well, it was nice to meet you, but I've remembered that root canal appointment at the dentist.' Instead, she peered at him with those fantastic gold-flecked blue eyes.

'No, Matt, you're not mental.' She appeared to be having a bit of a battle with herself, judging by the way her brow furrowed. She growled in frustration and then said, 'I don't see that I have any choice but to tell you. That piece of art I threw into the canal, it wasn't a piece of art. It's a ristag.'

'A ristag?' Matt repeated.

Karen shrugged. 'The best way I can describe it is a

poisoned Frisbee. It's one of the weapons of choice of a faction called the Ghoulshee.'

'What are Ghoulshee, for crying out loud?'

'Something that you do not want to meet, if at all possible, although you obviously already have. What happened out there this morning on Albert Street was no accident. I should have realised it when you found the ristag. It must have hit me as I pulled up to turn right. But it wasn't meant for me. They know it can't harm me. I think it was meant for you.'

Matt stared. Like a kettle on a slow boil, he could feel something building inside him. Something red and mist-like. He was still looking at Karen, but he was seeing her in an altogether different light.

'I know how it sounds.' she went on in earnest apology. 'But you need to take this seriously. The thing is lethal. It probably would have killed you on contact, had it struck. Of course, it's perfectly safe now, neutralised under water. You were lucky I was in the way. I wear a shield charm and a talisman most of the time, so all it did was throw me off-balance. But what it means is that they're after you. The weir is a quiet spot, even more so at seven-thirty in the morning. They're tracking your movements, I'd say. You're asking for trouble—'

Matt raised a hand. 'Okay, stop it now, please. I know the, "There are more things in heaven and earth, Horatio." speech back to front. I've been practising it in the mirror for the last two days.' Something sour had risen in his throat and was making it difficult to swallow the tea, let alone what Karen was telling him.

'But it's dangerous, Matt.'

'Dangerous?' Matt's face burned with colour. With the consummate lack of ease of someone having to struggle once again with facing several impossible things before breakfast, Matt grabbed the wrong end of the offered stick and began metaphorically waving it about his head like a demented hammer thrower. It didn't help that Silvy had played him like a gullible fish. He'd had enough of women—especially weird women—for a good long while, and he wasn't prepared to put up with this from some slip of a cyclist who couldn't ride a bike for love nor lucre.

'What's dangerous is me sitting here listening to this bollocks.'

'Matt, I know what it sounds like—'

But Matt had gone beyond listening. 'Weapon of choice of the Ghoulshee, did you say?' He shook his head with a sad little smile, but the muscles of his shoulders were bunched in anger. 'I know what I sound like. I know I must be losing my bloody mind, but ristag and Ghoulshee? They're not even good made-up names. At least you could have veered towards JRR a bit more. We are in Oxford, after all. "Nazggoids" is a good one, or "Stingrod" even. But ristag just sounds like a high-tech legal restraint.' He pushed himself up and away from the table, but then rounded on her with a pointing finger. 'I don't appreciate being patronised. You may think this is one bloody big joke, but I don't, okay? Just because you can't control a pushbike—'

'Matt, I'm not trying to make fun of you,' Karen said urgently. 'I could prove it to you, but I can't.'

Matt's eyebrows shot up so far, they almost fused with his hairline. 'You could, but you can't. You will but you won't. Yeah, right. Thanks for the tea, Kyearen, or whatever your bloody name is.' He grabbed his coat and helmet and hesitated for about as long as it took light to travel from the window to the sink in his micro-flat. Was that a look of genuine regret on her face as he pushed through the door? Well, if it was, good. Served her right. He'd gone ten yards when she called to him from the doorway.

'Matt, promise me you'll stay away from that weir. Please?'

There were people in the boatyard. They stopped to look. Matt put his head down and kept walking. 'Learn to ride a bike,' he muttered under his breath as he wheeled the bike back towards town.

CHAPTER TWENTY-ONE

MATT FOUND a bike shop open on Walton Street, bought a new inner tyre, and did his own repairs in the empty front car park of a derelict office building. By the time he'd finished it was mid-morning, and Matt knew that Ka...Ky...whoever she was, would be vindicated if he went up the towpath now. There would be joggers and dog walkers by the score. There would be people up at the weir out for a gander, too. His determination to revisit the scene of the watery crime had not waned, but he didn't want to do it in front of a gaggle of onlookers. If the urge to hurl himself into the water overtook him, the last thing he wanted was an audience...

As it had on many an occasion over the last few months, the self-destructive thought had popped up unbidden, yet it suddenly felt very odd. The legacy of a different mindset. Having escaped it once in so spectacular a fashion, death—whether the Silvy-assisted variety or the DIY type—was now off the agenda. What Matt wanted was an explanation and some sort of closure, not notoriety as the bloke who threw himself into the weir.

Thinking about all of this was making his head hurt, and so Matt cycled back to the centre of town, craving distraction. He parked and locked the bike, meandered on foot around the streets for half an hour, and settled in a café with free Wifi. There, he googled iron jewellery.

In the early part of the nineteenth century, it turned out, the Prussian government had made very fancy iron bling to exchange for gold, which the people (wasn't it always the people?) were meant to donate to swell the state coffers. *Ve haff vays of making you poorer.* Not that much had changed in two centuries, then. It was still the punters who were bailing out the Masters of the Universe, and not only in Prussia, either.

Yet, according to the Fair Isle-clad jeweller, his pendant was from a much earlier era than the Napoleonic uprising. Matt found nothing that looked remotely like it until he stumbled on a new-age jewellery site. There, he spotted a looped Celtic cross in sterling silver that bore a passable resemblance to the thing that Silvy had given him. But it was the flowery description of the piece that intrigued him more than anything.

The Celtic cross, Matt read, *symbolises the bridge to other worlds, high energy and knowledge. The vertical axis stands for the celestial world, the horizontal for the earth.*

Intriguing but useless when it came to explaining his predicament. He glanced at his watch, logged off and headed off to the Infirmary. After what he'd been through over the last twenty-four hours, going to work seemed even less attractive than unusual? Still, better to distract oneself with the mundane than either. And you never knew, now that Matt had his new weirdo vision thing going on, he might be able to while away the hours playing Spot the Zombie. Of course, there was also the risk that he'd cross paths with Roberro and the med student, but there was a chance they wouldn't be working.

And if they were, so what? They'd had their fun with the pink dildo. Having the med student, fun, and a pink dildo pop up in the same thought cloud sent Matt's imagination off on a brief, but not unpleasant little tangent until he dragged it, kicking and screaming, back to the task in hand. He'd work his shift as usual and in the morning, it would be Sunday, when no one would be on the towpath or at the weir. He could do whatever detective work he wanted to do there alone. If Kyearan's strident warning about staying away from the place rang any alarm bells in Matt's head, he ignored them and hoped she'd fallen into the canal trying to resurrect her bloody ristag…so long as she could swim.

———

THE FIRST PERSON Matt saw when he clocked on that night was Jim Staples, the porter he was supposed to be covering for.

'Thought you were off?' Matt asked.

'Stag do was called off.' Jim looked miserable. 'Groom's brother couldn't get a pass from prison.'

'So, what about me?'

'Oh yeah, Linda wanted to see you,' Jim said, grinning. 'She's hanging about for you in A&E.'

'Why the ear-to-ear grin?'

'You'll see,' Jim said, leaving Matt with a sinking feeling that went down to his ankles.

The Uruk-hai cheerleader was, indeed, waiting for him. She had her hair up in some sort of elaborate arrangement, which looked like a termite mound with combs stuck in it. Whatever it was she was wearing was having great difficulty containing her bulging muscles with its thin straps, and her face looked like a colour-blind seven-year-old's attempt at a Picasso. Ms Marsh was out on the pull.

'Jim's in. You're not in A&E,' she barked, which was, on the whole, what she did when she wasn't growling.

'So, do you need me at all?'

'The med students don't have anywhere for their soddin' seminars. Bollocks, if you ask me. Not one of them wears a tie and all the girls look like they've never eaten a decent meal. Still, the old dispensary needs clearing out by Monday. You're not here tomorrow, are you?'

'No,' Matt said.

'Never mind. Can't see you finishing it tonight, so put everything in the IT room. And be bloody careful. Some of the stuff in there is old and worth real money. In fact, with your track record for breakages, they're asking for soddin' trouble. Still, I don't give a toss. It's Saturday night and I'm in the mood for dancing.'

The broad face above a broader neck rearranged itself into what Matt suspected was meant to be a smile.

It sent a shudder through him. Linda Marsh in a good mood was almost worse than Linda Marsh in a strop.

'I'm off down the market for a skinful. Just be soddin' careful.'

Matt waited until she'd left and took a couple of steps out into the corridor that led back to A&E. It looked pretty normal, but he was disconcerted to see that Roberro and the buxom med student were both at the desk. He could have sworn he saw them look away as his face appeared in their eyeline. Matt cursed silently and put it down to paranoia. He was sure that Roberro's nights had finished on Thursday. But what did it matter, anyway? With a bit of luck, he wasn't going to see the git for the whole of the shift.

The old dispensary was a throwback to one of the hospital's many previous incarnations. A pharmacy when the NHS was in its infancy, for the last three decades it had been a storeroom—if 'store' meant bunging in every bit of unused and unwanted equipment that couldn't find a home anywhere else. Matt stood on the dusty threshold and flicked on the light. At least the bulbs lit up, but they revealed a daunting task. Through the metallic carcasses of wheelchairs and drip stands and the battered bits of equipment, he could glimpse stacks of glass jars and vials, some of them very large indeed. Once, they had contained salves and linctus, but even empty they looked heavy and cumbersome. They would be a challenge. Ah, well.

Matt got stuck in. The physicality of the removals was strangely liberating, once he got going. It freed his mind to ponder. And ponder it did, now that it had a whole new Pandora's box full of barmy data to ponder with. He couldn't help but pick over Silvy and the Carp, or Karen and the bike collision. The word 'supernatural' had never featured a great deal in Matt's lexicon because, essentially, he had inherited his parents' pragmatism, attitudes that included a humanistic approach to existence and that eschewed Intelligent Design and the presence of anything all-powerful as being about as believable as the Loch Ness monster. They were happy to celebrate Christmas and Easter, but mainly because of the chocolate.

Matt considered that most things—with the notable exceptions of tsunamis and elections—happened for a good reason, which, on balance, could be traced back to a logical series of events. When things happened for no apparent reason, it meant that you hadn't been paying enough attention when they did. When it came to Silvy and the tsunami, though, either it had been a fantastically elaborate practical joke involving thousands of pounds' worth of special effects for a hidden camera show called *Ordinary People Shit Their Pants* or, and this is where it became a little difficult, he had to throw the whole of his rational belief system out of the window and accept that Silvy came from somewhere a long, long way from East Germany, or Macedonia, or wherever the hell she'd said she was from (come to think of it, she never had, had she?). Somewhere that empowered beings with the ability to command an inanimate volume of water to behave like a steamroller on steroids. The plausibility of the latter was supported by Silvy's equally off-the-wall account of the car accident and, he admitted to himself, by Kyaren's ristag and Ghoulshee angle.

Matt ground his teeth. He wanted to accept all this about as much as he wanted a free life subscription to *The Annals of the Hitler Youth*. Because if he did accept it, it meant that his life was heading down the gurgler without touching the sides.

Worse, if he didn't, he'd have to tell the psychologist, who would invite him back for an all-expenses-paid stay at the

'Special Hospital.' He'd be back in limbo quicker than a rodent up the proverbial rain conduit, and that was not an option he was willing to contemplate.

But the dispensary beckoned. Matt bent to his task with grim determination. It was a bit like an archaeological dig without the mud, heavy boots and blokes with beards wearing inappropriate shorts and unwanted Christmas-present jumpers. And the time scale was measured in decades, not centuries. A yard in, and a bank of Seventies defibrillators the size of fridges suddenly appeared. Behind them was a layer of Sixties telephones amongst a collection of Nelson inhalers. After a while, he realised that the goal-oriented nature of the task was highly satisfying. This wasn't so bad. At least it kept him out of Roberro's way. At least, it did until about ten o'clock, when Jim appeared and asked if he could help lift a twenty-three stone man with chest pain from the ambulance trolley onto a bed.

CHAPTER TWENTY-TWO

A&E looked to be running along on autopilot. A couple of nosebleeds sat in chairs clutching paper towels to their faces. Someone was throwing up behind the curtains in Cubicle One and, judging by the screams, someone else was in real pain in Three. Matt did his lift and was on the way back to the dispensary when the med student, who was loitering near the central station, looked up and smiled at him.

'How's it going in the storeroom?'

Matt looked at her, unable to help a wary expression. 'Fine, thanks.'

'Sorry about the other day and the pink…thingummy. Giles thought it would be a laugh.'

'Oh, it was. Hilarious.'

Her smile faltered. That smile had probably got her through many a sticky patch of social awkwardness, together with those legs, that bum and those large and quite pointy—

'So, have you almost finished? Clearing out, I mean?'

Matt dragged his eyes back to her face. 'Not quite. But it's going okay. Should be done in a couple of hours, I reckon.'

The med student nodded and turned back to the notes she was reading, leaving Matt to wander back to the dispensary considerably perplexed. The med student hadn't ever spoken to him, other than to set him up for the pink dildo scam. Her role was to follow Roberro around like a lapdog. That she was in his thrall, there was no doubt. So, why was she so curious about how he was getting on in the dispensary all of a sudden? Okay, he was clearing it out for the med students, or so the Uruk-hai cheerleader had implied, so it could be as simple as that. On the other hand...

Matt sighed. Paranoia was such a waste of bloody time. Better he got on with it. After another ten minutes in the dispensary, he'd pushed the med student and Roberro to the back of his mind. But something was different. It crept up on him like the sun coming out from behind clouds; suddenly the day changes from dull and grey to warm and bright, and you realise that things aren't quite so bad, after all.

Yet things remained tantalisingly intangible until the moment he tried lifting out the carcass of a fold-up bed with one hand as he balanced a tipping operating light with another.

And then it dawned on him.

It was the clumsiness—or rather the marked absence of it. Nothing had slipped out of Matt's grasp the whole time he'd been in the dispensary, and neither had he knocked anything over. When the inevitable toppling of precariously placed items had occurred, he'd anticipated it and caught them. He'd been on top of his game, something he had not been for a long time. Not since before the accident. He thought about that, scrubbed it out and replaced it with not since before he'd met Silvy.

With that realisation came a little wave of euphoria, and he began to work quicker. Not throwing caution to the wind, but with more confidence. By midnight, he was through to the older, early twentieth-century stuff.

But this stuff did look old. There were huge glass bottles and jars, some three feet tall. Above them, on the racks and shelves of an old wooden display cabinet, lay tubes and vials and retorts and pestles and mortars and brass weighing scales, so that the whole display looked like a set from a *Jekyll and Hyde*, TV adaptation. Most were coated with thick dust, but some looked surprisingly clean. Right, so he'd move all the glass first to get it out of the way. There was less chance of knocking anything over that way. He'd start with the big stuff, one receptacle at a time.

He went for the first—a massive, red, round-bottomed glass jar. He got down on his haunches and put one hand round the neck, the other under the widest part of the base. It was all made more awkward by the proximity of an old wooden stepladder. Carefully, Matt moved the ladder, disturbing decades of dust and spiderwebs in the process, and repositio. ed himself at the jar.

He was about to take the weight of the thing when a gossamer patch of web drifted past his face to hang suspended in mid-air about a foot off the floor. Intrigued, Matt leaned in to peer at the floating web and saw that it had caught and folded on a thin piece of what could only be thread. He followed the almost invisible line and saw that it had been looped around the decanter, the tall jar next to it, some of the brass weights above, and then around the retorts and the test tubes. In fact, it connected almost everything on display. Then, the Uruk-hai cheerleader's words came back to him with a vengeance.

'In fact, with your track record for breakages, they're asking for soddin' trouble…'

It all clicked depressingly into place, like the thud of a guillotine at the bottom of its travel. The med student's feigned interest allied to that smug look on Roberro's face underneath the pretence of not noticing Matt when he'd arrived that evening. The one crumb of doubt Matt had was how much the Uruk-hai cheerleader had been in on it. For one sod-the-lot-of-them second, Matt had a sudden urge to yank on the fishing line to bring the whole lot crashing down. It lasted no more than a moment. He couldn't, *wouldn't* give them the satisfaction.

Instead, he reached out to touch the big jar's shiny and remarkably un-dusty surface. It felt slick.

Too slick.

Smiling to himself, he hurried off to the locked cupboard wherein lay the secret unguents and potions of the porter's trade. Inside were bottles of powerful disinfectants for the bodily fluid leaks that occurred from time to time in hospitals. The ones that were too vile for hotel services to deal with. Here was stuff that could kill 99.5 per cent of all known germs and strip the paint off your car in one container. Next to them were the glues for fixing waiting-room seats, glue remover for toilet-seat victims, gallon cans of WD-40 and specialist bottles of solvents and degreasers.

Appropriately armed, Matt went back to the dispensary. Whatever it was they'd applied to the glass was incredibly slippery. Liquid paraffin would be his bet.

Matt used a roll of industrial absorbent paper and one of the solvent-based products from the cupboard to clean the greasy film off. Then, he carefully cut the line that was wound around all the breakables. After that, he worked quickly, revelling in his deft sure-footedness. He was only interrupted once, when he caught sight of the med student loitering in the corridor as he passed through to the IT room laden with glass jars. He backtracked, still holding the jars, and caught her eye.

'Anything I can do for you?' Matt asked.

'Oh, no,' she said, with about as much conviction as a fox whistling past a henhouse. 'Just stretching my legs.' She gave him one of her hundred-watt smiles and disappeared.

By twelve-thirty, the dispensary was empty. Matt stood in the middle of the room with the last of the glassware in his arms, enjoying the way his footfalls echoed around the empty walls. Job done.

He could have gone up to the main porter's lodge, but A&E was the quickest place to cadge a cuppa. Besides, the med student's earlier appearance was bugging him. He sauntered straight into a stranger-in-the-local-pub moment. Everything stopped for three seconds of a momentary hush as everyone turned to look at him. From somewhere came the sound of a child crying, and everyone went back to what they were doing, pretending they hadn't seen him.

'Finished?' she asked with a horrified expression that would not have been out of place had he announced that a major pile-up from the M1 was headed their way. 'But…' she let the sentence hang.

'Did to want anything? I'm just getting a cup of tea, but then I'm off.' He paused, saw no reaction and turned away, but she put her hand on his arm.

'Could you wait one tiny minute?' She held up a finger before disappearing behind some curtains. Matt heard urgent whispering, followed by a bellowed, 'WHAT?'

The curtains flew open to reveal Roberro with a face like thunder. He strode belligerently across to Matt.

'You can't be finished,' he spat. 'Leanne, go and take a look.'

The med student hurried away.

'Do you fancy a cup of tea?' Matt asked. 'I'm parched.'

'You think you're so bloody sharp, Danmor,' Roberro snapped. 'You conniving, weaselly, ingratiating little piece of dog shit.'

'I'll take that as a no, then.' Matt didn't move. He was watching the staff, who were, in turn, staring at Roberro with much more than the usual interest in seeing an idiotic prat being an arse.

'Jim?' A light bulb lit up in Matt's head. 'You're running a book,' he said to Roberro with a mirthless smile. 'What is it, time to Danmor smashing the first piece of glassware?'

Jim found something else to do, and the anaesthetists might as well have started whistling, they looked so guilty. Meanwhile, Roberro's jaw muscles clenched hard enough to crack walnuts. Leanne reappeared, flushed and out of breath. She looked at Roberro and nodded.

'Shit,' he said and threw down his notes in disgust before thrusting his face three inches from Matt's and seething. 'You had help, didn't you, you sneaky little turd?'

'No help. But I *did* find this…' Matt raised his voice by

twenty decibels, '…almost invisible fishing line twined around all the breakables in the room. Lucky for me I did, or the whole lot might have come down around my ears.'

Jim and the anaesthetists turned to glare at Roberro.

'Shut up,' Roberro ordered.

'No,' Matt said. 'I will not shut up. You are what is known as an extremely sad case, Giles.'

Roberro didn't answer, but some very strange, high-pitched keening noises were coming from behind his clenched teeth. Matt shook his head and turned away, only to feel a hand clamp onto his arm.

'It wasn't me who paid a whore to walk in here the other night to make him look like he had a living girlfriend as opposed to one you need to blow up,' Roberro sang out, shrill as a choirboy.

Matt turned slowly. 'I didn't pay anyone anything. As it happens, she might not be all she was cracked up to be, but I'd be careful not to call her "whore" to her face, if I were you. She has a nasty habit of turning really ugly.' Matt dangled the fishing line, shaking his head. 'But this… You have serious issues, Giles. As it happens, I know a psychologist who specialise in hopeless basket cases. I'm sure they could help. I've even got their numbers here in my wallet.'

If cartoon steam could come out of people's ears, it would have been whooshing Flying Scotsman-like out of Roberro's at that point. All that was needed was some frothing at the mouth coupled with an aversion to water, and the word 'rabid' might as well have blistered itself on his forehead. Whatever comeback he was building up to deliver never materialised. He opened his mouth to speak, but before a word came out, his attention shifted to a woman who had walked through the doors of A&E, and who now strode towards them.

Roberro wasn't alone. Indeed, conversations involving males on all parts of the floor dwindled into a breathless silence as eyes turned to watch the visitor, who, unlike Silvy, seemed refreshingly oblivious of the effect she had.

'Excuse me,' she said to Roberro, 'sorry to interrupt the rutting. If you could lower your antlers for a moment, I need to speak to Matt on an urgent matter.'

They both turned to stare at her. Matt's face took on a resigned expression, but Roberro's was like a cat with the combination to the lock on the fridge, about to score a litre carton of double cream.

CHAPTER TWENTY-THREE

'WELL, HELLO.' Roberro gave the woman his best lounge-lizard drawl.

Matt's response was a little more underwhelming. 'Look, Kyaren,' he said, 'if you've come here to take the piss again, join the queue. This idiot was first.' He nodded at Roberro, who had gone from rabid dog to drooling pup in one brief moment.

'This can't wait,' Karen said, pulling Matt to one side.

Roberro, with skin as thick as an armour-plated rhinoceros, stepped between them. 'Hi. My name is Giles.' He grinned at the girl. 'Don't worry if you can't remember it now. It's written on my bedroom wall, so it could be the first thing you see on waking up tomorrow morning, if you play your cards right.'

Kyaren's face registered a kind of detached puzzlement as she leaned to one side to look around Roberro at Matt. It was an, 'Is this bloke for real?' look. Matt shrugged. Karen shoved Roberro to one side, stepped past him, and started talking at a hundred miles an hour, like one of those adverts with a thousand-word disclaimer at the end that they needed to get through before it finished.

'I know what you must be thinking I really do and this wasn't meant to happen like this I mean the accident this morning it was all wrong and I should have explained prop-erly… Oh blast. There is only one way this is going to work.'

'Work?' Matt asked. Even though he half-despised her for what she had done that morning, she *did* have the most amazing eyes.

'Please, I know it's hard for someone like you who has the pick of anyone you want, but if our foreheads meet, I can do the transfer.' She dropped her voice to a whisper. 'But it'll only look natural if we kiss, so…'

Matt's eyes narrowed. There was so much information in what she'd said that it would take a good ten minutes with very fine tweezers to tease it all apart. Instead, he zeroed in on, *the pick of anyone they want*, and let slip a wry smile. She gave good sarcasm, he had to admit.

'Is he putting you up to this?'

'He?' the girl asked.

'Him. The bloke with his eyes out on stalks behind you.'

Kyaren glanced at Roberro's jaw which was working again, but this time with overt hostility, and shook her head. 'No.'

''Cos I'm warning you, there's only so much humiliation—'

'Please.' She sounded desperate. 'Just one quick little kiss.' She turned her face up to his. Matt sighed in resignation. *Oh well*, he thought, *in for a penny*. He'd already kissed one stunner in this room recently and almost ended up as fish food, so what difference would one more make? He held up both hands in a gesture of acquiescence and saw Karen smile in relief. Could the world get any weirder? Not even, Matt decided, if Roberro turned into a quivering blancmange and started singing *Never Gonna Give You Up* in Spanish. Two seconds later, Matt knew that it could.

Kyaren's mouth was slightly open, and up close, her eyelashes seemed inches long. Her lips weren't bad either, soft and warm and tasting of black cherry. She cupped his neck in her hand and pulled him forward, so that as they kissed, the edge of her forehead met with his, and then…

Whether the earth actually moved or simply shifted slightly on its axis was a moot point. Bottom line: Matt *remembered*. He pushed back and stared at the girl, whose real name he now knew, and who'd developed the anxious look of someone waiting for the result of her driving test.

'Gggylah?' Matt said. ''owwsmmssssoobbliiip?'

Kylah breathed a sigh that was clearly one of huge relief. Matt was too busy with the new things in his head to worry about it. But then, they weren't new things really. Being memories, they'd been in Matt's head all the time. But like those annoying folders full of hidden files on your computer, they'd been unavailable for review. Until now.

'I know, I know,' she said. 'A billion apologies and all that. I promise, there will be time for explanations, but that time isn't now.'

'Innit?' Matt said, still confused.

'No. And neither is this the place.'

'Innit?'

'Look, rationalisation is not the way to go. Slow assimilation is better. I know just the place where we could share a nice warm drink.'

'Chilllllun…nnuncl?'

Kylah groaned. 'I hate this bit. Everything's jostling for position in your brain, looking for its correct order in the middle of all those other memories. It's best to do this lying down, with a towel over your head. Come on, let's go.' She pulled on Matt's hand and he followed with a gormless, lost expression.

Roberro, however, was still looking for his pound of flesh now that his smashing of the dispensary plan had foundered. 'This is pathetic,' he sneered. 'You another one of his escorts, then? Your rate the same as the blonde's, is it?'

Kylah kept walking, and Matt dutifully followed. He wanted to say something but couldn't; there were major mental road works on the neural superhighway connecting his thinking to his speaking. All he could do was shake his head in a desperate appeal at Roberro that was meant to say, 'Big mistake. Big mistake.' But which came out as an impression of a large, bleating lamb, 'Inngmmmeea. Inngmmmea.'

But he also knew that, even if he had been able to enunciate every word, it would have been like rain off a duck's raincoat. Roberro, angry and frustrated, had the bit very much between his teeth. And he now approached with all the subtlety of a yellow stretch Humvee.

'Fifty quid? A hundred? For that one snog?' He followed them and leaned in close to Kylah to hiss a lecherous whisper, 'What'll you give me for three hundred?'

Kylah walked past him at the kind of pace you used for roadkill, but now she stopped, let go of Matt's hand and turned slowly back to Roberro. His leer rapidly faded into mild panic. He wasn't used to anyone challenging his bellicose ranting. But she was just five-six in heels. And a girl. That, combined with the fact that he was a patronising chauvinistic arse of the first water, meant that any lingering doubts over the wisdom of his outburst were as short-lived as a worm in a trout hatchery.

'What did you say?' Kylah demanded.

'I asked, girlie, how much you were getting from that card-carrying idiot over there for making him look like he has a sex life, or any life, outside this place?'

'Let's get this straight. One, you just called me "girlie" and two, you're implying that I'm for hire?'

Roberro knew that everyone was watching now. It was all the egocentric fodder he needed. 'Oooh, very PC. Yes, for hire. So, how much do you charge to buzz the brillo with me watching, eh?'

Kylah looked across at the sister in charge and said, 'Better get a suture kit.'

She turned back to Roberro and offered him one dazzling, and very dangerous, smile. Then she kicked him hard between the legs and, as he doubled up, let fly with a stabbing punch to his forehead using only the knuckle of her middle finger. It was like poleaxing an ox.

It was over that fast. No one moved, least of all Roberro,

who lay crumpled on the floor. Kylah did a dismissive wiping off the dust from her hand gesture, which was a touch theatrical, but well worth it, before walking back to Matt and taking his hand again.

'We'll be gone for a while,' she said to the sister.

In return, she got a double thumbs-up and a small round of applause from the other female staff, none of whom were rushing to Roberro's aid.

―――――

THE COLD AIR was like a slap in the face when they got outside. There was a taxi waiting with its engine running. Kylah helped Matt in and he heard her tell the driver to take them to Canal Street.

'Whaooinohhhn?' Matt said.

'Give it a soupçon longer,' Kylah said, sitting back. 'It gets easier, believe me.'

The taxi took no more than five minutes to get to Jericho, pulling up outside Hipposync Enterprises. Kylah paid the driver and helped Matt out. Two minutes later, he was sitting in an office, one half of which was full of the most bizarre antiques he had ever seen, whilst the other half looked like an IKEA showroom. Of course, he had seen the office before. In fact, he had sat in this chair before. Matt shook his head like a wet dog, trying to get those disjointed thoughts to settle into place. Kylah was fussing with a drinks cabinet and came up with something deep purple in a small glass.

'Drink this,' she said. 'It'll help.'

Matt took the glass and sniffed the liquid. There didn't seem to be any alcohol, but the herbal bouquet reminded him of autumnal walks in the woods as a child. Warily, he sipped it. Yep, definitely no alcohol and so, mindful of his med student training, he necked the rest. A warm buzzing began to spread outwards from a point below his sternum, through his abdomen, and out into his limbs.

'Wow,' Kylah said in a faintly horrified tone, 'that was meant for gentle medicinal sipping.'

Matt wasn't listening. His mind was clearing faster than a Weight Watchers' conference lecture hall at the sound of the dinner bell. His bulging eyes stared at Kylah with untrammelled inquisitiveness. Whatever was in the purple stuff, it had cleaned and polished all his jumbled thoughts and put them back in date order in the trophy cabinet of his mind, where they glistened and gleamed, ready for inspection.

'Right,' Matt said. 'You've got three minutes before I tear off all my clothes and run screaming into the street.'

'It's almost worth keeping quiet.' Kylah grinned.

'I bloody well mean it,' warned Matt. 'There'll be police and ambulances and little old ladies screaming and you'll have to explain yourself to the authorities. If my memory serves me correctly, which I'm still not sure it does, that's something you want to try to avoid.'

'Three minutes isn't that long.'

'Two minutes and forty seconds.' Matt tapped his watch.

Kylah held her hands up. 'Okay, okay. You remember the bit about rescuing my uncle in the play area?'

Matt thought for a moment. 'Yep, you can skip that bit. What I want to know is, what happened after you stuck that thing on my head?'

'The pentrievant?'

'That's the one.'

Kylah squirmed. 'What you have to bear in mind is that it's company policy. I wanted you to understand that—'

'People use "company policy" to make something that's crap sound official,' Matt said in a steely tone. 'Tell me you don't work for the Post Office.'

'The pentrievant,' Kylah continued as if she hadn't heard him, 'allows us to examine your memory, and is very useful as evidence, but it also allows us to eradicate anything of a… sensitive nature.'

'Sensitive?'

'You're doing it again,' Kylah said.

'What?'

'Turning my last sentence into a question.'

'Does it irritate you?' Matt demanded. 'Oh, I'm so sorry. I'll just go and stick my head in a bucket of water for three days, shall I?'

'Sarcasm is such an unattractive trait.'

'So is me running naked down Walton Street.'

Kylah sighed. 'It's a security issue. We can't have any Tom, Matt, or Joaquin blabbing to the *Oxford Mail* about trans-dimensional incursions, can we?'

'Can't we?' Matt echoed.

'You're doing it on purpose now, aren't you?'

'Am I?'

Kylah gave him a slitty-eyed glare. 'There'd be panic and mayhem in the streets. People would be crying and wailing. Violence would be rife.'

'You're describing a normal Saturday night in my place of work.'

'Well,' Kylah said, 'it's something that *we* see as a security issue. I was only doing my job.'

Matt snorted. 'Oh, I see. And how many atrocities down the centuries has that little nugget of misguided fealty covered, I wonder?'

'I can see why you might be a little angry.' Kylah squirmed under his gaze.

'I'm so glad, because for a moment there I was beginning to think I was being unreasonable. You didn't think that perhaps being the only witness to a bunch of child-sized psychopaths attempting to sacrifice your uncle might have put me at risk of reprisals, by any chance?'

It was like throwing pebbles into a pond. Kylah was on the back foot now; he could see that.

'I can explain everything, but it's going to take more than three minutes,' she said, her expression full of pleading.

Matt sat back in his chair and folded his arms so as to enjoy her discomfort. 'Go ahead. I'm all ears. Do your worst, *Kyaren.*'

CHAPTER TWENTY-FOUR

'WOULD YOU LIKE SOME COFFEE?' Kylah asked, in an attempt at conciliation.

'White, one sugar,' Matt replied. He toyed with asking for something a bit stronger, but if the breakfast he'd had before was anything to go by, the coffee would probably be excellent. He needed something; the weirdness needle on the gauge in his head was flickering dangerously near the red zone.

Kylah picked up the phone and cleared her throat. It was only after she'd done it three times that Matt realised it was a language of some sort. She looked up and saw his pained expression.

'Mrs Hoblip still doesn't have a great deal of English. All she understands is "Full English," "sherry," and, "those blasted pigeons." At least, that's what Uncle Ernest claims. I mean, she's only been with him for forty years.' Kylah pursed her lips. 'Between you and me, I suspect she understands a great deal more than she lets on.'

There was a knock on the door. Kylah stood, opened it, and cleared her throat again before taking a tray that appeared about three feet off the ground. Matt couldn't help but notice that the fingers that held the tray had long yellow nails at their ends, that there were three of them, and that the hand itself was red and covered in tufts of orange hair. Kylah put the tray on the desk and saw Matt gawping.

'Wha..?' Matt was trying to swallow, but his mouth had become a saliva-free zone. 'Was that…'

'Mrs Hoblip, yes.'

'She's quick as baristas go, I'll give her that,' Matt said, his voice a little over-bright. 'Even if she *is* in dire need of a manicure.'

'You should see the rest of her,' Kylah muttered, but then checked herself. 'On second thoughts…'

The coffee was strong and fresh, with the slightest hint of fruit. All in all, truly delicious. Matt sipped while Kylah talked and he managed to only almost choke on his drink twice. The first time was when she called Roberro, 'that jumped-up piece of self-adoring pig effluent.' The second was when Kylah explained, with a sheepish expression, how she knew all about Roberro as a result of collateral spilled thoughts, courtesy of the pentrievant. 'There's often quite a bit of leakage,' she added.

'What do you mean, "leakage"?' Matt wiped spattered coffee off his shirt while trying to quell the shrill alarm creeping into his voice.

'Not that kind of leakage.' Kylah frowned. 'Neurosensory leakage. It's inevitable. Thought extraction is an inexact process, and often drags the odd unwanted memory with it.' She took a sip from her own cup and, with only her eyes showing over the rim, added in a throwaway tone, 'In your case, some very odd memories indeed.'

Matt stared at her in dull horror. Letting anyone into the recycled sock-drawer of his head without a chaperone was not his idea of fun.

'I should have twigged that something was up,' Kylah continued, unfazed. 'But it was only after you told me about the Carp yesterday that everything started to fall into place.'

It was meant to sound reassuring, Matt supposed, but it came across with the same conviction as a Post Office helpline.

'Oh, right. So, there is a place for everything to fall into, then? Only we've been so long in getting to this point that I thought maybe I'd missed a couple off pages of the script.' Mrs Hoblip's coffee, combined with Kylah's blasé admission of having poked about in his memories, was stoking the fire of Matt's state of irate confusion.

Kylah was taking no flak, though. She walked across to the window and perched her hip on the sill. 'Did it not occur to you that what happened at the weir with Silvy and her assassination squad was a bit odd?'

'Odd?' Matt said in a voice which, he was disconcerted to hear, sounded like it verged on the hysterical. 'Of course, it was bloody *odd*. My whole life for the last fourteen months has been the definition of *odd*. How do I really know that I am not at this very moment wired up to a machine on the neuro ward at the General in a bloody coma? How can I be sure that you and all of this.' Matt waved his hands about dramatically, 'aren't merely the product of a bit of my RTA-scrambled brain?'

Kylah's voice softened. 'I know why you want to keep visiting the weir, Matt.'

Matt stared at her and whimpered. 'Leakage?'

Kylah nodded.

'Great,' he said. 'That's just great. What else do you know about me that's totally humiliating?'

'I know you like dogs and hated peas as a toddler. I also know that your favourite dream involves a set of pole-dancing triplets and a tub of tequila ice cream.'

'Yeah, well, that one's straight out of *Rita Saves the Universe*. It's a film.' Matt's protest was a smidgen too vehement to qualify as aplomb.

'And is the one with the yellow hosepipe and the nurse in that very short uniform and the heels common knowledge, too?' Kylah's smile was wicked.

'You made that one up.' Matt squirmed.

'Yes, I did. The hosepipe was pink.'

Matt squeezed his eyes shut, cringed, and let out a mental

scream before sending Kylah his best indignant glare. 'Look, none of this is funny, or your business. I can't go back to Bristol and pick my life up off the deck until I get all of this sorted out. I've been a train wreck since the accident… breaking things, tripping over stuff. I've lost count of the glasses and cups I've dropped. I can't do anything right. I don't remember winning the title of "Mr Luckless Butterfingers." or even buying the raffle ticket. I mean, you need a bit of steadiness for surgery—' Matt caught himself, but it was too late.

'Is that what you want to do?' Kylah asked. 'Be a surgeon?'

Matt searched her face for signs of derision and was pleasantly surprised to find that there weren't any.

'It was on my list,' he admitted and cursed inwardly at letting it slip. It was one of the things he'd promised himself never to talk to anyone about. A secret goal kept in the locked cupboard of his brain under 'almost unattainable ambitions.' Like the way people might think about playing for their country at their chosen sport. Matt shook his head to clear it. 'The most ironic bloody thing of all is that tonight, having spent the morning seeing monsters and convincing myself I've finally flipped, I'm brilliant. I carried half a ton of breakables out from an old dispensary without a hitch. Didn't drop a single thing. Christ, life can be so fickle.'

Kylah walked across to a chair opposite Matt, eased herself into it, and sat forward. 'Matt, listen to me. You aren't in a coma, you're not mad and I doubt you're maladroit, either. Most of what's happened to you has been caused by someone or something. I still haven't worked out quite how you ended up gated, but—'

'Gated?'

Kylah sighed in the way you did when trying to teach a puppy not to stain the carpet. 'You do remember being here before? When my uncle was attacked?'

'Of course I bloody do,' Matt said with feeling. 'And it's nice to know it wasn't my imagination or a nightmare. In fact, you're making all my dreams come true, especially the one about Mrs Hoblip's lumbago poultice versus aspirin.'

'What?' Kylah asked.

'You're Fae immigration,' Matt couldn't resist adding. 'Sounds a bit like a silent film actress.'

'Did you have concentration issues before we used the pentrievant, or are you doing it deliberately, to make me feel guilty?' Kylah asked.

Matt bristled. 'I'm not that overjoyed that you took the memory in the first place, you know. I don't remember giving you permission to do that.'

'I did explain that we needed to borrow it.'

'So, how do I know it hasn't been tampered with?'

Kylah sat back, looking hurt. 'We only do what we have to. Look, the point is that you can see us. You've had the tenth gate opened for you. You know, nine gates, one for all the senses, number ten being the one that has to do with us?'

Matt stared at her blankly.

'You recall telling me all about Dean in the mobile shop yesterday morning?' Kylah asked.

'Of course I recall,' Matt said resentfully. 'Slippery Dean and his gastropod coat.'

'He's a Merrowman, by the way. Not a creature from the Black Lagoon.'

'Oh, sor-ry,' said Matt.

'The point is you could see him,' Kylah said. 'What I'm trying to work out here is why I didn't know that you'd been gated? Why didn't all that knowledge about Silvy show up when we used the pentrievant? It should have, because it's designed to pull out all relevant memories, give us the whole picture. But it didn't. All it showed us was that you'd harboured suicidal thoughts about the weir. That shouldn't happen.'

Matt looked about the room.

'What's the matter?' Kylah asked.

'I can still smell pine needles. Olfactory hallucination is a hallmark of temporal lobe tumours. That might explain all of this.'

'Oh, for crying out loud.' Kylah stood, strode to a wooden tub in the corner and picked out a handful of fresh green pine needles. 'Air freshener. It's from the forest near where I live.' She came back and sat down next to him. 'Paranoia is a known delayed after-effect of the pentrievant.'

'You would say that, though, wouldn't you?' Matt said. 'Okay, if this is all real, prove it.'

'Prove it how? You want me to turn that chair into a cat?' Kylah shook her head. 'I'm not licensed for that. I'd have the rat-squad down on me like a ton of bricks.'

'Rat-squad?' Matt searched the database of his extensive knowledge of crap TV police procedurals. 'That means internal affairs, doesn't it?'

'Yes. Except that, for us, they really *are* all rats.' She kept an absolutely straight face as she said it. 'Oh, come on, Matt. This is the truth, bizarre and weird though it is. I mean who the Valchak could make this stuff up?'

Matt toyed with challenging her about Valchak, but decided he didn't want to give her the satisfaction.

Kylah shook her head and then looked up. 'How about Mrs Hoblip?'

'Like I said, she's very quick off the mark.'

'No,' protested Kylah. 'I mean as your proof.' She went to the desk, picked up the phone and dragged up a bit of phlegm. Three seconds later, there was a gentle knock on the door. Kylah stood, opened the door, and in walked…

'Mrs Hoblip,' Kylah explained, 'is a bwbach.'

CHAPTER TWENTY-FIVE

She was about four feet tall, with red and very wrinkly skin, covered by wispy tufts of orange hair. Two spindly arms and legs stuck out from a shift that looked as if it were made of hessian. She had battered curly-toed leather slippers on her feet. Above all of that was a pumpkin-shaped head covered in tight orange curls, and a mouth which had not very many teeth, but which seemed to smile, under a pair of large and mournful-looking yellow eyes.

'Doesn't look like any girl guide I've ever seen,' Matt said, trying to make it sound as if he didn't want to scream.

'Bwbachs are symbiotic. They live off Prana—you know, stuff we give off in the form of unseen energy. They need to be near humans to survive. As such, they make excellent housekeepers.'

'She's a slave, then?'

Kylah fired over a sharp, horrified glance, and Mrs Hoblip's cheeky grin turned into a frown.

'Absolutely not. It's a great honour if a bwbach chooses you. She appeared one day and began doing things for my uncle. She does them very well, and in return gets paid and lives with us.'

'Here at Hipposync?'

'Yes. She has a self-contained cupboard for the eight of them in the basement.'

Matt's brows went skywards, but all Kylah did was shake her head. 'Don't ask. The important thing is that there is no contract, as such. It's a mutual arrangement. However, they tend to be with you for life.'

'So, it was you who made that amazing breakfast I had the other day?' Matt said to those huge eyes.

They lit up in response. Literally, glowing like two small headlamps. Mrs Hoblip scooped up the coffee cups, sent Matt one coy little look, giggled, or at least made a noise like a jolly garbage disposal, and hurried out on those spindly legs.

'Now you've done it,' Kylah said.

'I meant it.'

'Petrol on a bonfire. She'll be plugging you with experimental recipes from now on. Mrs Hoblip can make any TV chef look like a short-order cook, if you let her.'

Matt said nothing, but Kylah pressed him. 'Well? Will that do for your proof?'

He gave a small, grudging nod. 'I admit I haven't seen anything like that in a fancy dress shop.'

Kylah nodded. 'Right, good, that's settled then. Like it or not, she is real. Or, at least, a different real. You are not insane, Matt, merely unlucky enough to have come into contact with some of our more unsavoury residents. The question is, why?'

She walked back to the chair and sat with her legs crossed, her mouth turned down in concentration.

Matt shrugged and tried to get his head around it all. First the Ghoulshee, and now bwbachs. It was a lot to ask anyone to believe. But the worst of it was that it all made a bizarre kind of sense now that it had been explained to him. He found himself willing to buy into it, because it did explain every weird, out of kilter thing.

More than once over the last year, his imagination had strapped itself in and taken off on a flight of fancy in search of some sort of explanation. Now and again, it even felt like he was on the brink of finding the elusive luggage key that would open up the locked trunk of understanding and reveal its secrets.

But these were fleeting, ephemeral moments. Just the day before, there'd been one. It was as he'd stood behind the witch with the pile cream. He'd been looking at some stuff on the shelves in Boots, earrings or friendship bracelets or some faddy dross of that kind, when it had almost struck him. He'd seen something there that had almost popped open the lid of that trunk. But now that his brain had been made to do the hokey pokey, thanks to Kylah's memorable kiss, there seemed even less chance of him remembering what it was that had stuck its head up like a pocket gopher in the desert of his confusion.

Come on, he cajoled himself. *What was it I saw?*

He'd been looking at those bangles and wondering about what was different in his life that day to make him see all those bloody weirdos everywhere. Of course, the main difference was that he'd been washed into the boughs of a tree by a freak river wave conjured up by Silvy and the Oompa Loompas from Hell. Then, Matt thought further back, to the goat woman holding his hand in the MRI suite after the accident. She'd been the very first inexplicable creature he'd ever seen.

'You okay?' Kylah asked.

'No,' Matt replied. 'After the accident—the Silvy accident—I saw something in the hospital. A woman with a grey face and blonde hair and amazing green eyes and…hooves. I thought it was the morphine at the time—'

'Glaistig,' said Kylah. 'Lots of them work in hospitals. Scottish, very nice. They love helping people.'

'Well, I saw one,' Matt said. 'And that was months ago. Whatever this is, it can't be recent.'

'Did you knock your head at the weir?' Kylah asked.

'No.' Matt thought frantically, but there was nothing. No link between being in that room after the MRI and queuing in Boots. How could there be? He let his hand stray, as it often did when he was concentrating, to worry at something in a familiar tactile habit. Except that this time there was nothing to worry at…

He sat forward so fast he almost toppled onto the pine-scented carpet. It was there in his head. Of course. 'The pendant.'

'What pendant?' Kylah asked, alarmed.

'Silvy gave me a pendant to wear. She made me promise to wear it always.'

'Always?' Kylah demanded.

Matt nodded. 'She could be very persuasive.'

'I bet.'

'What's that supposed to mean?'

'Ghoulshee high priestesses are trained in certain…arts.'

'She was quite…artful,' Matt admitted.

'That must have been hard for you,' Kylah said, with a brittle smile.

Matt nodded and before he could stop himself, a little eel of innuendo wriggled out of a crevice in his brain. 'Hard and Silvy did seem to go together quite easily, I have to admit.'

Kylah made eyes at the ceiling and exhaled. 'We're looking for a comedian for our spring ball, so don't bother applying. Tell me about the pendant.'

'That's the point. Obviously, I didn't have it on when I had the MRI,' Matt said, the words spilling out. 'And then at the weir, the necklace broke when I was thrown into the tree. I took it to a jeweller and he said that it wasn't actually a gold pendant, anyway. He said it was gold leaf over iron—'

Kylah jumped up like she'd seen a funnel-web spider under the toilet seat. 'I *knew* it. I knew it! That day you were here, we kept getting a reading on the ferrinous. And don't tell me, you started to see the Fimigrants when you took the pendant off?'

'Fimigrants?'

'Answer the question.' Kylah looked serious.

'Well, come to think of it…yes. I'd taken it off when I met your uncle, 'cos the leather got wet from the saline, and then I started seeing weirdos the day I took it to the jeweller. I haven't put it on since.'

Kylah was pacing. 'It all makes sense now. Didn't you tell me that in one of your dreams Silvy appeared to you as something unpleasant?'

'Oh, yeah. That *Twilight Zone* movie moment in the car. Unpleasant's a bit of an understatement.'

'I've got news for you, Matt. That is what she really looks like. She's a Proturan shape-changer. Their caste have sworn obeisance to the Ghoulshee's gods. They're supposed to be priests, but their aggressive tendencies make them ideal for the elite guard.' Matt saw a hint of satisfaction flare in Kylah's expression.

Images of what had actually lain in the dunes next to him, and done those extraordinary things to him, froze his throat so that he had to have four attempts at swallowing before any saliva found its way through. He tried to let off an expletive, but someone had turned his voice off at the mains, and all that came out was a strangled. 'But why?'

'Because dreams are like mobile phones to us,' Kylah said. 'Easy ways of communicating. What's more, once someone from our side reveals themselves, it opens up a bit of the brain that is normally quiescent in humans. A sort of dormant inner eye in the parietal lobe somewhere. It opens the tenth gate.'

'But I've been having that dream of us in the car for months. How come it's only yesterday that I saw Silvy as that…thing, and that I started seeing the Fimigrants for what they were?'

'Because you've been wearing an iron pendant, that's why. Cold iron negates Fae power. Like jamming a radio signal, or stuffing uranium into a lead box. Having opened the gate, she tried to shut it again by making you wear iron.'

There were more questions than answers there. It made Matt's head hurt. 'Would it have had an effect on clumsiness and balance and stuff, too? Because I wasn't clumsy tonight. Not in the slightest.'

Kylah stopped pacing and pivoted to look at him. 'Maybe.'

'And there I was thinking that the damned thing was a lucky charm.'

Kylah glared at him. 'That charm is to luck what The Pogues were to glam rock, but it still doesn't add up. Why did she give you a suppressing iron pendant and want you dead?'

An unwelcome thought sat up and slapped Matt in the face like a slimy herring. He scowled. 'More importantly, why are you telling me all this now? It didn't seem to bother you before to string me along and then clap a gagging order on my brain.'

Kylah scowled, but then her expression melted into one of contrition. She sighed. 'Believe it or not, we are not a bunch of thugs.'

'On the showing so far, I'm reserving judgement,' Matt grumbled. 'That doesn't answer my question, either.'

She came and stood in front of him, folded her arms and then swung them out to the sides before bringing her hands in to slap against the outside of her thighs. 'Look, I know you're angry and feel used, but the thing is, I'm telling you all this now because…because we need your help.'

'My help? That's a good one.' He let out a hammed-up laugh. 'Why on earth would you need my help?'

'Because…'' She hesitated, looked away for a second as if to gather herself, and then turned back and pierced him with eyes that had become suddenly moist. 'Because my uncle is missing. They've kidnapped the Doorkeeper, Matt.'

CHAPTER TWENTY-SIX

As a conversation stopper, it was a metre-thick, steel-reinforced, ten-storey-high concrete wall. The silence that followed was equally as dense until Matt broke it with a swallow. 'Your uncle's been kidnapped? When?'

'This afternoon. I was away from the office and he decided to go out for some air.' Kylah shook her head, tears welling.

It took Matt completely by surprise. Seeing hard-as-nails Kylah with a heart was like finding a milky praline surprise in a bitter dark chocolate Easter egg. When she spoke, her voice rose with every word until it petered out altogether. 'I've lost count of the times I've warned him. He's so stubborn. I should have stayed here, but I had a meeting in London, and—'

'Is it the lot that were in the play area?' Matt asked.

'Yes.' She blew her nose into a tissue. 'Definitely a Ghoulshee snatch squad.'

'At least they didn't try and sacrifice him this time.'

'No. They're threatening to do that later, along with all the other captives.'

'Shit,' Matt said, registering the word captives. 'I'll do whatever you want me to do.'

'Thank, you,' Kylah breathed, but her eyes wouldn't quite

meet his. 'There is another reason I decided to tell you all this. I felt you deserved to know what's going on, considering.'

'Considering what?' Matt asked. There was something about the tilt of Kylah's head that suggested he wasn't going to like what was coming next very much.

'Considering they've tried to kill you three times already.'

'*Three* times?'

'The car crash, the weir, and the ristag attack on the bike.'

He frowned and looked at his shoes as the truth of it sank in. Not only was it unpalatable, but it pressed the big button marked 'unprovoked attack on innocent party' in Matt's head. The result was an outpouring of angry whining.

'But what the hell have I got to do with a bunch of bloody Ghoulshee, for crying out loud?'

Kylah looked uncomfortable. 'I have no idea. You'll have to ask Silvy that yourself.'

'As if that's likely to happen,' Matt scoffed.

Kylah stayed ominously silent.

'Is it likely to happen?' Matt asked.

She kept looking at him with those big gold-flecked eyes.

'It's going to happen, isn't it?'

'From what I saw of her in the photo on your phone—'

'I don't remember showing you that.' Matt frowned.

'Let's not get bogged down in the detail of what you have and haven't shown us,' Kylah said hastily. 'From what I saw of her, she looks like a seventh-order priestess. That's pretty high up in the necromancy hierarchy. Plus, she's a soothsayer. Makes it quite difficult to take her by surprise. She's acting under the zealous guise of a religious order, and you, for some reason, appear to be a fly in their holy ointment.' There was no mistaking the distaste in her tone.

'So, are you saying that they see me as a threat?'

'I can't think of any other reason they'd come after you. But they are a determined bunch. The thing about the Ghoulshee is that, to achieve what they have achieved in getting themselves over here through an inter-dimensional rip—'

A sudden gust rattled the windows.

'Okay, back to the rip. A door has opened and let in a few Ghoul—a few of them. Is that a big problem?'

Kylah tilted her head and pursed her lips. 'Not if it were just a few of them. The fact is that they're *all* over here. Lock, stock, and shrunken head decorated barrel.'

'I thought you said they were a disaffected socio-economic group, seeking cultural independence.'

'They are. But tied up with their demands is a belief in a few very unsavoury gods, who they have to appease on a regular basis through human sacrifice. Added to that is the prediction of one Greck of Bibilia, who prophesied that 2024 would be the year of The Rendering.'

Matt frowned. 'Rendering? I know you can buy rendered chicken nuggets at Cheap Save…' Matt dried up when he saw Kylah's expression. 'That's a funny smile you've got there.'

'Do you know what rendered means, Matt?'

'What's left after you take the normally edible bits away?'

'Exactly. Added to the Ghoulshee's very short list of charms is a penchant for cannibalism. The Rendering is a ceremony whereby they take what's left after the prime cuts are gone and make it into a kind of human porridge. In very large batches.'

Matt swallowed loudly. Human porridge was not an image he relished filing away in his imaginings' cupboard. He zeroed in on something else she'd said. 'When you say "prime cuts" do you mean—'

'I mean that I think you'll agree that stopping them would be a good thing.'

Matt nodded. Three times. Stopping them seemed like a very good thing indeed.

'The problem is we don't know where they are,' Kylah added.

'How many are we talking about?'

Kylah looked up to the ceiling as she calculated. 'About a million and a half.'

Another silence followed.

'You can't find a million and a half Ghoulshee?'

The rattling got a bit louder.

'It's not as simple as it sounds,' Kylah said.

'Obviously.'

Kylah pushed away from the desk and started pacing again. She moved with ease, well balanced, like a dancer. 'This inter-dimensional rip, which is highly illegal in and of itself, is via an extradimensional field. It means they're here, but at the same time, they're not.'

'Glad we've cleared that one up, then,' Matt said with a little shake of his head.

Kylah paused and bit her lip. Finally, she raised a finger. 'Think of it like a tiny hole in a baked bean tin, through which an invisible bubble of botulism has grown. In the middle of your lunch is this lethal ball of toxin. From the outside, there's nothing to see. And, unless you can find the tiny hole the poison got in through, you have no idea there's even anything wrong until you start seeing two of everything and your muscles forget how to breathe.'

'So, we're looking for a tiny hole?'

'Yes. Somewhere, there's a tiny hole through which they've squeezed a bit of their own dimension. It's outside normal space and time, so it doesn't take up much room unless you're actually in it, in which case it does. Got it?'

'I may need a diagram.' Matt frowned. 'How big a tiny hole are we talking about?'

'Big enough for them to get in and out of.'

'So, a man-sized tiny hole?'

'Yes.'

Pause.

'That's not what I'd call a tiny hole.'

Kylah sighed and started pacing again. 'What I mean is that it needs to be big enough to get one person through, not a million and a half. They'd have walked in a line.'

The thing with Kylah, Matt realised, was that he was still not quite sure when she was being ironic. Sometimes there was a minute clue in the way she shot him little glances, but not always. It would have been much better if a little light lit up on her head every time she used sarcasm. Come to think of it, it would be a bloody good idea to have one whenever you spoke to someone from Germany.

'All I know is that I'm never going to eat baked beans again,' he muttered.

'It's likely they'll have chosen somewhere remote and quiet,' Kylah said.

'Like Colwyn Bay?'

'The fact that they've been active and abroad here attests to them being close by. That's where you fit in. You're unique in that you've had actual physical contact with one of them.' Kylah sounded like she was forcing the last sentence out through glued-together incisors.

Matt slumped back in his chair. 'Don't remind me.'

'Doesn't sound like it was too much of a hardship.'

'That's not fair,' Matt said.

'Anyway, I'm still clueless as to why they singled you out.' She tilted her head again to look at him, eyes narrowing. 'What you'd dismiss as superstitious timewasters, the Fae would revere as being highly gifted, even magical.'

Matt shook his head, trying to ignore that last word. 'My dad was from Cornwall. My mum was Welsh. She sometimes wore headscarves, but that was about as exotic as she ever got.'

Kylah shrugged. 'Well, anyway, the point is that Silvy would have left her mark on you and we can use that to trace her.'

'What do you mean "left her mark?"'

'It's a bit like a fingerprint, only in Fae terms. From what I saw of you and her together, I expect it's all over you.'

'Look,' Matt bristled, 'that stuff was meant to be private.'

Kylah smiled, pleased at the response she'd got. 'That was a joke. And I'm only talking about the time in the Carp.'

Matt decided to drag the conversation back to the point, because he couldn't stand her smirk. 'So, this supernatural fingerprint thing, how do you get at it?'

'Well, back at the institute we have scanners and aura separators that would tease yours out from hers, but we can't do that here.'

'Can't we go back to yours?' Matt asked, trying to be helpful.

'Yes, but it would mean killing you, because we don't have time to get you there any other way.'

Another silence. Twins.

'That seems a bit drastic,' Matt croaked.

'Really?' Kylah said with a mischievous glint. 'I thought that would be right up your street.'

'Well, it would have been,' Matt said, feeling like he was riding a bike backwards, 'except that now you're telling me that all this stuff, which no one else can explain and I've put down to a doolally gene, may in actual fact be explicable, so long as I—'

'Buy into the existence of the Fae.' Kylah watched him closely.

'Exactly,' Matt said.

Kylah gave him a sympathetic little nod. 'I know it's hard for you, but if it's any consolation, you're not alone. Some big names have struggled—Arthur Conan Doyle, Oscar Wilde, C. S. Lewis, Vlad the Impaler. Even Jung wrestled with it. Of course, he went down the road of meaningful coincidences when what he meant was that he couldn't explain how or why certain things happened unless someone made them happen. Synchronicity, he called it. That's us in a nutshell.'

CHAPTER TWENTY-SEVEN

KYLAH WENT BACK to the window and faced him, both hands on the sill behind her. The light threw her shape into silhouette. 'We can make things happen that appear inexplicable to you, but to us it's like turning on an electric light. It's simply a different kind of "natural." If it has a name, the boffins at the university call it the Gweuswyn.'

'Grey swine?'

'Gway, as in grey with a 'w' and soo-een. Celtic, your Welsh comes closest. A force that interlaces with the fabric of existence. The power is simply there, like gravity or sunlight. It's an altered contextual reality, that's all.'

Matt remained perplexed, but his headache was beginning to downgrade from crushing-anvil to gnawed-at-by-a-rabid-badger and he was thankful for that, if not for the unsatisfying explanation. And there must have been moronic pleading in his expression, because Kylah was willing to offer more.

'Look,' Kylah said, 'it's a bit like your lot and nuclear power. We look at what you're doing and can't understand how anyone can mess around with anything so bloody dangerous. Mind you, that Higgs Boson ride at the Large Hadron Collider is the best ever.'

Matt looked for signs of the sarcasm light but realised

after fifteen worrying seconds that there wasn't going to be one.

'That's just physics,' he said, trying not to sound too lame.

'And what we do is just—for want of a better word—supernatural. The same but different. Okay, some of it is pretend, an illusion. A way of making people see things the way we want them to. But the real stuff, changing the way things exist in the world, that takes a bit of practise. It isn't easy. That's my point with the inter-dimensional rip.'

'The baked bean tin,' Matt said, pleased with himself for remembering the analogy.

'Yes, something like that. It takes an awful lot of juice. More than any one person could provide. That's the thing about using Fae power: it's pretty draining. The Ghoulshee have harnessed it from lots of different sources. A million and a half sources, to be exact. To do that you need complete discipline, a rigid mindset. They live by controlling every-thing, leaving nothing to chance.'

'Bit like the Nanny State, then?'

'I was thinking more Nazi than Nanny, although I see where you're coming from. They will try and eliminate any risk to their crusade. And you obviously pose a threat.'

Matt made a scoffing bulldog face. 'Why?'

'You already asked me that one.'

His shoulders slumped in defeat. 'But what can I do?'

'Silvy's trace. With a bit of luck, that should lead us straight to wherever it is they're hiding.'

'What about your uncle?'

'We're in desperate need of intel. We have no agents over there, so what we need is a quick reconnaissance. Small squad, in and out, find out as much as we can.'

Matt nodded. It all sounded very military and about as appealing as cold stew. Mr Porter's part in this remained a niggly little stone in his sock. 'Why, exactly, do they want your uncle, again? I mean he struck me as a very nice chap, but what sort of clout does he have? Politically, I mean?'

'Let's just say he's a bit of a figurehead.'

Matt leaned back in the chair, pondering. Finally, he said, 'I can't believe I'm actually saying this, but I think I'm beginning to believe you.'

Kylah smiled, and it lit up the room. 'Good. Now, can we get a look at that pendant of yours?'

'Of course, but it's back at the flat and my bike's at the hospital and—'

'You won't need your bike. We can use this.' Kylah crossed to a green metal filing cabinet and pulled open the top drawer. From it she took a polished blue and purple doorknob, which looked well used and old.

'Australian onyx,' Kylah said, in response to his unasked question.

'Right,' Matt said. Onyx was one of those words, like clerihew or dwile flonking. He'd heard of it but hadn't a clue what it meant. 'But how's it going to help us get to my flat? Doesn't look like it would seat two. Okay, that bulbous end might fit somewhere anatomical, but probably not both of us at the same time.'

'I think you've worked in that A&E of yours for far too long,' Kylah said, shaking her head. 'It isn't for transporting, it's for gaining entry.'

'You mean it's a ticket?'

'Sort of,' Kylah said. 'It has its limits, in that it can only take you to places you've been before. You have to be able to see where you want to go. There are other devices for unknown destinations, but this is an Aperio. A very valuable tool.'

'So,' Matt said. 'You hang on to the handle and say Aperio-here-we-go and Robert's your mother's brother. I see.'

'Sarcasm is such an ugly trait,' Kylah said, narrowing her eyes. 'Here, hold it. What does it look like to you?'

Matt ran his fingers over the smooth, polished surface. 'A glass door handle?'

'Exactly. What we need is a door.'

'But the door we want is in my flat.' Matt pointed out with exaggerated patience.

Kylah walked to the office door and placed the handle at hip height on the hinged side. She pushed hard, and when she took her hand away the handle remained.

'Very impressive. You've got some sort of Velcro thing going on there?'

'Since I've never been to your flat, you will have to do this,' Kylah said, ignoring him.

'Do what? Chant some gobbledygook? Throw fairy dust? What?'

'How about pretending that it opens into your flat and opening the door?'

Matt put his hand on the doorknob. It felt surprisingly firm. He turned it and pushed. To his utter amazement, the door opened. But at the same time, he could see the original office door still sitting in its place.

'That's...interesting.'

'Go on,' Kylah urged. 'We haven't got all night.'

Matt stuck his head through and gasped. Through the open doorway stood his pokey, damp bathroom as seen from the doorway from his bedroom. He half-stumbled, partly from shock and partly because he forgot the step down. 'Shit,' he said, and quickly scooped up some underpants, throwing them behind the towel rail. With more than a little trepidation, he peeped into the toilet pan and almost screamed with joy to see clean, clear water nestling at the bottom of it.

'Hmm,' Kylah said as she joined him in the tiny space. 'Interesting smell. Mushrooms, I think.'

'It's an old flat,' Matt mumbled.

'Maybe, but it still makes Mrs Hoblip's cupboard look like a loft apartment.' She stared at the interesting shapes the mould had made halfway up the wall behind the shower tray. 'There's one cardinal rule with the Aperio. Always bring the handle with you into the room. Doors have a tendency to be self-closing when you least expect them to. It can be very embarrassing to be locked in somewhere a thousand miles away from where you just left. Very expensive, too.' She reached around for the knob, removed it, and shut the door.

When she opened it again with the proper bathroom door handle, Matt's unmade bedroom, with its very unmade bed, was there in all its glory.

'Um, maybe you should stay here,' Matt said, trying to remember when he'd last changed the sheets.

'Maybe I should,' Kylah agreed.

'I'll only be a minute.'

————

THE PENDANT WAS where he'd left it in the sitting room. Matt picked it up and stuffed it in his pocket. By the time he got back to the bedroom, a genuine miracle had taken place. His bed was made, all the CDs and books were back on the shelves and in some sort of size order, the curtains were open, and the windows had been cleaned. Matt dropped his bag and knew his jaw was doing an impression of a basking shark.

'How did you—'

'First thing you learn where you're old enough to do stuff on your own. Boys generally can't be bothered, but it's a simple transformational charm. You imagine what it might have looked like the day you moved in. We're borrowing from a state of previous temporal existence. I've merely superimposed that over today's reality and there you go.'

'It's bloody impressive,' Matt said in genuine awe. 'I wondered where that mobile phone charger had got to, and that umbrella, oh and that chair. Shame you can't do the same for the bathroom.'

Kylah stood back and pushed open the bathroom door to reveal a gleaming, shiny, fungus-free bathroom. 'Ta-dah.'

Matt collapsed onto the edge of the bed. 'I think I'm going to cry. Can you do anything else?'

'I have a few other tricks up my sleeve. Though I'm not in Silvy's league.'

There it was again. Another sly little dig at what had happened between him and Silvy.

'What do they call you when you're at home?' Matt said

as he rummaged for a change of clothes. He aimed for charm but ended up at borderline inappropriate. 'Witch, is it? Or nymph, maybe? Not as in a nympho, I mean that implies something altogether…different.' He saw Kylah's eyebrows arch dangerously. 'I was just wondering if there's a name for your type of supernatural creature,' Matt said, quickly.

'I'm just a girl,' Kylah replied, with the tiniest grimace to indicate a nerve gingerly touched. Yet Matt sensed that it was not because of the clumsy reference to female stereotypes that he'd made with his size-tens; it was subtler than that. After all, she had every right to call him a chauvinist warthog. But she didn't. Instead, she opted for lifting up the edge of the conversational carpet and, using a neat little brush, sweeping everything underneath it.

'I'm just one of the Fae,' she said, before composing her face into a rueful smile. 'Labels are so limiting, don't you think?'

Suitably admonished for his attempt at small talk and befuddled by the combination of not being called an idiot and her wry smile, Matt sat up and went straight into feckless-bachelor-chancing-his-arm mode (one he was much more familiar with).

'Umm, the lounge could do with a quick once-over.'

'Done,' she said.

Matt walked back in and threw himself on the nice, clean, fresh-smelling sofa, unable to stop grinning. 'I actually think I could live here now.'

Kylah followed him in and leaned in the doorway, smiling. 'It could do with a few touches, but I've seen worse.' Then she looked at Matt's Warhol-print clock and her expression hardened. 'Matt, I'm sorry to hurry you, but I'd like to look at that pendant.'

'It's here,' he said, holding it out to her.

Kylah backed away. 'No, not here. We need a controlled environment, as well as an expert or two.'

'Hipposync?' Matt suggested.

Kylah nodded. Two minutes later, courtesy of the

Aperio, they were back in Kylah's half of the office. Matt watched, fascinated, as she produced a contraption made up of a small metal plate on struts spanning a tilting stone tablet, over which a thin stream of water constantly ran. The whole thing was about as big as an oversized soup bowl.

'Put the pendant on that, please,' Kylah said, pointing at the plate.

'Dare I ask why?'

'Iron over running water. It diminishes its effect significantly. It's all to do with density and magnetic flux.' She put on some odd-looking gloves and used a wooden stick to tease apart the coils of leather necklace enough to prod at the pendant. 'This is Ghoulshee, all right.'

'Not that surprising, since one of their priestesses gave it to me.' Matt pointed out. 'Is that why Silvy wanted me on the footbridge? Iron over running water and stuff?'

'Probably, but it's mind-boggling all the same. Taking you to the river would negate the pendant's effect and allow the attempt on your life, that I can understand. But making you wear it in the first place would make it twice as hard for them to do whatever it is they wanted to do to you.'

'I suppose it's too much to expect any sense in all of this,' Matt muttered.

'Well, anyway, this pendant stays here over running water. It can't do any harm there.' The phone rang, and Kylah picked up on the second ring. 'Are they here? Good, send them in straight away.'

The door opened, and the two beings who entered were very definitely not like anything Matt had seen before, Mrs Hoblip included. They had khaki-coloured skin and their sinewy legs, which gave them extraordinarily wide strides, were twice as long as their bodies. Their arms were angular, powerful, and nut-brown, while their faces were long and smooth, with swept-back foreheads and startling green eyes. They wore brown uniforms that marked them out as some kind of military.

'Matt, these are Sergeants Birrik and Keemoch from the SES.'

'I daren't ask.' Matt tried not to stare.

'Special Elf Service, although they're seconded from the Hemlock regiment, so strictly speaking they aren't elves at all. They're Sith Fand, and you have been warned. They won't say anything if you call them the E word, but they won't forget…ever.'

'Hi,' Matt said, forcing a smile while wondering what the hell a Sith Fand was.

'Hello, Mathew,' Birrik said, holding out a knotty hand.

'Matt,' Keemoch did the same.

Matt frowned. There was something terribly familiar in their voices and intonation.

'Of course,' Kylah explained, 'You know these two by their human pseudonyms.'

'Dwayne and Alf?' Matt asked. He slipped on his stone glasses and the two sergeants transformed into pierced Dwayne and lumpy Alf. 'Well, I'll be buggered.'

'Careful what you wish for, Matt,' Birrik said. 'You're on Fae ground now, and things like that have a way of creeping up on you whilst you're leaning over the sink washing a dirty teaspoon.'

Matt grinned, but Dwayne's lips remained firmly clamped together and he felt his own smile die, before the two of them started howling with laughter.

'You should see your face,' said Birrik, wiping his eyes.

Matt shook his head. Like Kylah, the Sith Fand were about as easy to read as the Epic of Gilgamesh.

CHAPTER TWENTY-EIGHT

SOMEHOW, knowing that there were Fae working in the hospital was even more flabbergasting than accepting that there was a bunch of murderous Ghoulshee secreted in a baked bean tin wanting to kill and eat half of Britain. Matt wasn't at all sure why, other than a bizarre kind of NIMBY denial as to what it implied. Who else was incognito at the General? Admittedly, he'd had his doubts about one or two.

There was, for example, that strange phlebotomist with the Dutch accent and the ponytail who'd tried to convince Matt of the musical merits of four recorders and a Mandolin. Being stuck in a kind of folk time warp was the norm for a surprising number of bearded, flower-bedecked people banging out *The Trooper and the Taylor* on Thursday nights in the back rooms of pubs all over the country, so Matt had been content in accepting benign eccentricity as Willem's label. But now that Alf and Dwayne had come out in the Fae sense, it did make you wonder.

'But why is it I never saw you like this?' Matt asked, perplexed.

'When was the last time you saw them?' Kylah asked.

'Couple of days ago.'

'Where you still wearing the pendant then?'

'Wearing the pendant would have shut the gate,' Matt said, realising his stupidity.

He saw Kylah nod in approval, which made him feel like someone had lit a coal fire under some cockles in his thorax. 'But what the hell are you two doing working in the mortuary at the General?'

'Recruitment officers,' Birrik answered. 'It's the best time to catch potential crossovers. Of course, sometimes it's a bit late. Not much left to cross over if you've been dead in your flat for three weeks and had your ears eaten off by your cats. Your spectral essence has worn a bit thin by that time. But on the whole, we try not to be too judgemental.'

'You've lost me.' Matt threw his arms up.

'Okay,' Birrik said, leaning against the desk. 'Fae/human rules 101. Death is the way into the Fae world for most of your lot. Very valuable, your death, 'cos it's a tradable commodity. Once you die, your place can be taken up by one of our lot. In fact, it's the metaphysical law. So, once corpses see the benefit package…' Birrik let his sentence hang in the air like a stunt plane at the apex of a loop-de-loop.

'This I've got to hear.' Matt sat back with his arms folded.

'Don't mock. You get your choice of reincarnation. Top three are canine, avian—usually a falcon or an eagle—or big cat. Hardly ever human, because most people have had enough of having to buy food and working. Besides, once they have the tour and see the variety of manifestations on offer, the human form doesn't seem all that special anymore. So, generally they opt for your noble animals.'

'Although, last week, there was that tax inspector who wanted to be a reticulated python,' Keemoch said.

'Old habits,' Birrik muttered.

'Dare I ask about conversion rates?' Matt ventured. 'I mean, people actually take you up on this?'

Birrik nodded. 'Compared with a hundred years ago, I'd say it's almost doubled. Rise of secularity over religion, success of *Most Haunted* on TV, you know the score. Although there are still quite a lot of people hung up on faith. Especially at that point in their lives.'

'Or deaths,' Keemoch added.

'Is it justified, that faith?' Even though Matt was not a believer, he knew lots of people who were. Being presented with the chance to ask a question that had intrigued two millennia worth of theologians was not something to scoff at.

'Yes, if you have faith in oblivion and an unending darkness,' Keemoch said.

'Laughingly known as the afterlife,' Birrik chipped in.

As a reply to the burning question of the age, it lacked a lot. Before Matt had a chance to press them for details, especially as they were both stifling laughter, Kylah clicked her tongue.

'Look, could we leave the metaphysics until a bit later?' She looked a little strained and kept glancing at her watch. 'Keemoch here is our tracing expert, and Birrik specialises in human technology.'

'Oh,' Matt asked, impressed. 'Where did you train, Birrik?'

'QVC.'

Matt opened his mouth, but no words came out. He did it three times in a passable impression of a goldfish, until they put him out of his misery.

'Okay, Matt,' Keemoch said, unpacking a rune-covered bag. 'Let's get you set up for the trace.'

'Tell me it doesn't involve pressing a green stone against my head,' Matt said, scowling.

Birrik chuckled and pulled out something the size and shape of a large chicken's egg. Matt eyed it suspiciously and got an evil smile from Birrik in return.

'Not your head, no. Don't look so worried. Touch of Vaseline and it slips in, no trouble. Has to be within the body cavity to work, see?'

'That's not even funny.' Matt's voice emerged half an octave higher than it was meant to be.

'Would be if you could see your face.' Birrik giggled.

'These are lode stones,' Keemoch explained, removing another egg, this one flinty blue compared to the other's light granite grey. 'All you need to do is hold one in each hand. The scan will show a map of your movements and everyone you've been in physical contact with for seventy-two hours. You run through everywhere you've been to during that time, we subtract that, and everything should be—'

'Tickety boo,' Matt said, trying to convince himself.

Keemoch unpacked a shallow stone dish and poured in some liquid that looked identical to mercury. 'Once we have the trace, Birrik will do his thing with a hand-held GPS, and that should be it.'

Matt watched as the SES set up. Kylah was busy preparing, too. Mostly by sliding thin and evil-looking knives into slots on the belt she'd put on. She was concentrating hard, which made her look lithe and professional and altogether pretty damned good in her tight black top and combats. Strike that, not just damned good, damned *outstanding*, especially when she arched her back to slide the knives into the rear of the belt. Maybe it was something to do with this tenth gate stuff, Matt mused. Not that he cared. It was just that every line of her curves seemed perfect and full and—

'You're drooling,' Kylah said.

'Am I?' Matt replied with a futile stab at nonchalance as he searched for a lie to save his embarrassment. 'It's this wisdom tooth thing I have. Gives me gyp sometimes.' Even to his own ears, it sounded cringe-inducing. In the absence of a convenient crack in the earth into which he could plummet, he reasoned that distraction might be his next best move. 'Um, there is one thing that I don't understand—well, there are several hundred if I'm being honest, but we'll go with this one for starters. Why don't I see you any differently when I put on the stone glasses?'

'I'm different already.' Kylah dropped her gaze and went back to arming herself.

'In what way?'

Kylah let out a sigh. 'Okay, I'm not strictly what you'd call Fae. Even though I was brought up amongst them.'

'So, you're human?'

'Not exactly.' Kylah frowned. 'Look, what does it matter?'

'It doesn't,' Matt said, sensing eggshells underfoot. 'If you'd rather not talk about it—'

'It's not that, I…it's difficult conceptually.'

'Try me,' Matt said. 'Conceptualise away.'

'I'm a Postlapsarian,' she said.

'Well, you'll be glad to know it doesn't show.'

Kylah shook her head in exasperation. 'I knew you wouldn't understand.'

'I'm trying,' Matt pleaded, searching his mental thesaurus. 'Postlapsarian. Post means after something, right?'

'Right. How are your scriptures?'

'I've got some ointment,' Matt said. It did earn a faint smile from Kylah, which seemed miraculous to Matt under the circumstances.

'Okay, think of it in these terms. You're in school. Everyone is happy in one big class. Then, one kid falls out with another and that divides the class into name-calling factions, so the teacher splits the class into two to avoid further confrontation. After my gang fell out with the other lot, we had a choice of living either in the human world or with the Fae. My family chose the Fae.'

'What school was this, exactly?'

'Big Bang Elementary,' Kylah said.

'So, we're not talking recent history here, then?'

Kylah shook her head. 'Think two thousand and then add as many noughts as there are in a city banker's pension.'

Since Matt was already at Weird Central, this little gem of extra weirdness didn't, to his amazement, surprise him much at all. 'So, you're in exile?'

'In a way, yes.'

'You're not a bloody princess, are you?'

'I am not,' she snapped. 'And can we leave it at that,

please? I'm not in the mood for discussing my roots at this moment in time.'

Matt had touched another nerve. Common sense told him to avoid the subject as if it had caused huge black boils and was transmitted by rats.

But she looks so delicious when she's miffed.

Kylah turned to Keemoch. 'How's it coming along?'

'Almost ready,' Keemoch mumbled. Birrik was pretending to hold a handbag in both hands while sucking in his cheeks behind Kylah. It was all Matt could do to stop from giggling.

'Right, Matt,' Kylah said, 'you're on. And if I catch you doing that one more time, Sergeant Birrik, you will not need to put that lodestone back into the box, because you'll be the one carrying it somewhere dark, moist, and unpleasant.'

'We're going to Reykjavik, then?' Birrik said, earning a withering glance from Kylah.

The aura trace wasn't that difficult. In fact, it wasn't anything at all, or so Matt thought, feeling more than a bit foolish as he sat in the centre of a rope-drawn circle on the floor, holding a lodestone in each hand as Birrik waved a wooden dowsing rod at him. Keemoch peered into the stone bowl and threw questions at him like, 'After Starbucks, where did you go?'

He tried to give them a blow-by-blow account of his day, but it proved to be amazingly difficult accounting for every minute. Matt found that it was best if he closed his eyes and tried to retrace his steps visually. He felt absolutely nothing except the odd tingle in his palms where the stones rested. After half an hour, Keemoch said, 'That'll do it.'

Birrik put down the rod, picked up a hand-held GPS gizmo, and began punching in coordinates while Kylah peered over his shoulder.

'The subtraction pattern shows a focus south of the city,' she said. 'Near Donnington Bridge Road. Damn, it looks like it's in the middle of the river.'

'Maybe not,' said Matt, who had walked out of the circle to join them. Birrik was already pulling up a Google map on an iPad. 'That's Long Bridges,' he said, recognising the curve in the river. 'People used to swim there. There's an island of sorts in the middle.'

Kylah looked at him hopefully. 'Don't suppose there's a door anywhere near there?'

'Well,' Matt said, 'it was an official swimming spot at one time. There even used to be changing rooms, but they've all collapsed. When I was there in the autumn, all that was left was the toilet block. It was still just about standing and there were doors of sorts, although most of them were hanging off the hinges.'

'Right, that's where we're going through,' Kylah said. She turned a serious face to Matt. 'The trouble is, you're the only one that's been there. So that means…'

'Give me that Aperio thingy,' Matt said with a sigh.

Kylah beamed. 'Matt, you're a star.' She kissed him chastely on the cheek. That close, she smelled of exotic spice, and her lips were soft and sensuous on his stubble. He knew it was nothing more than a gesture, a grateful affirmation of his local knowledge, so what the hell were all those butterflies doing flying about in his stomach? Keemoch and Birrik made several lewd gestures out of Kylah's eyeline, much to Matt's embarrassment. Kylah, meanwhile, had gone back to choosing weapons.

'Will I need anything?' Matt said, watching her put something that looked like a wand with a pointed metal end in her belt.

'No. Stay close to me. That's all you need to do. This is a stealth op. This stuff,' she waved a hand at her knife-laden belt, 'is purely precautionary. And anyway, you'll be perfectly safe, since you'll be totally invisible.'

There was a long pause while the three Fimmigration agents busied themselves and Matt's voice went AWOL. Finally, he recovered enough to ask, 'Did you just say I'd be invisible?'

'Yes, in Uzturnsitstan, which is where we're going. To them, at least. It's a Krudian anomaly of the inter-dimensional time-space issue. So long as there is no physical interaction with the environment. Best protection there is. Slip these on over your shoes, please.'

She distributed some gossamer-thin elasticated overshoes and, seeing Birrik and Keemoch slide them on, Matt did the same.

'Krudian web wrap. Think of it as insulation,' Birrik said, seeing Matt's frown.

Kylah walked across to the window and peered out. 'Almost dawn. Enough light for us to see by.' She went back to the green filing cabinet and took out the onyx handle. 'Everyone ready?'

Birrik and Keemoch stood, relaxed and ready. Matt shrugged.

'Then, let's do it.' She moved to the door, placed the handle, and stood back for Matt to open it.

CHAPTER TWENTY-NINE

HE'D BEEN to the old swimming spot at Long Bridges just the once. He'd hired a canoe and explored. The south side of the river was still a fairly popular tying-up spot, but on the other side, the only trace of previous activity was the metal ladder leading up the concrete bank of the swimming hole. In the heavily overgrown undergrowth beyond lay the abandoned toilet block and the doors that Matt thought of as he turned the handle. Two seconds later, he was trampling on dead bracken and brambles as he emerged into a freezing January morning. Kylah followed with the two SES agents behind. A narrow path led down to the edge of the concrete plinth, all that now remained of the changing area.

Keemoch pushed past with his dowsing rod held out in front of him. 'Down here,' he said.

They followed him in the grey light of the still-struggling dawn toward a collapsed brick wall, beneath which was a dark and very uninviting gap.

'That's it,' Keemoch said.

'Okay,' Kylah said, all business. 'Matt, you've been a great help, but this is where you go back. Birrik will take you to the office, and Mrs Hoblip will let you out.'

A wave of bitter disappointment washed over him. 'You mean, that's it? After all I've been through?'

'I'll be in touch as soon as I get back, but this is too dangerous for someone like—'

A woody snap from somewhere above killed her words. She shot a glance up to the left of the path they'd followed and bade Matt be quiet with a slender finger on his lips. Her hand moved swiftly to the weapons on her belt. Birrik was already backtracking lithely, making no sound at all. He looked back and made some hand signals, which Keemoch interpreted in a deep whisper.

'Returning Ghoulshee patrol. Twenty, at least.'

'We're totally exposed here,' Kylah said, looking around and zeroing in on the wall and the gap beneath. 'Come on, we're all going in. We'll hide until they're gone and we can get you back out.'

Decision made, Matt allowed himself to be pulled along and in through the gap. The space beyond had a strange, feral smell that suggested it had once been shelter for something mammalian and furry. Matt followed in an awkward crouch for what seemed like a long time, but the change, when it came, was pretty sudden. One second, it was a chilly Oxford morning; two duck-walking steps later, it was hot and humid, and they were hurrying through a small clearing surrounded by thick jungle vegetation. Keemoch headed straight for the greenery and pulled Matt in after him, yanking him down into a low crouch when he tried to stand. Kylah joined them two seconds later.

'Hot, isn't it?' Matt whispered.

'It's the way they like it.' Kylah stared back the way they'd come.

Matt found the whole thing exhilarating, despite the circumstances. 'Who'd have believed we're under the Thames?'

'Strictly speaking, we're not,' Kylah corrected him. 'We're in Ghoulshee-held Uzturnsitstan.'

'Oh, yeah. Baked bean tin. I forgot.'

'Quiet,' Birrik whispered.

Matt ducked a little lower. Through gaps in the fronds

ahead he could see nothing, but when he glanced behind him, lights sparkled in the darkness. There were thousands of them, glittering like stars. The other three were busy watching for the patrol, so Matt moved backwards until he was a good three metres away. There, he found that he could pull the ferns back to get a clear view of the moving lights. When he did, he let out an involuntary gasp. They'd come through onto a high mountain ledge in a very alien landscape. To his right, a rutted path led down like a dark ribbon through the greenery, but directly below, flanked by magnificent, white-tipped peaks just showing up on the edge of the red dawn, stretched a valley. A river, glittering silver and gold like the skin of a snake, ran its entire length. Between the peaks, a red sun was about to emerge. As it did, ochre light flooded the valley.

Matt's scalp crawled.

The moving lights were beings. Small beings, all with hooded cassocks, just like the choir from Hell standing on the banks of the river at the Carp that night with Silvy and in the kids playground trying to sacrifice Mr Porter. Each one had a fiery torch, which glowed as they moved through the jungle on a curving path to a vast plain next to the river. There were thousands of them, all moving in time, a well-organised, perfectly choreographed procession. Every few yards, the line of white hooded figures was broken by a ghostly angular shape. In the dim light it was difficult to make out details, but the strongest impression Matt had was of the blurry image captured on his mobile phone the evening he had kissed Silvy outside the A&E.

Memory of that little romantic interlude sent a shiver though him. As the light grew, the sheer scale of the procession became clearer, as did the detail of the valley bottom below. There, rank upon rank of hooded acolytes waited in a vast semicircle, the mass of bodies swelling all the time as more joined from the procession along the path. They stood on banks of what looked to be a natural amphitheatre, and in front of them, centre stage, was a sight that made Matt want to be sick. Serried rows of posts had been hammered into the ground, and tied to each of those posts was a person. Ordinary people. People like him.

Matt found that if he narrowed his eyes, he could almost focus in as if he had his own binoculars. *Krudian phenomenon*, he mused, with no idea of what the words meant. But the increased magnification revealed something that made his bowels cramp. There were more of those insectoid, grey-winged creatures mingling with the tied victims, taunting them with sharp sticks. He wasn't sure what all this was, but what it most definitely was *not* was a Boy Scout gathering, so the chances of them all bursting into a rendition of *On the Crest of a Wave* were slim.

As the light strengthened, he saw something that almost made him cry out. There, in the middle of the captives, was a portly figure in an incongruous tweed jacket and a woollen tie.

Mr Porter.

Matt turned back to the others but couldn't see them through the dense foliage. Instead, he whispered out into the forest, 'You've got to see this, Kylah. I think I've found your uncle.' He turned to look again at the gathering below, hearing a faint rustle behind as the others joined him. 'He's down there, in the middle of that little lot of wailing and crying people. Make your eyes into slits. It helps.'

'Keep talking, Mathew,' said a voice.

Matt's skin tingled. It was as if a hundred ants were crawling all over him.

The voice was familiar and female. But it definitely wasn't Kylah's. Her voice didn't have that harsh, Germanic edge to it.

'Silvy?' He slowly turned around.

She stood right behind him. Blonde hair, legs, the lot. But there was something about the way she was looking at him. Or rather, not looking at him, because her head was tilted at an odd angle, which put her gaze three feet to his left. It reminded Matt of the way a pigeon might look or a visually challenged dog. Because this was definitely not looking. It was listening.

'Where's Kylah?' Matt asked.

The instant he spoke again, Silvy changed.

Matt's heart became a revving engine doing its best to come up through his throat. *Twilight Zone* déjà-vu. Only this time she was close. Within striking distance close.

The nightmare face from his dream appeared on top of a body that was a foot taller than Silvy was as a girl. With that change came pale limbs and leathery folded wings. From a clawed hand she threw a handful of ochre dust at his face. Matt coughed and spluttered while Silvy towered over him.

'What the hell did you do that for?' Matt coughed.

'I prefer to see my victims,' she said.

Matt watched as something akin to a smile broke over her face. It wasn't pretty. Lots of very sharp teeth and what looked like bits of old meat. It was at that point that she struck.

There wasn't any pain. In fact, it was more like a punch. But when he looked down, he saw a very large handle at the end of the very sharp blade that was protruding from his chest. It was jet black with silver symbols all over it.

'My destiny is fulfilled,' the Silvy thing said and raised a lower appendage. She leaned in close. The smell of *eau d'abbattoir* was overpowering. 'The vultures will pick your bones clean,' she spat and booted him over the ledge.

———

MATT FELL FOR A LONG TIME. Well, probably a very short time, as measured by a ticking clock. But it was a long time in his head. Within seconds he tasted blood, and there was a rattle when he tried breathing.

The ledge was two hundred feet up. His weight from that height took mere moments, with the help of gravity, to reach the ground. Yet, he had time to think a hundred thoughts while he fell. The winner, by a mile, was his overwhelming feeling of disappointment. Somehow, this wasn't the script he'd imagined. The plan had been to qualify as a doctor, work hard for another ten years, and then hopefully reach his goal of a fulfilled and meaningful existence, which only ruled out proctology and dermatology as specialties. No part of that curriculum included being stabbed through the heart and pushed off a cliff, not even in the difficult second year.

It all seemed such a terrible waste. Matt thought of his mother and mentally apologised for not making more of himself. At least she wouldn't be traumatised by hearing of his death. There wouldn't even be an obituary, since the authorities were unlikely to find him in Uzturnsitstan. Not a chance in hell, since it didn't even exist in his universe. There'd be no cards or expressions of condolence, even. Perhaps Kylah might spare him a thought. He clung on to that little iota of comfort as he plummeted. It brought him a brief but sweet moment of succour to think that she might regret his absence from the world just one tiny little—

His back hit something hard, followed by his arm and then his head. Each time he hit, it hurt like hell. Finally, he crashed into the base of the cliff. They say that you know when you hit rock bottom, but that wasn't true for Matt. By the time he hit rock bottom, he didn't know anything at all.

Dead people generally don't.

CHAPTER THIRTY

IT WAS difficult to know how long the blackness lasted, since time was meaningless without context, and the only thing Matt was truly aware of was a vague shuffling and tapping, coupled with the odd squawk. The change, when it came, was slight but perceptible. It was like surfacing through a lake, but without the damp or the worry that the wispy thing touching your leg is not in fact a bit of weed, but the tentacle of some horrible underwater creature.

Things were coming back, but not all at once. Matt sat up, realised that the reason it was so black was that he'd had his eyes shut, and another flurry of struggling activity kicked in on his right. Once again, he ignored it. He let his lids crack open. It looked like he was in some sort of park, in that he was sitting on green grass surrounded by clumps of odd-looking lilac plants. Further away, there were trees. Lots of trees. And not just trees, but tall and elegant poplars. He was naked, apart from his M&S jockey shorts. From behind him, he could hear the reassuring, lulling lapping of a gentle ocean.

'Squawk!' That NOISE came from his right side, and the struggling, unpleasant sensation in his hand returned, this time fainter. Matt looked down and saw that his fingers were clamped tightly around the neck of the ugliest-looking red-headed vulture he had ever seen. Alarmed and not a little disgusted, he immediately let go. The bird pulled away, staggered, coughed and squawked several more times before glowering at him.

'What the effin' eff do you think you're playing at?' the bird demanded.

Matt didn't reply at once. He was too disconcerted. Partly by the bird's baleful stare, but mostly by the fact that it was talking.

'You could have bleedin' strangled me, you are effin' bee. I was just mindin' me own business…'

Memories of the tapping and shuffling flooded back to Matt, and with them, now that their origin was evident, came an unpleasant realisation. 'I think you'll find that you were trying to locate the softest spot in my anatomy to start hacking at, if you were being honest.'

'Well?' said the vulture. 'What do you effin' expect? It's in the job description, you cee.'

'Cee?'

'They slapped a no-swearing order on me when I was reincarnated, the effin' bees. Anyway, there was no need to grab me like that. Because in so doin', you've pulled me across with you. You cee-in' a-hole.'

'Cee-in?'

'Yeah, active participle of the cee-word, all right?' the bird snapped.

Matt gazed around at the vista once more. 'Where are we?'

'Oh great. That's effin' brilliant, that is. You drag me back 'ere, which incidentally is totally effin' illegal, and you don't even know where we are? You total tee.'

There was something oddly familiar about this place. A vague recognition that wasn't quite visual but there, nevertheless. Matt stared at the plants, the poplars, the blue sky. 'Are these flowers asphodels?'

'They're such crap, aren't they?' the vulture said. 'Be much better off with some nice effin' tulips, I reckon.'

Matt sat up, fragments of half-remembered Homeric mythology he'd studied as part of his English degree. 'It can't be. Is this…is this Elysium?'

'Ooo-effin'-ray. Give that man a cigar. Now, can you tell me who the effin' 'ell you are so's I can get back to doin' what I'm supposed to?'

'But Elysium?' Matt persisted. 'Does that mean I'm… dead?'

'As an effin' dildo, mate.'

'Dodo.'

''Xactly.'

'So, that means that you are, too? Dead, I mean?'

'Oh no. No effin' way. I've already been 'ere, got the soddin' T-shirt.' The baleful stare returned. 'I was supposed to be in an effin' witness protection programme back in that jungle. "No one will find you there." they said. "You'll be safe as effin' houses." Bunch of cees.'

The horizon canted weirdly and Matt's stomach almost went with it.

'Feelin' a bit dodgy? Does that to you,' said the vulture with a jerky tilt of its head.

Matt looked around again and saw a gate in the corner of the field. 'I remember going through the hole in the baked bean tin and seeing Silvy, and then…'

The vulture glared at him warily.

'Look,' Matt said, 'I'm sorry if I hurt you. I wasn't really in control.'

'You mean you are now?'

Matt almost fried in the glare the bird gave him, but he ignored it as his situation began to find a foothold in his brain. 'Can this really be Elysium?'

'Yeah. Well, Elysium Place, anyway. They went all 'olly-wood about five hundred years ago. Tees. I mean, poplars and asphodels? S'all bollocks.'

'So, do we go through the gate?'

'Suppose so. Quicker you get your interview, quicker we get this sorted.'

Interview was an interesting word, given the context. It registered in Matt's head, but he decided to let it go for now in a *que sera* moment. His eyes were drawn instead to some clothes laid out on the grass. He put them on.

'My name's Matt, by the way.'

'Rimsplitter,' the vulture said.

Matt had one arm through the green T-shirt. He stopped in mid-thrust, peering at the vulture through the neck hole.

'I know, I know. I'm a specialist, see. S'vulture culture. You're named for what you do. I was tapping to find out the soft spot, I admit. 'Ave to do that when corpses are on their effin' backs. But when they're prone, I go in first. The way is mapped out for me.'

Matt stared, sensing he had a sucking lemons expression on his face.

'Do I need to draw an effin' diagram of the chosen route of entry?' Rimsplitter snapped.

'No,' Matt said. 'Your name tells me everything I need to know.'

'I 'ad no say, mate. They all 'ad a good laugh, them bees in reception. Thought it was effin' 'ilarious. But what can you do? It was this or an effin' dung beetle. Cees.'

They headed for the gate. Or rather, Matt walked and Rimsplitter hopped.

'You'll forgive me for saying this but…well, your job sounds more like a punishment to me.'

'What, splittin' rims? Maybe. But I wasn't goin' to take the risk of finding myself in the other effin' place. You know, eternal oblivion.'

'You mean Hell?'

'No, Southend. They wanted to send me back as a seagull, but I wasn't 'avin' any of that. Them bees would get me if I was in Southend, seagull or no seagull. "Get me to another world." I says. "Use your effin' imagination." I says. I wasn't to know their imagination could be used to take corks out of wine bottles, was I?' Rimsplitter sent Matt another baleful stare, which didn't mean a great deal, since vultures looked baleful all the time.

Matt hardly noticed in any case. He was too busy trying to piece together the significant elements of Rimsplitter's rant. It was like trying to find the one unmistakable landmark in a thousand-piece jigsaw of the Newfoundland coast.

'Who would get you if you were a seagull in Southend?' he asked.

'The others that came across after the fight. They weren't at all 'appy chappies.'

'Fight?'

'Yeah, spot of bother with the Russians,' Rimsplitter muttered. 'W'ers. They didn't like the Chechnyan vodka I got them cheap. Just because there was a bit of anti-freeze in it.'

'A bit of anti-freeze?' Matt glared at the bird.

'Well, quite a lot of anti-freeze. Enough to kill ten of the a-holes. Anyway, my name was mud. Lots of death threats. After-death threats, even. So the men in grey suits say, "We'll find you somewhere safe." Safe, all right. Effin' vulture colony. Like I say, I think they were deffo takin' the pee. Bees.'

'Why would they do that?' Matt asked.

''Cos they're jealous. Successful entrepreneur like me? Brings out the effin' green-eyed monster.'

'Is that what you did before? Entrepreneurially sell cheap, tainted booze?' Matt tried to keep his eyebrow from arching too much.

'Import-export, glamour photographer, runner for a Russian football manager—you name it, I did it.'

'So, you were a chav pimp?'

Rimsplitter unfurled his wings in a gesture that Matt interpreted as anger. 'That's what they said at the desk.' He lowered his head menacingly. 'But I resent the word "pimp" That girl from Prague just liked blokes. A lot. Especially Middle Eastern ones with lots and lots of effin' oil.' He glared at Matt again, this time with suspicion. 'You've seen my file, haven't you, you cee?'

Matt shook his head. 'Never been here before in my life.

Or my death. You did say I was dead, didn't you? Only I don't feel—'

'You looked effin' moribund when I got to you, mate. Effin' great knife in your chest, more broken bones than Evel effin' Knievel.'

They walked through the gate and Matt stopped. Ahead on three sides was a vast plain, dotted with the same asphodels. Behind, he could still hear the ocean. All around, the blue sky fell to the horizon, but that was where the alien nature of the landscape became obvious. Along its length ran a ribbon of inky blue, within which twinkled stars.

'Course, there's no effin' real day or night 'ere,' Rimsplitter explained. 'They 'ave both at once. Easier to walk about that way.'

The endless plain was broken by three buildings: one to the north, one each to the east and west. They were all identical in size and shape.

'It's your basic inter-dimensional way station. Why they've chosen to make it look like an effin' East German Seventies apartment block, your guess is as good as mine. But at least it looks a lot better than it effin' did. Five hundred years ago it was all volcanoes and high winds and lightnin'. Took long enough for the cees to get plannin' permission but look what they come up with. As superimposed architectural contexts go, it's acceptable, but what was wrong with a bit of effin' Gaudi, or even Dali? I mean, if not 'ere, where the effin' 'ell else, eh?'

'Right,' Matt said. There wasn't much else to say. Except one thing, of course. 'Uh, which way?'

'West,' Rimsplitter said and began hopping in that direction. 'North is out of bounds unless you want your effin' soul divided up into forty pieces and shared out amongst demons whose favourite aperitifs are Plymouth Dry gin and essence of life. Cees. East is for elementals. Sylphs and undines and all that ess-aitch. We go west.'

Matt followed, and although it looked like it was a long way off, three minutes of walking brought them up to the front door of what Matt decided looked very much like a Holiday Inn Express.

'Don't effin' ask,' Rimsplitter said. 'All you need to know is that this is the physical manifestation of the multiverse, and each effin' room in 'ere is a way into a separate universe. Where you and me came from is on the bottom two floors.' Rimsplitter hopped towards the main entrance.

Matt pushed the front door open and walked in to a cavernous lobby which was open to the roof, except the 'roof' looked like it was a mile up. On each side of the lobby were balconies leading to hundreds, no, *thousands* of doors.

Right in the middle of one wall on the ground floor was a small mahogany desk with a bell on it. Rimsplitter nodded towards it. 'You'll be needin' reception. Go on. And you'd better 'ave a good story, 'cos they are goin' to be mightily pee'd off with you, sonny Jim.'

Matt walked across the empty lobby and stood at the empty desk. He took a deep breath in and out through his nose and pressed the bell. Nothing happened immediately, but he could hear someone moving about in a room behind the desk. The partition wall had a one-way mirror right in the middle of it, and Matt sensed that whoever was behind the wall knew he was there. He waited, looking around while some inane muzak played in the background.

He glanced over his shoulder and saw Rimsplitter pacing up and down. Whoever it was who decided on the zoomorphic reincarnations in this place, they'd got it smack on with Rimsplitter, in terms of reflecting attitude and personality at least. Matt found himself almost smiling. When he turned back to the desk, he was not alone. A man wearing a white shirt and black tie stood there. His hair, thin on top and short on the sides, was plastered greasily down on his skull, and his skin was a shade less grey than his suit. He bared large yellow teeth in a weak attempt at a smile and squinted at Matt over a pair of glasses balanced on his nose.

'Yes?' he said, with about as much warmth as a snapping turtle.

'Oh, um…Danmor. Mathew Danmor.'

The man peered at him. He held his head at a slight angle that implied irritated expectation. The man blinked once and then said, 'Yes?'

'Rimsplitter said I should report to the desk.'

'Rimsplitter?' The man made it sound like something memorable and disgusting at the same time. Matt nodded over his shoulder and saw the man send Rimsplitter a disapproving glare before adjusting his glasses and peering down at the ledger in front of him on the desk.

'No,' he said and shut the heavy book with a dusty flourish. 'No Matt Danmor booked in for today.'

'What do you mean?' Matt asked.

'I mean that there is no official record of you needing to be here. You are obviously a mistake.'

'You mean I shouldn't really be here? Shouldn't really be dead?'

The man sucked in air and tilted his head. 'Hmmm,' he said 'that may be putting it a little too strongly.'

It was one of those moments when, faced with the immutable force that is a bureaucratic bungle, it seemed like there was nothing to do but walk away. At least, that was the impression the man behind the desk gave with his resigned look and bloodhound eyes. It was like turning up at an NHS hospital for an operation, holdall packed with PJs and half a dozen books, only to be told that there wasn't a bed. In that situation, part of everyone wants to scream maniacally at the flushed and harassed-looking twenty-three-year-old nurse delivering the news, because of all the hassle they've been through in organising the kids, the dog and the job. But a part of them knows full well that it isn't the nurse's fault, and it wouldn't be right to take it out on her.

What they want to scream at, of course, is the 'system'—that nebulous, invidious, tentacled thing that has its hands and fingers in every pie of daily life and that takes every opportunity to make people feel like they're a pair of skid-marked underpants in the spin cycle of a washing machine. It was enough to drive you mad. Enough to make you scream like a Ghoulshee—well, maybe not exactly like a Ghoulshee, but scream, nonetheless.

'Right,' Matt said, giving up any thought he had of being able to get that all into a sentence.

'Those idiots upstairs have cocked up again,' the grey-suited man said, slowly and very clearly, like he knew that someone else would be listening. 'I'm going to have to get hold of my supervisor, but that could take a while. There's been an earthquake in China and a train derailment in Pakistan, so we're busy elsewhere at the moment. Can you come back in, say, three months?'

'Three months?' Matt did his best affronted punter impression.

The man sighed and shook his head. 'All right, let's say two hours. I'll see what I can do, but I am promising nothing. And could you take that vulture of yours with you? He's making an awful mess on the carpet.'

A note of alarm crept into Matt's voice. 'Take him where, exactly?'

The man gave Matt a very old-fashioned glance before looking up at the lobby wall with its thousands of doors. Then an idea struck him.

'So, can I go back to Uzturnsitstan?'

The man's mouth made the shape of a smile, but his eyes were full of derision. 'Of course not. I mean, think of the overcrowding if we allowed that to happen every time someone asked.'

'But...'

'No exceptions, I'm afraid.'

Matt's frustration was on the point of boiling over. 'Then what's the point of me being here?'

'Excellent question, and one that I hope we'll be able to find an answer to within the next couple of hours.' The man pulled out a piece of paper from under the desk, stamped it and pushed it across to Matt. 'Temporary universal visa to anywhere you'd like to go.'

'Anywhere except Uzturnsitstan,' Matt said, bitterly.

The man nodded. 'And, of course, terra firma, since that is where Uzturnsitstan is also currently dimensionally situated.'

Matt looked desolately over his shoulder at the wall of doors, his heart now somewhere around the level of his laces. He had to face up to the fact that he was dead and in no position to help anyone. Not Birrik, not Mr Porter, and especially not Kylah.

He squeezed his eyes shut and let fly a silent scream before giving the man behind the desk a resigned smile. 'Okay. Well, thanks for your help. See you in a couple of hours.'

CHAPTER THIRTY-ONE

As Matt walked slowly back across the carpeted floor, wondering what he was going to do, he was reminded of those interminable breaks between exams in medical school. No second chances there. It was pass or sling your hook. Oral exams were the worst. There was no point and not enough time to go back to your room to study in between each one, so it was a matter of treading water until your number was called. It was impossible to relax because of the churning adrenaline, but pointless trying to do much else, either. If anyone wanted to invent a torture to rival waterboarding, they wouldn't have to look much further than the wait between med school vivas. Except, of course, here at the Holiday Inn in Limbo Land there weren't any exams to take. That meant he wasn't going to have to spend time on soul-destroying activities in the company of snide, superior people trying to catch him out with unanswerable, impossible questions.

'Think that bloke's a deconstructed vampire?' Rimsplitter demanded, preening himself as Matt approached. A second later, he added, 'Why've you got that funny smile on your bleedin' ugly mug?'

Discretion being much the better part of the virulent desire Matt had to bellow obscenities and realising that he was going to be dependent on the vulture as a guide, Matt decided it was best to maintain the smile and keep schtum as he turned towards the lifts.

Rimsplitter was having none of it. 'What'd 'e effin' say?' he squawked as they headed across the lobby.

'I'm supposed to come back in two hours. I'm not in their system, apparently.'

'Effin' w-ers.'

The lift door opened. Matt stepped in and confronted the most extensively buttoned lift console he had ever seen. 'Have you ever been to any of these places?' he asked desperately.

'One or two. Uzturnsitstan, I know pretty well. Never short of food there on account of their strict effin' sacrificial policy. Cees.'

'Yeah, well, that's the one place I can't visit, apparently.'

'Okay, no need to get effin' shirty.' Rimsplitter stuck his head under his armpit, searching for a tick with great vigour.

'By the way, did you see what happened to the girl I was with?'

'The small, dark bint with a nice arse?'

'Small, dark bint with a nice arse is hardly—'

'Oh, yeah.' Rimsplitter leered. 'You saying you wouldn't? 'Cos I bleedin' would, no worries. If I wasn't a vulture, anyway.'

Matt shook his head, letting his shoulders sag in defeat. 'Yes, her.'

'Saw her being dragged away by the acolytes.' Rimsplitter cackled at his own joke. 'Pretty good that, eh? By the bleedin' acolytes. See what I did there?'

'Will she be okay?' Matt said through gritted teeth.

Rimsplitter cocked his head in what Matt assumed was a sardonic glare. 'As okay as any prisoner of a cannibalistic jihadist effin' group of religious cees ever is. The straight answer is no, she's effed.'

'I don't suppose you know where she's from?'

'Since she's the head of bleedin' Fimmigration security, I've got a rough idea.' Rimsplitter consulted the console and tapped with his beak. Matt saw the button marked 'Floor 123, Door 97' light up.

The lift doors shut. There was absolutely no sense of movement at all, but three seconds later they opened again, and Matt and Rimsplitter stepped out onto a balcony. Matt risked a glance down and pulled straight back on seeing the vertiginous view of the lobby below.

'This way.' Rimsplitter hopped along to door number 97. 'What do you want to visit where she's from for anyway, you old bee?'

Good question. Why indeed?

Yeah, Mathew, why are you so interested in visiting Kylah's country of origin? See if she has any sisters?

No, it wasn't that. It was because of…

Come on. Spit it out.

Attraction, okay? It was because he fancied her. Which was laughable. Hysterical. He hardly knew the woman. Yet even when he subtracted lust from the equation, he was left with the square root of the irrational divided by the cube of incredible over pi, and no matter which way he did the maths, it added up the same.

Attraction.

Thinking about Kylah left him with that familiar, queasy feeling in the pit of his stomach that could only mean he fancied her utterly. Unfortunately, he also vividly remembered what she'd said the first time he'd met her.

'Fae and humans are not a good mix. And I haven't had any reason to question that maxim so far.'

Hardly a sonnet. Certainly not the basis of a long-term relationship, but there'd been something in the way she'd said it. The merest suggestion of a softening of tone that he'd interpreted as wistfulness. Then, there was the fact that she was a girl—well at least mostly a girl—and she didn't consider him either a complete drop-out loser or a lunatic. She was the only woman in the world who truly understood his situation regarding Silvy, when you took out the catty remarks and scathing glares whenever he mentioned her name. And, of course, she'd kissed him.

Twice.

Okay, she'd glossed over the first time by insisting that it was also the quickest way to reinstate his memory, but the second time, it had been genuine. And that, Matt knew, had been the deal closer. Yet, holding it up for mental inspection like this did little to reassure him. It all seemed such a paper scaffolding upon which to build a relationship of any sort, let alone one to pin his hopes to.

Of course, when it came to emotional constructs, many a diamond anniversary owed its existence to a lot less in the way of substantial beginnings—the echoing clatter of a pencil as it hits a library floor and finally draws a glance from that shy girl in 4B. Or a mutual craving for midget gems on a long bus journey. Or even the opening chords of *All Right Now* at the college disco.

Matt's stomach clenched. All the vague feelings and long-ings he hadn't known he'd had instantly coalesced into one solid conclusion.

He was in love with a small, dark Fimmigration officer (he was too well brought up to ever use 'bint with a nice arse). A very nice arse, indeed.

Ah, joy of ironic joys. So, there it was—besotted with a girl who was in another dimension, about to be ripped apart by a group of cannibalistic freaks. And to cap it all, he was dead. Dead and unable to do a single finger-lifting thing about it. Danmor luck, again. The one shot he might have had at finding a little bit of contentment in this shit-awful existence had been snatched away in as much time as it had taken for a blade to pierce his heart. Tragic. Very Shakespear-ian. And about as funny as a Belgian joke book.

'Wossammatter?' Rimsplitter asked. 'Cat got your tongue?'

Matt shrugged, wishing there was a convenient dark hole to climb into. It was as if the crushing unfairness of it all was about to compress him into a speck of worthless dirt. 'I don't know. It would have been nice to have got to know her a bit better, that's all.'

'Well, not much effin' chance of that, is there? Still, you can say goodbye to her town for her.' Rimsplitter came to a halt and cocked his head again.

'Right,' he said. 'Door number 97. Go on, then.'

Matt twisted the handle. The door opened onto a short corridor with three other doors. 'Always take the left door from 'ere,' Rimsplitter explained in a voice tinged with bitter experience. 'Right is security, and they always ask awkward questions. Like, "Whose wallet is that?" Or, "Where did all this blood come from?"'

Matt opened the left door, and they stepped out onto a grey cobbled street that was damp with fresh rain. The air was cold but…different was the word that sprang to mind. The look, the feel, and oh, the smells. Matt sniffed burning wood, roasting food, and something else a bit less appetising.

'Right, what is that smell?'

'Chestnuts,' Rimsplitter said. 'They like chestnuts.'

Matt did smell chestnuts, but that wasn't what he'd meant.

'Oh, and remember the name of this street in case we get effin' separated,' Rimsplitter added.

Matt walked a few paces along, trying to exist in the moment and forget about Kylah. He was useless at it. But he got to the end of the road and read *Prestige Street*. He turned back towards the vulture. 'This is Britain, then?'

'Sort of. Geopolitically it is. But not like the one you know. Eff me, no. S'all city-states 'ere. This one's the effin' biggest. Bleedin' 'uge, it is. As big as London.'

'Does it have a name?'

'Yeah. Nodlod.'

'Wow, that's an anagram of Lond—'

Rimsplitter convulsed with vulture laughter. Well, either that or he was about to be violently sick. 'Got you there, mate!' he spluttered. 'You should see your effin' face.'

'So, what's it really called?' Matt tried to keep his voice even, when he really wanted to kick the bird until it screamed.

'New Thameswick.'

Matt gave him a glance.

'No, that's the God's effin' truth, that is. 'Onest.'

Matt walked a bit further and saw what was causing the smell. A large brazier burned, and he could see others on the street corners to either side. Each one sent up smoke redolent of fresh pine.

'What are these for?' Matt asked, half-turning back to where Rimsplitter watched him with an odd, expectant expression.

'It's to mask the other effin' smell, innit.'

'What other smell?' Matt asked, navigating around the brazier and putting one foot in the road as he did so. Only it didn't feel like road when his foot hit soft and squelchy ground.

'Horse dung,' Rimsplitter said, squawking with laughter again.

This was going to be a very long couple of hours.

CHAPTER THIRTY-TWO

MATT STEPPED BACK onto the pavement and tried his level best to wipe off the majority of the green slime on the kerb-stone, sensing a bitter smile curling his lip. It seemed that he couldn't escape crap in his life, even in another dimension. At the same time, he heard the rattle of wooden wheels and the rhythmic clip of horses approaching. Three horse-drawn carts passed each other in the roadway. None of them had drivers.

'Cars?' Matt asked as Rimsplitter finally managed to stop laughing enough to join him.

'No one has effin' cars. No need, mate.'

'Are you telling me they're horse and carts?' Matt asked.

'Just to transport provender.'

'It's a bit…retro, isn't it?' Matt took in his surroundings. There were buildings, but not much in the way of modern styles. They were mainly wood and brick, some with walls that looked as if they were leaning into the wind off Beachy Head. There didn't seem to be many people around, either. Those there were looked disappointingly ordinary, other than the fact that their dress sense was a little eccentric. More Vivienne Westwood than Gap. Capes were in vogue for both sexes, with long, multi-coloured scarves for the men. The women wore skirts, and some hid their faces behind gossamer veils under brightly coloured hair.

Other, more colourful sights drew the eye once Matt and Rimsplitter started along the streets. Matt spotted a group of dwarves with painted faces and elaborately curled facial hair, out on what looked suspiciously like a stag do (judging by the balloons and the star-tipped wand the one in the middle was carrying). Although, come to think of it, this might be them on their way to the office in normal dwarven business dress. But, since one of them was singing, 'I'm a pink pix-ee, you're a blue pix-ee.' quite loudly and swaying all over the pavement as Matt and Rimsplitter passed, a stag do went back to the top of the list.

Further along, there were four tall, bespectacled beings Rimsplitter explained were Northern Wood Elves, which he qualified with, 'Bunch of stuck-up, shortsighted effin' w-ers.' And once, when a large brown mountain blubbered along the opposite pavement, Rimsplitter muttered, 'Troll, fat git. They're into real estate.'

After a while and having encountered most of the mythical beings he'd ever read about, Matt became intrigued by the shops lining the streets. He suggested that they take a closer look. To get to the other side and avoid the two-foot-deep layer of horse dung steaming in the gutter, it was important, Rimsplitter explained, to choose a crossing place carefully. Matt found one at an intersection, in the form of big stepping stones, between which the cart tracks ran in worn furrows.

The shops on the other side were all bedecked with coloured ribbons and lights against the grey of the day, and had curious, almost familiar names. There was Bloops the Alchemist where, Rimsplitter explained, 'You get your potions and your effin' pills.' At Dependablehams, it was clothing and a big section of jewellery organised in racks according to function. Matt read signs like *Obsidian Evil Eye Brooches* and *Friendship Amulets*. There was a special offer on *Free The Seventh Circle Six* necklaces. Matt didn't even want to guess what that was all about.

Starstrucks, meanwhile, was a coffee shop and soothsayer

centre. Matt counted five in a quarter-mile stretch. There was a Mage and Sceptres, which had a big picture of underwear in the window. Well, it looked like underwear in that it was black and frilly; it was just that the thing modelling it had five legs and was roughly the size and shape of a wheelbarrow. Matt window-gazed at Transmogrify Us, which, Rimsplitter explained, was a 'kind of fancy dress shop for w-ing weirdos.' The strange-looking get-ups in the window included an ordinary man in a business suit carrying a briefcase with a neatly handwritten sign saying *Scary Banker* underneath it. There was a tariff of sorts hanging on the door. It read:

**Let us transmogrify you. Guaranteed charms.
Money back if someone recognises you.**

Four hours 2 scruples.
Eight hours 4 scruples.
Twenty-four hours 10 scruples.
*Midnight special this week: Turn back into yourself
at the stroke of twelve for that extra-exceptional
surprise. Only 5 scruples.*

BETWEEN THE SHOPS, musicians played in little squares, and street vendors sold a variety of hot drinks and things on sticks, which Matt didn't find the least bit appetising. Quite a few beings (it was the easiest and least offensive noun Matt could come up with) were coming in and out of quite a modern-looking shop—in that it had straight up and down walls—called 'QUINSECT'. It had a white logo of a piece of fruit with an ant crawling out of it over the doorway.

'What's that?'

'Ah,' Rimsplitter said. 'That's direct cross-marketing, that is. They love our technology, the bees. 'Cept they 'aven' got any to speak of, so they use what they got to make it look like what we got, see?'

'Clear as mud.' Matt narrowed his eyes. He was still struggling to work out when Rimsplitter said, 'see' he meant the verb 'to look' and not 'cee' the rhyming derogatory euphemism involving people from Berkshire with a propensity for red riding jackets and hounds.

Rimsplitter shook his head in vulture exasperation. 'Tell me what that thing effin' looks like.'

'A piece of fruit with an ugly-looking insect climbing out of it.'

'Exactly, you tart. What iconic famous piece of bleedin' fruit do you know from back 'ome?'

'It doesn't look anything like an apple,' Matt said.

'No, that's 'cos it's a bleedin' quince.'

Matt decided that he had to see this. In the window were all sorts of gadgets, most of them little shiny white boxes of varying sizes. Most were billed as Mocks. There were small MockBooks and larger Quinsect EyeMocks. The sign next to one read:

Get this latest desktop Mock Pongcluetor with three hundred gigamite processor and an LEG (Light Emitting Glow-worm) screen for just 399 scruples.

'Pongcluetor?' Matt asked with an expression akin to a boxer chewing a hornet.

'Chinese invention. There's a million elephant mites in the box. And you know what elephants have got.'

'Long tusks and trunks?' offered Matt.

'Brilliant memories, you tart,' Rimsplitter snapped. 'Every one of these mites is trained by the Pong family. Ask 'em anything and they'll tell you on the screen thingy. Little bees.'

'I thought you said they were mites?'

'Not real bees—bees as in illegitimate bees. You know, term of affection.'

Matt could only shake his head in wonder. Not at the pongcluetor, but at the thought of a brain that considered using the colloquial word for illegitimate as an endearment.

But by that point, there were other things in that window that drew his eye, things that made you want to own one of them even though you had no idea what they did.

'What's an Impod?'

'Ah, for the music aficionado. Same kind of thing. Effin' Pong family again. Basically, it's a matchbox full of parrot fleas. They have this synbionic relationship with a parrot—'

'You mean symbiotic?'

'That's what I said,' Rimsplitter said, rolling vulture shoulders in a huff. 'Means they take on bits of the parrot's ability for replaying stuff. So, they play the effin' parrot music, and then 'arvest the fleas and stuff 'em in the matchbox. Stimulate the fleas with a bit of parrot blood by pressin' a little white button thing on the front, and away they bleedin' go. Means you can listen to whatever you like. Brilliant, eh?' He sighed. 'Such a simple idea, carrying around your effin' music in a box. Wish I'd effin' thought of somethin' like that when I was back 'ome.'

Matt turned his head very slowly to look at Rimsplitter, praying for a sign that the vulture wasn't serious. Unfortunately, he found none, and so they kept walking.

A couple of doors down stood a large frontage with nothing but a black canvas sheet with a silver moon and three stars emblazoned upon it. The austere window displayed small phials and bits of old parchment on plinths. Above each was a runic symbol. No one was going in or out of the large oak door with its ornate brass handle, and Matt saw no name above the door.

'What's this? Apothecary? Mind-reading?'

'Nah, you get them in Bloops. Don't even effin' bother tryin' to get in there, by the way. That's Harpy Nix. Heavyweight effin' stuff in there.'

'It's not very popular, is it? I don't see any activity at all. It's like the Prada shop on South Molton Street.'

'No one in there 'cos they can't get in. Don't need security 'cos the doors are charmed. You got to be somethin' special to get in there. Think of it like an effin' arms dealer. Only qualified people can use what they got in there. People with ability and years of trainin'.'

'Really?' Matt said. Normally, he stayed away from places like this, staffed by snotty salespeople who were chosen on looks and their ability to hover with disdain as you riffled through clothing that cost more than three months' salary for a shirt. But today, he didn't care. Today, he wanted not to have to think about what was happening in Uzturnsitstan, and brazen curiosity was as good a distraction as any. On impulse, he tried the door. It opened silently. Inside, subdued lighting and the smell of incense greeted him. He walked through a velvet-draped antechamber into a circular room.

'How d'you do effin' that?' he heard and turned to see the vulture hopping after him. As it tried to follow Matt across the threshold, it was as if a plate of glass had suddenly been shoved in its way. Rimsplitter rebounded backwards onto his backside with a squawk.

'You *effin'* cee-in'—' Mercifully, the door shut with a click, blocking out any more of Rimsplitter's invective. Inside, the walls were covered with strange symbols—twelve in all. Beneath each was a glass cabinet with a variety of vials, carefully labelled pouches, and little tied sacks. The room was also perceptibly colder and, Matt sniffed, moister than the street outside. He tried reading the labels, but only a few were in a language he could decipher. He read one: *Powdered bile duct of three-toed troll-newt: Jehovia.* As he straightened, Matt sensed a presence behind him. A very pale and very thin young man with slicked-back hair stood there, looking as if he'd had his smile trowelled on by a plasterer in the back room.

'Can I be of assistance, sir?'

'Just browsing,' Matt said.

The man's eyebrows lifted, but the smile didn't move.

'Really, sir? How…unusual.'

'Just visiting town. Having a bit of a wander, you know.'

'No, sir, I do not. We have never had anyone *wander* into Harpy Nix before.'

'Right,' Matt said. He flicked his gaze back to the cabinet. 'I was interested in the powdered bile duct,' he lied.

'Of course, sir.' The man held out a hand to invite Matt closer to the item in question. 'Only of the purest and highest quality, as I am sure you will appreciate. A vital ingredient for any of the higher-order curses and, it goes without saying, essential for all the demonic-cleansing spells, including the *Rinten Noir*. But then, of course you would know that, sir.'

'*Rinten Noir*. Yes, of course,' Matt said, aware that he was canoeing in a pool of treacle without a paddle. 'Well, I'll certainly think about it. Thank you ever so much.'

'Not at all, sir,' the shop assistant said. 'Please take our card. My name is Luga, sir. If I can be of any further assistance, please do not hesitate to contact me directly or via cybersomnulence. My dreamweb site is on the card.' Luga reached into a drawer beneath the cupboard. 'Please also accept this small sample. A little *Bachau Oma* from the Welsh coven of Offa. For those especially awkward moments. Self-opening packaging. Point and throw deployment.'

Matt thanked Luga and took the offered crumpled muslin with a smile that matched the shop assistant's.

CHAPTER THIRTY-THREE

Rimsplitter was pacing outside.

'Thanks an effin' bunch,' he squawked as soon as Matt emerged.

'Look, I had no idea—'

'No one gets in there. No one but the effin' big nobs. Them profs of wizardship an' wossname from the Uni. Or Mr Pong and his bleedin' family. Not bleedin tossers like—'

Matt didn't squeeze the vulture's neck *too* tightly, but it was as effective a gag as any he could come up with.

'Just shut up, okay? I have as much idea of what's going on as you do. So, let's cut out the insults and walk.'

———

The biggest shop in the street was called Herod's. It had ten doors and six floors. Matt stood outside and gazed up in wonderment. Beside him, Rimsplitter sulked.

'Let's go in,' Matt suggested, by way of further distraction. He'd got over the vague anxiety of having a vulture with him; many of the things that walked the streets had animals of various descriptions with them as familiars. Rimsplitter didn't object, but his silent agreement was very grudging.

Inside, the air was pungent with incense. The bottom

floor was given over to a perfumery infested with the usual gaggle of female salespeople dressed in short black skirts and dresses; each one was made up, in this case, to look like an extra from *Halloween 4*. Three of them approached with samples as they ran the gauntlet of the closely packed aisles.

'Care to try some Inflagrante, sir?' asked one with chocolate-coloured lipstick.

'Umm,' Matt said, as usual, hamstrung by his desire not to seem rude.

'Guaranteed to render the wearer irresistible to the partner of their choice for twenty-four hours.' She offered a seductive smile. 'Today only, special offer, three scruples of gold for two ounces.'

She did have a lovely smile, and the smell of her made Matt feel a little strange. Suddenly, he was not in a hurry at all. How could he be? He had all the time in the world. Well, this world anyway. The sales assistant's badge read *Naomi*, and the heady mix of rich amber with a hint of patchouli emanating from her was tantalizingly reminiscent of something—or was it some*one*? Gosh, Naomi really did have one very big eye, and under the caked makeup, she had quite a cheeky little scar that ran from one side of her temple to the other. Matt licked his lips and wondered what she was doing after work. Perhaps they could meet up for a drink somewhere and Matt could tell her all about his adventures and see if he could charm his way into her…

A sudden sharp pain in his leg grabbed his attention. He looked down to see Rimsplitter gnawing at him with his wicked beak. 'Oi,' Matt protested. 'What's wrong with you?'

'Effin' zombies. Can't stand 'em.'

'They're zombies?'

'Course they effin' are. Some things are the same 'ere as back home.'

Matt stared at him. 'You're not saying that—'

'I'm not sayin' nothing,' Rimsplitter said. 'But the next time you're in Selfreesers, take a look at 'em. Nothing behind them made-up eyes, mate. They're all effin' doorknobs, I'm telling you. 'Ere, get a whiff of this.'

The vulture hopped over to a stand and picked up a wallet, which he thrust at Matt. Matt held the leather to his nose and with two sniffs, Naomi became less Kate Moss and a lot more an evil Michelle Pfeiffer in *Stardust* after three weeks face down in a river.

They got through the perfumery, a little voice nagging in Matt's head for him to remember where he'd come across Naomi's smell before. He stood stock still, his eyes like fog lamps as the synapses fired in his brain.

'Silvy,' he whispered.

Rimsplitter was more interested in the wafts coming from the food court, but half heard and looked up. 'What'd you say?' The vulture hopped back to where Matt was standing.

'Silvy,' Matt repeated. 'That's what she was wearing in the Carp the other night. Bloody Inflagrante. That was how she got me to bury the hatchet.'

'Lucky it was only the hatchet you buried, mate. Forget Inflagrante, should be called Shotgun Effin' Weddin', if you ask me.'

'I've been a total idiot,' Matt said.

'Well, you're not going to get any bleedin' argument from me on that score. I mean, walkin' straight into the Ghoulshee lair like that, knowin' they were out to get you. Takes a special talent, does that. Only found in total effin' morons. You're an effin' liability, you.'

Matt sighed. Rimsplitter was right. He had been an idiot, wandering off from Kylah's side. And now here he was on a jolly with a vulture while she was stuck to a post somewhere, waiting to be turned into offal porridge. But there wasn't much he could do about it. Matt forced himself to get back to the moment and looked around, his eyes darting from one bizarre thing to the next. 'So, where is everyone?' he asked, feeling the need to comment on the absence of bodies.

'What time is it?' Rimsplitter replied.

Right at the centre of the far wall were two massive hour-glasses next to a pulley and chain system with numerals. 'Says half past one on that clock.'

'That's effin' it, then. S'lunch time, innit. Everyone's effed off.'

'To where? I haven't seen any restaurants.'

'Ah. This is where it gets effin' good. What do you fancy? Italian? Thai?'

Rimsplitter hopped off towards some gently vibrating stairs. They weren't an escalator, but they did move upwards of their own accord once you stood on them. Disconcertingly, once they'd reached the next floor, they kept on going, hovering just above the ground.

'Where are we going?' Matt asked, still a little unsure of his balance.

'Food mall. You got to effin' see this.'

It was not like any of the food malls Matt had seen in his travels to the States or in any of the big British shopping centres like Cribbs Causeway or Bluewater. For a start, it was almost empty, there was no seating, and the only things remotely similar were the garish signs advertising food from different parts of this world—but there didn't seem to be anywhere to buy the food, unless it was from the stunningly dressed temptresses who wandered up and down with samples on trays. The signs were a bit different, too. The oriental flavour was provided by The Great Well of Thailand; there was a Parisburger and something called Insect Bap. Matt made for the girl who stood in front of House of Hinduria. She was smart in a colourful sari, and the food she had on the tray drew him like a moth to a matchstick. He took something on a cocktail stick and munched away, making cooing noises to Rimsplitter as he did so.

'Okay, okay, I get the message,' the vulture said. 'Effin' vindaloo village, it is. Bit too cooked for my effin' liking, though. And the spices play bee-in 'avoc with me—'

'Where do we order?' Matt interjected.

'Oi,' Rimsplitter said to the nice girl, 'table for two.'

She smiled, revealing two incisors with needlepoint sharpness that looked quite capable of aspirating two quarts of type O per minute. 'Follow me.' She shook her head from side to side.

They walked towards a plain door at the end of the House of Hinduria booth, and Matt realised that all the other booths had similar doors. The girl, or whatever she was, opened it and ushered Matt and Rimsplitter through to a candlelit antechamber full of sitar music. A flap of heavy burlap in front of them was pulled back by the biggest bloke Matt had ever seen. He must have been eight feet tall and was bare-chested and bald except for a pigtail lock of hair in the middle of his head. He wore sandals the size of small tugboats and Ali Baba trousers. With a theatrical wave of an arm, he ushered them through into…

Matt's jaw did an impression of a larded guillotine. With one step they were on the shores of a great lake at dusk. The wind was warm and gentle, and banners decorated with strange lettering fluttered overhead. In the middle of the lake stood a white marble palace, whilst ahead, leading down to the shore, were tables covered with white tablecloths, most of them occupied. To their right was a tented kitchen with waiters and cooks working like bees to prepare the food.

'Told you it was effin' impressive, didn't I?' Rimsplitter said.

A waiter appeared at Matt's elbow. 'Can I show you to your table, sir?'

'Um…'

'Need a minute, pal,' Rimsplitter said.

The waiter bowed and moved away.

'But what…how?'

'Transport, mate. That's the effin' truth of it. They can go anywhere at any time through them effin' doors. Bees.'

'But…' Matt was well aware that his contribution to the conversation wasn't improving.

'Don't ask me. S'not physics, but it's pretty effin' neat. Breakfast in New England, dinner in Italy, supper in Calcutta. Effin' brilliant.'

'So, no cars. No energy issues. It's—'

'Un-effin'-believable, I know. Took me a while to get me effin' 'ead around it.'

They wandered down to the shore and back again. Matt explained to the waiter that he wasn't feeling well. He was, in actual fact, famished, but he realised that he had no money. So, they left the restaurant and went back to the street with Matt still buzzing. They wandered again past Mage and Sceptres, and Matt realised as he glanced inside that it was packed with people.

'Hang on,' Matt said. 'What's going on here?'

'Exotic goods sale, mate,' Rimsplitter said. 'Innit.'

Matt went inside. It was laid out like all the other 'real' stores he'd been in back in England. Men's upstairs; women's on the ground floor. There was lingerie, sweaters, even driving gloves. Driving gloves? In a world without anything to drive? Still, that shouldn't have been much of a surprise. They were still selling harpoons in parts of Japan. But this was bizarre. Things he thought of as ordinary were exotic here.

'So, they like this stuff?' Matt asked as a witch with half a dozen witchlings in tow wheeled a trolley overflowing with Spiderman outfits to the checkout.

'They love it. Tees.'

'But if this stuff is so popular, why can't we buy any of their stuff?'

Rimsplitter, spotting a dead mouse under the chinos, gobbled it up. 'We effin' can, you pillock,' he said with his mouth full. 'What about them effin' gift shops with scale models of mythical beasts and tarot cards and dream catchers and whossnames?'

'That's just tat,' Matt said.

'Agreed. But it ain't tat over 'ere. Them things effin' work 'ere. Trouble is, our lot 'ave banned anything in the slightest effin' bit magical, on account of the fact that it might undermine effin' society.'

'They've got a point, I suppose,' Matt considered. 'If

everyone started knowing their future accurately, things would grind to a halt. But this transport thing is… I mean, it would revolutionise travel.'

'Yeah, dream on, Gandhi. The car manufacturers and the bee-in' oil companies are goin' to let that happen, right? Bollocks they are.'

'But no pollution, no global warming—'

'Exactly.' Rimsplitter spat out a bit of fur that had once been the mouse's head. 'Effin' disaster for capitalism and the world economy. Nah, better stick to what we know and watch our world eff itself, I reckon.' Rimsplitter glanced up. 'Eff me, is that the bleedin' time? Come on, or that poncey clerk at the hotel will 'ave my guts for effin' garters.'

CHAPTER THIRTY-FOUR

RIMSPLITTER HURRIED out to the street and Matt followed, along an unfamiliar route that took them off the main drag.

'Where are we going?' Matt asked.

'Shortcut.'

'Are you sure?'

'Yeah, yeah,' Rimsplitter uttered a belligerent squawk.

Matt followed the hopping bird in silence, his thoughts moving at twice the speed of his legs. It was a lot to absorb. That this place existed was a pretty challenging concept to start with, let alone how he'd got here.

Rimsplitter noticed his pensive mood. 'Wossamatter? You're like one of them effin' zombies.'

Matt shrugged. 'It's a lot to take on board, isn't it? I mean, this could all be nothing but a construct of my fevered imaginings. Maybe I'm still in a coma ward having a bed bath. Or maybe they've upped my drugs.'

'Look, you tee, I like you.' Rimsplitter paused, considering. 'Well, at least I don't think you're a total cee. What's 'appened to you is pure bad luck. Crap karma. Ess-aitch 'appens, sunshine. Get over it.'

Matt shook his head ruefully. 'I just wish I knew my place in all of this, that's all.'

'Like me, you mean?'

'Well, not quite like you, but you catch my drift.'

They were still walking. Rimsplitter's shortcut was taking them down ever narrower and darker lanes, flanked by tall buildings that leaned in so much they almost touched at the eaves. Neither of them noticed the figure lurking in a doorway. At least, not until it stepped out into their path and growled. Matt jumped; Rimsplitter squawked. The figure rumbled deep in its throat. It wasn't easy to see any detail, but two yellow eyes gleamed in the darkness under its hood.

'Well, well, lost your way I see, gentlemen. Need any help?'

The voice was gravel and dust. Rimsplitter made an extremely unsavoury noise, and promptly deposited something green and white on the pavement. Matt, having walked home on many an occasion through St. Paul's in Bristol in the early hours, knew the score.

'We're fine, thanks,' Matt said, keeping his head down and walking on. The hooded figure didn't move.

'You look a little anxious,' the figure croaked. 'Perhaps you might feel less anxious if you relieve yourself of those heavy possessions you're carrying.'

'Ah,' Matt said with an apologetic smile. 'I'm in transit, you see. No possessions. None at all.'

'A man always has possessions,' said the figure. 'A few scruples? A nice gem amulet, perhaps?'

Matt shrugged, and Rimsplitter squawked.

'Your parrot doesn't say much,' the figure said.

'Mouth like a sewer. Believe me, it's better when he's like this.'

'Well, if you have no worldly goods, perhaps I can have something else. A little blood, perhaps? Easy enough to trade in these parts.' The figure shifted and allowed a bit more of itself to be seen. Matt shuddered. What was on view included nails like claws and long, curved teeth under the yellow eyes. It reminded Matt a little of Silvy, in her less-guarded moments.

'Not today, thank you,' Matt said and prepared himself to bolt.

'I'm not sure you understand,' the thing replied, and this was accompanied by as disgusting a sucking noise as Matt had ever heard. 'It's not a request.' It fell into a crouch, ready to pounce.

Anxious dread took hold of Matt's neck and poured a glass of ice water down his collar. His fingers tingled. His breathing seized. He should have collapsed in a shivering mess. But something, be it anger or plain stupidity, put all that on hold. He did breathe, and in doing so realised that several thoughts were stampeding through his head.

In the lead was a shard of curiosity. He'd already died once that day and he wasn't sure if, under the rules, he could die again. Still, by the look of those claws, whatever was going to happen was not going to be pleasant. Added to that was the sad realisation that this world, like his own, operated under the same rules of criminality. It seemed that there were victims and perpetrators in all manifestations of the multi-verse, and here he was with a starring role in the age-old story of preying on the innocent. Although thinking of Rimsplitter as innocent made his head hurt. But more than anything, Matt felt a burgeoning anger as the injustice of it all bubbled up inside him, and he heard himself mentally voice the two most plaintive words in the English language.

Why me?

He hadn't asked to meet Silvy, or be almost killed in an RTA, or end up stabbed through the heart in a baked bean tin. Now, to cap it all, here he was being mugged by a Nosferatu look-alike in an alley in Deity alone knew where. It took the effin' biscuit, as Rimsplitter would undoubtedly have said. Matt looked his assailant in the eye and saw the pupils constrict into vertical ovals. There was nothing he could do. The thing was twice his size and had home-grown weapons and teeth like tusks. There was no one about. No witnesses. No help to call for.

Matt shook his head again. It was like all those pornographi-cally voyeuristic TV programmes that showed CCTV footage of feral youths on the streets attacking innocent bystanders. Programmes with names like *Night Cops: War On The Streets*, or something equally reassuring. The kind of programme where you wished that once, just once, a group of revelling rugby players would come around the corner at the very moment the hooligans started beating up on the old granny. That, just once, the victim got lucky and the bad guys got what was coming to them.

Take the here and now. All that needed to happen was for a bolt of lightning to come down from the sky and strike old nosy here on the head. Or for the git's cloak to get caught on a rusty nail sticking out of the street sign above its head so that, as Matt and Rimsplitter dodged, it would snag. Snag and tighten so that the knot holding it tied around its neck would depress the pressure point in its carotid and send a message to the vagus to slow its black heart enough for it to pass out.

But things like that didn't happen in real life. Fate, in Matt's experience, had nothing to do with fairness, and was more like Cruella De Vil on amphetamines. Yet a small glimmer of understanding began to glow in the dim recesses of Matt's brain. Something trapped in the corners of his memory stirred and stretched and turned over, something that had happened in Oxford with Mr Porter in the kid's playground. He'd heard crows cawing and…there was an odd pricking sensation somewhere behind his eyes.

'Rimsplitter,' Matt hissed. 'Do exactly what I do, okay?'

There was no reply from the bird. Matt risked a glance and saw the vulture cowering, his feathers ruffled and his head bowed.

'Shit,' Matt said. He grabbed the bird by its neck, feinted left but went right. The thing before them, unaccustomed to any sort of resistance from its terrified victims, stood momen-tarily confused. But having twisted left, it read the feint and lunged right, its timing instinctively perfect. The claws were out and primed to meet Matt's neck as he ran beneath the outstretched arms. Once in the soft flesh, they would not let go, and were destined to find those vital veins and arteries to sever and pop.

But that initial turn to the left induced by Matt's feint *did* cause the thing's cloak to billow upwards.

Was it— Could it—

Matt didn't hang about to see what happened next. He kept his head down and ran. But he heard the sound of material ripping. Heard a strangled gurgle as he passed beneath the reaching arms. Heard the *whoosh* as the claws somehow missed their target and flailed at fresh air inches from his jugular. Fuelled by adrenaline and terror, and with Rimsplitter under one arm, he covered a hundred yards in less time than it took Usain Bolt to pack his lunch box.

When Matt eventually slowed enough to look behind him, the thing was lying in a heap on the ground with its cape ripped and torn. Dangling from the street sign above, a matching fragment of material fluttered in the slight breeze like a trapped moth in a spider's web.

CHAPTER THIRTY-FIVE

AFTER TWO MORE SPURTS OF don't look behind you stitch-inducing sprinting, Matt finally let the vulture go. Rimsplitter took off and flew upwards, squawking as he went. Matt followed until they reached Prestige Street. There, the vulture glowered on the cobbled pavement, parading up and down, unfurling and furling his wings. It reminded Matt a lot of his five-year-old nephew when he wanted to pee.

'Wow,' Matt said, gulping in air. 'That was a bit close.'

'*Close*? Effin' *close*?' Rimsplitter spluttered. 'That's like saying Hitler was a bit naughty. That was Jock the effin' Reaper, man. You just laid out Jock the effin' Reaper.'

'I didn't lay him out,' Matt gasped, hands on knees as he sucked in air. 'We were lucky.'

'You did something, I effin' saw you. He was ready to make us into an 'uman-vulture sausage mix, but you, you was doin' effin' calculations. I saw you. What did you effin' do?'

'I don't know,' Matt said. 'I just thought that it would be great if luck was with us for once, and if I went left and his cape got caught on that nail and…'

Rimsplitter tilted his head with wary suspicion.

'Look, it was a fluke,' Matt said with a shrug.

'But it weren't, were it?' the vulture said, his beady eyes

narrowing. 'I could see it in your effin' face. It was like you remembered somethin'. It's 'appened before, 'asn't it?'

'No…well, maybe.'

'See, I effin' knew it. P'raps you're hortistic, you know, like one of them servants.'

'Savants.'

'Yeah, that's them. You've got the gift, mate, that's what you got.'

'The only gift I've got is that I can touch the tip of my nose with my tongue. Let's go.' Matt didn't like where this was all going.

'Oh, no. You're comin' with me. Come on.' Rimsplitter hopped back up to the main street.

'I thought we had to get back.'

'Five effin' minutes. Come on.'

A long sigh escaped Matt's lips, but he followed the vulture anyway. Because the truth was that he had nothing to rush back for. Whatever was waiting, it was waiting as a Kylah-free existence, and there was no point in hurrying towards that. Rimsplitter flew up, circled twice as he waited for Matt to catch up, and then landed again.

'Next street over. This bloke's got a shell and pea game goin'.'

'Shell and pea?' Matt groaned, but the vulture was already moving.

It was a classic set-up—a card table covered with a baize cloth, three walnut shells, a dried pea, and a hand-drawn sign that read:

Onley 5 scruples a bette

A good crowd of thirty or more had gathered. At the front of the semicircle of onlookers was the hustler giving the spiel. Matt surmised that there would be a ringer or two in the audience and, judging by the exaggerated congratulations being heaped upon a youngish man with a jauntily battered hat, one of them had won a game. Matt watched as a few mugs put down their money and lost. They might as well have had signs that read *Gullible Punter* pinned to their backs.

'What's this all about?' Matt whispered to Rimsplitter.

'Time to see what you're made of mate.'

'This is a scam. I'm not interested.' Matt turned away.

'No? What about this poor bee? Ain't you the slightest interested in 'im?'

An elderly man with a walking stick and a shabby cloak pushed his way through to the front and pointed a knobbly finger at the hustler.

'How come that man won?' he demanded. 'You've taken fifty scruples from me and I haven't won once.'

'Luck of the draw, Granddad,' the conman said, his cheeky smile not slipping a millimetre. 'Now, put down your money or make room for someone else.'

'You've got all my money,' the elderly man said, scowling.

'That's the way it goes, old-timer.'

Matt watched as one of the henchmen in the audience took the old man's arm and pulled, none too gently.

'Let go of me.'

'Piss off,' said the henchman, easily sixty years younger than the old man.

Matt bristled. 'What do you want me to do?' he hissed at Rimsplitter.

'Win his effin' money back for him.'

'With this lot? They're crooks.'

'Give it a go,' Rimsplitter said with conviction. ''Ere, look, I found twenty scruples on the floor over there.' The vulture dropped a purse in Matt's hand.

'You didn't nick this, did you?'

If vultures' eyes could ever become innocent ovals, Rimsplitter's did at that moment. Matt shrugged. He'd never won anything in his life, but it wasn't like he had anything of his own to lose.

'Leave him be,' he said to the henchman manhandling the old man. 'He's with me.'

A slight but definite look was exchanged between the

hustler and the heavy, who let the old man's arm drop. It was a look of pure 'spot the mug' understanding of the kind one shark might give another with a shoal of tuna balled up between them. The hustler began shuffling the walnut shells around, deftly covering and uncovering the pea. Matt put the money down and the hustler stopped. 'What'll it be? Left, right, or middle?'

Matt had no idea. He'd never won so much as a ring in a Christmas cracker. But he didn't like this little bunch of crooks. Not when they were preying on innocent old men. He stopped guessing and tried to think back to what had happened in the alley. He'd imagined the best-case scenario, hadn't he? Right. Wouldn't it be brilliant if he got the shell game right for once? And got it right ten times in a row.

'Left,' he said. The shark smile on the hustler's face didn't falter. He picked up the shell and the crowd applauded as the pea was revealed.

'It's your lucky day, my friend. How about another game? Double or nothing? You've already won once. Maybe you're on a lucky streak.'

'Maybe I am,' Matt said and watched as the hustler did his thing again. Matt went for right this time, and again the pea was revealed. Again, the hustler went through his spiel and Matt could hear the audience begin to whisper with excitement.

'This time he'll palm the pea and drop it under whatever shell you don't chose,' Rimsplitter whispered out of the side of his beak.

'How come you know so much?' Matt asked him. The vulture shrugged. Matt guessed that, if his beak had allowed it, he'd have started whistling. Matt waited until the hustler had finished and then said, 'Middle.'

The hustler smiled and turned over the middle shell. There was no pea. Then he went for the reveal. He turned over the left and it, too, was empty. He sent Matt an arched eyebrow smile full of mock commiseration, turned over the right shell and…there was still nothing. Laughing airily, he looked into the shell and put a desperate finger in to see if the pea had stuck to the bottom. But it wasn't there.

The hustler's epiglottis made a gurgling noise as he tried to swallow. He held up his hands to the crowd in confused entreaty and in so doing dislodged the pea, which trickled out from inside his sleeve, hit the table, bounced twice and finally came to rest next to the empty shells.

'Cheat,' shouted someone from the back.

'Oh, dear,' Matt said, feeling that slight prickle behind his eyes again. 'Silly pea.'

The crowd murmured in an unpleasant way. One that that spelt mob.

The hustler's smile had done a bunk; from the look of him, he desperately wanted to do exactly the same. But a glance at the mob told him that would be a very bad mistake.

'Once more?' Matt offered. 'Why don't we make it for a hundred scruples this time? Tell you what, double or quits.'

Matt could feel the presence of the two henchmen encroaching behind him. He watched the hustler move the shells. He was good, slick and smooth. But as he neared the end of his little show, he began sweating and the smile slipped again. Matt saw an exchange between the henchmen and the hustler once more, a little panicky flick of the eyes and a half-hidden mouthed word inside the toothy grin. 'Stuck.'

Something was obviously wrong, but the hustler was a pro. After all, Matt had one chance in three of being right, even if the pea wasn't doing what it should. The odds were with *him*, not with Matt.

'Left,' said Matt and the hustler shuddered.

'Are you sure?' asked the hustler in a warbly attempt at smarm. 'Take your time. I'm a fair bloke, me. I'll give you one more chance to change your mind.'

'No, thanks,' Matt said and was pleased to see a bead of sweat run down the hustler's forehead in a single, fearful rivulet as he lifted up the left shell. The pea nestled there, vibrating slightly, as if something were making it stick where it was instead of flying off where the hustler had wanted it to go. The crowd cheered. The hustler looked like he'd swallowed a live tarantula.

'Aren't you the lucky one?' he said, sounding as if he was trying to bring the tarantula back up.

'Okay, I think that will do for today,' Matt said and scooped up his winnings. He gave half to the elderly man and half to Rimsplitter, with instructions that he find the owner of the purse. Rimsplitter's beak split open in what would have been an ear-to-ear grin, except that he had no ears and, with a beak instead of lips, couldn't grin. As Matt walked away, he was suddenly flanked by the two young heavies that had been a part of the shell and pea gang. They joined in with his step and leaned in close.

'We ever see you 'round in this vicinity again, we're going to give you a new hole to breathe through. Right below your Adam's apple,' one whispered, with a steely glint in his eye.

Matt looked at the man threatening him. He was short and squat, with an unpleasant, gummy smile. His companion, meanwhile, had more scars than Bill Sikes's bull terrier and carried a lethal-looking four-inch stiletto in his hand.

'Threatening people is such a negative way of dealing with situations, don't you think?' Matt said. He stopped and faced them on the pavement. 'Oh, and by the way, I'd be careful of that knife in case you cut yourself.'

'Funny man,' said the one with the scars. From the way his mouth kept working, it looked like what little patience he had was wearing as thin as the strap on a pole dancer's thong. 'They call me Jimmy Blades, 'cos I'm really good with knives,' he added.

'Yeah,' said the toothless one. 'Likes sharpening them on other people's rib cages.'

'Really?' said Matt. 'Well, don't say I didn't warn you.'

'Funny man,' Jimmy Blades repeated, the knife glinting in the light of the afternoon sun. It was still glinting as the protruding leg of a very large wardrobe tied to the back of a trundling cart hit him square on the side of the head. He yelped and stumbled, depositing the knife in the toothless one's thigh as he did so, causing his fellow thug to hop violently, lose his footing, and land headfirst in the mountainous pile of horse shit steaming in the gutter below.

Matt walked away and left them to it.

Rimsplitter joined him at the entrance to Prestige Street. 'Spot of effin' bother, was there?'

Matt shrugged. 'Bit of bad luck, that's all.'

'Yeah,' Rimsplitter said. 'Luck. Funny thing, that.'

'It is, considering the way mine usually goes.'

'But that's in your world. Over 'ere, looks like you make your own effin' luck.'

Matt frowned. 'What, exactly, does that mean?'

'It means that we need to find a casino that admits vultures.'

'No way. Come on, let's go back to the concierge.'

CHAPTER THIRTY-SIX

Rimsplitter protested all the way to the lifts, but Matt was having none of it. His mind was made up. They retraced their steps and emerged through door number 97 onto the balcony in the Trans-Dimensional Holiday Inn. Rimsplitter, still sulking, hopped to the balcony edge and looked down to the floor of the lobby below. Whatever it was he saw cheered him up no end.

'Aye-aye, something's up,' he said.

'What do you mean?' Matt asked.

'There's a cushion on the seat at the interview table. Must be hexpectin' someone bleedin' important.'

Matt didn't say much going down in the lift. His palms were sweating. And the ingratiating smile that the stroppy clerk now had wasn't helping in the slightest. It looked like it had been cut out of a magazine entitled *Grin and Bear It* and stuck on with glue.

'Ah, Mr Danmor, sorry to have kept you waiting, sir. Interesting visit, was it?'

'Very…enlightening,' Matt said, frowning at the 'sir.'

'Excellent. Um, since you were here, instructions have come down from head office.'

'Head office?'

'And may I say, sir,' oozed the grey man, 'what a pleasure it is to meet someone as gifted as you are, sir.'

'Has Rimsplitter put you up to this?' Matt demanded. 'Gifted' sounded like one of the vulture's euphemisms for something highly derogatory.

'I'm sorry, sir?' The clerk's smile slipped into confounded innocence.

Anger bubbled away in Matt's head. Didn't anyone give a straight answer anymore? In a tetchy voice, he said, 'Can you please tell me what the hell is going on?'

The grey clerk turned a shade greyer and tried to swallow. 'Me? I…oh no, I couldn't possibly. I…'

'Oh, for crying out loud,' Matt said. From somewhere, a breeze rattled through the building.

The grey clerk let out a high-pitched trill of laughter. 'Please, Mr Danmor, please calm yourself. I'll get someone, shall I?'

He disappeared into the back room. There was the sound of scraping chairs and urgent whispering. An instant later, another man appeared. This one had a jowly, round, poached face with droopy eyes that made him look disconcertingly like a bloodhound. Like the clerk before, he wore a white shirt and funereal black tie, but this time, the suit was a darker shade of grey. The man held out a hand.

'Mr Danmor, my name is Thornton. Can I be of assistance?'

Matt took the hand. It was papery and dry. 'I hope so. Can you please tell me what I'm supposed to do next?'

The pleasant smile froze on Thornton's lips. 'Ah. Perhaps, if you'd like to take a seat at the table here?'

Thornton indicated the seat with the cushion. Sighing, Matt sat and watched warily as Thornton sat opposite him and took an expensive-looking pen out of his pocket.

'You see, we don't have many like you through here,' Thornton began.

Matt didn't let him finish. 'See, that's precisely what I mean. Someone like me? What, exactly, am I like?'

Some papers on the desk riffled in the wind where there could not have been any.

'I am so sorry about that,' Thornton said, running a finger around the inside of his collar. The pen in Thornton's hand began to ooze black ink.

'You're leaking,' Matt said.

'Yes,' said Thornton with a fixed smile. 'Fancy that. Lucky I took it out of my pocket when I did, eh?'

'Very.' Matt's eyes narrowed. 'Almost as if you knew it was going to happen.'

Thornton shifted in his seat. 'The truth is, Mr Danmor, we're not entirely sure what exactly *is* going to happen next. To you, I mean. Not to my pen.'

'Is that usual?'

'No,' Thornton said with a vehement shake of his head, 'it isn't. Not at all. When I said before that we don't get many like you through here, that was not strictly true.'

'Oh?'

'The fact is that we've never actually had *anyone* like you. You see, you're not in our system, and that shouldn't happen.'

There was a crack as one of the legs of Thornton's chair popped out of its joint. Thornton threw out a hand and managed to stop it from displacing entirely. His fixed grin didn't falter. Matt stared at him.

'If I'm not in your system, what am I doing here?'

'Exactly. We've been into the archive and looked through all the files. There is some record of "travellers" who can flit between here and there,' Thornton said.

'You're saying I'm one of them?'

'It's possible.'

'And what about what happened to me in New Thameswick?' Matt quickly explained about Jock the Reaper and the shell and pea game.

Thornton whimpered.

'Well?' Matt asked.

Thornton swallowed loudly. 'Textbook. Though I never thought I'd see it.'

'See what?' Matt yelled, finally abandoning patience.

The chair under Thornton collapsed, depositing its occupant on the floor. Matt stood and held out a hand, which Thornton politely declined. He fetched another chair and sat again. But a small coin slowly began to roll along a tortuous and sloping path towards a ledge in Matt's brain.

'Did I just do that to your chair?' Matt asked quietly.

'I think so,' Thornton said and then added, 'the clue's in your name.'

'Mathew?'

'No, your surname. It's Celtic, from the Cornish and Welsh. It means "from the sea".'

'Right,' Matt said, doing his best to contain the frustration that continued to build.

There was an ominous cracking noise from the leg of the table. Thornton looked alarmed. 'If I could ask you to try to remain calm, Mr Danmor, it would help.'

'I *am* calm,' Matt said. It sounded a little forced coming out through his gritted teeth.

'Danu was a Celtic God, and she had enemies: The Formorians. As I was saying, your name, Danmor is an amalgamation of the two. Rare in itself, but not much different from Shipwright or Potter, which do what they say on the tin, as it were, or at least did at one time.'

'But that's a load of bollocks,' Matt said. 'My dad was an accountant and my mother was a part-time teacher. Mythical gods don't come into it.'

'Ah, yes, but we are talking of origins here. From a very long time ago. I'm suggesting genetic threads that can weave through many generations until they wind their way to the surface.'

It made Matt sound like a piece of old carpet. 'Okay, so what were these Danu and Fomor gods *of*, exactly?'

Thornton's smile was joined by two bushy, arched eyebrows.

'They weren't exactly comfortable bedfellows. The Danann were supposedly all for civilisation, whereas

Fomorions revelled in chaos. The result of their unlikely alliance resulted in offspring who were very talented when it came to controlling their own destiny.' He paused and then added, drily, 'Especially when it came to the matter of chance.'

The rolling penny in Matt's head navigated a couple of bumps before finally plummeting over the edge and clattering loudly into place. 'Luck,' he said, half to himself.

'For want of another word, yes,' Thornton swallowed as he said it.

'Rimsplitter's right. I make my own, don't I? Here, at least.'

'We think it may not be wilful. There appear to be other factors involved.'

Matt let out a leaden sigh. 'Can I have that in English, please?'

'There is an emotional element,' Thornton explained. 'Anger or sadness may trigger what appear to be random or chaotic occurrences, but which tend to be beneficial to you.'

'Synchronicity,' Matt said.

'Pardon?' Thornton looked confused, and that pleased Matt enormously.

'Another word for it. What happened to your chair and almost to the table…it's because I was getting a bit tetchy?'

Thornton nodded.

Matt thought furiously. 'Let me get a couple of things straight. First of all, am I dead?'

'Corporeally, yes. But then again, given your situation, that's up to you.'

Matt took a deep breath and tried not to let the riddles get to him, but the table leg creaked again. 'How can it be up to me? Either I am dead or I'm not. Either I can go back to Uzturnsitstan or I can't.'

Thornton squirmed. 'If you wanted to go back, no one could stop you. But what state your body might be in, I couldn't say.'

'So, if I'd had my head chopped off…'

'That would make things quite difficult.'

Matt's brain was travelling at a hundred and fifty on the flat, trying to catch up with the implications of Thornton's words. 'But my head has not been chopped off, has it?' Matt mused. 'What if someone took the knife out of my chest and levered up the worst of the depressed skull fractures?'

Thornton made a hand gesture that suggested nothing was impossible.

'One more question. Can I take *him* with me?' Matt nodded towards the vulture.

'Would you want to?'

'He's good in a crisis.'

'From what we've seen, he's usually the cause,' Mr Thornton muttered. 'But in answer to your question, yes, you can take him with you. Mr Danmor, you're something of a 400 lb gorilla when it comes to situations like this.'

'A 400 lb gorilla?'

'As in, "What does a 400 lb gorilla do with his spare time?"'

'You've lost me.'

'"Anything he bloody well likes",' Mr Thornton said and nodded sagely.

CHAPTER THIRTY-SEVEN

Rimsplitter was standing next to a pot plant, staring at his reflection in the polished surface of a black marble pillar as Matt strode across the lobby.

'Think the wattle's a bit too effin' red?' Rimsplitter asked, lifting his chin. 'Could 'ave gone a tad more bleedin' orange if you ask me. But like, red goes with me eyes. What do you think?'

'I think you look exactly like a red-headed vulture should,' Matt said carefully.

'Yeah, that's what the effin' ladies all say.'

'So, you do have lady friends, then?'

'Wouldn't call them friends exactly. If it moves, eff it, I say.' Rimsplitter turned and glared at Matt. 'Anyway, never mind about me. How did it go with the bleeder at the desk?'

'Um…it went surprisingly well, I think.'

'What you comin' over as? Halsatian? 'Usky? Black Lab? Everyone wants to be a bleedin' dog. 'S that loyalty thing. I got money on you bein' an effin' canine person. Although, why anyone would want to be dependent on others for their food effin' beats me.'

'As opposed to depending on other people dying for their food, you mean?'

'Oi, we're the ultimate recyclers, us vultures. Bleedin' green all the way through.'

'The only thing that's green all the way through, in your case, is what comes out of your back end.'

Rimsplitter did a broody shoulder hunch, which, being a vulture, wasn't that difficult. 'Come on, what sort of effin' dog?'

'I'm not coming back as a dog. In fact, I'm not coming back at all. I'm *going* back, instead. As me.'

Rimsplitter let out a squawk and began flopping around. He squawked and flopped so much that Matt thought he was having a fit. Finally, he calmed down enough to say, 'You're an effin' comedian, did you know that? I haven't laughed so much since my mate Elvis—so called 'cos he likes to eat 'em while they're still shakin', rattlin' and a-rollin'—landed on that effin' bloke thinking he was in his death throes, when actually 'e was just asleep and dreamin'. Got made into an 'eaddress for his troubles. You stupid cee. No one goes back. It's im-effin'-possible. Everyone knows that. Even cees like you should effin' know that.'

Matt waited for the tirade to finish. 'Well, I asked, and they said yes. There's the gorilla factor, you see.'

'What effin' gorilla?'

'Me. I'm the gorilla.'

Rimsplitter shook his head. 'You're goin' back as a gorilla?'

'In a way. I've got a free pass. I can do what I want. And what I want is to go back and reclaim my body. I was wondering if you'd come with me?'

'Me?' Rimsplitter choked on the word. 'Me, go back? Them Ghoulshee aren't too bleedin' choosy about what they eat, or use to check the weather. Don't want me entrails on the six o'clock news, thanks very effin' much. They used Tarquin to check for squalls and then 'ad the rest of 'im with some bleedin' yams last week. Bees. What the eff do you want to go back for, anyway?'

Matt shrugged. 'Mr Porter, Keemoch, and Birrik. Kylah. Mostly Kylah. Maybe I can do something.'

'You against a million-plus Ghoul-effin'-shee? 'S like a bunch of nuns playin' Argentina in the World Cup final. Effin' suicide.'

Rimsplitter was, of course, right. An alien looking in on such situations would have been laughing like a kallapsian tree venk at the very thought. But what did aliens know? This was a peculiarly human bit of insanity Matt was contemplating. Because there was a good chance this wouldn't work. Every other human he knew was meant to be descended from chimpanzees, but that didn't mean they could hang from a tree with one arm and peel a banana with their feet at the same time, at least not without a lot of practice and a safety net. So even if Matt *was* descended from the gods of chaos, and even if he *could* get robbers to tie themselves in knots and fraudsters to mess up and expose themselves in New Thameswick, there was no way of knowing if he could do any of that at home or in Uzturnsitstan.

He'd had no evidence of being able to so far, but he had to try something. It was the same instinctive, illogical feeling that made ordinary people jump into icy rivers to save drowning kids. Leaping fully clothed into freezing water did about as much for your chances of survival (even if it is likely to up one's sperm count by a notch or two) as drinking the venom of a beaked sea snake. It flew in the face of every Darwinian principle ever espoused. Yet, people still did it.

Bloody human nature.

Matt looked over at Thornton, who continued to beam at him across the lobby.

'Nah, forget it.' Rimsplitter was still blathering on. 'Let's you and me find a nice little gamblin' den. Now we know that you're the luckiest bee in existence; we could take the cees to the effin' cleaners. There's this little country called Vietlombardia, nice-lookin' girls who can play ping-pong without bats for you, and sweet young, hooded vultures for me.' He made a noise that was presumably the avian equivalent of a lasciv-ious grunt.

Matt winced. *God, he's insufferable. What he needs is a short sharp shock. Like, if his feathers all suddenly fell out, that would certainly shut him—*

It happened so fast that Matt could only gawp in horror.

'Is it me, or has it become effin' cold in here all of a sudden?' Rimsplitter said. 'As I was sayin', Vietlombardia—'

'Rimsplitter,' Matt said, cutting the vulture off mid-flow.

'What?'

Matt nodded at the polished marble pillar, and Rimsplitter swung around.

The vulture leapt three clear feet in the air. He let out a strangled squawk and flapped his wings frantically. But being featherless and consequently aerodynamically knackered, he landed flat on his naked backside with a thud. The tirade that followed contained more 'bees' and 'cees' than a list of brassicas.

'Rimsplitter,' Matt said after a long two minutes.

'Don't even effin' *look* at me,' the vulture wailed. 'Gallopin' halopecia, that's what I got. Ess-aitch a brick, I'm *bald*.'

'Rimsplitter,' Matt said, more firmly this time, 'look at me.' Matt thought about how much better the vulture might look re-feathered.

'What for? Effin' 'ell, I'm effin' bald, I'm effin' ruined, I'm...' Rimsplitter turned to look at himself again and stopped. There followed a frantic three minutes of pacing up and down, while wings, breast, and tail were inspected for damage and the feathers that were now once more in place got preened. Rimsplitter swivelled his head, very slowly, back towards Matt. 'You did that, didn't you?'

Matt nodded.

'So, if I don't come with you, I can stay here, but effin' naked, is that it?'

'I need someone to do the repairs,' Matt said, hands up in apology. 'You're all I've got.'

'Repairs? What effin' repairs?'

Matt explained about what he had in mind and the vulture listened. When he'd finished, Rimsplitter told him, 'You're effin' mental, you know that?'

'Probably. But I need your help.'

'Fine,' Rimsplitter said. 'What effin' choice do I have?'

'You have a choice. I did the feather thing to shut you up.'

The vulture glared at him and slouched in his usual position. 'Nah, I'll come,' he said. 'Why not? Besides, if I stay here and go for an optimal environment like the Kruger National Park, I'll only get effin' bored waiting for a tiger to mangle an ibex so I get fed. At least I'll get some effin' action with you. Though I can't see it lasting very bleedin' long.'

'Thanks,' Matt said, before heading back to Mr Thornton to get directions.

On his instruction, they exited the lobby through a door to the left of the reception desk and found themselves in a smaller lobby, which looked much more opulent. On the desk was a sign that read 'VIP Guest Services.' Another grey-suited man, complete with sycophantic smile, greeted them. It was clear that they'd been expecting him. The concierge gave Matt a small pill.

'For the pain,' he said, with a very knowing smile, and pointed them in the direction of a door marked *Returns*.

'Thing is,' Rimsplitter said, hopping towards the door, 'I'm not sure what the eff I'm supposed to do. I mean, *you're* okay 'cos you're a bleedin' freak, but I'm not certain I'm meant to do inter-dimensional travel.'

'It's okay,' Matt assured him. 'Really.'

'Really?' Rimsplitter said, 'So—'

Matt put the pill in his mouth, put his right hand on the door handle, and shot his left hand out to grab onto the vulture's neck. Rimsplitter let out a strangled squawk as Matt dragged him across the threshold and fell. Matt flailed into emptiness and let go of the bird as everything went black. It lasted no more than a few seconds, and then falling was replaced by a searing pain in his chest and shoulder. It was the sort of pain that left you speechless in a gagging, open-mouthed, can-someone-please-kill-me kind of way, a horrible sensation of drowning and choking all at the same time. There was no air, just the pain and a vague awareness of how stupid an idea all of this was. He remembered the pill and swallowed it. The pain in his chest grew, if anything. In fact, it was as if someone was trying to yank a six-inch blade from between his ribs.

Oh, right.

There was a disgusting sucking noise, and air began to rush in through the hole. Matt tried to breathe and couldn't. The feeling of drowning got worse. Matt forced himself to think. Think about how he might have been really lucky if the blade had slid between the organs instead of through them, and how it might be if the sucking wound in his chest suddenly sealed itself and if bushes had cushioned his fall instead of those hard and craggy rocks. All one in a million chances, he knew, but...

CHAPTER THIRTY-EIGHT

MATT OPENED HIS EYES. He was lying on a narrow bank near a river, surrounded by half a dozen vultures. Some of them had bits of his scalp in their beaks, while one had a long and wicked-looking blade.

'Thanks,' Matt croaked.

The one holding the blade dropped it and said, 'Don't mention it, you effin' bee.'

'Was it difficult?' Matt asked, gingerly moving his bruised, but no longer smashed, shoulder.

'Took four of us to drag that blade out. Nearly sliced off me effin' talons.'

'Sorry.'

'The skull fractures, they were the worst. S'been like effin' ER. Lucky Jeremy 'ere was an effin' dentist, once. Struck off for fondlin', he was. Still, knew his way around your 'ead. Couple of them shards of skull was in deep, I'll 'ave you effin' know.'

'I appreciate it.' Matt felt his skull. There were a couple of impressive bumps, but it seemed intact.

'So, no broken bones, then?' Rimsplitter asked.

'No,' Matt said. 'I suppose I'm just lucky.'

The vultures all laughed.

'What's so funny?' Matt asked.

''S just we don't usually get to see marinade turn back into walking flesh and blood. 'Effin' 'ysterical, that's what it is.'

Matt nodded, delighted to have provided an afternoon of entertainment for a bunch of scavengers. 'I'm here all week. Now, I need the quickest way to the Rendering, please. Once I'm there, your job is done. I don't expect you to do anything else.'

'Okay,' said Rimsplitter. 'The boys 'ave already been to check out the picnic site. Follow us. Oh, and it might be just as well if you 'ave an effin' dip in that there pool. At the moment, you're all dust and blood, and there are things in that jungle that would consider them the equivalent of a bleedin' sherbet dip.'

Matt got up with great caution and shook out the stiffness. He caught his reflection in the pool and splashed water on his face. When he looked again, there was no reflection. He'd completely forgotten the Krudian anomaly but felt a lot better once he remembered it. Being invisible might have all kinds of advantages. His clothes, though, were very badly stained, and it would have taken a whole box full of Radiant biological and two cycles on the industrial-waste setting to get them clean. He took them off instead and stood up, completely naked.

The thing about being naked is that you feel such an idiot with all that stuff flapping around. He hoped that the Krudian thingy was permanent, and that it wasn't going to wear off when he got close to Kylah. If it did, he'd either feel very foolish or have somewhere temporary to hang his hat.

He sighed. No, it was no good. Naked wasn't going to work. What were the chances of him having brought across the clothes he'd worn in New Thameswick, which also, through sheer luck, would be Krudian'd up? No reason why it should have happened, but you never knew your luck. Except that, right now, Matt did. He looked back and saw a neatly folded pile next to where the vultures congregated. He slipped them on. They felt fresh and clean.

'Any better?' he asked Rimsplitter.

'Where the eff are you?'

'I'll take that as a yes, then.'

There was a path of sorts. Matt kept an eye on the circling vultures above, just to make sure he was going in the right direction. The jungle was a dense wall of greenery, and Matt would have given much for a machete. It was all made worse by the myriad of large insects that kept flying or slithering or crawling into him, making him feel like a windscreen on the A40 in June. After a struggle, Matt arrived at the edge of a rise. Here, the vegetation thinned and, looking down, he could see the vast plain before him. What was on it made his innards constrict with aching dread.

There were many more captives than he'd thought, upwards of two hundred. Kylah, Keemoch, and Birrik had joined their ranks, all tied to wooden stakes, all facing the hordes of robed acolytes. Between them stood a dozen or so brightly attired officials doing ceremonial things with chalices, urns, and bits of offal.

'Bugger,' Matt said to himself. Stealthily, he made his way down through the bamboo and grass to the valley floor. He moved slowly, conscious of the grey-winged elite guards patrolling the perimeter of where the captives were being held. Although Matt might be invisible, disturbing the grass too much was going to be a sure giveaway. The closer he got, the more he could sense the dread and fear that hung over the captives like a pall.

———

THEY WERE AN ECLECTIC MIX, many of them dressed in exotic clothing, captives from other parts of the Fae world. But some wore Aquascutum, and Matt knew they were from closer to home. Several of them were moaning and crying, hopelessness etched into their faces. Right at the front was Mr Porter. He seemed strangely resigned to his fate. On the far side, Kylah looked defiant and angry as she fought in vain against the ropes that tied her.

Matt crept forward in a low crouch and turned his attention to the priests. A variety of animal carcasses lay at their feet, surrounded by clouds of flies. Most of them had been gutted, and their entrails lay in gently steaming piles over which the Ghoulshee shamans crouched. Occasionally, one or another of these idiots would stand up and shout. It was a lot like watching *Today in Parliament.*

One (whom Matt assumed was their leader, since he wore by far the most ornate costume) put up his hand and turned to address the hordes. Everyone, including the guards, turned to look. Matt took his chance and slipped between two of them, carefully averting his eyes. They were hideous things, complete with arthropod limbs and leathery folded wings. A single appraising glance was more than enough, thank you very much, since the memory of having been intimate with one was pushing through in disquieting Technicolour. A minute later, he was standing on the killing field itself, mere yards behind the head priest, awaiting his pronouncements.

This ought to be good. Just so long as they don't start screaming.

Somehow, Matt knew he would understand what was going to be said, even though he spoke no Ghoulshee. He stared at the high priest, feeling extremely exposed. But since no one was taking a blind bit of notice of him, he assumed that the Krudian anomaly was still firing on all cylinders. The high priest was two feet taller than everyone else, thanks to an elaborate headdress constructed out of feathers, bones, and an animal skull with its jaws prised open. Why, oh *why,* was it always a bloody snake? Mind you, it had been an impressive snake, judging by the size of its fangs.

Matt shuddered.

'Children of the mighty Cthran,' the priest bellowed. Cthran came out sounding like he was trying to cough up a swallowed fly. 'Today is an auspicious day.'

The acolytes all cheered. Well, it was more of an ululating yodel, but Matt got the gist.

'Our harvest has been bounteous.' The priest swivelled and waved a stick adorned with bones and shrivelled reptiles at the captives. 'Soon, there will be blood. Soon, there will be the tearing of flesh and the stretching of sinew. Soon, there will be the RENDERING.'

The ululating volume doubled.

'After years of struggle, after years of patient waiting, the followers of Cthran the Mighty will be appeased. The infidels—'

Matt groaned. Snake gods and infidels. For crying out loud.

'—have tried to crush our faith. In silence we have endured, and in silence we have reviled them for their smug ignorance. We have watched them and waited for our opportunity. For we are Cthran's children, whose spirits will pass into Virhana while the infidels burn.'

Virhana? It sounded like a Japanese people carrier to Matt. Yet the way the acolytes all screamed hysterically in response, the thing must have either won car of the year on *Top Gear*, or was an afterlife that promised eternal joy and an unending supply of rendering refills. Whichever it was, the snake-headed priest was on a roll.

'We are the chosen ones,' he bellowed. 'We shall be silent no more!'

Oh, *puh-lease*. Not another monotheistic religion peddling an afterlife of milk and honey (or blood and human flesh, in this instance) and sod the here and now? Judging by the downtrodden, clone-like appearance of their followers, the priests and the guards were doing an excellent job of repressing any kind of individuality amongst the faithful. Was it some sort of theistic law that gods had to have jealous streaks? A decree that they should all have green eyes that made them view anyone who didn't believe in them, and them alone, as blasphemers? Love me, and salvation is yours; hate me, and death will visit you with sharp macharas and bloody renderings.

He couldn't even blame the Fae, because Matt could think of a million examples, from crusades to pogroms, which proved that Homo sapiens were just as deluded. All in the name of someone's faith. This little circus was another bloody example of what had about as much to do with what was real and meaningful and good as sitting under a box in the shape of a pyramid had to do with curing cancer. What it boiled down to was another way of saying, 'Join my gang, or look out!' All nothing more than a way for some elite bunch of twats in headdresses to impose their bloodlust on a group of gullible, hapless sheep. In fact, Matt was so incensed he couldn't resist the urge to shout out.

'Bollocks.'

He knew it was a mistake immediately. The high priest jumped so far off the ground he nearly lost his headdress. The alabaster guards all swung in his direction, sniffing the air and peering. Swiftly and silently, Matt changed position, keeping moving to confuse the guards. From the way they kept turning this way and that, it was working too. Emboldened, he tried another fusillade of words.

'There is no Cthran,' he yelled.

The acolytes all looked at one another and started burbling. High above, the vultures circled.

'It's just a bloody big snake. Just a bloody, great, greedy old snake, that's all.'

'There is a djinn amongst us. Do not be deflected from the path,' the high priest bellowed.

'The path is crooked,' yelled Matt. 'The Rendering is codswallop. These are people. People who deserve to live.'

'Infidels!' yelled the priest.

'Rubbish!' Matt yelled back. He'd had enough of this jumped-up Quetzalcoatl look-alike by now. He moved in closer so they could have a little one-to-one.

'I know all about your lot,' Matt said as he closed in on the terrifying Anaconda Head. 'Proselytising berks peddling fundamentalist fantasy because of words on a piece of parchment. Grow up, for crying out loud.' He was within ten feet of the high priest now and saw how ugly a bugger he was. Blue paint on his eyebrows, bone earrings dangling from his elongated lobes, two rows of teeth modelled on mud-coloured tombstones. If he didn't have this gobbledygook to occupy his time, no one else would have him, at least not within a length of a bargepole.

But his preoccupation with the high priest had diluted Matt's vigilance. He didn't see one of the alabaster guards moving towards a wooden bucket, and only saw the moving bucket as a blur in his peripheral vision as it was thrown toward him. But the bucket didn't come through the air; the throw was merely a move to launch its contents at speed. A gout of dark red liquid spewed out, and the edge of it caught the high priest on the face and shoulder. He screamed and pawed at his eyes. When they opened, they went straight from fear to narrowed in fury, without passing go. It took Matt three seconds to realise that the fury was aimed in his direction. He glanced down and saw, to his dismay, that half of him was also now covered in dark red stinking boar's blood.

'Shit,' he said.

As all-encompassing and succinct words went, that one was a doozy, since it covered the smell that assailed his nostrils, his predicament, and the contents of his bowels, which were threatening to emerge unbidden.

CHAPTER THIRTY-NINE

THE HORDES OF ACOLYTES BAYED. The priests roared. Matt turned and ran. He made it as far as the beginning of the bamboo forest before the guards caught him. He tried to think about them all toppling over and how lucky he might be if that happened. One or two of them did trip up, but that might simply have been due to their haste in getting to him. Besides, he couldn't think straight; his mind still fumed from the injustice of it all. As they piled in on top of him, all he heard was a blood-curdling yell from the high priest.

'Bring him back alive!'

The ensuing scuffle broke Matt's nose, and his struggles didn't do him much good anyway. There were far too many of them. They dragged him back to the clearing and tied him to a stake. He caught Kylah's desperate glance before they yanked him up and secured his hands. One of the grey-winged insectoid guards took charge and, when it was finished, leaned in close, transmogrifying into sinuous, silky-haired Silvy.

'I homed in on your voice again, Mathew,' she said, grinning. 'Speaking was a very stupid thing to do.'

'Yeah, well,' Matt said. 'It was worth it to get all that off my chest.'

Anaconda Head appeared before him. He looked almost apoplectic with glee as Silvy fell to her knees in supplication.

'Blasphemer!' he roared in Matt's face. The stink was even worse than the stagnant boar's blood. 'As punishment for taking Cthran's name in vain, you will be the first.' He turned back to the unsettled crowds. 'We have awaited a sign,' he sang out, waving a hand at Matt. 'Behold. Here is a non-believer sent to taunt us. Yet Cthran, in his wisdom, has delivered him to us, soaked in the blood of a pig.' He held up both hands theatrically. 'THIS IS OUR SIGN!'

The crowd let out a chorus of ululations.

Matt looked around. Behind and to his left was a woman. She wore a wax jacket and a skirt, an ordinary middle-aged, middle-class woman plucked from a Sunday walk in the country. A pair of broken glasses sat awry on her nose and she was white and shaking with terror, crying softly while murmuring to herself. Matt strained to hear what she was saying. As the crowd's noise fell towards a misguidedly respectful silence, the woman's words drifted across to him. But it wasn't a prayer that he heard; it was a simple, sobbing goodbye.

'Charlotte, Jake, Abby…Mummy loves you.'

Matt wanted to say something to her. He wanted to tell her not to cry, but what could he do? What words did he have that could succour her? And what was worse was that no one would know. There would be a spate of disappearances, but no clues as to why they'd happened. And the disappearances would continue, with no Kylah and Mr Porter to guard the doors. Even worse, the authorities in the Trans-Dimensional Holiday Inn might even give in to these barbaric, snake-loving idiots and make this the Ghoulshee's Glastonbury festival.

Doubt and fear crowded in on Matt. What the hell had he been thinking of, blundering in here like this? There were hundreds of thousands of them, not just one bloke with yellow eyes and a cape. Understanding spread like thick oil through his head. The things that Matt made happen, like making the pea stay where it was under the shell, were possibilities. Improbable possibilities, perhaps, but still possibilities. They weren't miracles. But with a hundred thousand acolytes and more screaming for blood only yards away, what could possibly happen to change things? Even if the Danmor mojo *did* work here, what the hell could he do to a crowd this big?

For years, he'd been plagued by bad luck. Women (well, woman, anyway), career, and now rescue attempt. Naïve and idiotic, that's what his plan had been.

Matt squinted up at the blazing sky. High above, he could see the vultures circling. Rimsplitter was up there, probably laughing his vulture head off and saying, 'I told you effin' so' at the same time. But even as these uncharitable thoughts jostled for position in Matt's tortured brain, he saw one of the birds break formation and start to dive. The thing fell like a stone to a height of a hundred feet, at which point it tapered into a glide and began circling, above the high priest's head, in ever-decreasing loops.

The priest, still busy trying to whip up a good old acolyte frenzy, halted in mid-rant as a lump of vulture guano the size of a hen's egg landed squarely on his shoulder. The priest looked up and waved a fist at the bird, who in turn, made a noise very much like a crow cawing, which was odd, since it definitely wasn't a crow. Matt squinted a bit more. Yep, it was a vulture all right, but why was it making a noise like a crow…

It was Matt's moment of epiphany. That cawing was no accident, nor, indeed, was the little present deposited on Anaconda Head's shoulder. Rimsplitter was sending him a message. Matt had been here before and Rimsplitter had decided to remind him of it. The vulture knew about the kids' playground on Clarendon Street, knew about Jock the Reaper, knew about the fraudster and his henchmen. Rimsplitter was the most unlikely of cheerleaders, and yet… Hope, almost extinguished from Matt's tortured spirit, flared into a flickering bright-blue flame. The odds were massive, the chances minimal, but it was time to find out.

'Oi, Anaconda Head!' Matt yelled to the high priest.

A guard scuttled forward and stabbed Matt in the leg with a spear. 'Careful how you address your betters, infidel.'

'No,' said the high priest. 'Let him speak. It amuses me to hear the whining of a dog who is about to die.'

'I just wondered,' Matt said through gritted teeth and watering eyes, 'Once we're rendered. What then? What else does Cthran want, besides our blood?'

'Cthran is wise. We will send the Doorkeeper's head to the infidel rulers and ask them to meet our demands. If they refuse, we will visit them with our wrath.'

'The wrath of Cthran? Wasn't that the full name of *Star Trek II*?'

'Again, you take Cthran's name in vain. Retribution will be swift, and I guarantee it will be painful.' He half-turned back to the crowd.

Matt coughed to get his attention. 'One more thing. I see that there are no women priests. Why is that?'

Slowly, the priest turned around, his lips pulled back in a dreadful parody of a smile. 'Ordinary women have no place in the priesthood. Cthran decrees that they be mothers...or whores.'

'Decrees, my arse. Little tip—don't use that one in your talk to the Women's Institute.' There was a familiar pricking behind his eyes, and the little blue pilot light flared into a brilliant white flame. 'Oh, and here's a newsflash. The infidels won't give in to you.'

'You are wrong.' The priest smiled and flashed his grave-yard dentition again. 'There are many in the Fae world who consider you vermin. We will be doing them a great service. In return, they will see the error of their ways and follow us.'

Matt nodded. It all sounded ludicrous, but recent history had taught him that the irrational was not to be discounted as a viable belief system, in a fundamentalist sort of way. Too many people had died in concentration camps to deny the horrible truth of that fact.

'These people have families.'

'If you find a scorpion, you destroy it. You care not for its young. That is Ghoulshee wisdom.' The priest sneered with triumph.

'It's Ghoulshee bollocks, more like,' Matt retorted.

Again, the priest smiled horribly. 'It is time.'

Matt watched as the guards and the priests began moving to the edge of the killing field. They were making way.

'Oh, buggery,' Matt said. He was first in line. The first to greet the hacking, maiming, tearing, murdering mob as it swarmed forward. Weirdly, he found that he didn't care much about what they did to him. Having died once, he was getting a bit blasé. But what he did care about, what made all this all so unacceptable, was Kylah and—for some even greater reason—Charlotte, Jake, and Abby. He'd never met them but knew they didn't deserve the months and years of constant heartache that would come from wondering why their mother had left them. Wondering if she'd died or been abducted. Or worse—if she'd opted for an anonymous life away from them because, secretly, she didn't love them. It was a blight they'd be marked by forever. They didn't deserve that.

The bright-blue flame erupted into a spitting jet.

The high priest held up his death-head stick and screamed.

'Behold: The RENDERING.'

As one, the crowd moved forward—a screaming, blood-lust-fuelled, religiously myopic mob.

Matt stared and tried to quell his galloping heart. He thought about Jock the Reaper. He'd imagined the cape catching in the rusty nail, seen the possibility, but what on earth could stop a rushing horde?

Matt squeezed his eyes shut and thought very, very hard.

Ahead of him, the earth began to tremble under the tramping of hundreds of thousands of feet. Matt could feel it under him. Feel the ground resonating…

Resonance.

What if the vibration of those thousands of feet set up a harmonic frequency that matched exactly the natural frequency of some fault line in the limestone rocks beneath the ground, so that…

With a dreadful, rumbling groan, the ground in front of the mob shuddered, and a million cubic tons of earth underwent a seismic shift.

Matt's galloping pulse seized.

A huge pall of dust billowed upwards and blotted out the sun for several seconds. He squeezed his eyes shut. He could barely breathe. When he'd stopped coughing and dared peek, an adrenaline charge brought a triumphant 'Ha!' bursting from his lips.

A sinkhole opened where once had been bleached plain, barely twenty yards in front of the baying mob. It had to be a mile across, a hundred feet deep, and fifty feet wide. With hundreds of thousands of roaring acolytes behind, those in the front couldn't do much about it. Even as Matt watched, the front-runners tumbled in, their bloodthirsty cries giving way to yodels of terror.

It was a scene straight out of *Lemmings III: The Director's Texas Chainsaw Cut*.

The guards and the high priests had escaped the quake, but a new rumble shook the ground, accompanied by a very odd hissing noise. Beneath the priests, the ground bulged ominously. They started running, but it was too late. A huge spout of boiling water gushed upwards, taking most of them with it three hundred feet in the air. Matt dragged his mind back and wondered what these stakes they were tied to might feel like if they'd been made out of balsa wood instead of oak or teak or... Matt wriggled and realised that the stake was now feather-light; he could lift it out of the ground with impunity. He fell backwards. The thin wood crumbled to dust under his weight. It was a simple matter to then slip his arms around beneath him and loosen the knots with his teeth. He turned his attention to his fellow captives and went first to the woman with the crooked glasses. Swiftly, he untied her hands. 'They'll be fine,' he whispered into her ear.

She could hardly speak, but managed to splutter, 'Who?'

'Charlotte, Abby, and Jake. You'll all be fine.'

The woman turned to Matt and looked into his face with gobsmacked wonder. 'Did you do all...*that*?'

Matt could do nothing but shrug. 'I'll clean it all up later, I promise.'

'But who—'

'Just think of me as your average friendly 400 lb gorilla,' he said and left her speechless with relief.

CHAPTER FORTY

From then on, it was a domino effect. Matt and the woman released two more, who released two more, and within ten minutes all the captives were freed; the acolytes, finally having come to a halt on the opposite side of the divide, glared across at them like rabid dogs staring in through a butcher shop window. Matt untied Kylah himself, but instead of the wild embrace of gratitude and more he was hoping for, he got a muttered, 'I think we need to talk.'

'Agreed,' Matt said, watching as she rubbed her wrists to get the circulation going. 'But can I suggest we get out of here first?'

Mr Porter looked a little the worse for wear but was in good spirits as Matt released his bonds again, this time with one of Kylah's borrowed ultra-sharp knives.

'Goodness me, I've never seen anything like it.' Mr Porter massaged a bit of stiffness from his neck. 'Did you have a hand in all that, young Mathew?'

'I think so. It's difficult to be sure.'

'Not that difficult,' Kylah said without looking at him. It earned a questioning glance from Matt, but her expression remained stonily businesslike.

'I can honestly say that I could cheerfully murder a cup of Mrs Hoblip's special tea,' murmured Mr Porter wistfully.

'You mean the one that's not safe to have next to a naked flame?' Kylah asked.

'The very one.'

————

BIRRIK AND KEEMOCH led the evacuation with swift military precision. It was helped by the total absence of any pursuit. One or two of the Ghoulshee made it around the edge of the fissure as the captives began climbing out of the valley. But there was little danger. Even when one of the priests—out for the count after being geysered—sprang up, let out a blood-curdling cry, and lunged for Matt with a poisoned dagger in his hand, it wasn't a problem. He managed two paces before Kylah expertly pierced his neck with a precision ten-metre throw of a gleaming stiletto. The priest gurgled and fell with his arm outstretched.

'Thanks,' Matt said.

'Pleasure,' she replied with a workmanlike shrug as she thrust the retrieved knife repeatedly into Uzturnsitstan's rich soil to clean it.

'Armed and dangerous,' Matt murmured to Keemoch as they watched Kylah round up those priests who hadn't been turned into lobster Thermidor by the geyser, while they waited for reinforcements. He said it with a kind of grudging admiration, as you might describe a finely engineered piece of armament, something to be respected but also feared just a little.

'She's probably saying the same thing about you,' Keemoch muttered.

That left Matt's sails flapping in a dead calm. The implication was insane. Kylah was highly trained and capable, whereas he…he was simply someone who'd stumbled into all this and got lucky.

Extremely lucky.

Okay, rewind that one. Incredibly lucky. He tried to push

Keemoch's thought-provoking *Exocet* to the back of his mind, but all it did was sit there, fizzing like a lit explosive.

He tried to blank it out by busying himself, doing what he could with the shocked and traumatised captives. The last to be released was a young boy of eleven, who'd been snatched on his way home from a local Co-op in Preston, Lancashire, where he'd been buying some bread for his family's tea. His name was Wil, the same as Matt's friendly childhood neighbour. Wil was frightened and very weak from lack of food. Matt found a serendipitous Mars bar in the pocket of his trousers and watched as Wil scoffed it hungrily.

'Better?' Matt asked and got a very definite nod from a lip-licking Wil. 'Right, so follow those two nice Sith Fand.' He pointed towards Keemoch and Birrik, who were a few yards away with some elderly captives. 'Everything's going to be fine.'

'You mean those two elf blokes?' Wil said in his broad Lancashire.

'Yeah, those two elf blokes,' Matt said, grinning at the scathing look he got for his trouble from Keemoch.

They were at the very edge of the clearing, close to where the jungle was trying to march inexorably back to reclaim that which had been taken from it, at the spot where the path led back to the ledge and the baked bean tin exit. *She must have been waiting there,* Matt surmised later. Hurt and angry, waiting for an opportunity to strike back. And strike back, she did. With a vengeance.

Wil was halfway between Matt, who'd decided to wait for Kylah, and Keemoch, who was striding out in front, when Silvy launched herself. It was obvious she was injured from the way she skittered across the space between the jungle and the boy. Her movement reminded Matt very much of a wounded spider. But it was still too quick for anyone to prevent her grabbing Wil.

'We meet again,' she said, tightening her grip around the boy's throat so that he gurgled alarmingly. The snakes' heads at the ends of her cornrow hair all hissed in unison.

'Stop it,' Matt yelled. 'What can you possibly achieve?'

'This is not about achievement; this is about appeasement. Cthran is angry.' Her voice was strained, but Matt couldn't tell if it was from rage or pain. 'Cthran is grievously displeased. Otherwise, how could he have allowed this? Allowed you…' She tightened her grip on Wil's throat some more. 'I can begin the appeasement with this captive. One Rendering is better than none at all.'

A black knife appeared in her clawed hand. Her ice-blue eyes looked ragged inside the red rims of her lids.

Matt shook his head. 'We both know it's me you want. Let him go.'

Silvy spat with derision. It sounded like an angry viper. 'But you are their weapon,' she said. 'I know now that I cannot kill you, but if I kill this boy, I know a part of you will die. That will please me.'

A scarlet balloon of anger burst inside him. He wanted nothing more than to crush this abomination with the heel of his shoe. But he couldn't. He daren't.

'Do not move,' Silvy said. 'If you move, his death will be slow and painful. He will beg you to finish it for him. Do you think you could do that, infidel?'

'Please,' Matt said. 'This is wrong. He's done nothing.'

'The choice is not whether he lives or dies. It is *how* he dies that you will decide.' Ochre dust streaked her white, translucent skin. As visions of evil went, it was a real keeper.

'Please,' Matt said again.

'On your knees, djinn,' Silvy roared.

In his peripheral vision, Matt could see Kylah and the SES watching, inching closer.

'Tell them to stay where they are,' Silvy said.

Matt sent them a glance, and they stopped moving.

'On your knees,' spat Silvy again.

'I'm not a bloody djinn,' Matt said. 'When will you people realise that I'm just an ordinary bloke? I don't want any part of this shitty, mumbo-jumbo heavy—'

He cut himself off because someone opened the door to the fridge in his head again.

'Okay,' he said, trying his best to sound defeated. 'On my knees. Okay.'

Matt let his knees bend, wincing from the stab wound while at the same time twisting his body so that he was at a slight angle to Silvy and Wil. He kept one hand out as evidence of his cooperation and put the other on his blood-soaked thigh as if he was in pain, which wasn't difficult because, by this point, his spear wound was hurting quite a bit. But it also meant that he could slip his hand into his pocket. There was a fifty-fifty chance that it was the right pocket but he, of all people, could trust to luck on that one. His knees met with the ground just as his pocketed fingers met satisfyingly with a crumpled ball of muslin he'd been given as a free sample when he'd visited Harpy Nix in New Thameswick. They'd told him to use it in especially awkward moments. And as especially awkward moments went…

'Good,' Silvy said. 'The knife is quicker than choking. But it might still take a while.'

She brought the machara dagger to within two inches of the boy's right eye, all the while keeping her gaze fixed on Matt.

'Is "Thou shalt be cruel." on the core curriculum with you lot?' Matt asked, feeling his own fury boil inside.

'It's optional. But a girl has to have some fun, eh, Mathew?'

'You're an abomination.'

'I hope you like the sound of screaming,' Silvy said.

Matt saw her eyes slip away from his towards Wil's face. *She needs to see where the knife is going. She's going to bloody do it. Right, Harpy Nix. Let's see what you're made of.*

Matt pulled his hand out from his trouser pocket and, in one fluid movement, threw the *Bachau Oma* in Silvy's general direction. He heard his own breath freeze in his throat. Wil's struggles were buying a vital few moments, long enough for the muslin ball to reach the apex of its arc and begin to fall.

To Matt's astonishment, it stopped for a split second in mid-air before flying unerringly towards the Ghoulshee priestess, shedding its muslin wrapping like the heat shield on a re-entry craft as it did so. In its wake, a comet tail of fine yellow dust hung in the air.

The movement distracted Silvy, but only for the merest second while she registered its presence, and Matt heard her curse. She sent him a hateful glance and jerked the knife towards Wil's face. But it was too late. The single moment of distraction was enough. For at that precise moment, the *Bachau Oma*, which had stopped six inches above Silvy's head, exploded in a puff of yellow dust which fell like intelligent talcum powder, coating the priestess in her entirety whilst missing Wil completely. Everything in the Silvy/Wil vicinity froze. Except for Silvy's eyes. Something was moving frantically behind them. A maniacal anger combined with a silent scream of fear and, much to Matt's delight, sudden, undeniable defeat. No matter how she struggled, her limbs were locked down tight.

It wasn't quite a Wicked Witch of the West moment, but it was damned close. Okay, there was no wailing or collapsing cloak and no voice saying, 'I'm melting! Melting!' But it was just as effective. The yellow powder coating Silvy simply began to fade away into nothing, and Silvy faded with it, leaving Wil standing there, rubbing his throat and face.

Matt was on his feet in an instant and at the boy's side a second later. He pulled Wil's hands away and exhaled in relief when two frightened but intact eyes looked back up at him in bewilderment.

'You okay, Wil?'

Wil nodded. 'What was that?'

'A very bad dream,' Matt said. 'Come on, let's get you out of here.' He took the boy's hand and helped him over to Keemoch, who stood watching in admiration.

'Okay,' said the Sith Fand. 'The sinkhole stuff was good, I'll give you that. But what you just did to that Proturan dirt-bag.' He shook his head, a half-moon smile playing over his lips. 'I'd pay good money to see that again. You going to tell me how?'

Matt shrugged. 'I know some people in retail.'

———

ONCE OUT OF the toilet at Longbridges, they summoned a squad of reinforcements and soon had some tents set up. In one of them, they hung a wooden door, which they used to repatriate the Fae.

In the other tent, the British people were given cups of tea and debriefed, a process that always ended with them wearing a headband with a green stone in it as a 'check' for any head trauma. Once the pentrievant had done its stuff, they were whisked off by SES agents through another door with an onyx handle, to emerge on the streets near where they lived. Confused and a little dazed, but mercifully alive, not one of them was able to explain in detail what had happened. Alien abduction stories had a brief resurgence in the local press all over the UK for a week or two, but then everything settled back down.

Once everyone was despatched to wherever they were from, Keemoch produced a stick of what looked like modelling clay from his backpack and wired it up around the collapsed brick wall that hid the entrance to Uzturnsitstan.

'What's that?' Matt asked, 'Some sort of closing charm?'

'Works like a charm, I have to admit, but this is good old-fashioned modified C-4. They won't get out this way for a long time.'

The last of the SES reinforcements came out of the hole and nodded to Birrik. 'That's it, Sarge. The Ghoulshee, what's left of them, are about halfway up the trail and looking pretty hacked-off. Plus, there's this really ugly vulture who won't take no for an answer when I tell it to bugger off. Bloody menace. Took a couple of potshots at it.'

'I hope you missed,' Matt said, alarmed.

They all looked at him as he ducked back beneath the

wall. 'Give me one minute,' he said as he plunged back into darkness to emerge into the sweltering jungle heat.

'Psst,' Matt hissed. 'Rimsplitter, it's me.'

There was a rustling in the trees; a second later, a very large and cheesed-off vulture flew down. 'About effin' time, you cee. That bleeder shot at me.'

'Sorry, we've been a bit busy. Look, I'm grateful for what you did. That thing with the high priest and the crowing noise…'

'What crowin' noise?' Rimsplitter asked. 'It was me that splattered the snake man, yeah, but the only noise I made was me usual log-layin' strain. Like to build up to one with a bit of effin' vocalisation, you know?'

Matt shook his head. 'Did anyone ever tell you what a lovely turn of phrase you have?'

'Frequently.'

'Well, anyway, if you want to come back through, I'll fix it.'

'Too bleedin' right, I want to,' the vulture said. ''S not safe 'ere anymore. My guts will be some bee's guitar string by mornin' if I stay 'ere.'

Matt led the way and emerged with Rimsplitter in tow, earning plenty of suspicious glances, as well as several of disgust, from the SES boys. Keemoch and Birrik finished wiring up, and everyone retired to the undergrowth while the detonation took place with a satisfying *whump*. There was a bit more to do to ensure that the baked bean tin was well and truly sealed, but finally, Matt stood with Kylah at the broken toilet door, just as they had that morning. The only difference this time was that Rimsplitter stood with them.

'Right,' Kylah said, 'back to HQ. We've got a lot of catching up to do.' She led the way, with Matt bringing up the rear. As Kylah stepped across the threshold, Rimsplitter whispered in a voice that was probably only audible as far away as Birmingham.

'I think you're in deep effin' doo-doo, mate.' He swivelled his head from side to side, which, Matt realised, was a sign to indicate that he was enjoying himself at someone else's expense. 'But if you're goin' to get a rollockin', she's the one to get it from. Oh, yeah, no doubt about it, pal; I would, on a bed of nails with me leg in a bear trap.'

Matt shook his head, grabbed Rimsplitter by his scrawny neck, and yanked him through.

CHAPTER FORTY-ONE

THEY RECONVENED in the offices at Hipposync. Euphoria was in the air, and Matt lost count of the number of times his back was slapped, he was high-fived, or variations of the words 'horse' and 'dark' were hurled at him. Everyone was treated to one of Mrs Hoblip's full-English breakfasts, except for Kylah, who ate something that looked like grey sawdust with yoghurt.

Yet even while he ate—and the food was, once again, astonishingly good—Matt couldn't shrug off a feeling of vague anxiety hanging over him like damp fog. It was almost four p.m. on a Sunday afternoon in late January, and the light was beginning to die outside. It had only been nine hours since they'd left that very room to enter the baked bean tin that was Uzturnsitstan, yet Matt felt like a year had passed. He glanced out of the window and saw Rimsplitter trying to catch rats on the canal bank.

'Are you sure he doesn't look too conspicuous?' Matt asked.

'Put on your sexy glasses,' Birrik said through a mouthful of toast.

Matt slid on the lensless specs. Instantly, Rimsplitter became a very fierce and weather-beaten black and white tomcat. The type you did not want to mess with, judging by the bits of anatomy he was missing.

'An interesting fellow, your vulture,' Mr Porter said as he followed Matt's gaze.

'Yes. He's very…special.'

Mr Porter, having cleaned the egg and fat off his plate with a slice of bread, looked none the worse for his ordeal, although he had yawned a few times and was getting more restless by the minute.

'Well, I think I'd better be getting along,' he said, making a great show of looking at his watch. 'Mrs Porter, if she has not done so already, will undoubtedly notice my absence very shortly, as it is fast approaching G and T time.' He laughed amiably and levered himself out of the chair with difficulty. Matt stood too and noticed that Birrik and Keemoch were standing to attention. Mr Porter clutched Matt's hand.

'I'm not sure what the consequences might have been if those Ghoulshee rapscallions had had their way today. I daresay someone would have called in my brothers.' Mr Porter shook his head. 'And you know what family gatherings are like, especially when revenge is on the menu.' He winked. 'We're all very grateful to you, Mathew. Knew you were a good one soon as I set eyes on you. Kylah here will take care of you. Now, where *is* that door?'

Birrik opened the door, and Mr Porter ambled out after kissing Kylah chastely on the cheek. The two SES followed on his heels.

'Ah, I have chaperones, I see. Perhaps we could have a song or two as we go, eh, gentlemen?'

Matt saw a fleeting exchange between the two Sith Fand in which he read dread anticipation. A muscle began clenching and unclenching in Birrik's jaw.

'Now,' said Mr Porter, 'how about that one about the yellow submersible? How does it go? Oh, or how about that Scottish one? I've been a wild roamer, no—it's not roamer, but it is a dog's name…um, Rex, isn't it? Had a dog called Rex, once. Excellent for keeping away the kelpie, you know.

Of course, you don't get kelpie in Scotland anymore, so why they bothered writing a song about it, I don't know…'

The front door of Hipposync slammed shut and Matt and Kylah were alone.

'So,' Matt said after a long few seconds, 'who's going first, you or me?'

Kylah opened her mouth to speak, decided against it with a frown, and then said, 'You. But wait just one minute. I better make a note of all of this for DC Farmer's records.'

She reached into a drawer and pulled out a small leather-bound book with very thick pages. It looked a bit like one of those recycled paper diaries you found in shops that sold expensive fountain pens. Kylah noticed his stare and said, 'Special parchment. Self-scribing.'

'Two and a half scruples from Wellworths, I know.'

Her eyes widened in surprise, but all she said was, 'Okay. We're good to go.'

It didn't take that long, and she didn't interrupt him much, but she did want details of Jock the Reaper and the shell and pea game, as well as making Matt repeat all of that twice. Matt was fascinated by the way the pages of the little book filled with words as he spoke. Of course, it was bloody miraculous if you stopped to think about it, but then there *was* such a thing as voice recognition software, too. When he ended with a description of the mini earthquake that Kylah herself had witnessed, he thought he could see a slight softening around her eyes.

'Right, that's me,' he said. 'Now, I need it all explained.'

'Explained, yes,' Kylah said, looking everywhere but at Matt. 'It's difficult to know where to begin.'

Matt stared at her in exasperation. 'Really? Well, let me help you out with that. How about beginning with how it is that I'm sitting here able to talk to you, when I know I've been stabbed through the heart, fractured my skull, and suffered God knows what other injuries, after being shoved off a cliff? Shall we try that one, for starters?'

'Of course, but you've already been to the way-station, haven't you?' she asked, frowning.

'Yes, but I'm none the wiser for it. Gods of chaos and destiny I know about, but why me? What's so special about me?'

Kylah stood and went to fetch a condensation-smeared jug, out of which she poured two glasses of water. She handed Matt one and then turned away to put the jug back. She delivered her next line with her back towards him, so that he didn't have to see her face.

'I will tell you, of course. But if you want, I can slip on the pentrievant right now, and let you forget all about this.' She turned back, her eyes big ovals of doubt. 'Let you get back to your career.'

Matt let out a derisive little laugh. 'My career? For the last two years, my career, together with the rest of my life, has been sitting in the water at the bottom of the toilet bowl waiting for someone to pull the chain. All courtesy of the lovely Silvy, I may add. Let's get one thing straight: I don't want to go back to anything. I want to go forward, okay?'

Matt glanced at the glass of water in his hand with renewed suspicion.

'It's okay,' Kylah said and smiled. It was wry tinged with teasing. 'There's nothing in it except fresh snow melt. Comes straight from a mountain near where I live. It's very refreshing.' She sipped hers and let her eyes drop. 'You do deserve an explanation. It's the very least we can do, after what you did.' Her gaze came back up and there was no doubt about it this time; there was a kind of reluctant tenderness around her mouth and eyes. 'Not many people would have risked everything to come back and help us like that. And I don't know anyone who would have stood up to a Ghoulshee high priest and announced that his belief system was bollocks. You certainly knew how to put it to the instrument of Cthran.'

'I was invisible,' Matt said.

'Even if you were invisible, you had a choice. At the way-station, you could have gone anywhere you liked, but you came back for us.' She held his gaze, her laser eyes monitoring his, right to left. 'Why did you do that, Matt?'

'You say I could have gone anywhere, but I couldn't.' As a neat deflection of her question, his bluff only managed to nudge it a degree or two off course. Kylah used her unyielding gaze to bring it back on target.

'No?'

Matt reverted to his usual defence: if in doubt, flannel. 'I mean, there wasn't that much choice. Not really.'

Of course, that was complete pigswill, because there had been a huge selection of choices on offer—Vietlombardia with Rimsplitter, for one. But somehow, it was the truth, too. There really hadn't been a choice for any right-minded person who thought that he might make a difference. Even if that difference was the equivalent of one-tenth of a millilitre of spit in the vastness of the Pacific.

'It is possible to take this self-effacing act a touch too far, you know,' Kylah said in a school-mistress-peering-through-her-half-moon-glasses-at-him sort of way. 'I mean, coming back is not what most people would have done under the circumstances. Not in a million years.'

Matt shrugged. It was a good shrug, too. All it was missing was a beret, a stripy shirt and a Gauloises cigarette. Of course, he couldn't tell her the real reason. That would mean baring his soul, and he wasn't quite up to that yet. Just like a four-year-old novice with a yellow belt in karate wasn't quite up to splitting a breezeblock in half with a hand chop, much as he'd like to have a go. Still, the shrug seemed to satisfy her, even if the narrowing of her eyes said that the effect was likely to be temporary.

Finally, when it was obvious, he wasn't going to be any more forthcoming, she sighed and pressed on. 'My uncle, as you can see, needs a bit of looking after.'

Matt nodded. As understatements went, 'a bit of looking after.' was a good one.

'The trouble is, he's stubborn,' Kylah continued. 'He enjoys his little walks. He likes his little luxuries, mainly Mrs

Hoblip's tea and Hendrick's and tonic with cucumber. But the reason he lives here is that he can still walk the streets without fear of attack. And he can do all that because of who he is.'

'And who exactly is he?'

'The Doorkeeper.'

'You already said that.'

'I know, but perhaps its significance escaped you,' Kylah explained. 'If the Ghoulshee had succeeded in killing him— and they could have, because they have designed weapons for that purpose—it would have been apocalyptic for your world and ours. You've seen what they're capable of.'

'I have, indeed,' Matt agreed. If he ever got to be on *Mastermind*, Ghoulshee cultural mores could now be his specialist subject. But Kylah chose to slather his earnest agreement with an extra splodge of accusatory barbecue sauce.

'Of course,' she busied herself with a paper clip, 'I almost forgot how *capable* the delicious Silvy was. But now that you've experienced her cruelty first-hand, the fact that you've slept with her must make you feel terrible.'

There were two answers to that one. Matt decided on the more appropriate of the two, under the circumstances, and fibbed with a sage, exaggerated nod.

'Apocalyptic is a word I don't use lightly, either,' Kylah went on. 'You see, my uncle has four brothers, one of whom is my dad. They've all been around for a very long time.'

'How long?'

'Since forever.'

'So, a long time, then,' Matt said. But then he read the patient look on Kylah's face. 'You actually mean *forever*, don't you?'

'They're immortals, Matt. Common to all worlds. They appear in most religious texts in one form or another. With us, it's a benevolent interpretation. We have a light giver, a spirit healer, the balancer, and harmony—that's Dad. The Bronze Age version your lot prefer features them, too. Plague, war, famine—'

'The four horsemen?' Matt gaped.

'Yes. Uncle Ernest is the fifth.'

'Shit,' Matt said. He almost slapped his forehead. Five horses. Hipposync. Of course, it was a play on words. Hippo meaning horse. And sync, which he assumed was an adulteration of cinque, meaning five in all sorts of languages. His only excuse for not working this out earlier was that he'd had quite a lot on his mind.

'He lives here because he is the guardian of the way. For some reason, he likes Oxford. Something to do with all that lopsided intellect surrounding him. Seeing a palaeontology professor in shorts on a tricycle pedalling up Park Street makes Uncle Ernest feel as if he's not so much on the edge of society, after all. But it's his presence that keeps the barriers up. We, the SES, are permanently garrisoned to look after him. So, the fact that you saved him means that we owe you a very, very big one. Officially, there's a ticker-tape parade scheduled back home, as well as half a dozen medals, but I did warn them that you might not…' Her lip curled up.

CHAPTER FORTY-TWO

DESPITE THE FACT that Matt was still trying, with difficulty, to assimilate this new package of synapse-frying information, his automatic refusal-to-involve-himself-in-any-fuss alarm was still on full alert. 'No thanks,' he said. 'I don't do mass adulation.'

'Just as I thought. So, that brings us back to the point of "Why you?"'

Matt looked out into the waning afternoon light. Rimsplitter was tearing something with a long tail to shreds with his talons and beak, a look of pure delight on his face.

'We captured a couple of Ghoulshee guards and managed to get them to cooperate,' Kylah continued. 'They're cocky bastards, but we have our ways and means.'

'Unpleasant?'

'They have this thing about noise. A couple of hours of *Pan Pipes do Prog Rock* generally does the trick. So, yes, unpleasant. Anyway, of the things we've learned, quite a lot of them were about you.'

'Me?'

'The best way I can put it is that you're that elusive missing sock that turns up in a leg of the jeans after the next wash, Matt. Over the last two years, we've had several reports of suspicious incursions from operatives in the medical field, specifically in the medical records departments of hospitals and GP practices. There's a particular breed of imp that loves going into those places and losing vital reports or swapping labels.'

'There must have been a plague of the buggers in the General, then,' Matt said.

'They're a nuisance,' Kylah agreed. 'But these incursions were different. They were systematic. Now we know that the Ghoulshee were looking for something…or rather, some*one*.'

'Anyone we know?' Matt asked.

The silent look he got back was answer enough.

'Me?' Matt was unable to stop his voice from going soprano.

'This isn't easy, Matt. Your father was an accountant from Cornwall, yes?'

Matt nodded.

'And his father?'

'A tin miner.'

'What do you know about their family histories?'

Matt shrugged. 'I'm the youngest of our bunch. My mum and dad were getting on when they had me; Dad was in his forties. He was the last of his lot, too, and he died last year before he got to seventy, but as for the lot before him, I didn't know them at all.'

He'd seen old posed sepia photographs of his grandfather on his great-grandmother's knee. Her in a long dress and a high collar, him in knee britches and boots with a face as long as Red Rum's on account of having to dress up and sit quietly while someone with a camera the size of a fridge told him to hold still for four minutes.

Kylah got up and retrieved a rolled-up bit of parchment, tied with string, from the filing cabinet. 'I've had the back-room boys draw this up.' She undid the string and flattened the parchment on the desk.

Matt stared at it, recognition dawning on his face. 'My family tree? But this goes back hundreds of years.'

'They are thorough. I'll give them that.'

'Bloody hell, does that say, "hanged for stealing a turnip"?'

'Yes, it does. But it was the pig that did it. It's the three generations before you that you need to concentrate on.'

Matt ran his finger back up the tree and found his great-grandfather. Widowed at thirty-five, he had married again, and it was this second marriage that Matt was descended from.

'Did you know that your great-grandfather had Romany blood?' Kylah asked.

'No, but that does explain my father's fixation with caravans,' Matt muttered. 'The number of miserable summers I spent trundling up and down the M5 in a clapped-out Vauxhall, hoping the damned thing wouldn't stall on a hill, you would not believe.'

'Your great-grandmother had some secrets, too.' Kylah lassoed Matt's thoughts and brought them gently back to the point in question. 'She'd had three children before she met your great-grandfather and never told him.'

'How do you know that?'

'We asked her this morning,' Kylah said.

'Oh yeah?' Matt said with a sceptical little laugh. But when he looked up at Kylah, she was not smiling, and the laugh petered out into a loud swallow.

'Two of those children were boys, and your grandfather was one of six, five of them also boys.'

'Right,' said Matt, not knowing where all this was leading. 'So, I've got a couple of long-lost great-uncles somewhere.' A panicky thought struck him. 'Don't tell me that you and I are related somewhere along this line?'

'No, it's nothing like that.' Kylah stayed in breaking-it-to-him-gently mode. 'Your father had a big family, too, didn't he?'

'He certainly did. One of nine,' Matt said. He paused to let the tiny light of understanding flare into a flickering flame. 'Oh, I see what this is. And yes, he was a seventh son, but his father—'

'Was a seventh son, too. But, of course, he had no idea. Neither did you, until now.'

'Wow,' Matt said. 'Families, eh?' He still had no idea where this was all leading, but it was beginning to feel like there might be a flower bed and a rhubarb patch around the next corner, and possibly a nice gazebo at its end.

Kylah kept looking at him, saying nothing.

'What?' Matt said, almost managing to keep the annoyance out of his voice. 'I mean, it's interesting, yes, but I'm one of five. I have three brothers and a sister. Even if the seventh-son thing *is* somehow significant, it doesn't apply to me. How can it?'

Kylah gave him a sympathetic little smile and perched on the edge of the desk, her eyes suddenly interested in her feet, her mouth becoming wafers of amusement.

'Will you stop it with those funny little smiles,' he said and glared at her.

'The Ghoulshee have soothsayers, Matt. They'd predicted that a *Mora*, one of their words for a powerful wind, would bring death and destruction in 2024. But they also knew that this *Mora* would take the form of a being, and that it would come from the human world, not the Fae.'

Kylah pointed to the parchment and to the name Alice Danmor, Matt's mother. Beneath were the five siblings that made up Matt's family, but at the very beginning, and between the fifth and Matt, the sixth, were spaces filled with a faint symbol. Three faint symbols, in all.

'Your mother had five children, yes, but she had three miscarriages, two of them before she had your eldest brother. All three of those miscarriages were male foetuses.'

The world tilted on its axis again.

This was insane. This was even more insane than all the insane things he'd experienced so far. Insane cubed, in fact. His mother had never said anything to him about having had miscarriages. But why should she have? They were a big, healthy family. She was not the type to casually bring up her obstetric history over the Weetos at breakfast. Even so, this was all a bit much.

Kylah read his mind. Her smile was all sympathy. 'If you ask your sister, she'll no doubt confirm it. Mothers tend to confide in daughters much more than in sons about this sort of stuff.'

Matt sighed. 'So let me get this straight. I'm the seventh son of the seventh son of a seventh son?'

Kylah nodded. 'You're the Ghoulshee's *Mora*. You must know the implications?'

Matt made a face. 'Only that it's twaddle.'

'The kind of twaddle that appears in every religion, in every culture, of about a thousand universes. The seventh son is variously known as the healer, the maker of things, endowed with gifts of second sight, predicting the future, or luck. In short, a seventh son is a divine one who has a special purpose in life.'

Matt shook his head. 'Like I said, twa—'

Kylah cut him off. 'Those incursions into medical records departments? The Ghoulshee were looking for you. Or rather, your mother. Someone with a surname like yours who had records of giving birth to lots of children. They're patient, too. Reports go back thirty years. It was only a matter of time until they hit pay dirt.'

Matt went back to the parchment. The writing was pretty small, and there was a lot of it. The dates on the left-hand side went back a very, very long way. 'Surely, these dates are wrong?' he asked, squinting to make them out.

'No,' Kylah said. 'They go right back to the first great migrations. In fact, they go back to when other things paid rent on this green and sceptred isle.' She dropped her voice. 'Some of them even refused to move out when the humans moved in.'

'Bloody squatters,' Matt said.

Kylah nodded. 'All a bit too much fun to give up when you're a God of Chaos. Seeing those upright monkeys reacting to random events was entertainment like they'd never seen. And then, of course, the inevitable happened. One of them fell for a human.' Kylah glanced at Matt and then busied herself rolling up the parchment. 'Take it from me, a goldfish impression isn't a good look for you, Matt.'

Matt shut his mouth and took the second glass of water Kylah offered. He drank in silence.

'Quite a bit to take in all at once, isn't it?' she observed.

Matt didn't know whether to nod or shake his head. 'But what, exactly, does all this make me?'

'Luck, fate, charm, karma, call it whatever you like. It's already out there, of course, like the air we breathe. Little pockets of it wafting about, waiting for us to stumble into them. For the majority of punters, it's completely random access, and when it turns out well it's good luck, but it could just as easily be bad. It seems you attract those pockets like moths to a flame, Matt. And what's more, it seems you can make them do whatever you want. That's what you are. A conduit for whim. That's what Silvy was testing you for with the iron charm. With it on, with the exposed iron on the rim next to your skin, you were projecting unchannelled chaos onto yourself—in a very limited way, of course. All that bad luck was self-induced. Of course, over here your power has limited efficacy, but in the Fae world, it's a very different cauldron of cod.'

'So, does that mean—'

'That you can do anything you want? Probably.' Kylah offered up a pensive pout. 'These are uncharted waters, as far as we're concerned. It's a question of learning on the job, I'd say.'

Matt's thoughts were doing a fair impression of a dog chasing its tail. 'But I've never been lucky at anything,' he protested.

'Really? Wasn't everything going well before you met Silvy?'

'Well, yes, I suppose it was.'

Kylah's shrug dripped with, 'there you are then,' but she apparently wasn't finished. 'The Ghoulshee were trying to get rid of you, Matt, but you survived all their attempts. Even the pendant couldn't quite quash all that karma of yours. But they also had a fallback plan. A way of turning you against yourself.'

'The weir?'

'The weir.' Kylah nodded. 'We also found traces of something else on the pendant. It's a particularly nasty little potion. A kind of self-destruct poison known as Suicider on the black market. While you wore the pendant, it leached out, trying to get you to kill yourself. But even that couldn't quite break your lucky streak.'

Matt blew out air. It was as if he'd just come off an attempt at a world record for number of revolutions on a roundabout in ten minutes. 'It's all a bit much to absorb,' he managed to mumble.

'You have a very dangerous gift,' Kylah said, making her eyes large and questioning. 'My offer with the pentrievant is still on the table, if you want.'

Matt shook his head, but it *was* sorely tempting. Maybe muddling along as a porter at the General was safer than Ghoulshee incursions and blokes in black capes with yellow eyes. But that would mean not seeing Kylah again. He pushed the thought to the back of his mind and came up with another question.

'Does the seventh-son thing explain my being able to travel between worlds?'

'I would think so. Head office hasn't quite got that one sorted yet, though.'

Matt thought for a moment. It only hurt a little. 'What if I said I definitely don't want to go back to things the way they were? What then?'

'We'd love to have you.' Kylah beamed. 'The Ghoulshee are just one of many little thorns in our side. Your gift would be a pretty major coup for us.'

'I'd be a superhero?'

Kylah tilted her head and frowned. 'I can't see you in a

cape, underpants and tights, in all honesty. We see your role more in intelligence, but with a hands-on option, if needed.'

'Is that a job offer?' Matt asked.

Kylah smiled. 'Think about it, that's all we're asking.'

'Oh, I will,' Matt said, sipping the water, which was still as cold as the moment he'd been given it. The brain freeze that followed focused his thoughts. He looked at Kylah and she looked back. Now might be the right moment. 'It's just that—'

Almost on cue, there was a tapping on the window. They looked up to see an ugly red-headed vulture with the back end of a half-eaten rat dangling from its beak. Matt's focus changed like someone pressing the TV clicker to a different channel.

'And, of course, there's him,' he said.

'Don't you think he's a bit unstable?' Kylah asked. 'I mean, he's a Class A sociopath, unbelievably sexist, and has an ego the size of a small country.'

'There's a job for him in politics, then,' Matt said with a grin.

'I'm serious.' Kylah wasn't smiling.

'He's Rimsplitter,' Matt replied with resignation, 'which is probably a psychiatric category all of its own. But he did play his part in what happened today. Without him, I wouldn't have done what I did. He's already in the witness protection programme, I know, but he deserves some recognition. And maybe a change of direction.'

Kylah shook her head. 'We can't give him human form. He has so many bad habits. His enemies will spot him a mile off if we put him on two legs.'

'I was thinking of something a little less ignoble than a vulture, that's all.'

'I'm sure we can come to some arrangement.' Kylah looked at the vulture and shut her eyes in disgust. 'You're sure about this?'

'Not in the slightest,' Matt said, 'but I owe him. We all do.'

Kylah smiled at the vulture and waved. Out of the corner of her mouth, she said, 'Gratitude can sometimes be the most difficult of graces.'

Matt nodded. 'So, what now?'

'Now, you have a cooling-off period,' she said, collecting the water glasses and making herself suddenly busy. 'Go away and think about what I've said. But you also need to understand that, if you wanted to go back to university and finish your training, it would be fine. Or there's always the pentrievant.' She turned, and her smile seemed a tad too bright. 'Any time you want, we can wipe all of this from your memory and you could go back to being good old Mathew Danmor.'

Matt tried to see what lay behind her expression. It was softer than it used to be. But that little hint of irony colouring her phrasing was there still, and, so help him, Matt couldn't tell if it was a challenge or not. He groaned inwardly; he'd always been hopelessly dyslexic when it came to female subtext. Exhaustion pressed down on him like a lead blanket. His brain hurt. Resurrection certainly took it out of you.

'I think I'd better lie down,' he said. 'Somewhere warm and a long way away from here. Any chance I could borrow your Aperio?'

CHAPTER FORTY-THREE

HE HAD no way of knowing if the handle would work on the flap of a tent. Nor had he any right to assume that the tent would be there at all, since he'd packed the thing away into his backpack after his gap year trip. There was no earthly reason for a tent to be pitched on an Alpine meadow near the western slopes of Arthur's Pass on New Zealand's South Island. But there it was, in twenty-one degrees of heat, well stocked with cold beers and chicken for barbecuing. Luck was a very weird thing, indeed.

There was plenty of roadkill for Rimsplitter, too, down in the valley, and Matt didn't see much of him all day as he snoozed in the warm afternoon sun. That evening, he walked a high ridge, and though it was mid-summer in the Southern Hemisphere, he saw no one. He didn't even hear a single plane or car. He was in his sleeping bag by ten, exhausted. He dreamt dreams that were full of horrible snake-headed priests and bloodthirsty acolytes, not to mention dreadful battles and bloodshed and five apocalyptic horsemen who rode the sky. When he awoke, Matt sensed that it had been more than just a dream. It had been a warning of how things might have turned out. Stretching in the bright sunshine, he wasn't sure if the sweaty brow he'd woken up with was from relief or sheer terror.

As Matt cooked bacon on the Primus stove, Rimsplitter landed with his usual lack of grace and waddled over to where Matt was sitting.

'Okay, 's warm and there's lots of food and there's some cheeky-looking female parrots about, but it isn't exactly my idea of a bleedin' activity holiday.'

'That's the point,' Matt said, cracking an egg into the pan. 'I need solitude and tranquillity. A bit of breathing space.'

'Yeah, well, there's enough effin' breathin' space 'ere for the red bleedin' army.'

Matt sipped hot sweet tea and ignored Rimsplitter's moaning. 'I came here in my gap year. I was eighteen. I thought I could change the world.'

'I got news for you, mate. You are bleedin' can.'

Matt nodded. 'Yeah, funny that. Now that I know I can, I don't know if I want to.'

'What the eff does that mean? You can do anythin' you want. If you robbed a bank, I expect there'd be a faulty alarm button under the effin' teller's desk. Or you could have a threesome with some Brazilian pole dancers and not bleedin' catch anythin'.' There was something in the way Rimsplitter cringed when he spoke of the pole dancers that suggested more recollected regret than imagination.

Matt stopped chewing his bacon sandwich to stare at Rimsplitter. 'It's at times like these when we find out how little we have in common.'

'Come on, you ponce. You're the luckiest bee in the world. Comin' 'ere trying to find yourself. 'S all bollocks. You know what my old 'Ungarian granddad used to say? If you talk to God, it's praying. If God talks to you, it's bleedin' schizophrenia.'

Matt almost choked on his tea. 'Rimsplitter, that's almost profound.'

'No, it's somethin' he used to say over and over. Even when they took him away in the ambulance, he was sayin' it. But 'e was right. There's no bleedin' answer 'ere. It's all effin' ahead of you, mate.'

'Maybe. But I need a bit more time. Clear my head.'

'Yeah, well, when you do arrive at your cosmic answer, just let me know. 'Cos I miss the effin' action.'

'You miss Uzturnsitstan?'

'Not all of it, no.' Rimsplitter tilted his head, apparently pondering. There was a bit of congealed rabbit fur on his wattle. 'Definitely not the poisonous frogs and the snakes and the flesh-eatin' plants. And I can live without them Ghoulshee berks and the volcano. Oh, and the contaminated lake stinks and the salt desert is a bugger. You can effin' keep them. But me mates, I miss them cees.'

Matt nodded. 'Ever thought of working in the travel industry?'

––––––

ON THE SECOND NIGHT, Matt's dreams were just as vivid, but different. They weren't so much about what might have happened as about what would, instead. In his dream, he was having tea with Mrs Hoblip and had become fluent in bwbach throat clearing. She introduced him to her son, George, and when he'd got over that and steadied himself, he had an idea and discussed it with George at length. Then Birrik and Keemoch were disinterring bodies in a cemetery, and he took the opportunity to pick their jarhead brains about a few things. But although it was what he was longing for, he didn't see Kylah once. She wasn't answering her calls, it seemed. Either that, or he was on her blocked sender list.

––––––

THE NEXT MORNING, Matt got up and signalled to Rimsplitter.

'Come on, we're off.'

'Somewhere with a bit of bleedin' action, I hope?'

'New Thameswick,' Matt explained. 'I need to do a little shopping. But first,' he added, sealing the tent flap before applying the Aperio, 'we need to stop by the Holiday Inn.'

It turned out to be as easy as saying it. Matt applied the Aperio and thought about the lobby. A bit of him realised that, even in the rarefied atmosphere of inter-dimensional travel, what he was doing was pretty unusual, given the way-station's stringently fatal entry criteria. But there was no need for deep analysis; it worked, and that was all he cared about.

'Why 'ere?' Rimsplitter grumbled as they stepped in through the lobby door.

'Bit of unfinished business, that's all,' Matt explained.

'Yeah? Well, this place gives me the bleedin' creeps.'

'Just wait here while I talk to the concierge.'

He left Rimsplitter brooding and made for reception. The man behind the desk almost fell over himself in his effort to be deferential as Matt approached.

'Ah, Mr Danmor. A pleasure to see you again, sir.'

'You've had instructions, I take it?'

'Yes, sir. Room Four. On the ground floor.'

Matt took the offered brass key and held it dangling from his hand as he went back to the vulture.

'Woss that for?'

'We've had special dispensation,' Matt explained.

'Isn't that a big word for a bung?'

Matt ignored him and walked to door number four. He unlocked it and held it open for the vulture. Rimsplitter muttered as he hopped past. 'Went through Room Eight the first time I came 'ere. Walked in a bloke, came out a bleedin' vulture. It's bleedin' sp—'

Matt waited until the vulture was fully inside and then shut the door, locked it, and put the key on the floor. He waved at the concierge, who waved back with the enthusiasm of a demented four-year-old. Matt took the lift to the 123rd floor and headed for door number 97. Five minutes later, he was on the ground floor of Herod's making a purchase. Afterwards, he stopped by Harpy Nix to say, thank you. To say the welcome he received was effusive would be pushing things, but from the nod of the head he got from the salesman, the general impression he gained was that the feedback had been appreciated. Ten minutes later, he was back outside Room Four at the Holiday Inn, inserting the key.

'All done?' he asked the concierge.

'We trust it is to your satisfaction, sir.' The man beamed as he said it.

Matt opened the door.

'—ooky, that's what it is.' Rimsplitter paused and turned to look at Matt. He had a smelling-a-rat expression on his avian face. Nothing new in that, since smelling rats was one of his chief hobbies. 'Ain't you comin' in?'

'I've been.'

'What you talkin' about?' Rimsplitter squawked his way back out in double-quick time. 'You won't catch me goin' anywhere in this effin' place alone. No bleedin' way.'

'Fine,' Matt said, staring at Rimsplitter.

'Why are you smiling like that?'

'Oh, it's your wattle. Looking a bit pale, I thought.'

'Is it?' Rimsplitter hissed in frozen panic. 'Funny you should say that 'cos I'm not quite feelin' me bleedin' self.' He trotted over to the black marble pillar to peer at his reflection, muttering as he went. 'Been feelin' a bit off colour, to tell you the truth. Maybe I'm coming down with som…WOAH… WHAT THE EFFIN' EFF!'

The spluttering roar that escaped his beak made the foyer chandelier tinkle ominously and attracted a glare of supernova proportions from the grey-suited concierge. Matt watched with high amusement as Rimsplitter furled and unfurled his wings, which was no easy task since they now had a span of over six feet. He looked at himself and let out a long, low whistle as his talons scraped the stone floor, before turning a pair of sharp, almost black eyes towards Matt.

'I'm an effin' eagle,' he said in the harshest of whispers.

'Hope you like it,' Matt said.

'Like it? What is there not to like? Look at this plumage! Not overstated. Black and white with a touch of effin' grey. Very classy. Plus, I got me own effin' 'eaddress. I'm an eagle, that's wot I am. An effin' eagle!'

He started hopping from one leg to another before segueing into a moonwalk.

'A crowned eagle, actually,' Matt said. 'Top of the cool raptors list.'

'The girls'll be beating down the doors to me effin' nest. Ha! Wait 'til that ponce, Jeremy, sees this.'

'I'm pleased you like it,' Matt said.

Rimsplitter stopped and swivelled his head towards Matt.

'Thanks, mate. I mean it.'

'It's a pleasure,' Matt said. But he left it at that. You don't hug crowned eagles, and you certainly do not shake hands with them. Not if you want to keep all your fingers.

'But what about you? What are you goin' to get out of all this?' Rimsplitter said in a disquieting ejaculation of concern.

'That depends.'

'On effin' what?'

'On a little bit of luck,' Matt said, leaving Rimsplitter to ponder. Matt refused to be drawn in further. Instead, they went back to Arthur's Pass so that Rimsplitter could do some test flights and get used to his new manifestation, decimating the rabbit population in the process. But Matt didn't linger. With a wave to the soaring eagle, he turned the onyx handle once more and exited through the tent flap, driven by the need to tie up a few last dangling loose ends.

CHAPTER FORTY-FOUR

It was still January in Oxford. Still dark and damp and about as welcoming as an unswept corner of a fishmonger's van. At a quarter to five in the afternoon, the day's wintery light had all but leached away, and the General was lit up like a Christmas tree. Matt parked his bike and let himself in through the staff entrance. He had barely exchanged pleasantries with the charge nurse in A&E when he heard a familiar, drawling, carping voice.

'Well, well, if it isn't Mattanova.' Roberro emerged from the suture room with the buxom med student in tow (was she looking just a little bored with it all?), an insufferable, gloating grin twisting his arrogant mouth. He made a show of looking to the left and right of Matt before pouring on the astonishment. 'What, no accompanying slag today?'

The buxom med student winced. It was astonishing how much Matt wanted to slap Roberro's facetious face and turn it into moussaka. He could almost taste the satisfaction the pain in his hand would give him. But he didn't. In the great scheme of things, restraint was what was called for here. Matt shrugged and said nothing. Roberro took his cue.

'So, popped in to collect your cards, have you, Desperate Danmor? AWOL without a doctor's note,' Roberro tutted. 'Not good, Danny boy. Sackable offence, I've heard.'

'Just as well that I'm about to leave for good, then, isn't it?'

'Tragic.' Roberro beamed. 'If I'd known, I would have organised a whip round. Second thoughts, we *are* in a recession, and there's not much you can buy for fifty pence these days, is there?'

'Comedy platinum as always, Giles,' Matt said and enjoyed Roberro's irritation at being called by his proper name. 'Anyway, I'm glad I bumped into you, because I've got a little something for you. A small thank you for all your help.'

Roberro's smile slipped into quizzical doubt. Matt was betting on the man's ego winning hands down in a fight with implausibility. Indeed, it took only three seconds of internal musing for Roberro to accept the laughably flimsy possibility that Matt was grateful for all the name-calling and general bad blood. After all, he'd been doing Matt a great psychological service by treating him like a dishcloth, hadn't he?

Matt watched Roberro's face as the little cogs of self-justification all meshed together. Informing proles of their place in life's pecking order through derision and sarcasm was considered a genuine communication skill on planet Roberro; he'd said as much on more than one occasion. As such, Matt guessed that if it did cross his mind that this might be a wind-up, it would cross with the velocity of a speeding bullet to embed itself, well out of sight, in his egocentric, insight-free, pachyderm skin.

'Really?' Roberro asked, his face transforming into an expression of almost child-like expectation.

The image of a fisherman reeling in a big one popped satisfyingly into Matt's head.

'It's in my locker,' he said. 'Look, I have to go and see Linda. Why don't you meet me there in, say, five minutes? That's if you've got the time.'

'Always got time for a colleague, Matt. You know that.' Roberro's voice was syrup and treacle.

Matt ducked out before the nausea got too much to bear and headed for Hotel Services. On the way, he passed a porter transporting a wheelchair-bound patient along the corridor. The guy was fussing, tucking in a blanket around the patient's knees. But as he passed, the porter looked up and put a hand out to grab Matt's arm.

'Mike?' said the porter. 'Wait a minute, will you?'

Matt stopped and stared. It was Flynn. He hadn't recognised him, largely because Matt's brain wasn't geared towards putting two such improbable things as pushing a wheelchair and talking to a patient together under the label 'Horizon Flynn-job description.' Matt stared in speechless wonder as Flynn knelt and smiled at his patient, patting his arm. 'Hang on a minute while I have a word with this chap, Mr Spackman.'

Flynn pulled Matt to one side. When he spoke, it was in a sort of desperate whisper. 'Mike, how's it going?'

'Good,' Matt said. 'It's going good.' He couldn't help noticing that the muscle in Flynn's eyelid flickered constantly. 'You?'

'Funny you should ask, because since that visit to the mortuary we did the other day, things haven't been right.' Flynn glanced behind him nervously.

'What do you mean, things?' Matt asked.

'Weirdness is what I mean,' Flynn whispered. 'I keep havin' this horrible dream. Every night the same. There's this thing… Ah, Christ, Mike, it's all wrinkly and red with tufts of orange hair, and these big yellow eyes like lamps. Keeps bringing me food. Horrible food, with snails and bits of grub and roots and… Jesus.' Flynn shuddered. He looked on the verge of vomiting. 'Says it'll make me eat it if I don't…' He ran a finger around inside his collar. 'Says he'll do all sorts of thing to me if I don't…'

'If you don't what?' Matt demanded.

Flynn's eyes showed an awful lot of white.

'This is where it goes off the dial. It says I must win Porter of the Month. Oh, it's horrible, Mike, horrible.'

'I can imagine. Red skin with tufts of orange, you say?'

'What? No, not that. It's *this* that's horrible. This working, you know, properly.' He seemed on the verge of tears.

'You can do it, Flynn. I know it's in you.'

Hope, desperate and pitiful, flared in Flynn's expression. 'You reckon I can, Mike? Do you?'

'I do, Flynn. I really do.'

'What do you think it is, Mike? In my dreams, I mean? Have you ever seen or heard of anything like that before?'

Matt was saved from lying through his teeth by Mr Spackman's wracking cough. Flynn flinched. 'I'm coming, Mr Spackman,' he said and rushed over. 'Don't want you to be late for the bladder nurse, do we?'

Flynn pushed the wheelchair down the corridor. Every now and then, he'd throw his head around to make sure that no one, or no *thing*, was following.

Matt allowed himself the slightest of satisfied smiles and sent a mental note. *Thank you, George Hoblip.*

———

THE URUK-HAI CHEERLEADER was in her office when Matt knocked.

A disembodied voice said, 'Come in.' Matt pushed open the door. Linda Marsh ignored him and continued doing some late-afternoon curls with a heavy barbell. She finished her set and wiped the sweat off her neck with a hand towel before looking up with eyebrows arched. Even *they* looked muscular.

'Stone me, it's the soddin' invisible man.' Marsh let the barbell clunk heavily to the floor. 'Nice of you to call in. We thought you'd been run over by a bloody bus. I've been hopin' for an obituary so's I could rearrange the rota. Where the soddin' hell have you been?'

'Long story,' Matt said.

Linda Marsh snorted. 'You know what? I'm not even interested. You had your chance, sonny Jim. Not my problem that you've done a Paris Hilton.'

'Paris Hilton?'

'Blown it, Danmor. D'ye need a soddin' diagram?'

Matt smiled sweetly. 'So, you won't want my written resignation, then?'

'No, I will not. Collect your wages from General Office and piss off.' Linda Marsh turned away.

'I wanted to thank you for giving me a chance,' Matt persisted, pouring on the soft soap. 'Not many people would have done that.' It had worked with Roberro already; why not with a psychopath like Marsh?

'Don't thank me.' Linda Marsh turned back around and glared down her nose at him. On her forearm, a huge vein the size of a child's bicycle tyre became swollen with blood as she flexed her bicep. 'Thank that lily-livered soddin' equal opportunities commission. You filled my quota of educationally challenged employees for this year, Danmor. The fact that I was proved one hundred bollockin' per cent right to have doubts gives me no satisfaction. Well, not much, anyway. From the look of things, leaving doesn't seem to be bothering you that much.'

'Like I said, I am grateful. Despite being on all the worst shifts and getting all the crap jobs no one else wanted to do. That's the way it is, I suppose.'

Linda Marsh drew herself up. It was like talking to an inverted Cornetto. 'Too bloody true. And don't you forget it. Someone has to do them jobs, Danmor. So why not the soddin' imbeciles?'

'Why not, indeed,' Matt murmured with a fixed smile. 'And while you're at it, why not give them a nice yellow star to wear as well, just to make it easier for people to recognise them in the street?' He was surprised at how even his voice sounded.

'Yeah, well, there may be some mileage in that, too. I'll speak with my managers.' Linda Marsh's nostrils flared. 'So, what's next for you, Danmor? Burger bar? Mobile phone sales? Bin man?'

'Oh, I expect something will turn up,' Matt said, deflecting her vitriol. 'I'm feeling lucky.'

'Better watch out in case Dopey and Happy get jealous.'

Linda Marsh let out a croaky laugh that reminded Matt of tipping gravel onto corrugated iron. Announcing his impending exit had made her day, if not her year.

'Yeah,' Matt said and let it hang in the air while Linda Marsh stopped laughing at her own joke. It took a while. 'So, anyway, I got you a leaving present. Mate of mine works in France for an exclusive designer. They've got this new scent coming out. Hasn't hit the shops yet, but he sent me a sample and, well…I thought of you.'

Matt handed over a small and highly ornate glass bottle, decorated with a pink ribbon around the neck. Linda Marsh pulled out the stopper and inhaled. Her eyes lit up.

'Not bad. Not bad, at all. But I'm still not giving you a soddin' reference.'

'Wouldn't expect it,' Matt said and watched as she tipped the bottle up on her fingers, lifting her chin to apply some of the perfume to her throat. Matt, anticipating the move, had already taken a deep breath in and was holding it. He managed a strained, 'See you.' Before turning and hurrying out.

He'd taken two steps along the corridor when he bumped into Roberro.

'So? Where is it, then?' Roberro asked like a spoiled child at a birthday party.

Matt forced himself not to smile too much. 'I left it with Linda. Enjoy.'

Roberro gave Matt a huge smile. The sort of smug predatory smile a pool-table hustler wore after he'd taken the local wannabe champ to the cleaners for two hundred quid. As he pushed his way past in the narrow corridor, Roberro coughed. Inside that cough, Matt heard him enunciate, 'Loser.'

Matt didn't take any more steps. In fact, he waited until Roberro pushed open the door to Linda Marsh's office, then backtracked and craned his neck to listen.

'Danmor says he's left me something. Bloody idiot is giving out leaving presents.'

Throaty laugh. 'I know. He left me something, too.'

'What a pathetic moron, I mean...ooh, what *is* that smell?'

'That's his prezzy to me. Not bad, actually.'

'Linda, I've never noticed until now how much your muscles gleamed under this artificial light—'

'It's called Inflagrante.'

'The way your hair stays so stiff, even when you move your head.'

'Roberro, what the soddin' hell's the matter with you?'

'I've always liked really tight skirts.'

'Roberro, I'm soddin' warning you.'

'Linda, has anyone ever told you that you've got hidden depths and that I'm just the deep-sea diver to explore them for you?'

'Come one step nearer, and I swear I'll break your bloody legs.'

'Oh, Linda. You smell sooo good.'

'Do I? Oh good, because here's another aroma for you to try. It's called essence of soddin' PEPPER SPRAY.'

Matt walked away with a zipped-up smile of satisfaction curving his lips. Such was the matchmaker's gift of bringing joy and happiness to people's lives. As the noise of snapping furniture and Roberro's screams of pain echoed along the corridor, he even started to whistle.

He went back to the porters' locker room, removed all his stuff, and wandered back through to A&E. The med student watched him with suspicion.

'There's something different about you,' she said, looking him up and down.

He didn't bother answering her. She knew it. He knew it. Oh, what the hell. Abruptly, he turned and leaned in close so that only she would hear what he had to say.

'Little bit of advice. That stinging sensation when you pee? It's not due to overuse. I'd pay a little visit to the GUM clinic, if I were you. Oh, and stay away from the source. He's pure, unadulterated filth, and you know what they say about mud sticking. Ring your tutor and tell him you want to change mentors. After this evening,' he looked up as two security men ran in the direction of Hotel Services, 'I'm pretty sure he'll understand.'

She stared at him in horror, a crimson blush spreading up from her throat as she mouthed wordless protestations. But she didn't slap him. Instead, she turned away. He thought about putting his hand on her arm and asking if she was okay. Despite the well-packaged body, she was just a kid. But the touch never materialised. She had colluded with Roberro, after all. Even if, as Matt suspected, coercion had played some part in that, too.

She'd taken four steps before she stopped and pivoted. Her mascara had turned into dark wet clumps on her lower lids, and she looked embarrassed and miserable. She held things together enough to proffer a fluttering smile. 'Thanks,' she said.

'Don't mention it.' Matt nodded. 'I promise *I* won't.'

Her smile widened. It was a great smile. Under different circumstances he might have returned that smile with interest. But there was unfinished business to see to, and so, instead, he waved to her and turned away.

CHAPTER FORTY-FIVE

THERE WAS no doubting the sense of satisfaction he'd derived from being able to return the compliments, with interest, to Roberro and Linda Marsh. However, one remaining dangling string needed tying off, and it was the one he was least looking forward to. Rimsplitter had been right. Despite all Matt's procrastinations, it still all came down to a stark choice of the 'Should I stay or should I go' variety.

Much as he'd have liked to believe that he could continue to play the hero, that wasn't what he wanted. What he craved was that which he could never have, and it was time to confront that stark fact. Matt sighed. If only Kylah were here now, he could get it all over and done with.

'You rang?' Kylah said as she pushed open the doors of A&E. She was wearing one of her better smiles, this one warm enough to toast marshmallows on.

Matt grinned and raised a questioning eyebrow.

'Intuition,' she answered.

'Can you buy that at Harpy Nix, too?'

This time her smile was full of knowing, and warm enough to send his pulse up two notches. 'I came to buy you that drink,' she said. 'If you still want to?'

'I do,' Matt said, 'but we need to talk first.'

'Here?'

Matt shook his head. 'I know a place.'

——————

IT WAS morning on the alpine slopes beneath Arthur's Pass, the morning warm and noisy with buzzing insects. Matt found himself desperately resisting the urge to burst into song about the hills being alive.

'This is an amazing spot,' Kylah said, sucking in the unsullied air.

It was, too. Just the place to stroll along, distracted by the jaw-dropping beauty of the scenery and the robin's-egg sky, so that the real reason for them being there could simmer away on Matt's back burner for a few moments longer. After all, there was no point rushing at disappointment. That was like hurrying to school on the day of the exam results knowing full well that, instead of revising *King Lear*, you'd actually watched all the second-series reruns of *Breaking Bad* and *Everybody Loves Raymond* on Dave, instead.

'This is, without doubt, my favourite place in the world,' Matt mused. 'It's where I go to in my mind when I want to think.' He shook his head and let out a wry laugh. 'Now I can actually come here any time I like, with the Aperio.'

'And *have* you thought?' Kylah asked.

'I've been doing nothing else.'

She turned and pierced him with one of her furnace gazes. 'So?'

Matt looked at her. His face must have shown his confusion.

'What?' Kylah asked, and Matt thought she looked a little pink in the cheeks.

His pulse was drumming in his ears. She did have the most fantastic eyes.

He started walking again. It seemed to help. As did not looking at her for a minute. 'Okay, I might as well come out with it. I've decided not to be a part of the SES—'

He stopped and turned back. She hadn't moved, but her

features had crumpled. The distress and disappointment in her voice when she spoke took him utterly by surprise.

'But why?'

Matt shook his head and let it fall. 'It's tempting. Birrik and Keemoch are great guys, and I like your eccentric uncle, too. It's just…it's just that I couldn't stand being in New Thameswick or Hipposync or anywhere you were—'

'Oh.' Kylah looked at him with a face that was the definition of glum. Matt wanted to retrace his steps to get close to her, but somehow his legs had taken root. Amazing how a little word like 'oh' could stop two grown people in their tracks.

This isn't what's supposed to happen. Why does she look so unhappy?

He didn't have any answers. The script he'd rehearsed had Kylah feigning sympathetic understanding while mentally dancing a jig at the thought of being rid of him.

Still, Matt made himself finish what he wanted to say. 'I couldn't stand being in New Thameswick or Hipposync or anywhere you were, harbouring the futile hope that you and me…that we…' His mouth clamped shut. It was no good. He was bloody useless at this. He squeezed his eyes shut and looked away. 'I have no right to even say this. We hardly know each other, and I'm an idiot and…look, I'd rather forget the whole thing. Just stick that damned pentrievant back on my head and—'

Kylah took two steps forward to bridge the gap between them. The gold flecks in her eyes sparkled. She put her finger against his lips. 'Did you say "futile hope"?'

'Ysss,' Matt mumbled before pulling her finger away. 'Pathetic, isn't it?'

She put her finger against his lips again. 'Can you shut up for one minute? I like you, Matt,' she said in a low and tremulous voice. 'I liked you the very first time I laid you out on the floor of the office.'

'Thanks,' Matt said, frowning from behind her finger.

'You're smart and funny and maddeningly humble, and

okay, you think about things far too much, but I quite like that because it makes you vulnerable. And what's more, you're obviously one of us, which saves an awful lot of time in the travelling-between-the-two-existences scenario. But when a girl meets someone like you, she doesn't raise her hopes too high. I mean, I'm very ordinary—'

'Will you stop saying stuff like that?' Matt said, pulling her hand away, but not letting it go. Surprising how strident his voice sounded through gritted teeth, too. He hadn't meant to sound quite so vehement, but she'd said a couple of things that had pressed the spin cycle in his brain again. 'Someone like you.' What the hell did that mean? He knew what it implied—That he was different. Okay, the last 24 hours had proved that to be true. But did she mean in general or in another way?

That he could be special to anyone was a joke. And then there was her continuous, coy insistence that she was 'very ordinary.' That one definitely took the chocolate-coated hobnob.

Ordinary?

He suddenly wanted to scream at her, but good manners prevailed and instead, he said, 'I can't have my pick of girls, okay? They scare me. Especially the really good-looking ones like you.' He paused before adding in a resigned, pleading tone, 'So, please stop taking the mick. It's not funny anymore.'

For a single moment, they looked at one another with identical frowns of bemused confusion. Had Cupid been up there—and who was to say he wasn't, given how weirdly the rest of the week had gone—he'd have been tearing his curls out at their stupidity, while waiting, fingers drumming, for the first points on his archery scorecard.

But gradually, confusion gave way to dawning realisation. Perception, sputtering like a candle in the draughty breeze of destiny, flickered into life and lit, at long last, a Catherine wheel of blazing understanding in both their heads.

But Kylah couldn't resist the tiniest of teases.

'Is that why you came back to Uzturnsitstan?' she asked.

An odd excitement bloomed on her cheeks, her pupils black circles in the blue-gold of her amazing eyes.

'I've already told you,' Matt said. This close, she smelled wonderful.

'Tell me again.'

He sighed. 'I came back because I couldn't stand the thought of not being with you at the end, all right?'

It sounded crass and clumsy. Worse, it sounded completely mad. His actions were based on an unrequited infatuation stemming from nothing more than a couple of hurried conversations about attempted murder and a couple of perfunctory kisses—well, one perfunctory, the other literally mind-blowing. Still, they were not the ideal ingredients for a full-on, meaningful relationship. Yet the honesty of the admission was like lifting a hundred-ton weight off his shoulders. 'I had no plan. No idea of what I was going to do. Call me an idiot, but there it is.'

'You're an idiot,' Kylah said, but her eyes glistened as she said it.

'I wanted to be there when the shit hit the fan, and sod the rest of it,' Matt added. 'The definition of idiocy.'

'You could have been killed.' Her voice had a new, husky edge to it.

'Umm, excuse me. I *was* killed,' Matt pointed out.

'But you still came back.'

'Some things are worth dying for.'

She smiled. He smiled. And then they were kissing to the sound of an obligatory choir of angels and fanfare of trumpets. At least, Matt could hear them. When they quietened down, he was left with the strangest of feelings that for the first time ever, he knew his place in the world. Here, with Kylah.

Quite a bit later, after a very energetic forty minutes and much adjustment of clothing into a semblance of propriety, Matt said, 'Right. I could do with that drink now.'

'It *is* thirsty work,' Kylah said.

That made Matt laugh out loud. He *really* liked this girl.

'Well, it is,' she said and pulled him to her again. 'But we can come back here whenever you want. Give us a chance to get to know each other. Catch up on all those little secrets it takes years to learn.'

'What, like when I won the egg and spoon race at primary school?' Matt's eyebrows came together in a sceptical scowl.

'Exactly. The stuff that makes you tick. I want to know all the gory details.'

'Even the one about the nurse and the hosepipe?'

'Mine involves a centaur and a…never mind. Let's stick to egg and spoon races, to start with.'

They held hands as they walked back across the meadow.

'What about you? You ever win anything?' It didn't matter if she had or hadn't. He simply wanted to hear her voice again.

Kylah shrugged. 'I did represent my city-state in gymnastics.'

Matt's eyebrows shot skywards. There was no denying it; sometimes his vivid imagination was a curse.

'You okay?' Kylah asked.

'Never better,' he said, trying to swallow.

High above them a huge bird swooped, its shadow passing over their heads and racing across the meadow in front of them. Matt looked up to see the silhouette of an enormous, crowned eagle soaring majestically in the cloudless sky. Instead of an eagle's piercing call, a gruff voice shouted something down to them. Matt looked up and waved. The eagle looped the loop.

'Is he musical in any way?' Kylah asked.

Matt almost swallowed his tongue. After he'd recovered and wiped his eyes, he said, 'Rimsplitter? I don't think so. Why do you ask?'

'Because every time he's appeared since we've been here, he seems to be saying, "You lucky F in C." Does that mean anything to you?'

'Vaguely,' Matt said in a strangled voice and turned his

face away to hide his smile. 'And one day, when we know each other a lot better, I'll sing it to you.'

'Really,' Kylah said, pulling his head back around to search his eyes and narrowing her own in a way that told him she knew damned well he was tugging at her lower appendage.

'Yes, one day. Soon…ish.' As if on cue, Matt's stomach rumbled. 'So, where shall we go for that drink? I quite fancy somewhere that does food, too.'

'I know this bar on the beach in Goa,' Kylah suggested.

'Goa? Sounds amazing.' Matt grinned. He could get used to this.

Kylah reached for the Aperio, fitted it to the tent flap and opened it onto a warm and balmy Konkan night.

'Do they take Visa, you think?' Matt asked as he stepped through onto another continent.

'I don't think they do. But knowing you, I expect you'll find some money under the table.'

'Yeah. You're probably right.' He nodded.

On the other hand, they might not even ask a 400 Lb gorilla to pay at all.

You never knew your luck.

ACKNOWLEDGMENTS

As with all writing endeavours, the existence of this novel depends upon me, the author, and a small army of 'others' who turn an idea into a reality. A special mention to Bryony Sutherland for editorial guidance through the labyrinth. The Hipposync Archives are a work in progress. Special mention goes to Ela the dog who drags me away from the writing cave and the computer for walks, rain or shine. Actually, she's a bit of a princess so the rain is a no-no. Good dog!

But my biggest thanks goes to you, lovely reader, for being there and actually reading this. It's great to have you along and I do appreciate you spending your time in joining and the team at Hipposync and in New Thameswick where anything is possible.

CAN YOU HELP?

With that in mind, and if you enjoyed it, I do have a favour to ask. Could you spare a moment to **leave a review or a rating**? A few words will do, but it's really the only way to help others like you discover the books. Probably the best way to help authors you like. Just visit the book's page on Amazon and leave a few words, or a rating, if you have the time. Thank you!

FREE BOOK FOR YOU

Visit my website and join up to the Hipposync Archives Reader's Club and get a FREE novella, *Every Little Evil,* by visiting:

https://dcfarmer.com/

When a prominent politician vanishes amidst chilling symbols etched in blood, the police are baffled. Enter Captain Kylah Porter, an enigmatic guardian against otherworldly threats. With her penchant for the paranormal and battling against cynical skeptics, she dives into a realm where reality blurs. Her toxic colleague from the Met is convinced it's just another tawdry urban crime. But Kylah suspects someone's paying a terrible price for dipping a toe, or something even less savoury, in the murky depths of the dark arts.
She knows her career and the missing man's life are on the line. Now time is running out for the both of them…

Pour yourself a cuppa and prepare for a spellbinding mystery.

By signing up, you will be amongst the first to hear about new releases via the few but fun emails I'll send you. This includes a no spam promise from me and you can unsubscribe at any time.

AUTHOR'S NOTE

Once upon a time, in the swirling mists of the last century, my journey into the fantastical began. A devotee of the greats like Tolkien, I found myself drawn deeper into Terry Pratchett's Discworld and Tom Holt's tilt at the modern—the holy trinity of the Ts, if you will.

Two decades ago, I embarked on what I now affectionately call "the archives." But alas, life's currents swept me into real world. I found myself scribbling away in different genres. Don't get me wrong, I still do that. But those archives? They never stopped whispering my name.

Fast forward to now, with a bit more time on my hands and with newfound vigour and fresh releases on the horizon. We have new covers, new titles—everything's getting a makeover to match their quirky, satirical souls..

Now, if you've dipped your toes into one of these tales before, you know the drill. It's all about characters tangled up in the most bizarre situations. I mean, come on, this is fantasy we're talking about! But sometimes, in those quiet moments, I wonder... Could there be someone out there, playing guardian between our world and the great beyond? Someone keeping the cosmic order intact until things inevitably go haywire? Just a thought

All the best, and see you all soon, DCF.

READY FOR MORE

The Ghoul On The Hill

With a job he hates and his partner about to leave him, Darren Trott's world is turned upside down by the revelation of his true identity and a desperate request.

Now, with the help of warrior queens, a mischievous bwbach, and otherworldly allies, he must confront his past and save both his world, and the one he's drawn to.

But with enemies closing in, Darren must tread carefully —or risk unleashing an apocalypse of unimaginable proportions.

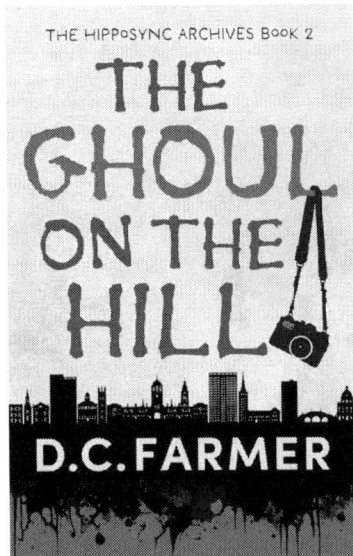

THE HIPPOSYNC ARCHIVES BOOK 2

THE GHOUL ON THE HILL

D.C. FARMER

Printed in Great Britain
by Amazon